PRAISE FOR THE

ROYAL MATCHMAKING COMPETITION SERIES

"An endearing coming-of-age story with plenty of romance amidst an assassin mystery . . ."
   -Independent Book Review

"The Royal Matchmaking Competition is a delightful young adult fantasy romance with a touch of intrigue and excitement . . . [it] combines coming of age with romance and mystery in a terrific contemporary fairy story."
   -Readers' Favorite Review

"Twelve eligible bachelors. One traitorous assassin. One naïve Princess. Who will she choose? In all, Galloay has created a vivid fairytale world, with bright and vivacious characters."
   -S. A. Reedsy Discovery

"Sweet and wholesome while also holding a fair amount of slow-burn, spicy romantic zest."
   -Reader Views on Prince Zadkiel

"One prince trying to find true love amongst a dozen eligible princesses is a lot of fluffy fantasy fun!"
   -Jaime Garner on Prince Zadkiel

"Cheeky in its approach, spirited and splendidly written The Royal Matchmaking Competition is a must-read for fans of Teen & Young Adult Romantic Fantasy and is highly recommended."
   -BookViral Review

"You can't always predict what will happen next. . . . "The Royal Matchmaking Competition: The Fate of the Empire" by Zoiy Galloay is a clever, fun, and dynamic work of entertainment that you should definitely put at the top of your feel-good rom-com list. Welcome to good clean fun with a sense of humor."
   -Tammy Ruggles from Reader Views on The Fate of the Empire

"Zoiy Galloay is a very entertaining writer and she seems to have found a good genre to continue in, with this pseudo-medieval fantasy setting."
   -Reedsy Discovery on The Fate of the Empire

Royal Matchmaking Competition

PRINCESS QLOEY

Other Books by Zoiy Galloay

The Royal Matchmaking Competition Series:
Princess Qloey
Prince Zadkiel
The Fate of the Empire
Princess Zoyechka
The Flight of the Gryphon

The Search for the Truth Within Trilogy:
The Wizard Code

More to come . . .

Royal Matchmaking Competition

PRINCESS QLOEY

ZOIY G. GALLOAY

For the One Infinite Source, for only you made it possible.

ICE PALACE
SNOW F...
VELAZIAN EMPIRE
CRYSTAL HOT SPRINGS
CENTAURUS CITY
CASTLE RUINS
PALACE
PEARL SEA
VELAZIA
PINECREST
CENTAURUS FOREST
SEAWEED COVE
RAINBOW MOUNT
BAYLOR
PHOENIX DESERT PYRAMIDS
PAYONNIAN QUEENDOM
MYSTIC LAMP OASIS
THE

PIXIELAND KINGDOM
BERRY FOREST
AIREIS
DWARVEN MOUNTAIN RANGE
ADONIS PEAK KINGDOM
LABRADORITE CAVES
MOONSTONE CITY
NOLOLAY
EMERALD CAVES
TILDON
ELDOREN QUEENDOM
OGARZ
AGATE WATERFALLS
Royal Matchmaking Competition Series

Royal Matchmaking Competition Candidates

Royals of the Foreign Realms
1. Zazan, Prince of Eldoren Queendom

2. Abdulla, Prince of Payonna Queendom

3. Octavio, Prince of Pixieland Kingdom

4. Hedgewood, Prince of Adonis Peak Kingdom

Nobles of the Velazian Empire
5. Edgar, Prince of Baylor

6. Alejandro, Prince of Ogarz

7. Qinrel, Prince of Nololay

8. Lancelot, Duke of Moonstone City

9. Clayton, Duke of Pinecrest, Velazia

10. Zaccaria, Baron of Tildon

11. McKinley, Knight of Centaurus City

Winner of the Velazian Commoner Competition
12. Kipp, actor

CHAPTER I

The List

It cannot be denied that I was fortunate to have this opportunity. Where many would complain about the lack of freedom given in marriage, I gratefully acknowledged that there were at least twelve boys to choose from.

For me, marriage was a duty, not a right. It was an obligation, not a dalliance. My parents, the empress and emperor of Velazia, were examples of this. They ate together, they sat together during public events, but when nighttime came, they went to opposite sections of the palace and slept alone, only to repeat this routine the next day.

This was expected of me.

Yet . . . who wouldn't be curious about love at seventeen?

My mind lifted into the clouds, daydreaming of the feeling of being in love and being loved, something that caused my heart to press against my chest and beat faster. When I came back to reality, I found myself staring intently at the three-layered glass chandelier hanging from my bedroom ceiling.

Quickly, I straightened my neck and brought my attention to the servants who were tightening my stays, polishing my shoes, and preparing to put my skirt on, hoping nobody saw me ogling.

I cleared my throat.

Really, all I knew of love was from watching dramas at the Orb Theater in town; tragedies really. Somehow, two people would develop feelings for each other and were met with impossible odds that kept them apart—yet how these feelings developed between two people was yet a mystery to me. Interestingly enough, these lovers were either enemies from different kingdoms or people of different social classes who fell in love, and almost every time, they both ended up dying in the end. Yet part of me always rooted for them to end up together, happily ever after, despite the fact that they unceremoniously defied social protocol.

Truly, love made no sense.

It seemed irrational.

Nonetheless, I would perform my duty to the empire and follow in my parents' footsteps by marrying a boy with the perfect image and profile.

I tried to end my thoughts at that, yet . . . I couldn't escape from the lingering curiosity in the back of my mind: what if I fell in love in the next four weeks?

The last servant finished plucking off a single black hair of mine that fell on my sleeve. After everything was perfect, they asked if there was anything else for them to do, but I wished to be alone with my thoughts before the ceremony, where I was about to meet my future husband. They curtsied and left.

My nerves shook enough to make my legs feel weak and I had to get the jittery feelings out before presenting myself to the world.

As the crown princess, destined to inherit the empire, perfection wasn't an option for me—it was a requirement. The entire empire was watching, and if I made a mistake criticisms were often harsh. Among many things I had to be: I had to keep a thin figure, have grace in my every movement, and speak with beauty, power, and sophistication. I had to be studious, knowledgeable in modern literature and military tactics, and keep up-to-date in all political affairs. I spoke five languages fluently *in their native accents.* I sang, danced, and played the harp. I fit the role of next ruling empress to the T. And because I played the part perfectly, my new husband had to fit the role as well. My demands were high. *Or rather, my mother's demands were high.* But I wanted to please her, so I complied. Thus, my husband must be supportive, faithful, generate positive press, and give me inspiration and strength during my reign. He must be sagacious, and know five languages, and be current in political affairs, and . . . and . . . and well, he must be *everything* a royal should be! Most importantly, he must provide me with several heirs to the throne.

All this, I felt would be an obvious trait to find in a partner.

For the hundredth time, I individually scanned through each of the twelve drawings of the participants in the *Royal Matchmaking Competition,* called the RMC, and I imagined what each boy was like in person.

Then I took a few deep breaths and let the jitters drain out of my legs and onto the floor.

The RMC was a month-long competition where the most eligible princes, dukes, and noble members from each of the Seven Cities within the empire—plus one peasant—competed for a chance to marry the next empress or emperor of the Velazian Empire; *which was me.*

The city of Velazia—now called "the capital"—was ruled by a rather ambitious ruler 200 years ago (my great-great-great-great-great-grandfather, Emperor Alexander). He conquered several surrounding cities, establishing our Empire's hold on the region. But our control was always shaky and the empire almost fell apart. The royal families from the conquered cities either wanted more say in the government or to secede from the empire (by force, if necessary). This was exacerbated by an internal peasant revolt from rising taxes for the war efforts. To appease everyone at once, a treaty was made between the Seven Cities to hold the RMC. And therefore, it gave each of these demagogues a hand at ruling. Including the peasants.

As the Crown Princess, I had a royal duty to satisfy these royal guests now arriving at the palace.

This was my coming-out ceremony. A chance to prove myself to my mother, to other nobles, to my people, and to the world.

After reading the profiles of my twelve competitor over the last month, I picked out the obvious forerunners. Half the contestants were already eliminated from my personal list of potential husbands. Although I was curious . . .

Could I really experience love with one of these boys?

Would a boy who I fell in love with be equally capable of ruling as the emperor?

Do people fall in love by choice or fate?

My fingers caressed the soft paper of the miniature sketches of each bachelor. The two elves, Zazan and Qinrel, attracted my attention the most, for their skin glowed, their hair glimmered, and they were awfully handsome! Perhaps it was the artist's rendition, except rumors stated that elves (royal elves in particular) were irresistibly attractive to humans, and thus it could be real. In any case, I was eager to meet them. It was always a fantasy of mine to marry an elf.

Love or not, I could marry someone attractive to look at from across the dinner table.

With a smirk, I put their portraits down and took up another.

Each bachelor was chosen by their own people to enter the competition, but they had to match a certain profile. They must come from a noble bloodline, must be of a certain age range, and they must be willing to abdicate the seat of power in their own city if the opportunity arose. Although Velazia held the seat of ultimate power, each city had a ruling royal family to oversee the operations of the government. As part of the RMC agreement, they were allowed to retain the titles of king or queen.

There were seven noble contestants within the Seven Cities of the Velazian Empire, plus one commoner, which made up eight contestants. However, many people didn't like my family, both internally and abroad. My mother ruled with an iron fist and showed little mercy. This, combined with her policies—which were very profitable, so I didn't know why others complained—made anyone who couldn't benefit from her regulations angry. Marrying me, after all, meant that my consort would rule as the next emperor, so the RMC was useful in satisfying our conquered and unconquered cities. In terms of foreign relations, we were on bad terms with the dwarf kingdom, after my mother humiliated their prince during her RMC. Plus, Payonna Queendom, in the south, didn't like our influence within the realm (some rumors claimed they were planning to conquer some of our weaker cities to gain control of our resources). So the four neighboring foreign queendoms and kingdoms were invited to the RMC in order to "satisfy their thirst for power," and keep positive relations with them. This made up twelve contestants in total.

I looked over the commoner's profile. His name was Kipp and he won the opportunity in a contest held by the crown, for we couldn't just allow *any* peasant to enter the palace. Unicorn forbid! He had to have public speaking abilities, honor and dignity, and be attractive. Allowing him to join the RMC was a show of compassion toward the people that the aristocracy was listening, but in reality, the aristocrats didn't take him as a serious competitor. Some saw his admittance as a sham.

Kipp's smile was rather cheesy as he showed off his big straight pearly white teeth. People didn't usually smile in portraits and they didn't usually have good teeth. That was probably why he was chosen. Nonetheless, the young peasant was likely to lack knowledge in any foreign or political affairs, and thus already off my list.

A sham, indeed, it was.

Out of the contestants, I had only met one before—my distant cousin Clayton, the Duke of Pinecrest. He was chosen as Velazia's contestant. Pinecrest was a province on the western outskirts of the capital bordering a lush forest. But I confidently told myself I'd never marry him because of our close relations. *Or would I?*

It was three years since I last saw him at a royal dinner where my mother publicly humiliated me for not being aggressive enough in my approach to the *Gremlin Gangs*. At the dinner, I didn't think much of Clayton. Now I wondered, was he filled out? Handsome? More mature? Less irritating?

Still, it was awkward. We were related. And I wanted to mend problems with *other* cities through this marriage.

Everyone at that dinner party would be here during the RMC. It was a chance to redeem myself. Yet, just thinking of seeing them made me want to crawl into a tiny hole, never to emerge again.

One of the most interesting contestant was the dwarf named Hedgewood. Being 5'4"—only an inch shorter than me—he was rather tall for his species. He wore glasses. *Most unusual.* And was clean shaven. *Don't they usually have beards?* It was a general bias that all dwarves had thick beards and a stocky physique, reaching a maximum height of 5', and they loved to work in mines. He did not fit that stereotype. Not at all.

Meeting him will be interesting.

Yet the dwarf was already off my list. After all, I didn't really need the alliance of the distant dwarf kingdom. Payonna was more important. But I'd allow the dwarf to attend the competition, regardless; a show of hospitality.

Prince Edgar was the most promising out of all the contestants. He had an impressive profile and fit my list of requirements of a husband perfectly! He was a high-ranking prince, wealthy, owned several mines, he looked regal in his velvet canions, and was rumored to have an astute understanding of the world and to be agreeable. I eagerly anticipated meeting him the most. The list of competitors went as follows:

Guests were already arriving, and the opening ceremony would begin within the hour. To me, this would be a quick and easy process. I would impress and inspire the guests with my grace and intelligence, find the perfect man within a few days, and make my parents proud of me with my good decision; then my rule would be the golden age of the empire.

I neatly arranged all portraits into a pile and set it on my cherry-colored desk, which matched my large bedposts, vanity, and various chairs around the room. Then I headed to the opening ceremony.

Chapter 2

The Grand Competition

My parents had planted within me the importance of impressing my guests with my poise, grace, finely spoken words, and of course, my wealth and beauty. My mother now stood to my right, with my father and younger brother on my left, as we took our places in front of the throne.

The throne room was so vast that it could nearly fit a thousand people comfortably. Today, all the aristocrats stood on either side of the isle, dressed in their fine diamond and ruby jewelry, along with silk, damask, or brocade gowns. They looked either toward the double doors where the contestants would soon enter or at me. The air was filled with anticipation and excitement from our guests from this opportunity to be in the presence of the reigning family and high-ranking nobility.

As I looked at my mother, she didn't smile or comfort me; instead, she glared down at her vassals as if they belonged to her.

For the ceremony, she expected me to act and behave perfectly without her input. Yet, if I did anything wrong, she would immediately point it out. Finally, her deep brown eyes looked over, wondering why I was looking at her.

"Stop looking like a frightened kitten," she criticized with a snarl. "Chin up, watch the entrance."

Already, I made a mistake.

Sometimes I felt meek in her presence. She towered above me by several inches, was bigger boned and stockier. In comparison, I was thin and lightweight like a feather. I wished to have her confidence, but didn't always know how. Right now I felt sick to my stomach. One of these boys that I was about to meet would become my husband. I had to impress all of the them and make all these guests happy with my decision. How could I have confidence at a moment like this?

There was one thing that always boosted my self-esteem, and that was knowing that my appearance alone would impress many without even trying. Fairy dust made my white and purple gown shimmer like moon beams. I was a twinkling star on the throne. Anyone who entered the room immediately set their eyes on me. A matching crown embedded with soft curves and amethysts gently rested on my head. But it was my massive black hair extension that took extra neck strength to hold up.

My lips were pink like soft rose petals invigorated with morning dew drops. I had matching nail colors made of magical fairy dust that glowed in the dark. Everything was in place; except for my nervous system.

My father, Emperor Ricardo, was originally from Tildon City and won the competition twenty years prior, during my mother's RMC. Next to him was my brother, Prince Farooq. He was only ten years old and silently stood with his hands behind his back, displaying perfectly obedient behavior like I should've been. But my mother would scold me again if I didn't look straight ahead, so I brought my attention to the double doors at the entrance just as the soldiers pried them open.

Trumpets sounded, and the first contestant was announced.

How wrong I was to think I had the center of attention. No amount of fairy dust in the world could compare to the beautiful creature who now approached the throne.

Prince Zazan of Eldoren Elf Queendom had violet-colored eyes and long white hair to his waist. His skin glowed against the candlelight in an unnatural way. But most impressive was his physique. He wore spaulders, which was a single plate of elven metal that covered his shoulders. It made his frame look broader and his waist thinner, which inevitably made him look more striking than one could possibly imagine. Additionally, he wore a white and blue skirt with a water-charming wand loosely hanging off his hip like a sword.

My pupils were the size of an orange as I tried to take everything in. It was the first time I set eyes on a royal elf whose radiance was supernatural. But I remained poised. It was imperative that he didn't see me lose composure. I was the next empress after all. And my parents would scold me for showing any weakness.

Zazan never took his eyes off me from the moment he entered the room.

Dear unicorns, help me. I prayed to God.

He bowed. "Your Majesty, Princess Qloey, no one told me your beauty competes with an elf Goddess."

I was in love.

From several feet away, I smelled his elven cologne. Strong, potent, and zesty, as if he stepped out of an eucalyptus bath. "You flatter me, Prince Zazan. For I could never compete with a Goddess," I said with a chuckle.

"Do not sell yourself short, Your Majesty. Your destiny is greater than you realize." He smirked.

I nearly collapsed right there. But luckily, his servants brought forth gifts, which gave me a moment to recover.

"Elf cosmetics, lotions, and perfumes to glorify your greatness. But I'm certain you don't need it anyway." He bowed again and gave me a sultry look as he turned to leave. His sister, the Crown Princess Luna, and their parents, Queen Biva and King Tolyn, stepped away with him.

Forget the other boys, I was prepared to marry him now! *And oh, will these lotions make my skin glow too?*

The announcer spoke again as the second contestant arrived taking my mind off of the goodies. Each contestant was introduced according to their status. First, the high nobility of outlying nations, followed by princes and lower ranked nobles within the empire. The peasant, having no rank, would be introduced last.

The RMC was the event of the decade. It took years to prepare and save up for, as the cost of hosting and feeding all these guests for two to four weeks was extensive, plus organizing the competitions. Everyone invited got an ego boost, and they arrived with their families and staff. Many of their extended family members were allowed to attend the events, but we only had a limited amount of rooms inside the palace, and we only gave it to the highest ranked nobles, plus the contestants and their families. Everyone else found hotels around the city to stay in. Some booked their hotels years in advance and paid a handsome price.

The second prince was from a powerful foreign queendom that would be a mighty foe in battle. In the fourteenth century, Velazia tried to conquer Payonna Queendom and failed. It would be advantageous to have them as an ally in marriage. Our empire would become invincible!

Prince Abdulla of Payonna had a dark goatee and thin mustache with colorful garbs. He, too, smelt delicious from frankincense and oils. He lived in a queendom rich in trade, and gifted me with handmade rugs, oils, and gold jewelry.

The third contestant, Prince Octavio of Pixieland Kingdom, was bright and cheerful, and had pure white skin like snow. Just seeing him approach brought a smile to my lips. Pixies were known for their joy and playfulness and it clearly rubbed off on Octavio.

He brought *universal fairy dust,* an expensive commodity, as most fairy dust had one purpose, like healing dust, or dust for clothing-dye, or dust for purifying water, etc. Only the creator of the dust could determine its uses. However, universal fairy dust could be used in a multitude of ways in one jar, all at the owner's discretion. I would have to safeguard this commodity.

Next came the dwarf. Prince Hedgewood of Adonis Peak Kingdom was more handsome than I had expected. *Who knew dwarves could be attractive at all?* However, I quickly discarded any thought of marrying him. There were more profitable matches to be had. He surprised me with gifts of literature, when I rather hoped he'd bring sapphires from their mines.

Oh well, books will do.

Next were the eight bachelors from within the Velazian Empire, the first being Prince Edgar of Baylor.

Sweat dribbled down my back. For a month, I had imagined how cordial our first interaction would be, of us falling in love upon introduction, of him saying some joke that'd make my family and myself laugh. Afterwards, I often daydreamed about us walking down the hallways together holding hands, all smiles and politeness, and possibly exchanging . . . *a kiss?* He had attractive curly red hair and cute freckles, but . . . a long straight plain face. When he smiled, his upper lip seemed to curl up in an unsightly manner that revealed his gums and two protruding buck teeth, all of which his portrait conveniently edited out. That was not how I imagined him.

No worries. No worries. He is still perfect husband material.

"I am most propitiously delighted, auspiciously tickled, optimistically enthralled to be here." Prince Edgar lifted his nose into the air before he gave me a slight bow.

"Oh, yes. Uh?" *Auspiciously tickled?* That was a rather peculiar way of describing our first meeting. Yet, I quickly brushed the strangeness off, knowing that his words only proved that he was well read and polished in his education. *He's exquisitely literate,* I affirmed his greatness in my mind. "Just as I am, uh . . . propitiously . . . delighted? That you're here."

That was weird, I shouldn't have said that. I imagined banging my head on a wall with such an idiotic response.

My mother smiled brightly at Edgar, taking no note of my awkward response.

Edgar's father, King Edward, had a business partnership with my mother to open ruby mines in the capital. The mines ultimately created great wealth and more jobs. Still, this led to the Ruby Riot of year 1555. United, Velazia and Baylor both brought in their armies and put an end to the troublemakers. Of course, I didn't understand why *anyone* would protest with all the jobs and wealth the mines brought to the capital.

But these details were unimportant. The event in the past. So I shrugged it off.

Edgar presented the largest ruby I ever saw. My hand caressed the translucent blood-red hue and the perfect cut before the servant whisked it away.

So wonderful!

The next contestant strutted forth with an air of confidence. He flung his cape behind him and bowed. Prince Alejandro of Ogarz winked at me while tossing his long hair about in a sexy way. His portrait didn't do his beauty justice. Alejandro brought chocolates and read a love poem to me, devoting his heart to me forever.

"You shall be mine, and I shall be yours. Forever our love will remain, till the end of time." Alejandro winked again and walked away.

My mother was overtaken by his charm and said, "We shall call him the *'Prince Charming'* of the lot."

Charming indeed. I didn't know how to begin taming a boy like that.

The second elf entered. Prince Qinrel was just as beautiful as the first elf, with jet black hair falling to his waist and piercing sapphire eyes, but his personality was lacking. He appeared annoyed to meet me, and slightly dazed from his carriage ride. He hardly looked at me, and his eyes almost drew into the back of his head.

Was he rolling his eyes or sick to his stomach?

He just stood there and his servant motioned to the gift. Qinrel nodded. "A gift . . ." His words trailed off as though he forgot what the gift was.

The elf servant finished the sentence for him after a few seconds, ". . . of elven robes."

Other than Qinrel, each contestant brought gifts and spoke impressive words, although they became redundant after a few bachelors were introduced, as they always complimented on my beauty being greater than this-or-that, or comparing me to an elf. I enjoyed it but . . . I rather hoped for something original.

Next, Lanselos du Pierre de Lune was introduced. The duke gave me flashy moonstones and stuttered on introduction.

"P—pleased to meet you, Your Majesty," Lanselos said. "You may call me 'Duke Lancelot'." His fluency in Velazian was remarkable, I could hardly hear his Moonstone accent.

Impressive.

My cousin Clayton gave me deep royal purple fabric. *My favorite color!*

"Zaccaria, Baron of Tildon," the announcer said.

Everyone waited for him to enter, but . . . nobody came.

Lack of punctuality, tisk tisk, he's going lower on my list. But Zaccaria was my father's favorite contestant since they were from the same city, so . . . I'd have to forgive him.

A loud tapping noise echoed from outside the room, followed by cries of, "watch out" and "make way." Zaccaria then entered the throne room on horseback. He came to the center of the room and performed several stunts on the horse, impressing the audience and myself.

The boys must capture my attention somehow, and this was definitely memorable.

After his display of horsemanship, he stood on top of the saddle and did a backflip off the horse. He was nearly the size of the dwarf, only an inch taller than me, muscular, energetic, and unruly.

"Zack, Baron of Tildon, at your service." *Then would come the beauty compliment . . .* "I've heard many wonderful things about your beauty, but never could imagine how immaculately gorgeous you are in person."

"It is an honor to meet you, Baron Zaccaria. I look forward to getting acquainted with you."

"Do call me 'Zack.' Please accept the gift of this Fusaichi Pegasus. A direct descendant of the Pegasus on Rainbow Mount from which I found her."

"A *real* Pegasus! How ever did you find one?" I stepped forward, eager to know more, and then saw small wings starting to protrude out of its sides. That was enough to get my mother's attention.

"Qloey." My mother warned. *"A princess is never eager, never excited, and never smiles too much,"* my mother always told me growing up.

I stepped back, placed my palms together, and spoke softly. "We shall go riding together. I wish to know more about your discoveries on Rainbow Mount." But inside I was jumping with joy! My feet danced in my mind.

Two more left. I couldn't wait to start the competition.

"McKinley, Knight of Centaurus City." McKinley appeared more proper than some of the princes. He was tall, buff, handsome, and rather stern.

Perhaps he's nervous, I thought.

"It's an honor to be invited into your presence, Your Royal Majesties. I hear you're skilled in archery. Thus, I've brought a bow made from petrified trees from the lost city of Atlantis."

"This is delightful." I beamed, but restrained myself from stepping forward again. "I invite you to try it with me and show me its mystical ways."

"My pleasure, Your Majesty." McKinley left the room with perfectly straight posture.

"Who knew he was so regal." I looked to my mother for agreement. He was only a knight, yet was definitely moving up on my list. My mind whirled as I compared my pre-competition favorites list to my first impressions on meeting them and some were vastly different.

The last contestant was the commoner, who had received a makeover and crash course on protocol over the last few weeks. His hands wrung together and his jaw clenched as he approached the throne with his family. Although he was given fashionably new clothes—a new leather jerkin, boots, and a clean white tunic—he was easy to distinguish from the royalty in both his posture and the fact that he wore no gems or regalia. Yet, he was attractive, with a good physique.

Poor boy, he will never have a chance. I remained composed and greeted him with dignity and honor.

"Your Majesty, I offer you a gift of literature."

He tried.

"A new, unpublished play from the great writer, Pippa of the Orb Theater," he said.

"An unpublished play?"

I knew all of Pippa's plays! This woman would go down as the most brilliant writer in all of history! Extraordinary. And now I had an un-published copy of her new play?!

I contained my desire to jump for joy, yet my cheeks were hurting from smiling. "How did you manage a copy? This must be worth a fortune."

"I'm part of the theater, Your Majesty. She heard I won the contest and wished to offer this gift on my behalf. It is my honor to deliver it to you."

Truly impressive!

I wanted to twirl around in circles, but I held back.

"I accept the gift with enthusiasm," I said. As soon as I returned to my bedroom tonight, where my parents wouldn't see me, I'd dance around my bed posts and shout in silence to express my exuberance.

But Kipp still has no chance.

After the last contestant was introduced, our guests gathered into the reception room for dinner and entertainment.

My family proceeded in a different direction. We went into the hall between the throne room and the reception room, where we could discuss our first impressions while the guests got settled.

"I could smell the dwarf from ten feet away." My mother sneered. "I'm repulsed the dwarf kingdom was added into the RMC treaty in the first place. No royal member will marry one, and it's a waste of our resources to house them." She peered out the door to spy on the guests as they settled around the tables.

Hedgewood wasn't so bad in person, I thought. His clothes were rich in embroidery with gold swirls, and his face was attractive. It might be real gold thread too. But she was right, that humans and dwarves rarely married. Humans married elves frequently, as elves were beautiful creatures and highly respected, but dwarves, having short stubby legs and being bigger boned, weren't considered attractive to humans. Being unappealing to the eye meant elves and humans treated them with less respect.

A door opened and my lady-in-waiting, Victorya, stepped through and curtsied to all of us. I stepped to the side with her and she asked, "So, who made the best first impression?"

Victorya wore a deep blue and camel-colored gown. It was one of my old gowns, but as my ladies made me new ones, I often gave the older ones away. They were always thrilled to receive such fine clothing.

"Prince Zazan," I answered.

"Of course." She squeezed my hand. "You stared at his portrait so much, you could've burnt holes in it."

Victorya was correct, but I wouldn't admit something like that out-loud. "Nonsense. I would never do such a thing," I said.

"And Prince Edgar?" Victorya held her hands to her heart, ready to hear how I fell head over heels for him.

"He . . ." What was the word? "He has an impressive vocabulary."

Victorya tilted her head, expecting me to say more.

Then my mind quickly found another boy to admire. "The Baron Zack was interesting, but he's so short!"

My father overhead me mention him and said, "I rather thought the Baron Zaccaria made an impressive performance. Plus, I've never seen a Pegasus before. This will go down in history. And Tildon will be known for it."

My mother made no comment about Zack, knowing that my father's opinion was biased. "I can't stand that Prince Octavio. Look at him now, all fake smiles. It's as if he's never seen a palace before." My father peeked out, then returned to stand with his hands behind his back.

I decided to add to the conversation. "Prince Octavio's cheery behavior seemed genuine to me. It was refreshing, actually."

My mother gave me a long cold stare, as though I overstepped my boundaries in disagreeing with her opinion. "I know your blasted fairy goddessmother bestowed compassion upon you as your christening gift"—her lip curled in annoyance—"but sometimes I think it affected your brain. Octavio is pitifully annoying and childish." And that was the end of my opinion on the matter as she peeked out the door again to observe the guests.

My parents didn't like that my fairy goddessmother gave me this gift and eventually forbade her from returning to the palace ever again. They thought I should be bestowed with the ability to influence others, strength in battle, or perhaps make money grow out of trees, but compassion? It was useless to them and often meant I had a different opinion than the rest of my family. Yet it didn't stop my curiosity. I spent a great deal of time in the library, reading fiction stories about characters who might've experienced it, how compassion worked in general, what if felt like, and what benefits it had for society, etc. Eventually, I came to the conclusion that I must experience compassion in its entirety before fully understanding it; but my parents rarely showed it to me, so I hadn't had the experience yet that I so desired.

My brother stood next to our father, mirroring his stance with his hands behind his back. The two didn't look alike at all; my father had broad shoulders and a square jaw, while my brother was short, even for his age, and had an aquiline nose. Wherever he got his nose from, I couldn't tell. Not that I looked like my mother. She became plump over the last few years and lost her figure. Since I kept to daily sword fighting and archery, I was strong but skinny and looked more like my father in that aspect. Plus, we both had more of a diamond shaped face than my brother.

Our councilwoman and advisor suddenly opened the door and approached. Yenna was a humorless, dull woman and showed this in her dreary gray and black clothing; with no flair or oomph. Plus, Yenna would report my every mistake to my mother, which put a bitter taste in my mouth whenever she was around. She was a petite and thin woman with muscular arms and a curvy waistline, a native to the capital with a long lineage of advisors who served the crown. A trusted woman to the royal family and given great oversight. Victorya, on the other hand, had more personality and zest, and always worked on giving me the latest fashions. She was the trendsetter of the empire and tested her mantuamaker skills on me. I loved her new creations, like my current gown, and wore them with pride.

"The reception is ready," Yenna said with a nod.

The reception room went quiet as my family was announced. We stepped inside and took our seats in the front of the room for everyone to see us the entire meal. The guest's tables lined up against the walls and left a space in the middle of the room for my performance. But first, the servants went to each of the twelve contestants and presented them with a gold pocket watch studded with small rubies.

The pocket watch was a new invention. We could keep time inside of your own pocket! It was extraordinary. Our empire recently opened new trade routes to various places around the world, expanding our reach, influence, and introducing us to new technologies.

After the gift exchange, the plan was to captivate them with an honorary dance. My outer skirt detached, revealing my hose and a small skirt underneath. I stepped into the center of the room when Alejandro and Zack started cheering wildly for me, causing me to smile.

My dance partner was a twenty-five foot-long purple ribbon attached to a handle. Throughout the dance, I performed standing splits while twirling the ribbon around my body, then leapt into the air doing the full splits again. Sometimes I'd throw the ribbon in the air, do a back bend or double spin, then catch it as it fell.

After a standing ovation from my admirers, the servants put my skirt back on, and I sat down at the harp and sang a soft melody while playing the instrument. The plan was to make my bachelors fall head over heels for me from the start with my fine-tuned contralto voice.

The hard part was over. After the strict formalities were complete, we'd all retreat into the ballroom, where I could casually mingle with each bachelor and get to know them better. Edgar was the first one I would pursue, followed by Zazan. But that never happened.

Near the end of my song, some aristocrats made supercilious remarks about how rude the guards were. And then someone screamed and shook me from my daydream of dancing with Edgar.

Right as I looked up, one of our palace guards lifted a bow.

His arrow was aimed directly at me.

CHAPTER 3

The Crystal Chambers

Everything happened in a split second. The entire room erupted in screams. I quickly ducked behind the harp as the arrow flew through the air, but I wasn't quick enough. Suddenly, I felt a fierce explosion of pain in my arm.

My guards rushed in, creating a blockade around me. Their light blue cloaks blocked me from seeing what was happening, but my head was spinning too much to comprehend anything, anyway.

The next moment, one soldier picked me up and rushed me out of the room.

"Qloey! Qloey!" My mother lost all composure. "Quick, get the healer!" But the elven healer was already running toward me. She took a clear quartz crystal and moved it across my wound as the guard carried me down the hall. "Are you hurt anywhere else?"

"I—I." Normally, I remained composed even under strenuous situations, but my arm was aching and my head felt dizzy. Guards were shouting. People ran in every direction. In the chaos, I didn't know up from down anymore and couldn't grasp how to respond.

"You're in shock. We'll move you into the red crystal chamber. I won't remove the arrow until we have supplies," the healer said.

"The arrow?" I asked, and looked over at my wounded arm to see what she meant.

The Crystal Healing Chambers performed wonders. I slept in a cave dug into the basement of the palace. There were multiple different rooms in the crystal chambers. Each room was filled with crystals of different colors of the rainbow, plus a white, a black, and a gold room. The gold room was indeed made of pure gold.

I was inside the red room; it had red tourmaline, rubies, and red garnet gemstones sticking out of the walls and making patterns on the floor. Each crystal helped heal different aspects of my body, mind, and spirit, but I wasn't knowledgeable enough in the art of healing to know it all. What I did know was that the red crystals healed shock and survival aspects. By the next morning, my nerves had calmed and no negative emotion remained of the event; even the wound on my arm was mostly healed, minus a small scar. When I returned to my actual bedroom, it was overflowing with flowers, gifts, and notes from my contestants concerned about my well-being. It gladdened my heart and almost sent a river of tears welling in my eyes.

I went about smelling each flower bouquet and reading the notes. *"My deepest fears came alive when I saw that man shoot his arrow at you . . ."* one note began from Clayton, and another, *"I wish only to be able to comfort you during this time, but your guards wouldn't let me pass,"* from Zack.

How sweet. I was filled with love. They cared, they really cared for me. Or was it compassion? Compassion, care, or love? I had to study the differences, but thought it must be love.

Each note was carefully read, then placed on the windowsill so their love could watch over me as I slumbered. But then my mother stepped inside the room with her usual cold expression on her face, taking the sunshine and warmth from the love letters like a winter storm. She didn't hug or smile. Instead, she sat on the bed as I clasped my hands together and found a seat on my favorite velvety royal-purple vanity stool.

Purple was all around my bedroom, in my curtains, and on my bed sheets. It was an expensive color, but so beautiful to the eye that I adorned myself in it daily.

"Her bedchambers are as big as my aunt's entire house," I once overheard a servant say. *"And these purple curtains could feed us for an entire year."*

My closet could fit three king-sized beds in it. This was normal for me, and I couldn't fathom how a human could possibly spend their life inside a house that small or manage so few clothes in their wardrobe, when, after all, it took over thirty minutes just to walk from end-to-end of the palace; my home. Yet I had no conception of how much food cost as my servants bought it all for me. A whole tour of the palace would take two hours if you didn't linger too long to admire the intricate gold geometry woven throughout the ceilings and walls, the many paintings and statues, or take a detailed look at the hand carved furniture. The palace was three stories high with a basement, a roof to lounge around, and was four million square feet in total.

"Have they finished interrogating the assassin?" I asked my mother.

My mother was a commanding woman and a strict disciplinarian. I never called her "mother" out loud, instead it was: "Your Royal Majesty," or under casual circumstances when she was in a good mood, the less sympathetic, "Empress Ezmorelda" and "Emperor Ricardo" for my equally severe father. Yet a part of me wanted the closeness of "mother" and "father" therefore, I usually thought of the two as such. Yet, I was also too afraid to tell them this in-person. What if they didn't approve of the way I thought of them?

Every word my mother spoke held power, and no one questioned her on any matter. I wished to emulate her greatness someday. However, I was different in many ways. I was soft and gentle, and because of this, others doubted if I would live up to my mother's strength. But I would prove to them that I could during this RMC!

"He killed himself after they captured him," she stated.

"WHAT! HOW?"

"Qloey." That's all my mother had to say for me to realize my exuberance was too much. Royalty never shouted. They never lost composure (*except last night when my mother panicked.*) But my mother could. I, on the other hand, wasn't allowed to.

Until I become empress. Then I can exclaim all I want!

She waited for me to erect my posture and place my hands in my lap again before continuing.

"Some sort of poison in his mouth. He bit into it and released the venom. The healers couldn't revive him as it was too strong." She spoke in an emotionless tone, lacking any compassion for anyone.

"By what means did he acquire such a powerful poison?"

My mother shook her head, meaning they had no leads. "No known poison anywhere in Velazia." Finally, she reached a hand over and squeezed mine. "For a second"—she breathed deeply—"I thought I lost you." A moment of silence remained between us. This was a special moment. This was the most affection my parents would ever show me. My mother's hand in mine. I didn't want to let go, and squeezed her hand back with a smile inside my heart—like a joyful sun ready to dote upon the morning sunflowers—but she quickly let go and the clouds covered up the sun once again. I longed for that moment's eventual return. "We're taking extra precautions. Including investigating each of the contestant's staff members and reducing their presence. You may choose to rest today and we'll move the schedule back a few days . . ."

"No! Uh . . . the competition must continue. On time." I didn't want to wait. Not with all these beautiful love letters. "They've come from so far and made great impressions on me. I wish to honor their time with my own."

"Very well then." She patted my hand. Again, there was that affection. Twice in a day, combined with the flowers and the love-notes, this was turning into a wonderful morning.

"What do you think the assassin's motive was?" I asked.

"We don't know. It could be any of the cities under our rule trying to gain independence by stirring the pot. Or one of the four independent nations trying to lessen our power in the realm. Or even someone starting an internal peasant revolt. There are too many agendas to narrow it down. But we *do* know that the assassin tied the bow underneath the table prior to the competition and reached for it at the opportune time."

"That extra second it took him to grab the bow is the only reason I had time to move behind the harp," I said.

My mother took a deep breath. "We don't think the assassin was acting alone and may have been taking orders from another. In order to achieve what he did, he had to steal a uniform from the armory, enter the palace before the competition began, and place the bow and arrow inside the dining hall *after* the tables were set up. All without being noticed by the female servants preparing the room. Unless it was a female servant who did it? There are too many variables to account for. One individual couldn't have achieved it all.

"As we go forward, keep in mind one thing: Allowing so many visitors into the palace brought an opportunity for others to upset things in the capital. Either someone traveled with a royal entourage under disguise so they could execute their plans, or one of the contestants has ulterior motives. They might target you again or one of us. So do be careful."

Qloey, Princess of Velazia

CHAPTER 4

True Concern

(The Bachelors)

"**S**he will be alright, my informants tell me." Prince Edgar snuffed, then picked up the *Royal Times Newspaper* which reported on the opening ceremony last night, the headline of which was a drawing of a soldier holding a bow as he prepared to shoot Qloey. "She's completely recovered, entirely healed, substantially alleviated of all her ailments," Edgar informed the room without lifting an eye off the paper.

"And who told you this?" Baron Zack asked. It irked his ego that Edgar had this information when he didn't.

"I have great connections," Edgar said and shifted to the next page and found an article on each of the bachelors. It detailed the positive and negative impressions each boy made during the opening ceremony. Edgar was high on the list of favorite bachelors according to *The Royal Times*. "See here, it even says, my connections with the royal family 'are above and beyond' your own. Making me 'the most likely candidate to win her hand'." He quoted and set the paper down with a smile that made his cheeks pucker up. "Seeing that my position is more palpably reputable, assuredly valuable, discernibly commendable than the rest of you, if you need to deliver a message to Her Majesty, Princess Qloey, do come to me first. I'll see that she gets it."

All the other boys scowled under their breath, as if any of *them* would go through *him* to get to Qloey! They all had their own plans for the competition. While Edgar took the time to gather his information through his father, King Edward I, who received his information from Empress Ezmorelda herself, the other boys took the time to order gifts of flowers, jewelry, and new hair pieces to be sent to the princess directly, which Edgar did not do.

Another who did not send any presents was Prince Hedgewood. He already finished reading the entire *Royal Times* and *Gremlin Times* before Edgar even reached the page on the *"Favorite Bachelors likely to Win Princess Qloey's Hand."* Hedgewood then moved onto *The Fairy Tale Times Newspaper*, which had an entirely different perspective on who was most likely to win based on the gifts the bachelors brought to the ceremony and on Qloey's facial reactions to these gifts—and while seemingly neutral at times, she occasionally gave away a hint of telltale emotion as to her heart's desires. Here, Zack was number one for his display of horsemanship and the rare gift of a Pegasus. But Zack wasn't a reader himself and was too busy doing his morning handstand push-ups and oiling his biceps to know what a great impression he made on the spectators. Kipp was second for Pippa's unpublished play, but Hedgewood was still last for giving her *"plain old books,"* as it said.

The two elves sat in a corner talking in the elven language. To the human ear, they appeared to be in a heated argument, but nobody else knew elven and thus ignored the pointy eared boys.

"Kipp." McKinley stomped his feet as Kipp entered the breakfast area, and rested his hand on his belt. "How was your first night in the royal palace?"

Kipp wore all new clothing that was given to him for winning the competition, but he still looked out-of-place next to the noblemen with rich velvety doublets, diamond rings, and the fact that most of the noblemen carried swords by their side. Kipp never welded a sword in his life and didn't understand the necessity for these other boys to be parading around with them like some savior. After all, it didn't help keep the assassin away.

"Thank you McKinley. Uh, Sir McKinley," Kipp corrected himself. "The accommodations are to my liking."

"McKinley will do; we're all equals here." McKinley made extra effort to go out of his way and make friends with the commoner, hoping he'd feel comfortable in his new surroundings, and this was much appreciated by Kipp.

McKinley, being the lowest ranked of all noblemen, knew that rank meant a great deal to *some* nobles, and they wouldn't bother stooping so low to associate with either a knight or a commoner—although it was too early to tell which ones in the room were like this yet. But McKinley wasn't interested in gaining privilege through connections by kissing another nobleman's rear end and preferred the easier, more comfortable connections of a humble friend. Thus, he tested the waters of Kipp's likely friendship before the others.

Another bachelor started playing music alone in the corner.

"Music in the morning?" Alejandro took a moment away from looking at himself in the mirror to protest this idea.

"Music *all* day long!" Someone behind him exclaimed. "Music brings joy to the world."

For some, like Alejandro, it was too much positivity for this early in the morning and gave him a headache.

"Breakfast is served." Alejandro interrupted the music by announcing the obvious fact that servants were bringing in hot sausages, eggs, toast, and cold fruit, and placing them across the large rectangular table. To his delight, the music stopped, and they all took seats at the table. Then the door opened and in walked the crown princess.

(Qloey)

The twelve boys stood as I walked into their breakfast room and joined them for our first breakfast together. The food was just brought out and not a single one of them took a bite. Without saying a word, I nodded for them to sit. I enjoyed being the one in charge instead of my mother, for once. *I get to make the commands.* It made me feel all grown up, as if I was already the empress.

"Are you alright, Your Majesty?" Kipp, the commoner, leaned over the table and spoke over his royal superiors . . . which wasn't proper. Nonetheless, it was endearing.

I smiled and answered him first, "I am fully healed. Thank you, Kipp." I remained standing to speak with them. "Last night was traumatic, and while the assassin is dead, we're continuing the investigation on some leads. Rest assured, we will find the mastermind behind this."

While talking, I took the time to gaze everyone in the eye. Suddenly, I forgot what I was going to say as my thoughts got carried over by what *their* first impression of *me* might be. *Did they find me attractive? Did they admire my performance last night? Did they feel a spark of chemistry between us? Could they sense my nerves right now? Did they want to fall in love with me or just want to gain the crown?* Perhaps it was hard to tell at this point since the ball was canceled.

Throwing all doubts aside, I tried to find confidence as I finished addressing them. "Yet, I wish to honor you all for the sacrifices you've made coming here. This is an opportunity to find potential compatibility between us and hopefully garner deep relationships between our people. And so the competition will continue as planned."

I sat down and a servant—knowing my favorite food—placed poached eggs, strawberries, cucumbers, and biscuits on my plate and handed me a glass of fresh squeezed orange juice.

Two seats down was the snobbish elf, Prince Qinrel. Just as the previous night, he failed to hide his annoyance in being here and didn't even acknowledge me the entire meal. Instead, he looked down at his food, or occasionally argued in elven with another over religious protocol.

Makes choosing a betrothal easier. I affirmed. *He's definitely scratched off my list.*

The dwarf sat nearby as well. Again, he portrayed abnormal attributes of a typical dwarf. Perhaps there was much to their species I had yet to learn. He wore round glasses, held perfect mannerisms like the emperor himself, and spoke with eloquent sophistication.

"I dare say," Hedgewood spoke to Lancelot, "the *Gremlin Times* is most vulgar and rather ignoble in their approach to the opening ceremony. The assassination was mere play and entertainment to them, not a single ounce of sympathy for those impacted by the pain of the event."

I silently agreed; the *Gremlin Times* was known for their unwashed opinions.

Should he move back on the list? I wondered. *Nah. He's still a dwarf and way too short.*

Prince Edgar, who sat to my right, looked superior in his rich purple doublet and large rubies studded along his neckline. Edgar's father, King Edward had four children: Edward II, Edgar, Edmond, and Ednnys whom had a powerful influence on the empire. Two out of four of my family members (my great and great-great-grandfathers) married someone from Baylor during their RMC. Here I could see why, for Prince Edgar was regal; he had good manners. He was a favored candidate among every aristocrat in the palace. But then breakfast began . . . and things swiftly went downhill.

"Money is wasted on road repairs. It is substantially wasteful, absolutely uneconomical, altogether prodigal," Edgar said stiffly, while slicing a sausage into a bird-sized piece to nibble on. "The road between here and my city, Baylor, was repaired just three years ago and again they're doing construction. Why are all our resources being allocated toward fixing the same roads?"

"There was a flood that washed out the road—" I informed, but he rudely ignored me and continued talking.

That. Never. Happened. To me before. Nobody interrupted me while talking; my mother was the exception. *But dear fairies. A prince interrupting me? I am the crown princess!* When my mother spoke, everyone went silent and listened to her. Generally, whoever was higher ranked in the room was the one talking, while everyone below them listened. But here, a prince interrupted me! How lowly it made me feel, as though I didn't really hold the title of "Crown Princess."

As Edgar continued speaking, I wondered what to do about this. Should I interrupt him and talk over him, or would that make a scene? If I remained quiet and listened, it may be seen as a weakness in me. My father would say so. This, right here, was why people often criticized me, for being too meek, because the empress would know what to do in this situation. In fact, she would . . . just start talking and others would quiet down immediately. But, how do I command such respect when I never did so before?

Herein lies my mother's disappointment in me. If only I was stronger.

In the end, I decided to listen in and wait for the right moment to add to the conversation.

Edgar continued to speak about increasing trolls on toll bridges in order to levy taxes, details on how taxes work, then the history of taxes, land taxes, food taxes, and roof taxes. Everyone around him grew bored; it wasn't just me.

Maybe I'm not meek, maybe the conversation is just boring?

After this, I began to develop the opinion that Edgar was rather stiff, too serious, somewhat wearisome, and quite humorless. He displayed every attribute expected of a wealthy and powerful aristocrat: someone who wanted more wealth and power.

Problem was . . . it was breakfast! Who talks about taxes at breakfast?!?

But, still Edgar had an impressive profile. I took a few breaths to calm down. *Maybe it's just this one conversation and everything will work out fine later. There's plenty of time to fall in love with him.* I convinced myself and turned to my other side and saw Lancelot, the Duke of Moonstone.

Lancelot didn't speak a word and just nodded to me. To compensate for his shyness, I inquired how his journey was and was met with a quick, "Wonderful."

Silence.

"And your comfort in the palace?"

"Wonderful."

More silence.

This was the most awkward breakfast of my life.

To my relief, Kipp pulled up a chair between us. The table went silent as all royal members soaked in Kipp's unruly behavior. "How is your arm, my princess?" A shock wave went through my body as he touched my arm.

Nobody, in my ENTIRE LIFE, had ever touched my arm without permission.

Although, it was . . . a kind gesture. Endearing. So I addressed him calmly. "The wound is no more."

"It's gone? No, I swore I saw you get hit by that arrow! You had a huge gash right here, bleeding out." He drew a line on my arm where the scar was,—as I wore a short-sleeved dress for our outdoor activities today—causing a tingling sensation rise up to my neck.

Interesting, no one else asked how I was. "You are correct, Kipp, son of Adelle and Bennson." He had no real title.

"Oh, just call me Kipp!" He smiled joyously. He seemed to be amiable and pleasant to be around.

"I healed last night in the crystal chamber."

"Crystal chamber?" He spoke too emphatically for my mother's approval . . . but . . . I enjoyed his enthusiasm. It was a relief to see him openly display emotions I was prohibited from expressing. A relief to have no bounds in conversation.

"You mean, you haven't used crystal healing chambers before? They heal wounds and chakras so one may maintain a perfect aura-chakra balance." I spoke to him as though he were a close brother whom I wanted to reveal a deep secret too.

"The what? And what, what? You're speaking elven language aren't you? I never heard of "sakra," but I would love for you to show me someday."

I chuckled. "It's called 'chakra'. It's . . . oh, I'll explain later."

Alejandro, the Prince who gifted me with chocolate, abruptly stood from his seat and yelled across the table, "How dare you speak to Her Majesty with such disrespect!"

The Baron, Zack, stood up to agree with Alejandro and defend my honor. It was a sweet gesture, but unnecessary.

Kipp defended himself. "Disrespect? Not a single one of you inquired about her well-being. She was almost assassinated! This isn't disrespect, this is compassion and concern for Her Majesty."

"That's because your manner is improper!" Alejandro wagged his finger at him.

"Lords, gentlemen, please, let us not tarry over simple matters," I said and gracefully turned to them with open arms; my every movement flowing like a gentle breeze. "Our dear Kipp has good intentions. Today, we have entertainment planned in the courtyard. If breakfast is complete, let's rejoin at nine o'clock."

Everyone stood as I left the table. Armed guards surrounded me at every moment and followed my every footstep. Alejandro ran up to me in the hall. Two guards immediately became defensive, pointing their swords or spears at him. I waved a hand, and they settled down.

"Do you have anyone to escort you back?" he asked.

"My guards."

"Well, they aren't real escorts! You need a prince. But deserve nothing less than a king." He held an arm out for me to take. "And if any assassins come, I'll be right here beside you, to protect and defend you until death."

My heart skipped a beat.

"But I must apologize for my behavior back there." Alejandro touched his heart with his hand. "I only meant to give you the greatest respect, and abhor hearing of anyone not speaking to you with the utmost honor."

"Oh." I gasped. My body heated up. His attention and admiration was unlike anything I experienced before; it made my heart flutter. *O' to be loved and cared for so much!* Even my brother never tried to protect me from other's gossip. If I were in danger, Farooq may or may not let me fall. But just the mention of the wrong title, and Alejandro became defensive and concerned over me. "Your concern is endearing." I looked into his face and noticed a most attractive crooked smile. "Kipp, no doubt, meant no harm. But I will never condemn such valiant chivalry from your, either. Thank you."

"My pleasure." Alejandro kissed my hand, then stroked it as we walked. "You know, after watching you dance and sing last night, I thought you were a forest nymph."

"Oh. Hah!" I burst into laughter; and was glad my mother wasn't there to witness my unprincessly behavior. "Music and dance is a princess's duty. I had no choice but to learn."

"Duty? What about fun? Hobbies. What do you *enjoy*?"

"Well . . ." I started to come out of my shell. "I do enjoy music and dancing. And Archery."

"As long as you distinguish 'enjoy' from 'duties', I'll accept that response. Perhaps we can find more activities we can enjoy together!" He raised an eyebrow.

I chuckled.

My parents didn't really do "fun activities" together. They talked during the day and entertained guests during the evenings. It was my plan to have a husband who had similar hobbies as myself, like archery, so that . . . well . . . so that we'd have more we could do together. Seeing my parent's lack of affection for each other made me desire *some* connection with another human being. After all, my parents were unhappy, and that was not a desired state I wished to live in, but I would never tell my mother that I was curious, even hopeful at times, to have love and affection. She wouldn't care for those things, and would immediately remind me that "marriage is a duty."

We stood in front of the royal hallway, and Alejandro leaned down and kissed my hand, getting a whiff of my passion fruit perfume that Prince Abdulla had given me.

"Thank you for escorting me," I said.

"No." He paused. "Thank you for allowing *me* the opportunity."

He spoke with such passion, like it was the greatest thing he could achieve in his lifetime. It was difficult to wipe the smile off my face the remaining morning. Was this love? No, it couldn't possibly come on so quickly. Yet my heart was ready to leap out of my chest. Whatever I felt was definitely something powerful that I couldn't put into words.

CHAPTER 5

Archery

The summer sun beat down on the nobility and guests who opened their umbrellas and tried to secure seats underneath the shade of the trees or tents that their families brought.

Our palace grounds were extensive; we had a large maze made of ten foot tall hedges. Next to that was our stable yard for training horses. To the north of the palace there was a bridge that reached across the large pond and led to a dirt pathway that weaved in and out of forested areas. There were little pockets where you could find berry bushes or crystals in the ground, and an indoor greenhouse called the Secret Garden, with fairies. To complete all of this, we had an extended porch that wrapped around the entire east side of the palace for the many nobles who gathered around to watch the events.

My family sat in the royal seating area, a wooden platform with a roof, with the families of my parent's favorite guests—those from Baylor, Velazia and Tildon—sitting nearby. The grassy area below was set up for the bachelors' archery competition.

Throughout the RMC, there was a daily competition. The winner of each competition would have a private luncheon with me. To mark the opening of the archery competition, I shot the first arrow, then found my seat next to my family.

Archery was part of my intense education. Another duty. But the idea of separating play from duties now overcame my thoughts. *Hobbies? Fun?*

Although I didn't know *play*, archery *was* meditative and *was* enjoyable as it helped organize my thoughts. So maybe it started as a duty, and over the years, transformed into a pastime.

The bachelors lined up on the archery range; each had twelve arrows. The contestants with the lowest scores in each round were eliminated from the competition.

"The knight, McKinley, has an impressive aim and a strong arm," my mother said. So far, he got bull's-eye every time. "Much to expect from a military man."

"Aye, and the Baron, Zack, is keeping up." I pointed the obvious to my father, who likely was watching the young chap from his hometown the entire time.

"It's because he comes from the best city in the empire." My father joked. He rarely joked.

"Well, they certainly know how to bestow gifts." I said with a smirk. "No other princess in history has owned a Pegasus before." *Now I would go down in history as the first!*

Every contestant was hitting the target—not always on center—except poor Kipp. It wasn't a matter of strength; it was a matter of technique.

Aristocrats sniggered under their breath as Kipp became the laughingstock of the group. "They shouldn't have allowed a commoner to compete. How embarrassing." Edgar's younger sister, Ednnys, amused herself from a few seats away with the Crown Princess of Tildon. Did she know her voice could be heard from there?

Isabella agreed. "Who would ever take that peasant seriously even if the crown princess chose him as a husband?"

"And who would take *the princess* seriously if she did?" Ednnys said. "He's only here to appease the peasants anyway."

How dare Ednnys talk about me that way!

"Yenna," I called the advisor over. Yenna nearly tripped on her dull gray garment, trying to get to me as fast as possible. "Was Kipp not educated on events prior to his arrival?"

"Uh . . ." Yenna searched for an answer. "He was educated on etiquette and other matters that took up much time. He had a lot to learn, Your Majesty."

"He was supposed to receive training on ALL matters to avoid this type of public humiliation. See that he's trained vigorously on *all* other events!"

I left my seat and walked to the archery range toward Kipp.

"Kipp, keep your shoulders down." I instructed him from the side. "And relax. You're too tense. Also change your aim. Do you feel the slight breeze? All your arrows are landing on the left. Also, position your fingers like this." I reached behind to reposition his fingers. When our fingers met, he turned to face me. His face was inches from mine.

"Thank you, Your Majesty." Then he continued to gaze deep into my soul.

I took a deep breath. "Uh . . ." Yet he continued to stare. "Try it." I stepped back to let him shoot another.

"Yes, Your Majesty."

The next arrow hit a random spot on the target. He wouldn't make it to the next round, but at least his aim improved.

After that, he turned to face me directly. A small smile of appreciation formed on his lip.

"Um . . . I should return." I backed away from his charming smile and found myself backing into McKinley.

"My apologies, Your Majesty," McKinley said.

He had quite the handsome face up close. And his large, strong shoulders only added to his appearance. He didn't smell like a sweaty military man either and had a slight hint of cologne on him.

"My fault. You have a wonder technique, by the way," I complimented. "I imagine you'll make it to the finals."

He was taken aback by my words and had a hint of blush on his cheeks. His mouth hung open, unable to say anything, yet he tried to hide all hint of his feelings by forcing his words out. "I hope to win for you."

There was a pause between us, with me thinking how that was the goal of the competition. He seemed to think the same and looked embarrassed by his poor choice of words.

"I mean, I hope to impress you . . . to please you . . ." His face turned red as he couldn't find anything good to say, but I only chuckled it off.

"You're impressing many of us." My words cooled him off as he realized I was not judgmental or easily offended. "I won't take up your time, besides, I have a good view of you from my seat." With that, I walked away with a smile, not looking back to see his reaction.

The second round was ready, and the target was moved further away.

When I found my seat, my eyes met Alejandro's. Already eliminated from the competition, he took to the task of winking at me. He was definitely one of the most handsome of them all, aside from the elves, with a v-neck shirt that showed off his muscles underneath and that long hair to his shoulders made him even more desirous.

The other boys were too engrossed in the competition to send me love messages with their eyes, so I discreetly offered Alejandro a flirtatious smile in return, knowing I'd have the honor of talking to him more later tonight.

"Clayton isn't as good at archery as I would've thought," my father said, turning my attention away from Alejandro.

"I do hear he prefers the caliver. It's a recent invention. A type of lightweight musket," my mother commented as my cousin also stepped out of the competition. "But I do say, it's made his aim in archery weaker."

"He hunts with the caliver too," I said. "But I think these new inventions of 'muskets' takes the fun out of hunting altogether." I watched as the dwarf's strong arm nearly broke the target in half. He was too powerful for this sport.

"The discovery of gunpowder has completely reinvented war," my father said. "That is how your ancestors conquered the empire, after all. They were the first to acquire such mechanisms. I say it also eliminates the chivalry aspect warriors hope to achieve."

That was true. Many new inventions were coming out during my time. I was glad to become the empress during such an innovative time period.

During the last round, only four bachelors remained in the running: Zack, Hedgewood, McKinley, and Lancelot.

I caught my little brother, Prince Farooq, laughing with our cousin in the distance. Behind Farooq, the moody elf flirted with an equally beautiful elven woman with long black hair falling to her knees, yet in my presence, Prince Qinrel remained stone cold. What the purpose in being here was if he wasn't interested in marrying me?

My mood improved when the other elf, Prince Zazan, approached.

Zazan was from the elf queendom that wasn't a part of the empire, and he was the most mesmerizing of all boys. My great x5 grandfather was rather ambitious—egotistical to some. Luckily for others, he died before taking over the whole world. Seeing the greed of their neighbors fighting each other, the Eldoren Queendom cut most ties to the rest of the world in hopes of sparing themselves the drama. Now, they remained generally aloof unless it involved important matters that influence the next reigning monarch, like the RMC. They didn't send correspondence or do trade with inlanders. Eldoren was a mixture of islands off the coast with gorgeous waterfalls, as I saw from paintings, and well protected by mermaids.

"Prince Zazan, it is my pleasure to have you here. Come, shall I get you tea or coco we imported from the New World?" I escorted him away from prying ears to have alone time with him.

"Why, dear princess, all I wish to have is you."

I blushed ear to ear. My parents smiled in approval as they watched us connect. To have such attention from an Eldoren Elf was rare.

His gaze held a magical presence, while his violet eyes pierced my every thought. His elven crown was made of an elven-alloy that humans couldn't reproduce. It was flexible and strong and dangerous in the wrong hands. Velazia tried to get their hands on it several times, but the price was intentionally set impossibly high.

"You excel in every area, archery, dance, music. Is there nothing you can't achieve?" Zazan asked.

"Why, there are many things I haven't attempted to master yet. These crafts took me a decade of practice to master. What of yourself, Prince Zazan, what areas do you excel?"

"Elven religious ceremonies. Spirituality is essential for all rulers. For a leader must remain pure-hearted and humble." Spoken like a true elf—always about spirituality.

"I would love for you to educate me on your spiritual knowledge so I too may become a better leader someday."

"I shall, my darling. I shall." With that, he kissed my hand and left.

That is all? "You're leaving?"

"I wish not to take too much of your time, Your Majesty."

What? He strummed me like a harp with promises for the future, then left me wanting. *But I want to discuss such things right now!*

Pegasus poo.

Once I was back in my seat, I noticed the elf Qinrel whispering into the elven woman's ear. They were close. Too close. They were flirting too. This competition already wasn't going how I imagined; and these elves were playing hard to get.

Hedgewood was naturally strong and could easily hit past his target. He was in the lead, but in the last few shots, he missed the target completely. It seemed odd, like it was intentional so that he wouldn't win.

After a few more shots, Sir McKinley was declared the winner.

Despite losing, Zack flexed his biceps to the crowd, then showed off his love for his muscles by kissing them.

Oh dear. I looked at Princess Ednnys and Isabella, and laughed erratically in embarrassment at his behavior. They reciprocated the gesture, then started gossiping about the boys.

After that, I stepped onto the field to honor the winner. Arm in arm, McKinley and I waved, walked along the path, waved some more, and then we made a final stop on the balcony overlooking the front of the palace where a crowd gathered. Like the ending of a fairy tale where two lovers set off for their honeymoon, we put on a show and gazed lovingly at each other while holding hands. The crowd shouted in glee.

Together, we returned to the pond and entered a boat with a canopy to shield us from the heat. To the side we watched as albino and green colored peacocks wandered about. We nibbled on grapes and delicacies as a servant gently rowed us to the deep end.

"I am well pleased to find someone to enjoy activities like archery with me. And I hear you enjoy horseback riding too?" I dipped a raspberry into some chocolate and savored the juiciness on my tongue.

"As a knight and officer of the Centaurian Army, I've mastered many arts. Archery is an area where I would only allow a dwarf's strength to prevail over me." McKinley sat on the embroidered cushions across from me as he explained.

"Ah, same as me. I am competitive in archery and every area of my life. In part, because my mother would be ashamed of me if I lost a match to another girl."

"I'll admit, you surprised me today. In a good way," he confessed. My eyebrows raised in question, but he answered before I could ask. "Helping Kipp was honorable, yet unexpected."

"I'm glad you think so. In my mother's RMC, the commoner was dominated in every event. He wasn't instructed much before arriving.

But because I singled him out, people will gossip about me later. Perhaps I'm weaker than my parents, but I just couldn't watch as Kipp was disgraced."

"Weaker? No! Never!" McKinley dared to question me, but in a way that reaffirmed my goodness. "Helping Kipp makes you stronger! Not weaker. For which is harder, helping someone in need or trampling over the weak? It takes a good leader to care about the least of us. For a leader is only as good as their lowliest subject. Today you showed yourself strong, honorable . . . and worthy of ruling."

My face went flush. This boy had high values, and that was an admirable quality to have. "And it takes someone with a good heart to praise this gesture," I complimented back.

"Many in the military put on a tough persona. But I had an experience growing up being the underdog. I once found a sword-fighting school for commoners, but my father was strict and wouldn't let me join because they were of a lower social class. I snuck out and joined anyway." He laughed. "While the upper classes are taught strict technique, it offered me an opportunity to learn about street fighting and helped me see things differently."

"Since the other students didn't know I was nobility"—he continued with a completely neutral tone of voice—"they treated me . . . well as their equal. They didn't go easy on me and even picked on me. After so many bruises and scars, my father found out about my activities and forbid me to return. But I realized the importance of treating the underdogs with respect. Besides, you never know who they'll grow up to become someday."

"A wonderful lesson." Every word he spoke garnered more of my respect and our conversation flowed; we never let a moment pass without sharing a smile or a well-formed thought. *What a wonderful option he was for me!*

"Also . . . it's better to have friends than enemies. So why not help the needy? Fewer enemies to worry about in battle. If politicians could only do the same . . ." he said.

"Nonsense." I toyed with him. "Politicians make great friends . . . when you're facing them. And even greater enemies when your back is turned."

We both laughed. "Too true. But enough about me; I wish to learn more about you." He turned the tide.

Another plus side to him, I affirmed. *He's open to sharing* and *interested in my stories. A good balance.*

"I've never done anything as adventurous as you, like sneaking out to fight. My entire life was spent in these palace walls."

"You mean . . ." His eyebrows raised in question. "You've never left these walls?" Although he was often stoic, he seemed to have a river of emotions beneath the surface that he continually tried to push back down whenever it emerged.

"Well, I have gone to the Orb Theater and the opera house. I once left Velazia for my coming-of-age ceremony at Rainbow Mount. And I go horseback riding around the palace . . . but not without an entire army following me or hiding in the bushes."

"My dear, let us hope your Pegasus grows those wings faster so you can fly away. If we find ourselves compatible"—he slowed his speech—"I'll take you sailing, or exploring the Centaurus Forest, or to the sand dunes near Ogarz. Wherever you wish to go, I will guide, guard, and hold you safe while setting you free from these confines."

Wow. Who knew a partnership could provide so much?

Alejandro, Prince of Ogarz

CHAPTER 6

The First Date

Alejandro, Prince of Ogarz. Human. Age 17. Loves chocolate, romantic evenings, & dreams about watching the sunset with Princess Qloey. Interests: Dancing the Paso Doble Pegaso & marrying the princess.

The first date was arranged with Prince Alejandro, the charmer who walked me to my door this morning. The memory still brought a smile to my face.

Alejandro was dressed in a V-neck shirt that showed off his chest and with trousers so tight, I didn't know how they didn't rip every time he sat down. His slick hair was gelled back. I got a whiff of his cologne as he kissed both of my cheeks in front of every reporter in the room. It was part of his homeland custom to kiss on both cheeks, but . . . it was out of my comfort zone. I feared that tomorrow morning's newspaper would say something scandalous about us. They were here to help boost the citizen's morale by publishing gushy romance stories. This one certainly started out sugary and sweet.

Alejandro put his hand on my upper back instead of holding an arm out for me to take. I tensed up as we left the entranceway and proceeded to the art room to paint. We sat on opposite sides of the canvas so that we could gaze at each other. A few reporters sat in the far corner drawing pictures of us. Everyone assumed he and I would paint each other, but I wasn't great at portraits and couldn't afford to paint anything short of perfection.

"Your profile didn't mention that you were a painter, Prince Alejandro," I said.

He stopped painting and put all his attention on me. "You cannot learn everything about someone from reading about them, Your Majesty. We must get to know each other *personally*." He winked.

"Well, I'm afraid reading about others is one of the few connections I have with the outside world," I admitted. "What are you painting?"

"You."

I blushed. "Do get my good side."

"Do you have bad side?"

I chuckled.

"And what are you painting, my sweet princess?"

"The sunset behind you."

"Ah. Say, let's make a bargain. Whoever draws the best painting gets to decide where to go after this."

"I'll agree to that."

We painted for the next hour while asking each other personal questions. "What's your favorite animal?" he asked.

"Animal? I've never thought of a favorite before." I scanned over every animal I knew. "Horses. Since I like to ride. What is yours?"

"A platypus."

I chuckled. "Why?"

"They're the oddest creatures. I'm surprised it's not under the mythical creature list. If you think about it"—he shifted in his seat to explain in-depth—"they're the cross between an otter and a duck, plus they spit out venom."

"I didn't know that."

"Yes, truly unusual. Okay." He moved onto a new question, but I felt so boring next to him. Alejandro likes platypuses and McKinley explored the world, yet all I could come up with was a barnyard animal because I saw them every day. Nothing was wrong with horses; I loved them dearly but felt so sheltered and closed inside the palace. Surely I could explore more exotic animals and add them to my list of favorites. He asked another question, "What profession do you want when you grow up?"

"What kind of question is that?" I laughed, "I am grown up, and I have no choice in the matter." My brush added a new layer of blue to the sky as he explained his question.

"But . . . if you had a choice, what would it be?"

"Such a thing never crossed my mind." I searched for something interesting to say, as I didn't want to seem dull again. "I'd be a mermaid."

"A mermaid isn't a profession." He raised a single eyebrow.

"But they seem so free. They can explore any part of the ocean they want and eat an abundance of squid. I'm sticking to my decision. I want to be a mermaid."

"I guess I'll accept your response." He pursed his lips, but it was all playful. "I, on the other hand, wish to have the profession of 'Princess Qloey's husband'."

"Oh, dear." I rolled my eyes.

His arms opened wide, questioning my rejection of his answer. "I am serious. But I don't want to be a fish-man. They're all slimy and can you imagine their fish breath in the morning? So you'll have to remain a human for me."

We were ready to reveal our paintings.

"You first," he urged.

I revealed the landscape. The same landscape I witnessed every day. For I knew little else.

"Impressive. Absolutely impressive. Now my turn." Alejandro turned his painting around to reveal the worst child's painting of a human I ever gazed upon.

I squealed in horror.

"I see you like it." He joked. I couldn't help but burst into laughter. "I take it from that reaction that I won the bargain."

"Oh, dear. It's so . . ."

"Amazing I know."

"Yes, yes, you definitely won." I went along with his silliness.

It was wonderful to see someone so comfortable with their imperfections. He turned his weakness into a joke and entertained the reporters at the same time. It was . . . refreshing.

He would make a fun husband.

"Even though you clearly won . . ." I joked. "You may keep my painting as a gift."

"Just as you may keep mine."

I chuckled. *Oh, dear. What would I do with such an ugly thing?*

Rose petals were strewn about the shiny marble floor that lined the hallway. Clearly, he planned this in advance. The rose petals led to a room resplendent in flowers, wine, and delectable chocolate morsels.

"You did mention chocolate and romantic evenings on your profile," I recalled.

"Yes, but as I said before"—he tossed his hair back like a half-naked Velazian God running nude on the beach—"there's so much more to learn about a person."

Any more romance and I'd burn up in flames. I couldn't handle him.

We sat on a rug in front of a fireplace and discussed our daily life. Of course, my schedule was dull: wake up, go to council meetings, eat, repeat. His life was more relaxed and casual.

"I wake up," he said. "Stretch, then lie in bed imagining my life by your side."

"You do not!"

"Alright, I'll admit I only started doing that after my invitation to the RMC was accepted."

"But what if you didn't end up liking me?" I asked.

"Impossible." He strummed his fingers through his hair and inched closer to me. His arm brushed against mine, but then he pulled away, acting like it was an accident. By the third time, it was clear his movements were no accident. His next move made me the most nervous, as he brushed a hair away from my forehead.

The guards in the room grew uneasy with his forwardness and shifted their eyes to meet mine, then looked away. The guards had to be on the lookout for the potential assassin in the palace. Yet these same guards watched me grow up and weren't instructed on what to do if a contestant . . . kissed me. It was unspeakable territory that my parents never brought up. I doubted that my parents ever kissed each other aside from their wedding day. These bachelors weren't expected to love me, just to be good politicians and help strengthen our empire with our union. If there ever was a kiss from one of these boys, one must ask: was it warranted or worthy of a warrant? Under any other circumstance, someone would be arrested just for accidentally rubbing his shoulder against mine. But we couldn't arrest RMC bachelors.

The heat of the fireplace made me sweat. Or was it him?

Alejandro stopped talking and gazed deep into my soul.

His face was inches from mine. His nose moved closer. My nerves fluttered. His lips puckered up. *What do I do?* He leaned forward. And then I heard a tearing noise, as if his trousers ripped open behind him.

He sat back on his rear and shifted uncomfortably for a moment before pursing his lips.

I opened up the awkward moment to assess the situation. "Did your trousers just . . ."

"Yup." Alejandro's cheeks flushed.

He slowly stood and backed up to the fireplace so nobody would see his goods, but the guards already knew what happened and silently muffled their amusement from the far wall.

"Perhaps I should—OUCH!" He yelped, then said a series of hisses out of his mouth. He had stepped on the brass fireplace poker, which flung a piece of burning ember right onto his exposed area.

"Are you alright?"

A silent moment settled between us. Then I wondered if I should help him. He just stood there, holding a hand to his backside.

"I'm just going to . . ." His voice cracked as he pointed to the door.

"Yes, do take care of your . . . uh, yes, that, that thing." *I shouldn't have mentioned that.*

He moaned, then grabbed a pillow and hid his rear end. He waddled all the way out like a duck, moaning and wailing. In a way, I was relieved that I didn't have to share a kiss this prematurely, and returned to my own bedchambers.

Once in my bedroom, I leaned against the door and laughed hysterically. That'd teach him to wear some proper clothes.

But what if he actually kissed me? What would I do? *This was too much, too fast!* I never imagined the possibility of such a scenario so soon. On the first private date! What if every boy tried to kiss me on our date? *Oh dear!*

But the memory of our chemistry returned. I sat at my windowsill and gazed into the distance, recalling that special moment by the fireplace, as passion rose within me, and then . . . the moment was shattered. Should I have kissed him? What would he think of me if I moved away?

Despite my hesitancy displaying intimacy this early, I liked him. He was charming and warm. But what about choosing the best political leader of the group? Or the most advantageous alliance? Alejandro was from the weakest city; marrying him wouldn't be the smartest choice. And McKinley was only a knight. Should my feelings matter more than politics? What if the bachelor who I felt the strongest about was the least capable of becoming the next emperor? Which one was the best at politics, anyway?

Before this began, I had the perfect plan. I already cherry-picked my favorites. Now my entire list just flew out the window. And this was just the first private date. But I had to admit, I loved the thrill of this new adventure. My dull life was ignited by a new reality, one more thrilling than the last. There was a real possibility for love in my life. True Love.

CHAPTER 7

Talent Show

The next morning, I was all smiles and giddiness as my fantasies stretched into the clouds. Yet, I was concerned over Alejandro's . . . misfortune and embarrassment. Hopefully the guards wouldn't gossip during break time, but I knew how these things worked. Plenty of times, I had overheard a maid or two spreading the latest juicy story involving the royals.

Before my ladies-in-waiting came in to do my hair for the morning, I pulled out a quill and parchment and prepared a "get well soon" letter to him.

Dear Prince Alejandro,
I wish your posterior a speedy recovery.

Oh, dear. I scribbled it out and started again.

Dear Prince Alejandro,
May you still bear fruit and multiply.

Yikes. That was even worse. The damage to his bodily functions wasn't that extensive. I crumpled up the parchment and started over.

Dear Prince Alejandro,

Let's put this unfortunate event "behind" us.

Now it sounded like I was making fun of him.

"Your date went well, Your Majesty?" Victorya asked as she and the other girls walked into the room.

Perhaps I'll just have flowers sent to him, along with a new pair of canions.

"Oh, Alejandro's so charming!" I sat at my vanity for her to do my hair. "I might as well end the competition now and say our 'I do's with Alejandro . . . and Zazan . . . and McKinley." But I knew a betrothal wasn't possible yet. The rules were: every bachelor gets a one-on-one date within the first two weeks, and only after that was there a round of eliminations. The remaining contestants got a second private date where we got to know each other better without competitions getting in the way.

There were political repercussions in proceeding with an elimination without forethought. I couldn't afford to harm relations with any other realms. That's where the mutual rescission came in; if another contestant and I agreed marriage wasn't compatible between each other, we could part ways on good terms.

"But I liked McKinley too!" I plucked hair out of my comb. Normally my servants did that, but I had to fidget with *something*. "He was mature, and respectable, and worthy of a princely title. But then Alejandro was . . . enticing and amiable. And did you see how charming Zazan was on introduction? Oh, what do I do?"

"Follow your heart," Victorya advised.

"No, follow your reason." Councilwoman Yenna walked in and ruined my romantic fantasies. "Your husband has a big role to fill. He must be sophisticated, proper, and an excellent speaker. Take Edgar, for instance."

Edgar? One more breakfast on taxes and I'd keel over.

How would it be if we had a conversation about taxes every morning for the remainder of my life?

Eek!

Despite being garrulous in conversation and hardly attractive, surely Edgar would show a more positive side to his personality today. I remained optimistic. *One hiccup doesn't mean we won't fall madly in love with each other.*

I had seven ladies-in-waiting, a dozen personal servants, and "Yenna," who kept me up-to-date on events and organized my schedule. Everything in my life was organized for me. My duty was to master my education and expectations of courtly life, which were often strenuous and uncomfortable. Thus, all the trivial details were attended to by my staff.

"What's the schedule today, Yenna?"

Yenna was the type to wake up at five every morning to get her sword fighting workout in, then ate a hearty meal of greens and fruits. Her frame was petite for all her efforts. "Breakfast first. Then a High Council meeting about the new fairy protocols for those who use fairy dust on unsuspecting victims, followed by the talent show and tea with all contestants—"

"The dates?" I interrupted, that was the only thing I was interested in. "Who's the private date with?"

"In the evening, your second date is with Prince Hedgewood," she said.

"The dwarf? Let me see the schedule. Who made this?"

Yenna handed me the piece of parchment with the competition schedule. "You asked *me* to make the schedule, Your Majesty."

"No. No." I complained. The dwarf was on my unqualified list of candidates, thus I wanted enough time to meet and choose out of the *real* potentials. "Move him to the twelfth date." I rolled up the schedule and handed it back. "Prince Zazan is today. Tomorrow, Prince Qinrel, no, he's aloof! Put Edgar tomorrow, then Prince Octavio . . ."

Yenna cleared my throat. "Pardon me, Your Majesty, but this will cause," she paused, "*controversy,* if Hedgewood is placed last in favor of the elves."

"He knows the schedule already?"

"All participants received a copy of this and it corresponds with group dates, activities catered to participant's specific talents, and reservations we've made. All was agreed upon by each participant's family to ensure fairness. A lengthy process that took months of back-and-forth correspondence," she said.

I refrained from expressing any discontent on my face, but inside I felt differently. "But why is the dwarf second?"

Yenna understood that I wasn't interested in him. "It's only *one* date. He's a bookish man. You read too. Make polite conversation."

"I will go tonight, but see if we can make amends to . . . some of the other contestant's schedules and put the most promising ones in the beginning?"

Yenna tried not to show annoyance and pursed her lips to hold back her frustration. "I'll try my best, Your Majesty."

Every nobleman was expected to be accomplished in some form of activity, whether it be singing, dancing, or a musical instrument, thus the talent show competition was a chance for the contestants to show their skills and impress the royal members of court. Unlike many of the other group dates, I would decide the winning talent.

Comfortable seating was arranged for the royals and extended family members to attend inside of the ballroom.

Prince Abdulla was first. Multiple musical instruments were set up for him and his staff. He performed a single song—an extended, and very . . . very long song—where he rotated between each instrument to show his diversity in musical talent. The crowd was absolutely delighted, and he received a standing ovation. He would be a hard act to follow.

"A good candidate in marriage," Victorya whispered to me. Although we sat in the front row, I requested the organizers put distance between us and the attendees so that we could gossip about the boys. "Plus, Abdulla's queendom is powerful and wealthy, and he's deadly handsome!"

"He's top on my list," I said. An alliance with Payonna would be wonderful.

The two elven princes, Zazan and Qinrel, joined in an elven folk song that elevated the audience directly to heaven. Their angelic voices soared to such high notes that they reached the female vocal range. Again, they received a standing ovation from their human admirers.

Edgar played an extraordinary piano piece, exemplifying passion and melodrama as his fingers nimbly flew across the keyboard.

Wonderful. So wonderful. See, he's perfect. I affirmed to myself, letting the tax-issue fall away.

Next, the three contestants, Prince Octavio of Pixieland, Duke Lancelot of Moonstone, and Kipp, took to the stage together.

Octavio addressed the audience. "We've combined our three skills to bring you a play. The play is based on my storytelling of an ancient pixie fairy tale, that's been rewritten by Duke Lancelot's extraordinary poetic prose, and will be performed by the extraordinary actor, Kipp."

"This will be interesting," Victorya said, unaffected.

Octavio continued. "Your Majesty, Princess Qloey, you may judge us independently based on the story, the playwright, or the acting. Or . . . you may choose us all."

The audience laughed.

Octavio narrated the story of the pixies who once roamed Pixieland before any human had stepped foot there.

Kipp didn't read off a script, instead he memorized every line and cited it perfectly despite the little time he had to prepare for this event. He gave the audience a confident and commanding performance. It was a story describing how humans arrived in Pixieland, stole every resource they desired, and ultimately caused an imbalance in nature.

Kipp stepped back as Octavio continued the narration.

"Remarkable memory. To have memorized Lancelot's play in a single day!" I exclaimed.

Victorya leaned in to respond. "He did say he worked at the Orb Theater. His mind has the practice of memorization."

Lancelot's poetry was quite spectacular, and if he were not a Duke, I'd order him to write plays alongside the great poet from Orb Theater, Pippa. For surely, Lancelot was among the best poets in Velazia.

The play ended with the pixies withholding all resources from the humans until humans could learn and be in harmony with the earth and themselves. At the end, they made an agreement to adhere to the wisdom of the pixies. To this day, the pixies gave the humans in Pixieland advice on how to maintain balance with nature. Some of the knowledge they passed down was healthy farming methods like organic horticulture, and spiritual insight into communicating with plant and animal spirits. No wonder Octavio seemed so kind and down-to-earth.

I stood in applause, but not all others in the crowd followed suit. Perhaps because a peasant was on stage, or because the idea of allowing a pixie to give advice to humans was offensive. Many elves and humans thought they were the wisest creatures on the earth and ignored the wisdom from the little critters, like birds, and trees. But spiritual practices (which not everyone followed) taught how consciousness is in all living beings, even trees, and the earth itself was conscious and had wisdom to teach us. Non-spiritual and skeptical elves, humans, and dwarves often only respected those with noble titles or great wealth.

My parents and Clayton glared at me, so I quickly sat back down. It seemed I wasn't allowed to let any of them win, for my family wouldn't approve, and I wanted them to be happy with my choice.

Zack, the Baron of Tildon, was next. My father cheered louder than all the others.

Zack strutted onto the stage, ostentatiously flexing his muscles, making some women swoon. Then he . . . performed acts of strength? *Interesting*. He displayed agility in calisthenics. First, he did push-ups. Then one-armed push-ups. Then resorted to hopping off the ground as he did the push-ups.

Victorya and I awkwardly glanced at each other and chortled. "This is uncomfortable to watch," Victorya said, slumping in her seat.

"I'm embarrassed for him."

After that, his skills became more intense. Like a gymnast, he did handstands, flips, and jumped on a metal bar where he swung around. He finished with backhanded pull-ups.

After displaying each skill, he bowed. Some women applauded wildly, while Victorya and I . . . acknowledged his great muscle strength with a slow, almost inaudible, clap.

To acknowledge the crowd, Zack alternated between pecking his chest muscles up and down.

"Dear unicorns." We gripped each other's hand for solidarity.

My heart thumped as Alejandro entered the stage next. After our date last night, I was ready for my wedding vows . . . but not ready to kiss him yet. *Is that strange?*

He wore an elaborate beaded jacket with no shirt underneath.

"Brace me." Victorya grabbed onto my arm.

"This talent show is getting dangerous!" I warned.

Alejandro also wore tight trousers and a red cape, making the damsels in the crowd nearly faint. Apparently, he hadn't learned his lesson regarding the tight pants and wore a new pair.

He danced the *Paso Doble Pegaso*. It was passionate and intense. He turned mid-dance and winked at me.

"My heart's been stolen." I fanned myself with my hand.

"If you don't marry him, I will," Victorya said.

He turned back to blow me a kiss. He, too, received a standing ovation . . . from the women in the room. The men, on the other hand, appeared feeble in the presence of this charming prince and scowled amongst themselves.

"Inappropriate display of masculinity," one man scoffed.

Another surprise took place as Sir McKinley and Prince Hedgewood performed a duet. Unlike the elves, these two were both basses, with deep throaty voices. Their performance was earthshaking and powerful.

The very last talent was my cousin, Clayton. I didn't remember him being a virtuoso at music, although he played piano. But there was no way he could outperform Edgar, so, perhaps his choice of art was a good one.

A painting easel was set up with an assortment of dark paint colors. With his back to the crowd, he began painting in swift movements, taking his long pinky nail and occasionally swiping the paint to create a certain effect. It was far more entertaining watching him create a masterpiece in fifteen minutes than I ever thought possible. It was a painting of Rainbow Mount in the springtime, which was a mountain in the south with a permanent cloud hovering above. Some claimed that a castle floated inside the clouds where unicorns roamed about, but I didn't see how that was possible. In any case, Clayton left the benevolent horse creatures out and stuck to a dark brooding landscape with gray and black flowers, and a cloud hovering above, sending a black shadow over the once happy forest below.

Everyone applauded. Entertaining, yes, but not worthy of first place.

"Whoever will you choose?" Victorya grabbed my hand in excitement.

"How about Zack's push-up show?" We both chortled together. "I just had a date with McKinley and desperately want another, but I want to meet the other boys too." Plus, I wasn't really interested in two dates with the dwarf today. *O' how short our children would be if we married!* "It would be widely acceptable if I chose Edgar, and would show others I have good taste."

"None of that matters. Forget politics. Or how others will judge you. What do *YOU* want?" Victorya postulated. She was a hopeless romantic who wished for me to fall desperately in love and have twelve unruly children. "Just one thing, you can't choose Alejandro because he's mine."

"Don't you dare steal my boys." I warned her with a smile, then took to the stage to address to the audience. "You all had remarkable performances. It's always difficult to take center stage and be judged, and I applaud all of you. If I could, I'd choose several of you for first place. But to limit it to a single performance, I must go with the marvelous and inspiring music from Prince Zazan and Prince Qinrel."

Everyone applauded. My mother nodded in agreement, approving of the choice of elves.

Good, I'm pleasing my mother for once. She will see that I'm worthy of becoming the empress.

CHAPTER 8

Hedgewood

Two elven princes all to myself! *What a wonderful idea to hold this competition!* I locked my arm around Zazan's while Qinrel sulked behind.

We were going to eat lunch together under a canopy on the roof. A perfectly romantic setting to start our relationship.

While Zazan granted me his full attention, Qinrel focused on his food. He kept putting his head to his temple as if he had a headache.

"You give us too much credit." Zazan flirted as we spoke in the elven language. "Our voices are average for an elf. You humans do impress us however, in how low you can sing. His Highness Prince Hedgewood and Sir McKinley performed wonders."

"Do you mean a human is capable of impressing a talented elf like yourself? For I thought elves were great at all things?" I buttered him up.

He chuckled. "Elves and humans are two entirely different creatures, yet compatible in *many ways.*"

I read between the lines and grew giddy.

"Historians claim we originated from the same mother," he explained. "But we have essentially evolved far beyond humans."

There was that elf ego. Then again, I pampered it.

"Evolved because you keep to spiritual ways while we often stray? Enlighten me on your spirituality, will you?" I urged him to continue.

Finally, Qinrel perked up. It seemed like I could *feel* his mood, as though his emotions were like an ocean current that swept over the room and crashed into me. Right now, I *felt* he was confused about being here.

"Water, Earth, Fire, Air, Ether. Each elf comes from a different race of elements. Like the fairies and pixies, we harmonize ourselves with our element in spiritual ways," Zazan divulged.

"So all of Eldoren elves are water elves, correct?" I asked.

"It is true." He waved his hand, and his wine swished around.

"But what does all that mean?" I grew wide-eyed, wanting him to explain more when Qinrel jumped in:

"That we can bring balance to the creatures of the earth with our element," Qinrel quickly said.

"Or creatures of the water." Zazan sounded irritated that Qinrel forgot to add his element. "If the water becomes polluted, it will communicate with us and teach us how to restore balance. Then we perform ceremonies to heal it and relearn how to prevent this from happening again."

"Sounds beautiful." I marveled.

"Or the land!" Now Qinrel was irritated, but I ignored him and found myself lost in Zazan's lavender eyes.

I seemed to become warped into some elven magic. My peripheral vision narrowed. Everything else around me became fuzzy. I seemed to be taken into the clouds and forgot the world existed around me.

"Lunch is over!" Qinrel abruptly stood, knocking over his plate of food.

Zazan stood up to face Qinrel with a clenched fist, testing his reaction. They looked ready to pounce on each other like lions fighting over a mate, except that Qinrel had no interest in me.

"Gentlemen!" I stood between them. "What is this behavior?"

"Pardon, Your Majesty. But I've lost my appetite." Zazan turned back to address me. "If I may retire?"

"If you don't wish to stay, I won't keep you . . ." He started to leave before I finished talking.

Then I turned to Qinrel. "Please, do explain."

"I apologize, Your Majesty. It is an elf thing. But I'm not feeling well, either. May I also retire?" He looked dazed and pressed his palm to his head again, and his eyes glazed over.

"You're dismissed."

Well, this was a wasted date. I should've gone with Edgar. My hands went to my hips.

Farooq and my mother were finishing a conversation with the Baylorian royal family when I ventured downstairs from the date. King Edward and Princess Ednnys were already walking away and didn't notice me approach. I expected my mother to applaud me for having good taste in choosing the talent show winners, but instead, she barred her teeth and sneered.

"The two elves returned from the roof looking angry. Why can't you behave yourself? What did you do wrong?" She nearly yelled.

"The date went smoothly—"

"No, it didn't! You hadn't even spent a full hour with them! Clearly neither of them are interested in marrying you."

"Nothing went wrong. I think—" I was about to say: *"Qinrel had a headache,"* but couldn't finish the sentence before she hissed at me again.

"You 'think!'" She barked. "Sometimes I wonder if you think at all. You're too stupid to think correctly most of the time. Farooq impressed Princess Ednnys with his piano performance after the competition, while you pissed off both of the elves!"

You're too stupid to think correctly most of the time. The words settled on my conscience.

"Everything is—" my words trailed off as she lifted her heavy skirts and stomped out of the hall.

Farooq remained staring at me for a moment, without any expression to denote what he was thinking about. We were strangers to each other's intentions; despite being siblings. He slowly turned to follow our mother down the hall.

The interaction was embarrassing. I didn't want to give my brother any reason to think he actually should have the crown instead of me and cause tension between us.

A part of me wanted to cry, but I wouldn't. I would hold it in and let the pain devour me.

Hedgewood, Prince of Adonis Peak Kingdom. Dwarf. Age 19. Fluent in three languages, politically active in all affairs within Adonis Peak. Interests: Reading, poetry, opera, berries, & sword fighting.

Hedgewood and I enjoyed a quiet stroll over the bridge of the pond as the press drew pictures of us from across the water. One fairy created a "light painting,"—a magically moving painting of us. It took a highly talented fairy artist to produce such wonder; and would sell for gold.

We continued across the bridge where goldfish puckered their lips and frogs leapt on lily pads. As the sun set on the horizon and fireflies came out to light the way back, we waved to the admirers and retreated inside.

Despite the romantic setting, and despite how we played the part perfectly, we were acting. It was a ruse for the press.

Hedgewood looked handsome and stylish in his thin circular spectacles, a sported feather hat, and a velvet embellished doublet. In fact, everything about him, including his mature attitude, impressed me. He wasn't so bad for company, after all.

We ate a four-course meal, while Hedgewood began the conversation. "Where did you decide to put Prince Alejandro's masterpiece of a painting?"

How did he know about that? "Oh, I didn't realize everyone knew about my date with Prince Alejandro," I said.

"Hmm," was all he said.

"Perhaps I'll put it in our portrait hall among the other royalty." I released a small laugh.

"If it means that much to you. And how was eating chocolate mousse while lying across rose petals?"

"Uh?" *Did Alejandro tell him everything? What about the possible kiss?* A shiver went down my spine. I didn't want others knowing the details about that, so I changed the subject. "I almost chose you and McKinley for your extraordinary performance today."

Hedgewood was surprised at first, but then nodded as if coming to some unknown yet unsatisfying conclusion, and continued eating.

Silence.

"You do surprise me, Prince Hedgewood." I ended the awkward silence with an intended compliment. "You sing opera and rumors say you read a whole book and three newspapers a day."

"Is it reading a book a day that comes as a surprise or that a dwarf is capable of reading?"

I nearly choked on my *zucchini gratin*; per his vegetarian health request.

He responded before I could. "Yes, many Velazians have developed a bias towards dwarves. Some even say that we 'love working in mines' and 'under the most oppressive conditions,' which can rightly be blamed on human-written fairy tales. But I will inform you, while the average dwarf is more robust and tough than even the strongest human male, we do participate in every aspect of our thriving culture, which includes politics, dancing, philosophy, and the art of writing and reading."

"I . . . apologize if I've offended you, only . . ."

He noticed the solemn expression on my face and looked down at his plate. "No, my apologies." He pushed his plate aside. "Such was rude of me. It is only, you see, my people aren't always treated with respect by other species. On my journey to the palace, I visited some dwarf communities in the empire and was disgusted by their treatment. You see, plenty of dwarves love to sing, some love to train horses, love to partake in all aspects of life and they're being denied that for the simple reason that *they're a dwarf*. And dwarves—in the eyes of most—should do the dirtiest labor and work in the worst conditions with minimal pay. Many cannot follow their passions simply because nobody in Velazia will hire them. That anger welled inside me and finally found an outlet. But it was improper to make a statement on our date and should be reserved for an official meeting with the empress. So I apologize."

"I had no idea dwarves were treated so poorly." My mind quickly raced over how I didn't know much at all about the dwarves living in Velazia, or the commoners, and how I too had biases against dwarves. I didn't want to marry him because his species was too short to be appealing to my senses. Now I felt bad for trying to push Prince Hedgewood to the twelfth date. *Oh, what a horrible issue that would've caused! How could I be so callous?*

My compassion took over. It was a wonderful yet unusual gift that often took me on adventures; for I would often think one way, learn a new perspective, and the compassion would then steer me in the alternate direction. It drove my family nuts, for it meant I was inconsistent in my ways. But compassion to me meant understanding multiple points of views without judgment; taking neither side and accepting both ends of the spectrum. Here was a new one on dwarves.

"Yes, well . . ." Hedgewood continued with his spectacles sitting on the edge of his nose, which he delicately pushed up with a single finger. "Velazian dwarves have one choice: to work in harsh conditions, with little pay. Or work in harsh conditions with little pay until they can afford to migrate back to their homeland. All while risking their lives, might I add, if they try to escape from your ruby mines. If the employers find out, they'd either deduct their pay or kill them without justice being served. Nobody will take up a penniless dwarf's case in court. They pay their bounty hunters more than the dwarves. Most never make it back to my kingdom alive."

"Oh?" The dinner took a sour turn. "That is . . . terrible." I was so senseless about the specifics surrounding these ruby mines that I never took the time to look into the matter personally. My parents always took care of this issue themselves. "Perhaps you and I can do something about it?" I remained optimistic, but a marriage contract likely wasn't on his mind either.

"I plan to bring awareness to the empress before my departure. Who, no doubt, will do nothing about it," he said.

My mother would never allow anyone, especially a dwarf, to speak to her in such a manner as this. Was it a weakness of mine, or a strength like McKinley pointed out? *Compassion must be my strength, but I can still work on my assertiveness.* I concluded.

The servants brought out a dessert of assorted berries drizzled in honey, and Hedgewood immediately dove in.

"You plan on leaving so soon?" I beat myself up for having such thoughts on dwarves before. "What about the competition?"

He popped a blueberry in his mouth and slowly chewed before answering. "Let us both admit, humans are attracted to tall, beautiful, sexy elves, not short, stocky dwarf men. I see the way your pupils dilate when Zazan walks by. And . . . I will admit, I do prefer a more meaty, and altogether, a shorter dwarf woman. We are of different species. Nothing wrong with different tastes. Ultimately, I'd rather leave early than be humiliated by the empress, or you, just as my uncle was when he competed in this competition with your mother."

Once again, he nailed me to the wall. I couldn't think of what to say, so we finished dessert in silence. Then I remembered the archery competition where he was winning, then suddenly seemed to miss the target on his last few tries. He intentionally lost because he also didn't want to go on a date with me.

My mother's date with Hedgewood's uncle twenty years ago was a horror story, to say the least. She made the dwarf sit at the far end of the table in case he *"infested her with dwarf warts."* He left ten minutes into the date, enraged by her constant insults of him. It was a surprise the dwarves returned this year at all. But, the RMC was also an opportunity for them to test the waters of the next ruler and eat fresh berries . . .

Seeing I was in deep reflection, Hedgewood spoke up again. "But I do thank you for your hospitality and for actually completing this date with me . . . unlike what happened to my uncle. I specially arranged to go second so I could depart quickly. It was a pleasure meeting you. I will take my leave and report many things about you back home, including your mesmerizing dancing." He stood to depart.

"Hedgewood!" I quickly stood. "Your Highness, Prince Hedgewood. Do stay. Please."

As I stopped him, *pleaded* with him to stay, he appeared deeply moved by my acceptance of him.

He listened.

"As next reigning empress, I wish to do something for your people. Our people. It would be much easier to create a plan while you're here rather than through long-distance correspondence. For the press, we can claim we're getting along in the competition. It'll ignite a positive impression on dwarves and their skills, and create overall awareness for your cause!"

He walked to the window with his hands behind his back. "You would do all of that to help my people?"

"Absolutely."

"It's not some trick?"

"Never! It is my duty to understand my people—*our people*—and help improve their livelihoods. I wish to create a more prosperous empire for all citizens. For, if rulers don't sincerely concern themselves with all of their citizen's highest well-being, then there's no reason to have a ruler at all."

I'd prove to the world that I was a capable leader.

"If you're willing to help me, then I shall assist you as well," he said. "Perhaps I can be your eyes and ears and assess your bachelors so you can choose the best husband. Boys are different behind closed doors, you know."

A smile stretched ear to ear as I opened my arms to him and reached for his hands. "I would love your guidance."

"My guidance?" He took my hand, but with hesitation and suspicion in his eyes. My mother would never. Ever. Touch a dwarf. Let alone take guidance from one.

"It's a deal," he said. "I'll write up a list of things needing to be addressed."

Prince Hedgewood of Adonis Peak

CHAPTER 9

Racing to the River

Large purple quill feathers stuck out from the top of my stylish hat. I was a fashionable girl and wished to capture attention with my decadent outfits, if not my regal presence. On this particular morning, I wore white leggings with a half mullet-skirt falling down the back. My purple brocade vest had puffy sleeves with peplums hanging down. A stunning haute couture. Even my saddle was purple.

Some boys cheered as I bid them good morning, while others remained gentlemanly and bowed. I kept a smile on my face, soaking in their love; enjoying the attention with a twirl.

The horses were all prepared by staff, but Zack personally brought out my Pegasus.

"I've been eager to ride her." I smiled at Zack.

"There's something magical in her gait," Zack said and helped me mount. I was an expert rider but accepted his assistance, just to make him feel like a gentleman. Zack then stayed nearby and wouldn't allow any other boy to ride between us.

It became immediately apparent that Kipp would struggle with this group date too. He received riding lessons, however, he appeared nervous just walking up to the horse and quickly jolted back after the horse shook its head from side to side. The trainer had to give him encouragement just to mount it. Then he closed his eyes and silently mumbled a prayer under his breath. Being nervous while riding a horse didn't do anyone any good.

"Stay confident." I rode to Kipp's side. "Even when you have none. The horse can sense your emotions. We will not press too hard."

"Thank you, Your Majesty."

"May I stay by your side and offer guidance?" Sir McKinley asked Kipp.

"Yes! Please." Kipp gripped the reins until his fists turned white.

"Start by taking a few deep breaths," McKinley instructed.

Oh, McKinley's so wonderful. My eyes sparkled in admiration for him. While some boys competed with Zack to ride by my side, McKinley sacrificed himself to help another, and this won him more points. *He might very well win the private time with me today.* I smiled in satisfaction.

Then I noticed as my cousin rode up on an impressive looking stallion with defined muscles, trained for speed. "Can he do tricks?" I asked.

"No, just for riding," he responded, then trotted ahead of me as though no longer interested chatting.

Our group was off.

"When will the Pegasus be able to fly?" I asked Zack as we rode off into the open field. The Pegasus started growing wings, but they were still small.

"In three years or so. It's only half-Pegasus and therefore will take longer to develop wings. But because of this . . . well . . . you may not be able to fly at all. But still! You look angelic."

"It's quite rare to capture one. How did you manage?"

"Uh . . ." Zack thought hard about how to answer, and his eyes shifted left and right. "They live in the highest and most remote regions on the floating castle of Rainbow Mount. Getting to them is hard, and capturing one is even harder."

"Then how did you manage?" I pried.

"Well . . . uh she's half-breed. A merchant nursed her. He offered a pretty price."

"So you didn't capture her yourself?"

He lied when he said he went to Rainbow Mount himself.

"No, Your Majesty. But I knew you'd love her!" He tried to save face. "Everyone said you like horseback riding."

"Indeed, I do. And I'll treasure her regardless. You needn't lie to capture my attention," I assured.

His head fell. "Understood, Your Majesty."

We rode for half an hour and then reached a picnic area set up for us. We were to enjoy tea and snacks while sitting next to the forest edge overlooking a hilly green field. Soldiers patrolled inside the forest to protect the royal guests.

After everyone got settled, I spoke up. "Who's up for a horse race to the stream and back?"

Zack, Lancelot, Alejandro, and McKinley took to the challenge.

"Prince Hedgewood, would you do the honor and start us off?" I asked.

"My pleasure." Hedgewood nodded in satisfaction. His body language showed he was more relaxed around me. Whereas before our date, he was severe and never smiled at me directly.

We were mounting the horses when we heard a strange, high-pitched bird squeal in the forest. "What kind of bird was that? I've never heard such a thing," I said and searched the skies.

"Maybe a Phoenix?" Alejandro brought his horse next to mine with a large crooked smile. He always wore the sexiest shirts, but this time, he wore loose canions over his tights to prevent any . . . accidents.

"A Phoenix! Oh, what a good omen that would be."

"The omen indicating a happy marriage between us?" Alejandro puckered his lips like he was going to kiss me.

"You're so silly."

"This will be the start and finish line." Hedgewood drew a line in the dirt with a twig. "Ready. Set. Go!"

I sped off, making sure each bachelor realized they better not go easy on me. For I wouldn't spare them a second.

The shy Lancelot was a surprisingly good rider. He came up on my left side and showed off his teeth with a smile. Lancelot may not communicate with words much, but his enjoyment shone all over his face.

We came to a fallen log. Lancelot swerved around it, while I leapt over it and sped on.

McKinley soon came up on my right. Alejandro was now in the rear, unable to catch up, as Zack raced along the forest's edge.

The stream soon came into view, it was marked by large cottonwood trees and cattails. But before we reached it, three palace soldiers galloped out of the forest. One man fell off the horse.

Then I saw the arrows.

"Back, Your Majesty! GO BACK!" One soldier screamed at us to retreat.

We came to an abrupt halt just as a herd of centaurs charged out of the forest in full armor, metal breastplates, and chain-mail with swords and bows drawn. They quickly drew more arrows and aimed at us.

CHAPTER 10

The Centaurs

Centaurs were very territorial and often preferred to shoot before talking. Any little disturbance or sign of trespassing into their territory and they whipped their arrows out. Little could be done to stop an angry herd of them as they came after us. The strange thing was, centaurs didn't live within fifty miles of this region. Why were they in our territory in the first place?

The centaurs soon overran the soldiers and chased after us. With the boys riding by my side, we raced back.

"They're gaining on us!" Zack shouted from behind.

Our horses were worn out from the horse race, meaning the centaurs definitely had the advantage.

We leapt over the log again, except Alejandro, who lost time by going around and came within range of their arrows. A centaur shot at him, but pierced the ground next to him instead.

I looked into the forest on the side and saw the soldiers trying to hold the centaurs at bay as arrows flew in every direction. Then we reached the top of a small hill and saw the other bachelors smiling and cheering. Then it dawned on me, between Kipp's lack of riding abilities, our tired horses, and other slow riders, we wouldn't all survive. That is, if any of us survived.

Some bachelors may be more practiced in riding, but centaurs weren't as lazy as regular horses. They trained in combat and racing, and had minds of their own. They were strong in the legs but weak in the arms.

Finally, more soldiers filed out from the forest behind us in a suicide attempt to block the centaurs.

"GO! GO BACK!" McKinley waved to the bachelors at the picnic. None of them could hear. Instead, they cheered us on. It wasn't until some centaurs got through the soldier's barricade and made it over the hill that the boys at the picnic realized what was happening. We weren't racing each other. We were racing to save our lives.

Kipp's horse became spooked as he tried to mount and ran off without him, while Zazan's foot then got stuck in the saddle as he mounted. Zazan was a water elf, they don't ride horses much.

"I'll get Kipp and Zazan." McKinley galloped in their direction. He risked his life to save the two! But three riding on one horse meant none would survive. I had to get one of them too.

This can't be happening. But I had to keep a clear mind to come up with something to save us.

Right as I reached the picnic area and slowed down to help Zazan, my Pegasus kicked up its rear in irritation. It soon went out of control and bucked me off its back.

I rolled across the grass and looked back at the crazed Pegasus completely out of control.

Zack, Lancelot, and Alejandro all came back to get me.

In one swift movement, Zack grabbed my arm and lifted me onto his horse.

"Someone get Zazan!" I yelled at the top of my lungs, and Lancelot immediately reached a hand out for Zazan.

Then, an arrow shot through my hat, flicking it off my head.

"GO. GO. GO!" I shrieked at Zack.

As we sped away, I saw McKinley come to a complete stop. He rummaged through each of his pockets.

"LET'S GO!" Kipp yelled.

But McKinley kept searching, then pulled out a small whistle and blew.

A high-pitched, eerie squeal shattered the plains, but as annoying as it was to humans, to the centaurs and horses, it was unbearable. The centaurs abruptly stopped to cover their ears. Some screamed, most dropped their bows and arrows and cried. I couldn't help covering my ears too; it was so irritating, like nails on a chalkboard.

McKinley drew another breath and blew the whistle again. More soldiers arrived from the palace direction. They surrounded the centaurs and confiscated their weapons as the whistling continued.

"We give up. Stop, please. Have mercy." The centaur leader cried.

McKinley stopped blowing.

"Did you have mercy on our princess?" One soldier flung a whip in the air.

"Enough!" I howled at the soldier and approached the centaurs on foot. Meanwhile, every bachelor nearby beseeched me to retreat into safe territory. Two of the bachelors were already halfway to the palace, unwilling to look back, while the others returned to our location, not willing to leave me.

"Every bachelor not in the horse race is ordered back to the palace NOW! Those in the competition, I need your assistance. McKinley, I don't know what that thing is, but hold the whistle ready in case something else happens." I wanted only the fastest and strongest boys with me for protection, in case we had to flee again.

"Allow me to offer diplomatic assistance, Your Majesty." Hedgewood stepped forward.

"Accepted." I turned to the centaur leader. "Why did you attack us?"

"*YOU* attacked us!" The centaur roared.

"You mean my soldiers attacked you?" I asked for clarification.

"Your . . . your person. You!"

"Please explain so we can understand. Which of our people attacked you?" Centaurs were ultra-sensitive, like horses. So I had to word everything carefully. Even suggesting that the centaurs were responsible for attacking *us* could make them want to attack again. After that, diplomacy would be even more difficult to achieve. Yet, the centaur was so belligerently enraged, her anger spoke over all reason.

The centaur continued explaining in broken Velazian language. When amongst themselves, the centaurs spoke mainly in the Centaurian language, which was what McKinley's ancestor's spoke long ago, but it was a dying language and was mostly used now only in opera, poetry, and religious ceremonies. Yet, their people seemed to adopt a little Velazian and a little Baylorian language so that they could communicate with the rest of the world. When their leader spoke, she would often add a Baylorian word in here and there. Since I knew both languages, I could understand the full sentence.

"Attackers carried Velazian royal flag. D'ey wore your blue uniforms." The Velazian colors were bright sky-blue and white. "And you STOLE our brethren!"

"You mean one of your people was kidnapped by my people?" I asked.

"YOU kidnapped him!" She pointed to me.

"*I* kidnapped him?" I asked. "It wasn't me."

"You did!" She repeated.

They were getting upset, so I had to tread carefully. They were clearly agitated enough to put on metal armor and travel all this distance with heavy war hammers and swords to attack. If they killed any of us, it would've been an international disaster, unless that was their intention. But centaurs didn't concern themselves with elf, human, or dwarf affairs. So there must be more to the story.

"Please, I'm trying to understand. We can help you find your people. How many centaurs were kidnapped?"

"Lies come out of your mouth!" The centaur spit on my shoe.

Seeing the centaur was too defensive to speak with me, Hedgewood stepped in. "I am Prince Hedgewood of Adonis Peak. A dwarf. My people didn't partake in this crime." The centaur calmed down. "I can talk to the imprudent blue-robed humans to make them understand." He failed to resist a smirk.

The centaur spoke in the next sentence in Baylorian, but Hedgewood looked at me, not knowing what she said, so I translated for him.

"She said: 'I lied. The brethren who was kidnapped is before our eyes. Yet, you claim that we don't understand'."

Hedgewood nodded and returned his attention to the centaur. "Where's the brethren? I'm not smart enough to figure it out myself, as I'm not part of those who committed the crime." Hedgewood proving was good at diplomacy. It took someone to put aside their own ego in order to successfully negotiate.

"There! The Pegasus you kidnapped is there!"

Everyone glanced at the Pegasus who was still bucking around by itself in the field. Then back at the centaurs. Then all eyes went to Zack.

Zack froze. "I . . . I didn't. I swear Your Majesty! I . . ."

He lied once already. Did he lie again?

I put my hand up. "Save it for later."

The dwarf continued. "Can you tell me the story so I may convict the wrongdoers?"

"D'ey will convict no one! D'ey commit blasphemy! D'EY LIE! Pegasus is before our eyes. And they lie. You lie now."

"They didn't tell *me* the truth." Hedgewood placed a hand on his heart. "Now that *I* know the truth from you, I'll help you get the Pegasus back."

Zack squealed. "You can't return . . ." I simply glared at him, and he shut up.

"How did they capture the Pegasus? By what means?" Hedgewood asked.

"Man came in light blue uniform during our 'right of ceremony' near Rainbow Mount, to honor our close relations with the Pegasus and unicorn. He used the whistle that man carries." The centaur pointed to McKinley and his whistle. "There was explosion. Everything was in chaos. Then the soldier took the Pegasus before its 'right of ceremony' to grow wings. You see, now it has small wings."

"But how do you know it was this girl here who captured the Pegasus?" Hedgewood asked. "You just said it was a man in a blue uniform."

"Eye witness." She stomped her hoof in the dirt like she was ready to charge me. "Someone claimed they saw a Pegasus being taken on the road out of the forest by a 'black hair woman in purple clothes.' He offered to follow the human woman for us and found where it was taken. Here! To the palace!" Sometimes it was hard deciphering what centaurs were saying, since their Velazian was broken, but we pieced it together in the end. "Eyewitness says to us last night where to find the Pegasus. In the forest. By the blue soldiers. On this day. We waited. He gave signal. Soldiers was hiding in the forest as human man said. And there we saw *her* riding it. INSOLENCE!" She spit on the ground again.

Whoever planned this framing job knew that I often wore purple riding clothes . . . what a perfect setup. I clenched my fist. Killing me is one thing, but all of these boys too!

"How can we solve this?" Hedgewood softened his voice, since they were upset at me for riding the Pegasus.

"Give us Pegasus back and kill she who captures and dare rides it." The leader pointed at me.

Chapter II

Investigation

"Y ou can't kill the princess!" Zack pushed his way forward in my defense, but it only startled the centaurs. Those who still had weapons on them reached for their daggers or swords again.

McKinley jumped in between them and myself, holding up the whistle in warning. They put the swords back in their sheaths.

Hedgewood continued in a gentle, calming voice. "The princess here was tricked. I saw who gave her the Pegasus. It wasn't anybody here." He lied a little. But the centaurs would never know. They were gullible, seeing how easy it was for the mastermind behind this to concoct a story with so many plot holes. But it was hard to explain that to these creatures.

"THIS IS GREATEST INSULT!" The centaur leapt up in the air, circled around another centaur, then came back to us. They all had large metal helmets with brown plumes on the top that made them seem bigger and more intimidating than they already were. "Humans have always respected Rainbow Mount until now. Why do you commit sacrilege now? And to do so on the Spring Equinox!"

Rainbow Mount was a sacred mountain to *all* creatures; humans, centaurs, elves, and fairies combined. It was said that bad luck would come to anyone who dared disturb the sanctuary. For anyone to commit a crime like capturing a Pegasus, especially to do so during a ceremony or on the equinox was blasphemy. I went there after reaching puberty to do a ceremony honoring my womanhood. The place was peaceful and happy. Their anger made sense now. But that wasn't the only reason the centaurs were upset . . .

"Then you ride Pegasus! You humans and dwarves take horses to ride; horses agree to this, but not a youngling. Pegasus is not of age." I never thought of that, how the Pegasus was really too young to ride. "Give Pegasus and princess to us or we'll overrun the palace for your crime!"

Back in the fourth century A.D., there was a war fought between people called the Hovarts and the centaurs. Long story short, the centaurs won and nearly wiped out the Hovart people, which was proof that we didn't want to go to war with the mighty centaurs, who were most valiant knights. Plus, they worked as a unit, not as individuals. If we went to war with one herd, all others from the north, south, and east would join in the fight. It would be a domino effect.

"Your Majesty . . ." The lead Velazian soldier pulled the royal members aside to discuss this matter further. "If we allow the centaurs to go now, they'll attack again, especially knowing that you rode the Pegasus. We have to solve the issue right here and now. We must kill them all."

"No," I said, not allowing a slaughter of these sacred yet imprudent people. "I won't stoop to such levels. We have but one option. We must return the Pegasus to them and let them be on their way."

Zack squealed but said nothing. My word was final.

"Allow me," Hedgewood said. "We will make an agreement; we will free you and return your Pegasus. Then justice will be served."

"We want her!" They pointed to me.

"She did nothing wrong." Hedgewood assured, but the centaurs were insistent.

"She captured Pegasus on sacred day!"

"I assure you"—I stepped forward—"that I did not go to Rainbow Mo—"

"YOU LIE. YOU COMMIT BLASPHEMY." All the centaurs leapt up onto their hind legs.

McKinley put the whistle to his lips and blew once. The centaurs immediately stopped to talk again.

"Our dear princess was framed," Hedgewood said.

They glanced at each other in confusion, not understanding the word "framed." I spoke the Baylorian word for "framed" but they still didn't understand, so Hedgewood tried to explain. "The person who told you that a black-haired woman in purple captured the Pegasus was lying."

A different centaur stepped forward to defend their leader. "You insult our leader." They stomped their hooves at me.

"No. No, it's not—" This was getting complicated.

"NO JUSTICE until princess is punished for crimes! Give us her." They wouldn't back down.

Hedgewood tried to explain over the next ten minutes what "framed" meant, and questioned the source of which they received their information. "The person lied to you when they said a girl in purple captured it, yet you yourself saw a soldier in sky-blue." After some time, they seemed to understand the concept but also had no Centaurian equivalent to the word. Then, Hedgewood offered a bargain. "How about we capture the real criminal and hand him over to you? Then justice would be served."

The centaurs spoke to each other, neighing and snorting for a few minutes before coming to a consensus.

"This is another trick! Hand over princess now."

"We must *find* the thief first. Give us time. Then we'll deliver him to you."

They spoke to each other again, then said, "One week. You must hand criminal over or we'll attack the palace."

"Four weeks." Hedgewood bargained.

"Two."

"Three."

"Two and a half."

After further negotiation, it was clear the centaurs wouldn't wait longer than two and a half weeks. And they might not even keep that agreement as they weren't great at telling time. They counted by days of the moon, which probably meant we had from now until just before the next new moon . . . or so . . . in order to find the mastermind behind this and hand the person over. Otherwise, Velazia would become a battlefield.

Ice ran through my mother's veins as she looked down from her throne onto the alone and defenseless baron. Zack now stood in front of the High Council for interrogation, with his shoulders slumped and his eyes downcast.

"Tell us everything!"

"I lied. I mean, I told the truth, but I also lied," he stuttered. "I didn't find the Pegasus at Rainbow Mount from a merchant, a merchant brought her to court and sold her to us. He said it was the rarest gift one could ever offer and would guarantee I'd be noticed by the crown princess if she received it in the RMC. We paid a high price for her. Truly. There are records of this. Many in my palace witnessed this transaction. My father and brother can testify. The staff . . . many were there."

"'Noticed,' yes, you were 'noticed' for your fatuity!" Despite how livid she was, she tried to calm down; after all, Zaccaria was from her husband's home city. "Let me get this straight." She began pacing about with her fingers on her temple. "A merchant came to your doorsteps with a young Pegasus and offered to sell it for the *sole* purpose of impressing the crown princess of Velazia, which she'd no doubt ride the first opportunity she had—during the group picnic. And you did everything he suggested without suspecting a thing?"

"What was there to suspect? It was a great gift! I didn't mean to harm my beloved Princess Qloey. I love Her Majesty." Zack fell on his knees in a moment of desperation. "I want to marry her! Please forgive me. How can I ever repay you?"

My mother looked at me, then to our advisors. "Send the fastest messengers to the city of Tildon and confirm the story. Interrogate Zaccaria's family. If it fits, you'll be pardoned. If not . . . we'll hand you over to the centaurs ourselves and your entire family will be stripped of their titles and wealth. In the meantime, you're under house arrest. Dismissed."

After Zack left, McKinley was brought forth for interrogation. His expression serious and dutiful, as usual.

"Sir McKinley of Centaurus, do you know why you're here?" My mother tried to strike fear in the military man with her dark brooding glare, but he seemed unmoved.

"Because I'm of Centaurus, the closest city to the capital, of which the centaurs who attacked today reside."

"And what is that whistle you have?"

"There is an ancient legend called: *The Princess and the Sailor.* Have you heard it?"

"No. Explain."

"One of my great ancestors, a princess, was lost at sea after a terrible storm. She was saved by mermaids in the Seaweed Cove by being transformed into one herself. Long story short, after being kissed by her true love, a sailor, she transformed back into a human. Her journey helped develop a positive relationship between mermaids and humans in the Pearl Sea. As a gift for saving her, the humans offered them a golden trident with magical powers. In return, the mermaids gifted the princess with three shells. While mermaids call these shells 'musical instruments,' we call them 'whistles,' because they sound different on land than they do underwater."

"I hear they're quite irritating, yes. Go on." My mother's hands remained on her hips as she listened.

"It is our belief that the mermaids actually knew that these whistles could be used in defense against a centaur attack. These whistles have saved our people many times. I always carry one. There are only two others, one at the Centaurus palace and the other in safekeeping. We keep them secure since they can be easily abused."

A crease formed around my mother's eyes as she narrowed them. "Yet this same whistle was used by the thief to kidnap the Pegasus from the centaurs. Did this culprit get his whistle from the mermaids too?" She angrily blurted out the last part.

"If one of our whistles *is* missing . . . it means that it was either stolen, or one of my people—or myself—are now suspects in this assassination attempt. I take all responsibility for the misuse of our seashell whistles if it belongs to us, Your Royal Majesty." McKinley remained humble, but he should never have given my mother such leverage over him.

"You're right." A cunning smirk formed at the edge of my mother's mouth. I knew he just walked himself into a trap. "You and the others responsible may very well be tortured alive if found guilty. You better pray you're not."

McKinley took a moment to soak her words in, then continued. "If our whistles are accounted for"—he inhaled deeply—"it's possible there is a fourth whistle from the mermaid queendom. I offer my services to investigate the matter. "

"Very admirable of you. But if all your whistles are accounted for, then your people are no doubt guilty. But I wonder, could you be offering your services in order to hide the evidence?" McKinley said nothing as she paced back and forth, trying to intimidate him. Still, he remained unmoved. "Our constable, Sir Takaya, will take charge of the investigation. Do you agree to allow him unlimited access to your files in Centaurus and fully comply in the investigation?"

"Absolutely, Your Royal Majesty. And if I may offer a lead." He was eager to serve us, like a chivalrous and loyal knight. Every word he spoke, every action he took, made me fall deeper for him. A prince charming in a knights armor. "There are other whistles used to communicate with forest creatures, including centaurs. When we were at the picnic getting ready for the horse race, we heard a bird screeching. It was not the shell whistle, but another type."

At the mention of a "horse race," my mother gave me a disapproving glance. I was about to be scolded! "Reckless." She snapped at me. "Perhaps I'll hand you over to the centaurs myself since you don't value your life anyway. It's you they want and one less headache for me if you're gone. Maybe then I can stop worrying about the future of the empire."

My muscles became stiff, yet I said nothing to defend myself. She always had the final word anyway. Best not to dig myself any deeper into this hole.

But the fact that she said that in front of the entire council and Sir McKinley was humiliating.

McKinley looked at me, then back at my mother, yet I couldn't discern what passed through his mind. Perhaps he now saw how pitiable I was standing next to the great empress.

"I'm also trained in fighting centaurs," McKinley said. "I wish to offer your officers advice on fighting centaurs if a war ensues."

"Very well. You may leave with Sir Takaya to discuss further. You're dismissed," my mother said and waved him off.

After he left, another councilwoman named Sonya spoke up. "I can confirm this last account. All soldiers recalled hearing a high-pitched bird squeal prior to the centaur attack, but they didn't see where it came from. Aside from that, we have another alarming development. Before handing over the Pegasus to the centaurs, the soldiers saw a rash on the Pegasus' hindquarters. The soldiers described the rash to our herbalist who identified it as *toadstool poison*. It's found all over Velazia."

An epiphany suddenly came to me. "During the attack, the Pegasus began acting out and flung me off. It continued to buck around for nearly ten minutes as we negotiated. But . . . Zack was the one who retrieved the Pegasus from the barn for me." I alerted them. "Did he do it?"

"Pardon, Your Majesty, it wouldn't be him then," Sonya clarified. "Apparently this poison takes three to five minutes to begin taking effect and causes severe itchiness. So someone had to have done it while at the picnic."

We all went silent.

Three to five minutes.

There was no doubt. One of the contestants was trying to kill me.

"Did you rub against any plants during your . . . horse race?" Yenna asked. Couldn't she have said "picnic" instead of "horse race?" Just mentioning the horse race again in front of my mother made my mother's eyes twitch.

"No. And you said the plant must be in a moist area under shade, like a creek or heavily wooded area," I said. "We were in an open field most of the journey."

"Did you see anyone go near the horses before your *horse race*?" my mother probed.

"Everyone," I recalled. "All the horses were grouped together."

We all took a deep breath at the same time.

"Clearly, Zack and McKinley are the biggest suspects." My mother concluded. "Or was it one of the bachelors who ran back to the palace like frightened idiots?"

"Nonetheless," I changed subjects. The situation was chaotic, so I couldn't expect the boys to wait around for me to catch up. Their lives were in danger, and they needed to escape quickly. "The mastermind of this attack will clearly want to cover his tracks and try to divert attention *away* from him. He already succeeded in framing me to the centaurs. Could we then speculate that neither Zack nor McKinley are the culprit, and it's someone less obvious?"

"A possibility, but let's not discount them yet. This gives us more leverage to make demands on Tildon and Centaurus." Her eyes turned green with greed. "We'll consider them all guilty until we find the one, or the group of them, whoever organized this."

"Pardon me for bringing up a controversial question." Sonya stepped in, "But we should find a motive first. For instance . . . what would happen if Her Majesty *was* assassinated?"

My mother barred her teeth and looked ready to smack Sonya, so I interceded.

"My little brother would become crown prince," I said.

"And that would benefit the culprit how?" Sonya asked, but no one answered. "And . . . what would happen if you *and* several of the princes were harmed or killed in the attack?"

"How dare you suggest . . ." my mother growled.

"A very good point!" This was an important question to look at, so I quickly answered to tame her anger. "If Prince Abdulla died, it could lead to war. If we were busy at war, the other cities in our empire would revolt. In this, we can see a motive." I looked at my mother. "It's starting to look like someone from within the empire is trying to start a revolution."

"No." My mother immediately shot down my point as if it wasn't valuable. "It's someone from outside the empire trying to lessen our power in the region."

My mind ran down the list of bachelors and their motives. *Qinrel clearly didn't like me. It could be him.* Then I remembered how Hedgewood was upset about his people's work conditions. He, too, could easily wish for the empire's destruction. Especially after his uncle was treated so badly during my mother's competition. But I quickly threw that thought in the back of my mind. *No. He wouldn't go so far.* In any case, I wouldn't bring Hedgewood up in this conversation. One mention of *the dwarf* and my mother would use it as an opportunity to publicly humiliate him too.

"Is there anyone we can assume isn't the mastermind?" I wanted to narrow the list down.

My mother continued the analysis. "Let's leave Zazan and Abdulla out. We can't afford bad relations with them." Either she thought Pixieland or Adonis Peak was the culprit, or her own opinion about the culprit being from *"outside the empire"* was no longer her opinion. She then started listing those from within the empire as if her previous suggestion wasn't valid anymore. "Edgar, of course, would never."

Sonya and I glanced at each other. We wouldn't cancel any of them out, but couldn't say that to my mother.

My mother continued. "Clayton is of Velazian nobility and wouldn't benefit from a war in his own home, and Kipp . . . I cannot see how Kipp could start a war. He's just a lowly actor's assistant."

We brainstormed for another half-hour, or rather, my mother narrowed down her own list for half an hour, but every time we found another possible motive, more questions came up. Truly, it became too difficult to pin down one and I was better off talking to Sonya alone about this later in order to voice my true opinions.

"Should we cancel the competition?" Sonya asked.

"No! If we do, we won't have the opportunity to find who's responsible," I spoke up before anything else was said on the subject. The truth was, I was confident the right husband for me was among this group. We had to keep going.

"Agreed. We need to sniff this criminal out from hiding and get more leads. This person is determined. He'll try again and you will be our bait. Perhaps we'll host a horse race to draw him out."

I clenched my fists, knowing I screwed up again.

If only I could do something right for once.

Prince Abdulla of Payonna

CHAPTER 12

Prince Abdulla

For the next two days, I was busy working on the investigation, creating defensive strategies against a centaur attack, rearranging the group schedule, and working out my fears that I might end up choosing the assassin as my husband.

Reports came in that centaurs were antsy and on the constant move. Some were migrating from great distances into Velazian territory, yet we only had two weeks to find the perpetrator—or someone else to blame—and hand them over, or an all-out war was imminent.

Zack was pardoned, as his story of the Pegasus merchant was confirmed by several sources, but there were nearly no leads on the merchant's profile and current whereabouts. The group and private dates were altered entirely, and a new plan was created as we realized it was too much of a risk if the bachelors knew the entire schedule. Nobody except the reigning family and Yenna knew whose date was next. It also gave me more leeway to choose who I wanted to see next.

I snickered in delight to myself.

"You've been a wonderful asset to our preparations with the investigation and centaurs." McKinley walked me to my door after our last meeting so I could prepare for my date. He was the only bachelor I saw in the last two days.

He remained professional and stern during meetings, but afterwards when we'd sometimes talk, his face became softer and his eyes sparkled as he put his undivided attention on me. Perhaps it wasn't fair to the other contestants for us to have extra private conversations away from the RMC, but my decision in a husband would affect the rest of my life, so I'd soak in all the time I could get with the boys whom I liked without guilt.

McKinley's chest rose and fell as he listened to me speak. "I hear the vocalist Sophya is your favorite opera singer," I said.

"Indeed, her voice is so crisp and powerful."

"Well, maybe she'll make a surprise appearance." I teased him as I bit my lower lip. "A show of appreciation for all of your hard work."

He seemed to lose his words.

In the meetings, he talked fluently, but when romance came up, he stumbled; but in an adorning way. Yet he tried as hard as possible not to let it show. It was as if love was a poker game and he was taking a risk by revealing his emotions. So he quickly withdrew them. I was afraid he lost all interest in me after my mother's public criticisms, or developed a negative opinion of my leadership abilities, but at the end of the day, he remained by my side and showed no signs of running away.

"I'll see you later." I batted my eyelashes, then I turned inside for my ladies to do my makeup and put on an evening gown for me.

Abdulla, Prince of Payonnian Queendom. Human. Age 17. Fluent in Payonna and Velazian languages. Interests: Plays five instruments, sings, & has mastered over ten dances.

The scent of essential oils and perfumes filled the air as I entered the room for my third private date. Prince Abdulla insisted on hosting the date so I could relax (even though my staff did everything for me anyway). He was only given three hours' advance notice, yet he did a marvelous job (or rather, his staff did) in preparing all the food and decorations. Unbeknownst to him, they sent several poison testers in to sample *everything* his chefs cooked.

I spent a moment soaking in the beauty of the scene. Abdulla sat on a handmade rug with intricate geometry and wore a suede garment that hung over one shoulder, revealing part of his chest. If that wasn't irresistible enough, he was tall, muscular, and handsome with a black goatee, and he smelt like delicious frankincense. *Yum.*

As if cupid stung me right there, I forgot all about the activities of the last two days, along with my first date with sexy Alejandro, which I was certain nobody could outdo in the romance department.

I was wrong.

"Come, my princess." Abdulla took my hand and led me to some pillows on the floor. "Are you well after the centaur attack? We were all worried after you canceled all dates and activities and disappeared."

"We are taking greater precautions and had to shift things around. But I'm glad to be here with you now. How splendid all this is. And you did it on short notice."

"It is my tradition to give before receiving. Yet, for a woman of your caliber, it's impossible to give too much."

"You flatter me, Prince Abdulla."

"I speak only truth." He tamed me with his licentious eyes. "You have remarkable beauty and grace. Yet, you balance it with strength and courage."

"I could only hope to have those attributes." I looked down, almost in shame.

Everyone flattered me so much since the beginning of the competition, but after the centaur incident I started to wonder if all of it was all an act.

Prince Abdulla's queendom wasn't a part of my empire. Payonna was wealthy because of their exotic merchandise and decadent artwork. My ancestors exhausted resources attempting to conquer them and went on to attack the elf kingdom of Nololay instead..

What if a marriage between us was an opportunity for Payonna to assassinate me? I wondered.

"I wish to offer you gifts," he said. "You danced and played music for me on the first night; now I'll share music with you. And hopefully, I can hear the sweet sound of your voice again." He pulled out a *kamanche, a* musical instrument that resembled a guitar . . . but different. "I fill my spare time with the *kamanche, nay,* and *dotar* musical instruments; often entertaining the other bachelors. We need music and dance to keep our spirits moving."

"Indeed." I couldn't agree more.

He played a song and then switched instruments, then asked me to play the harp and sing with him. Together we found rhythm and discovered our own song.

After we were both high from the music, dinner was served. Luckily, he didn't nudge closer like Alejandro did, for I wasn't ready for that much intimacy with anyone yet.

"The best time to eat is when you're happy. The food acquires healing powers through joy. That is why it's our custom to play music and dance before eating."

"And it does well for digestion." I chuckled, but he didn't reciprocate the amusement.

"Tell me, princess, how shall you manage through this competition with so many engagements? I personally want to place all my attention and energy on you alone, yet you have twelve to entertain."

"The days are draining and you're only the third date," I admitted. "Unfortunately, if all the dates are as wonderful as ours, finding the right husband will be impossible."

He fiddled with a pink rose. "I willingly admit, if this competition wasn't to take place, I would've sought your hand anyway. With a reputation in music like you have, who could not?"

"A match like ours would benefit both our people as well."

"Bah. Politics and love don't mesh." He sniffed the flower, then placed it in a bowl of water. "Your decision should be one of love, not duty."

Why couldn't he be unattractive and unromantic? Then my choice would be easy. Everything he said and did was based on deep philosophy and passion. It was beautiful and helped me escape from reality. I liked three boys now, yet they were all so different.

I inhaled deeply. "The balance between duty and love is something I'm still learning."

"It's easy. Duty is public, and shall be accomplished in the day; love is private, and should be reserved for the night." He swiftly glanced at me. "Just as a third of our lives should go toward rest, a third should be dedicated to responsibilities, and a third to joy and play. Or . . . we can simply forego all duties and have fun our entire lives."

"Such is not possible for me. I wake up thinking of daily tasks and fall asleep planning the morrow. But I will try. Can you teach me a song from your people?" I said.

He smiled. "Certainly."

We spent the remainder of the evening sharing our favorite music, which took a great weight off my shoulders from all the stress and responsibilities in my life.

Chapter 13

The Secret Lover

"How do I choose? This is impossible!" I sprawled across the bed while Victorya sat next to me.

"I've never seen you this way," she said.

Yes, I was refined, even behind closed doors, but I was now wrestling with my thoughts and my pillow.

"My heart feels many things it has never known before. Alejandro was charming and handsome. Then Abdulla was charming and handsome. But both in completely different ways." I smothered my face in the pillow, then flung my head back up. "Perhaps Abdulla is the better of the two in terms of solidifying our hold on the region. And the Ogarzian Plains where Alejandro comes from is weak; they're almost a burden to the empire. But Alejandro is so warm toward me. I cannot possibly let him go!"

I rolled about, my blankets were about to slip off the bed and my legs sprawled about. "But then McKinley's personality and values are pure. And we work naturally together. He'd be a great choice to strengthen the military . . . unless he's the assassin and is tricking us! In which case, I'm royally confused and should send all of them home."

"You have *nine* dates left, plus group dates, and then a round of second dates," she said.

I moaned and shoved my face into the pillow again.

"Plenty of time to delve deeper into their natures and intentions, *and* your feelings." Victorya smiled warmly.

"But . . . what if all twelve are charming and handsome *and dangerous assassins?*"

"I can tell you at first glance, not ALL are charming OR handsome. Nor would they make good assassins." Victorya's comment made us chortle. "But I'm most curious, what are your feelings on Edgar? You haven't talked about him since he arrived."

"Oh, he's . . . a disappointment. But I still have hopes for him . . . " My fingers made circles on the bed covers. "My opinions are changing. Before they arrived, I thought nothing of charm, or considered they'd each have different personalities. Why is it my thoughts were so far from my heart?" My hair now stuck up like a wild child.

"Because you've lived a secluded and controlled life, with only your parents as a role model, and never met a man outside of work. Now, let me do your hair or you'll look like a vagrant at breakfast."

"I don't want to see them again. Just give me the best one and off with the others." I waved her off.

Councilwoman Sonya came into the room, telling me it was time to sit at my vanity. She was one of the High Council members who catered more toward "the future empress"—getting on my good side—than the "current empress." I knew I could trust Sonya with things that Yenna should never know. "We have concerning news about one of the contestants, Your Majesty."

"Good."

"Good?" Sonya's eyebrows rose.

"It'll make it easier to eliminate one or two . . . or three."

"Oh?" She questioned. My comment flew over her head. "Prince Qinrel, of Nololay—"

"Anyone but him." I cut her off mid-sentence. Then I remembered the elf's prickly attitude. "Never mind, he's okay."

Now Sonya looked royally confused, but she shook it off and continued, "Prince Qinrel . . . we have found . . ." She sighed. "Has a secret lover in the palace. Shall we dismiss him from the competition?"

My mind raced over my interactions with the disinterested and cold elf and the elven woman he flirted with. "Does my mother know?" I shifted my eyes without moving my head so that Victorya wouldn't mess up my hairdo. I liked impressive styles to make a grand appearance.

"Not yet . . . Your Majesty."

"Good. You did good coming to me first. Keep it a secret. My mother cannot know ANYTHING."

Qinrel's entire family would be humiliated if this got out, expelled from the royal courts, or even excommunicated. Infidelity was bad enough, but to be an RMC participant and cheat on the crown princess was an unforgivable crime.

"Um . . . there's one more thing. Qinrel's mother arrived. She secretly pulled the elven mistress, Glynnda, Qinrel's lover, out of the palace. She now wishes to seek an audience with you this morning. We suspect she's trying to keep the situation under wraps."

"Does *she* know that *we* know?"

"Not that *I* know, Your Majesty."

"Hmm." My mind raced. "I'll accept her request before breakfast."

Queen Typa bowed before me in the throne room. She brought a large emerald as a gift. Qinrel didn't present much in terms of gifts at the opening ceremony, as the elven robes he offered me were used and smelly. Now I wondered if he *intentionally* forgot to bring these precious gems with him?

The Nololay emerald mines were almost empty, and they were quickly running out of financial resources. That meant they'd have a weaker army as well. This emerald would be a prized possession, telling me she was desperate. Being only half-part of the empire meant that the Nololay elves didn't have Velazia's protection, in case someone decided to take advantage of the situation. Alternatively, the political vipers in my own court might also use the opportunity to undermine them. I felt sorry for their elven kingdom as my compassion desired peace.

No doubt the elves would benefit from a marriage with me; then I could offer them assistance without controversy. It's too bad that Qinrel not only didn't try, but seemed to intentionally harm their reputation.

"Your Majesty, I come far to wish you good tidings and a prosperous marriage to whomever you choose." The widowed elven Queen was playing it safe, probably trying to determine if I knew about the secret lover or not.

"Thank you, Your Royal Highness, Queen Typa. But you needn't come all this way to wish me good-tidings, not when your son resides in this very palace."

"You are correct, Your Majesty." Her voice was soft like a dove. "But our nations must continue our good relationship, of which we simply don't do enough to maintain."

As the future empress, I needed this practice in decision-making. Without my mother here, I was in charge and felt more confident in expressing my views without her incessant criticisms. This was fun. And I knew how to play the game from here.

"I look forward to my time with your beautiful son. So far he's proven to be a great candidate in the Matchmaking Competition. And I hope you visit more often. Do make my palace your home for the remainder of the competition. You may join the royal table for dinner. I accept your gifts with gratitude." I stood to leave.

Queen Typa perked up, realizing now that I wasn't privy to Qinrel's transgressions. "Thank you for your gratitude, Your Majesty."

"Sonya," I called the councilwoman over as Queen Typa walked away with her lavender silky robes fluttering behind her. "Tonight I'll have the date with Prince Qinrel. Tell Yenna about this alteration."

As the next empress, I would decide these things.

Everyone jumped to their feet as I entered the bachelor pad. Hedgewood's demeanor was altered; he was quite attentive toward me after the recent events and even smiled as he bowed.

"Hedgewood, Alejandro, wonderful to see you again. Abdulla, Lancelot, Edgar . . ." Everyone greeted me kindly as I individually acknowledged each bachelor and spoke their name.

"It has been too long since we've met. I hope you're all comfortable in your quarters. Please sit," I said. "It cannot be ignored that our lives were threatened. And, I'm sorry I couldn't see to your comfort and needs the last two days, as we've been diligently gathering intelligence, creating defensive and diplomatic plans in accordance with the centaur attack, and running an investigation on the assassin and his accomplices. Speaking honestly, we're uncertain how this will play out. I understand what concerns you have. If any of you feel unsafe and wish to leave, you may sign the mutual rescission and leave before the competition today. I will hold nothing against you."

The table was silent for a moment.

"I feel safer with you," Kipp blurted out.

"Thank you, Kipp."

"It's 'Your Majesty'," Alejandro corrected Kipp.

"Let us not fight at breakfast." I sat down. "We'll eat together and then join the festivities outside."

CHAPTER 14

Physical Challenge

To the guard's detriment and anxiety, the palace grounds were full of aristocrats and paparazzi, ready to judge the bachelors and cherry-pick their favorites. The boys had three different obstacles to overcome. In each round of the physical challenge competition, four of them would be eliminated.

"That elf Zazan is the most handsome creature I ever laid eyes upon." I overheard Ednnys say to Princess Marie-Avignon of Moonstone this time. "What I would do to marry him!"

It was strange hearing other girls ogle after my boys,—or was it just Ednnys?—but I supposed that since eleven of these eligible bachelor boys would return home without an engagement, some of the other aristocrats might try to marry their children to them while the opportunity remained.

Then I saw the elf, Glynnda, coddle Qinrel. The elven woman's dress swung like a bell, like some magical presence lifted her up. She stroked her fingers seductively across Qinrel's cheek and slithered her bony hand up his arm. She wasn't even trying to be discreet in public. Then Glynnda's eyes met mine.

There was something devious about the way one lip curled in a vicious smile. Like she wanted to challenge me to *her* mate.

Supposedly, Qinrel's mother already removed this elf; why was she still here?

"Sonya," I called the councilwoman over. Sonya hadn't the most attractive facial features but made up for any deficiencies in her intelligence. "Do you see what I see?"

"Yes, Your Majesty. Glynnda is supposed to be on her way back to the elf city right now."

"Investigate. And keep it under wraps. I don't want anyone to notice their indiscretion."

The first competition was a three-legged race. The four boys, Kipp, McKinley, Hedgewood, and Lancelot, huddled together like they were coming up with a game plan. I was glad to see everyone working together and was worried that the peasant and dwarf would be singled out as undesirable partners. But instead, Kipp and McKinley joined as teammates, while Hedgewood and Lancelot made another team.

Secretly, I was rooting for the McKinley and Kipp to win this first race. Yet, there was cause to wonder why my focus kept going to Kipp. *We could never be,* I tried to convince myself. *I really just want McKinley to win.*

The trumpet sounded and everyone was off. The two elves, Zazan and Qinrel, were a miraculous team and worked in unison, almost as if they were telepathically linked. They jumped over a small log in perfect timing, zig-zagged around obstacles, and ran through the finish line in first place; without a single misstep.

Everyone else either didn't run in unison, or as in Zack's case, ran too fast and kept yanking at Alejandro's leg.

Then Edgar and Clayton tripped and face-planted in the mud.

"Ooh!" Everyone gasped, then laughed it off.

The two sullen royals untied their legs in defeat and walked to the finish line.

The sweltering sun didn't deter the crowd's roars of excitement, nor did our non-gambling rules prevent people from passing money under the table.

The second round in the competition for the boys was an obstacle course built over the pond, so if anyone fell, they'd get soaked; much to our amusement.

Alejandro took off his doublet, revealing a sweaty white tunic underneath for the women to gawk at.

He just wants to show off. Not that I'm complaining. I smiled inside.

To compete for attention, the other boys took off their doublets as well, causing the women in the audience to become giddy with delight.

"Zack and McKinley are so strong and handsome," Ednnys said again to Marie-Avignon. "They're my favorites."

First Zazan, now them? Fine, look all you want, but they're my boys. I decided to let go of the jealousy. I would rather be proud of my boys than envious of the girls.

Hedgewood, too, was robust, toned, *and* handsome. His biceps were the size of my quads; toned and powerful. Of course, dwarves were naturally stronger than humans and could easily outperform them in a race. But I wasn't expecting him to win because of our agreement. He was here to help me find a husband. Still, he was attractive to look at . . . with or without a shirt on.

But the elves! They were shining beams of light, the most handsome creatures on earth. Qinrel threw his black hair back as the cool breeze brushed across his sweaty chest. The elves were lengthier and more toned than they were buff.

"I intentionally lost." I overheard Edgar tell my father as he wiped mud off his face with a towel. "A prince should never partake in such unruly activities."

He wasn't a very good sport, that's for sure.

The boys prepared themselves. Only four would continue to the finale. Anyone who fell into the water would be automatically eliminated. The horn sounded and they ran off. They had to navigate across a rope course and then jump across slippery logs with plenty of opportunities to fall.

Hedgewood was fast! He was the first to reach the rope course where he'd swing across. A few times he almost missed the next rope, but his strength endured.

Qinrel, came up in the rear; if I didn't know any better, he was taking his time, intentionally losing. I knew from the three-legged race that he was faster.

Hedgewood now reached the last section and jumped across the slippery logs like a frog hopping on lily-pads, and ran across the finish line in first place.

Zack and McKinley fought for second. Zack took a chance and leapt across McKinley, cutting him off. But this caused him to slip on the log and fall head-first into the pond. Now McKinley struggled to regain his footing. Everyone sat on the edge of their seat waiting for him to fall . . . then he made a daring leap onto the grass and rolled into a somersault.

The crowd roared.

Alejandro and Lancelot came up behind, passing Zack and making it into the next round.

Once Zack emerged from the water, he ripped his wet shirt off like a raging werewolf. Then he flung it around in a dance with his hips, as girls squealed.

"Dear unicorns." I uttered under my breath.

My mother's face turned pale in embarrassment, while my father just bit his tongue and kept his gaze straight ahead, not daring to comment on Zack's uncouth behavior.

My attention now returned to Qinrel, who now stood next to Glynn-da like a sad puppy. Glynnda stared over his shoulder and licked her lips at me.

Disgusting. I thought. *Qinrel could sabotage his crown, humiliate his people, and shame himself. Why is he doing this?*

And where were the elven guards? I scanned the premise. Sonya was busy talking to them. I would have to take care of this myself before it got out of hand.

Not to draw any attention to myself, I snuck behind the royal seating area to reach the two lovebirds.

Neither of the elves greeted me with the proper respect. Just the opposite; Glynnda cocked her head to the side, measuring me up. Nobody ever treated me with this much contempt in my life.

"Prince Qinrel." I ignored her and addressed him. "Qinrel?"

While his eyes were normally ice blue, right now they were dark brown. He stared straight ahead in a trance, not seeing or hearing me.

"Prince Qinrel, what's the matter?"

"Tell her Qinrel." Glynnda pressed her body against his. "It's time for the princess to *get lost*. Ha ha ha."

"How dare you . . ."

"It's time to get lost," Qinrel said in a monotonous voice, repeating her words.

Glynnda had an ominous laugh. "You heard him, shoo, little spoiled brat."

"Perhaps you don't realize the repercussion—"

"Ya-da, ya-da." She moved her hand as if imitating my lips moving. Then we heard guards marching toward us in perfect unison. The elven leaders were here. "Time to go, sweetie-pie." She turned to flee with Qinrel. But guards were approaching from behind her too.

"It's too late. You're surrounded. Give u-h-h . . ."

I never finished the sentence. My eyes glazed over and everything became like a dream.

White smoke floated everywhere. "Where am I?" I spoke, but my lips wouldn't move. Every muscle in my body froze like ice.

Then my mother magically materialized in front of me. "Qloey, take the sword."

Something cold went into my hand. I held up an elven sword. It was beautiful, sharp, and deadly.

"Kill him," my mother ordered me.

"Kill who?"

"The assassin. He's right in front of you." Instantly, Qinrel appeared in front of me.

"Prince Qinrel? He can't be the assassin? What is going on?"

"Take the sword and pierce his heart," she urged.

"Wait, I can't—" then my hands moved like I were a puppet attached to strings, and I pointed the sword at Qinrel's heart.

"Do it now. Kill him before he kills you."

CHAPTER 15

Glynnda

"How is Qinrel the assassin? How do you know?" None of this made sense. Where was I? What was happening?

"Don't ask questions. Just kill him. Quickly!"

"But . . . where are the guards? We need to hold a trial?" My legs shook in fright, more so because I was disobeying my mother.

"Kill him now. Do it. Before he kills you. Quickly!"

Again, a magical force pulled the sword into the air so I could swipe at him. "Are you sure?"

"YES! NOW!"

Then someone grabbed my hand right as I tried to swipe at the assassin.

"Your Majesty. Your Majesty." I heard Sonya's voice but couldn't see her.

"Sonya? Where are you?" I asked.

"Your Majesty." The mist suddenly went away.

I was back at the competition with the hot sun beating down on my obsidian-colored hair. The boisterous noise of the crowd returned to their usual cheers and claps. The third competition had already begun, with McKinley clanking swords with Lancelot on the field. I was also holding a sword. Ready to swing at Qinrel.

"What? What am I doing?"

One elven soldier held up a crystal to my face. It helped dissolve the remainder of the mist in my mind. Qinrel was also coming out of his trance, and Glynnda was detained by the guards.

"She had you two under an elf charm, Your Majesty," the elven guard said.

I almost killed Qinrel.

"You would've had me kill the prince?" I turned my anger onto Glynnda.

Glynnda looked away, having nothing to say for herself.

I didn't understand her motives or Qinrel's history with her, but now wasn't the place to make a scene.

"You disgust me. Take her out of my sight." I looked around; people were watching, wondering why I pointed the sword at the prince, including my mother.

"Wow, what beautiful craftsmanship." I laughed.

Sonya and the guards gave me a curious look.

"Play along, let's not make a scene," I whispered, then admired the sword. "Elven metal is stronger than a diamond." I raised my voice so the onlookers could overhear.

"Thank you, Your Majesty." They bowed and took the sword back.

"Tell Queen Typa I'll meet her after my date to discuss *elven metals* with her. Understand?" Meaning: we'll discuss what just happened.

The leader nodded, reassuring he understood the message.

Sonya and I walked back to our seats, trying to maintain an appearance of normalcy, while Qinrel was taken inside to receive medical attention. I put on a smile and nodded to everyone.

"Queen Typa and several other elven guards who were guarding Glynnda's room were found fast asleep under an elf tonic," Sonya explained. "They were too afraid I'd make a scene if they approached him, but then you did and we had to act."

I pursed my lips. "And destroy their prince's reputation in their hesitancy! What was Glynnda's motive?"

"I'm not yet certain."

"Tell the elven authorities nobody is to know. I'll seek them out after the competition to get a detailed explanation," I demanded.

She immediately turned to leave.

The first round of sword-fighting was already over. McKinley lost to Lancelot. From what everyone said, it was a close match, but Lancelot was lighter on his feet. I took my usual seat next to my mother just as the next round was about to begin.

Without looking at me, my mother spoke in a cold, disappointing voice. "It looks pathetic when you run after boys. As future empress, people come to *you*, when you demand it."

My stomach twisted and turned in frustration, so I tried to defend my position. "I was discussing a business deal on acquiring elven metals."

"A useless occupation. You'll fail like everything else you do."

I took a deep breath and watched as Hedgewood stepped onto the field. *Someday, I'll do something right. Someday.*

Alejandro approached Hedgewood in the ring and spit on the ground before him.

Alejandro! I was disturbed by this ignoble gesture. But he'd get a good rear-end whooping in a minute. Dwarves were mightier in everything physical. Even a female dwarf could compete with a fast human male. Maybe that'd teach him to respect a dwarf?

Hedgewood's arm swings were so powerful that Alejandro kept stepping backward and lost his footing until he inevitably lost the round. On the second round, Alejandro almost fell over. The third round wasn't any better for the Ogarzian prince, as the dwarf pierced the armor on his side within a few seconds and was immediately declared the winner. But Alejandro wouldn't have it, while Hedgewood was stepping off the floor, he charged him. Hedgewood still had his weapon and swatted it with such power that Alejandro's sword went flying onto the grass. Alejandro then charged him with his fist, but the soldiers stepped in to separate them.

"Dear unicorns, what's gotten into Alejandro?" I sat at the edge of my seat.

"Hedgewood probably said something inappropriate," my mother said, defending Alejandro.

Next up was Hedgewood and Lancelot. Lancelot was a reigning champion in sword-fighting in Moonstone. He always came so close to winning every group competition, but hadn't won one yet. During the fight, Lancelot was light on his feet and wouldn't be intimidated by Hedgewood's powerful strokes. He came in and tapped Hedgewood's side and won the first point.

Hedgewood understood balance and was well grounded in his stance and wouldn't let Lancelot get another jab at his armor. After a good show, Hedgewood was proclaimed the overall winner of the competition. *I thought he was here to help me find a husband? Now he stole Lancelot's time away from me.*

Lancelot did the honorable thing and bowed to his opponent.

As eager as I was, the elf issue would have to wait. My day was packed from dawn-to-dusk. After the competition, I spent an hour talking to aristocrats, and then I was off to my date in the Secret Garden where Hedgewood awaited. He was refreshed from a quick bath and dressed in new clothes after the sweaty afternoon.

"Dear Prince Hedgewood" My arms reached out in a warm greeting. "You were first in almost every event today, which is why I'm baffled that you didn't win the archery competition on the first day?" Even though I already knew the answer, I wanted to hear his response.

The guards opened the greenhouse for us. It was a magical place where fairies pollinated plants, invigorated the flowers with deep colors, pruned the bushes, and offered berries for us to munch on. And then there were fairy cats—cats with wings—who flew about, making mischief like nibbling on plants, pooping in the soil, and offering no practical value except being cute and adorable.

"My aim isn't the best and I rarely practice. In fact, I dislike athletic activities in general. But my brothers, you see, were quite indignant that if I remain here after the private date, and win at any event, then it ought to be in sword-fighting. If I had not won, it would've been an insult to my people and I would have to face all five of my brothers' ridicule; especially Juniper. Best to avoid all that."

And he wasn't planning on being here this long.

Still, I wanted to focus on the *real* contestants. I only had so many days to find the right husband.

"Nonetheless . . ." He saw my dismay and responded accordingly, "We must meet to discuss things, as we agreed on. This is as good a time as ever. Otherwise, I might as well take my leave." He looked ready to stand back up, but I put a hand on his arm to reassure him I would work with him on our agreement. He looked at my hand on his arm and then back at me; surprised.

"And you're right, this is a perfect time. We have privacy. No need to worry about the fairies overhearing. These fairies work for no humans; they come to attend the garden and in turn, we protect the waterfalls in northeast Velazia from invasion by other species. No humans are allowed up there. Good for them anyhow, as this is a lovely community for the fairies to grow up."

A glowing blue fairy flew in front of our face and waved, then fluttered off, leaving a trail of sparkles.

The servants brought over a basket of fresh berries, berry pie, berry cakes, and berry jams for us to enjoy. As we bit into the warm, chewy cherry pie, a fairy cat jumped on the table and stared at us.

From our private dinner, I knew Hedgewood loved berries. "Perhaps you won because you heard a rumor that the winner got berries; I see your strategy now."

He laughed. "Caught red-handed. Now tell me, who do you like so far, and I can give you a rundown on their real characters behind the scenes. Boys do act differently around girls, you know."

I devoured a single raspberry and savored the taste. "So far, my dates have been with Alejandro. And, oh, he's so charming."

"Charming yes. But charming doesn't make a good husband or emperor," he critiqued.

"Yes but, my heart goes out to him. He's romantic."

"Romantic, but that is all he's good for?"

He was sounding more like my parents, trying to crush my dreams of love. Then again, my flame for Alejandro started to wane after his bad conduct during the sword competition. "I am sorry about how he acted today. That was awful. Do you not think he has other good attributes?"

"I'll let you know if I find one."

Ouch.

"Well . . . what of Sir McKinley? He's regal, and he's not even a prince."

"He would provide the image your mother would want."

I didn't like that answer either. I mean . . . I did. That's what I always wanted . . . until I met the boys. Now I wanted . . . well, I either didn't know or wasn't ready to admit to myself that love mattered the most to me now. Perhaps someone to support me emotionally through all the chaos that was happening.

"He is studious and mature," I added.

"Very. It would be a suitable match for you if it wasn't for his low rank."

Did Hedgewood know me so well to interpret that rank meant so much to me?

A servant served him a biscuit with blueberry filling. He took one bite and blue goo oozed out onto the plate.

I erupted into giggles.

"Pardon my manners." He grabbed a napkin.

"And what do you think of the elves?" I moved along.

"They keep to themselves. Zazan is mysterious and haughty, while Qinrel . . . Qinrel has his mind and heart elsewhere. I sincerely warn you against either of them."

Did he know about the secret lover? Did all the boys?

I didn't like any of his answers.

He noticed my change of countenance and grabbed my hand. "I apologize. Your heart is open to many, and it's a beautiful thing. Perhaps you should just follow your heart?"

"Thank you, Prince Hedgewood." I placed my other hand on top of his. "But I don't know what my heart wants."

"You've only had three private dates. Give it time."

"Is there anyone you do like?"

"The Duke Lancelot of Moonstone. He has a pure heart, brilliant mind, and good intentions," he said with a nod.

"Yes, if he would but talk."

He chortled. "He's a little shy at first, but warms up."

A fairy cat with a big spot across its eye stared at us while sitting on a napkin. Then it swatted a bowl of mulberries off the table for no good reason.

"Silly little thing." I chuckled.

Hedgewood's eyes glistened. "After what happened to my uncle twenty years ago, you surprise me."

"I am sorry about what happened with your uncle. I'm not proud to be associated with that type of behavior," I said. "It's embarrassing."

"You need not apologize for others. I only meant to point out that you and your mother's personalities and way of thinking are very different," he said.

"Everyone always said I was different. It's all I heard growing up." And it hit a sore spot too. Sadness welled up inside me remembering all the criticisms I've received about being the black sheep of the family, but I pushed the sadness back down, not ready to face it yet. "I'm still not sure if that's a good thing or not."

"I think you're perfect, just as you are."

I blushed and didn't know how to respond. To alleviate our moment of silence, he changed topics.

"Did you know we have three hundred and sixty-nine varieties of berries in Adonis Peak?"

"How is this possible?"

"We are very connected with the fairy and earth realm; therefore, they gift us with sweet joys like berries. Not all are edible. If you respect Mother Nature, she provides the most delicious wonders in return. Dwarves don't build their homes from dead trees either, we use clay. Clay helps to ground ourselves to the earth. It is quite calming and preserves our forests. You should visit me sometime. We will receive you gladly."

"That would be wonderful."

His eyebrows raised in surprise at my enthusiasm.

"Tell me more." All of my attention was on him. "I seem to know very little about my own people, let alone the people of the world."

He described his kingdom and the untouched landscape around it. Then he shared stories of his family growing up, and how in his society, the hardest labor jobs like mining comes with the highest pay and respect. Next was my turn to share.

"My little brother, Prince Farooq, and I aren't close. He's currently in an intense learning stage, just as I was. It was exhausting. We never had time to play or casually chat. I remember, my mother once brought the best archery teacher in all Seven Cities to teach me. She wouldn't let me 'have fun' until I defeated her. It took several years, and by that age, the only thing fun for me to do was more archery."

"That is terrible. There are better ways to learn," he assured. "My family is closer. They raised us, unlike human and elf royalty. You're given a governess, tutors, nannies, and the lot, and while we do have tutors and the like, our parents spend more time with us as part of our filial piety. There is a saying that 'a parent must build a relationship with the youth through play in order for the children to develop respect for the elderly.' It seems to work."

"That's beautiful. I shall incorporate that into my children's education."

Our conversation lasted three and a half hours. There was always another topic to discuss, like our favorite foods, hobbies, books, and plays. He discussed the difference between dwarven and human plays, which was more like Octavio's play on the pixies, and we never got around to our original purpose, to discuss dwarves in Velazia, when Yenna entered and spoke in a monotonous tone:

"Your Majesty, sorry to interrupt, but you must prepare for your date."

"Oh, yes. Tell the Nololay Prince I'll arrive in an hour." I turned to Hedgewood. "I had such a wonderful time. Here, take as many berries with you as you wish."

"That is a dangerous statement."

We shared a moment of laughter. He wasn't what I expected. I could spend many more hours discussing nonsense with him.

"Until next time." He stood, kissed my hand, and bid me goodbye.

Prince Qinrel of Nololay

CHAPTER 16

Second Chances

Prince Qinrel and Queen Typa fell on their knees at my mercy. "Please forgive us," they pleaded.

They were from the elf kingdom that was half under the Empire's control—half because Emperor Alexander didn't conquer them. After a long battle, the emperor was injured. The two sides signed a treaty to end the war. The treaty stated that the elves must pay gems and taxes to the Velazian Empire, but they could maintain suzerainty over most, but not all, of their own political affairs. What the elf kingdom didn't know was that Alexander was mortally wounded from the battle and died three days after the treaty. If the elves had known how close to death's door he was, they never would've agreed to it. To this day, it was a sticky situation. Some zealous politicians wanted Nololay's economy to crumble so they could fully conquer them. That's why the Velazian court intentionally stripped them dry of whatever wealth they had.

And I wielded the power to either save their reputation or destroy it, but compassion was forever my superpower.

"Your Royal Highness," I spoke in a soothing whisper. "I'm not here to reprimand you."

The two had foreboding looks on their faces. They likely expected me to throw them out on the street, shamed and humiliated, then demand more taxes; based on my ancestor's reputations. Or even hold them prisoner and blackmail Nololay into giving up full control. I had to explain that was not my intention.

"My parents don't know about the incident." I nodded to them. "And I intend to keep it this way. Now stand, please."

"Why? What will you have us do?" Typa's voice wavered with trepidation.

My mother once told me that other aristocrats would take advantage of me if I didn't remain tough, cold, and decisive. But I didn't want to hurt these already broken elves. Hedgewood's comments earlier today gave me confidence by validating that it was okay for me to be myself.

"If others find out, this will turn into an international scandal, and it won't bode well for you or myself. What I want to know is: was Glynnda the one to arrange the assassination attempt on my life and the centaur attack. What were her motives?"

"Glynnda may have abused her elf-charm, but there's no reason to suspect she had *that* much influence to instigate an attack, Your Majesty. She was acting alone. We've known her for years. She comes from a lowly yet ambitious family. Two years ago she tried to hypnotize my son into marrying her so she could become queen. We tried to talk Qinrel out of it, only to discover the state of hypnosis that he was trapped in." Typa held her hands in prayer. "We put her under arrest, but she escaped."

"Glynnda made me think I was in love with her," Qinrel confessed. "But the feelings only came when I was around her. Often I would do things unbecoming of my true nature, and I would have no memory of it. Once there was distance between us, I thought clearly again. Please believe me when I say I was honored to partake in the RMC. My people entrusted this to me. However, when I entered the carriage to come here, Glynnda was there waiting for me." Qinrel's shoulders slumped. "She stole the gems I had as your gift. Truly, I don't remember the entire journey here."

"So you were acting under her influence the entire time?" My voice went soft.

Qinrel took a large breath, hoping not to have to admit this. "Yes. But I will confess, after being around her again, I no longer wished to marry you. I behaved dishonorably."

His mother jumped in, "But it was just the charm. Not his true feelings. Right, Qinrel?"

"Indeed. I never wished to disgrace my people or yours, Your Majesty."

"It was not his fault," the queen said, still seemed concerned I would react harshly.

I turned to Qinrel. "Your Highness, because she also hypnotized me, I understand its effect. I almost killed you. This would've been a tragedy. Therefore, we both have mistakes to repair. Let's put this behind us and forgive each other. It was out of our hands. Prince Qinrel, you're under no obligation to continue the competition and may sign the mutual rescission and leave—"

"No!" He reached out to me, then pulled back, realizing he over-stepped his bounds. "Pardon, but I wish to be every part of this competition!"

"What of your feelings . . ."

"Please, Your Majesty"—he bowed his head—"I beg you to let me stay. I meant no harm to you or your reputation. Nor to ruin your contest."

"So . . ."

"If I haven't destroyed myself in your eyes, I wish to start over and see if something forms between us. At least to remain until the first eliminations. If you'll accept me. Hopefully . . . to be a real contestant," he said.

There it was again. In the beginning, I only gave half the contestants a chance. But this competition was changing me. Even though my heart belonged to a few others already, I'd grant him this.

"I will," I said.

His energy lit up the room.

"Tonight was supposed to be our private date. Shall we?"

His cute smile reached ear to ear. And he took my hand.

Qinrel, Prince of Nololay. Earth Elf. Age 17. Went spelunking for a month in the emerald mines. Interests: Spending time in nature, spirituality, & relaxing evenings.

Prince Qinrel took small bites of his glazed duck and rarely looked me in the eye. I *felt* his shame and embarrassment from across the table.

He wore the usual extended elven spaulders that shaped the attractive frame of his male body. Plus, his shiny long hair fell to his waist in a seductive way.

Their pointy ears are so cute. I admired from across the table.

However, Hedgewood made a lasting impression on me. While elves were delicious eye-candy, there was another type of "beauty" that only came from the inside. I learned that judging others could cause a lot of harm. Outward appearances or sex appeal shouldn't be the defining factor in finding a partner. I smiled while thinking of Alejandro.

But . . . I won't complain if I end up with a sexy stud.

"Everything became cloudy when I was under the charm." I opened up our awkward supper to conversation. "It was similar to my experience with Prince Zazan."

Qinrel clenched his fist around the goblet of wine. "I apologize on behalf of all elves. I told him not to do that ever again. It was wrong."

"So he was charming me?"

He nodded. "All elves have charms. We use it to connect with nature in religious ceremonies. But some elves use it wrongly."

"What would Zazan have done to me?"

"Glynnda creates illusions, but with Zazan, it's the opposite; he reads your thoughts," he explained. "Zazan dug into your mind to see if you're right for him, or even to find your secrets. But I think love should come naturally, not something to be pried out."

"And what is your charm?" I perked my head to the side curiously. *What a beautiful complexion he has.*

"Empathy. I feel others' emotions. And they feel mine."

I twirled my glass of red wine. "I definitely feel your emotions."

He blushed, but when I chuckled, his shoulders relaxed a bit as if all the tension was drawn out.

"We can share our charm like a blessing bestowed on others," he explained. "For instance, I can hold the energy of some emotion, like joy, and those around me are blessed with it."

I felt this before. It seemed whenever he had a strong positive emotion, I felt it too. But would it work the same with negative emotions?

"But this is a natural way. See, I put joy out and others around can choose the joy or not to. But it's in their free will. Whereas, Zazan's way is invasive."

"I like your version." I took another sip of wine. He was a beautiful being on the inside too. "But I thought you and Zazan had a good relationship?"

He grew hesitant. "Not particularly. We disagree all the time," Qinrel admitted. "Perhaps because he's a water elf and I'm an earth elf. Our elemental philosophies are different." He put his fork down and changed the subject. "You surprise me, Your Majesty."

Hedgewood also said that.

"In what manner?"

He pulled the chair closer to gaze directly into my eyes. Up close, I could admire the glow of his bright eyes that looked like the deep sky on the clearest day.

"I feel your intentions toward my mother and myself; they are genuine. You're compassionate. But I expected . . ."

"A public flogging?" I answered for him.

He nodded. "You know, my love for Glynnda was never consistent. When around her, I felt so passionate, but when we separated, my feelings for her fled. It confused me, for I thought she was the one for me at one point. But I should've loved her no matter the distance or time apart." He looked down, trying to figure it out. "I feel so heartless."

"Nonsense! I don't know much about love, but . . ." After developing feelings for some of the boys, I realized that love was readily available at all times, I simply had to take the time to nurture it. "It seems like her charm was a type of brainwashing, so trust me, you are *definitely* not heartless, Prince Qinrel."

"When I do fall in love, I want it to be consistent, no matter the distance between us." He looked directly at me when he said that. A jolt of electricity pumped up my spine.

"As do I."

Zack, Clayton, and Alejandro sat on the balcony goofing around in a way only a child would. First, they arm wrestled. Then, Zack showed them how to do a back flip. This display was followed by a comparison of their biceps to see whose was largest.

Do boys always act like this? I wondered. My ten-year-old brother was more mature than them.

Zack now taught them how to move their peck muscles up and down.

Dear heavens.

Then I wondered if I could . . . I looked down at my . . .

Nope! I'm not going there.

And that was the end of that.

Hedgewood sat alone in the corner reading a book. He became fed-up with their immature behavior and retreated inside and was surprised to find me standing at the door watching.

"Your Majesty." His face lit up. "How was your date?"

"It was a successful dinner. Oh, but I was thinking about you. I don't remember if I thanked you for your diplomacy with the centaurs. What would we have done without you?"

"Oh dear, I was certain you were offended."

"I don't have an ego that big, I hope," I said. "Centaurs are difficult to handle, and you managed to solve one issue."

"Solve one and create another. We don't have much time to hand the criminal over or all our lives are at risk," he admitted.

"Do you have time? I thought we could discuss plans for helping dwarves."

His eyes drew larger, but he didn't fail to notice the circles under my eyes. "I'm glad you remembered, but you look tired."

"Of course I remember, Your Highness," I said. "We agreed to this. But our conversation earlier got so carried away. This is an important issue that's gone far too long without redress. It is my royal duty to improve the lives of all citizens."

He tucked the book in one arm and held out his other arm to escort me somewhere private.

"But our conversation earlier was good, nonetheless. And please, do call me Hedgewood." He pulled out a piece of parchment from his doublet pocket, outlining various issues in such small print I'd need glasses to read it. "I prepared a list of issues to address and potential solutions." Each note he wrote was a beautiful masterpiece; all lines were perfectly straight and aligned. One could frame his writing on a wall.

"The first is a general outlook on dwarves. It's imperative to improve the way humans *see* dwarves, not as forces of labor, but as living beings

CHAPTER 17

The Game Show

The people cheered wildly as our royal carriages rolled to a stop. The contestants weren't aware, but they were being judged on their popularity. Yenna waited at the entrance of the public stadium with a quill, writing down the reactions of the crowds as each boy arrived, as the next emperor must be popular with the people to strengthen our image.

People rushed to get front-row seats. Some would draw pictures of the contestants and sell them to fans. Others might write stories and put on puppet shows in the city square. While musicians would make new love songs based on their favorite contestants.

The crowds screamed as the charming Prince Alejandro exited the carriage. One wink and a line of women nearly fainted to one side; which he laughed off. Halfway up the steps, he stroked a hand through his long glossy hair and let it fly loose against the soft breeze. The women released more orgasmic screams.

Before he retired inside, he swiftly glanced back at the cheering women and kissed the air between them.

My carriage was in the rump, but I could still see everything that happened from a distance.

Despite the roaring excitement, once Prince Edgar stepped out of the carriage, the enthusiasm died. His family was associated with the Ruby Mines and subduing the Riots of 1555, which gave him a bad reputation. He didn't once look at the people. With his aquiline nose stuck high, he immediately entered the stadium with, what seemed like, no other thought than himself.

"Not good. Not good," I muttered to myself. Edgar's lack of popularity meant he wouldn't improve my image with the people if we married, which was very important to me. But how would my mother react if I eliminated him after the first two weeks? There was a dance of turmoil inside. Now I felt like I *had* to like him because high officials expected me to choose him. Yet, we had no chemistry. I wasn't attracted to him. He was boring in conversation. *But he must be innocent to the dwarf issue,* I made excuses for him in an attempt to draw out my feelings for him; as if they were secret even unto myself. *There's no way he knows about their enslavement and poor living conditions, otherwise he wouldn't support it. And my mother too. It'll all get cleared up once I inform everyone of this atrocity.* I remained optimistic.

Hedgewood, surprisingly, brought a large following. It seemed every dwarf and gnome in Velazia squeezed their way between participants to get a view of their distant prince. Hedgewood clasped each of their hands with a heartfelt joy. It was peaceful until the dwarves pulled out a large poster-scroll protesting the ruby mines.

The guards stormed the protesters and pinned them to the ground in handcuffs. Hedgewood intervened, offering a diplomatic solution: the protesters would peacefully leave, and in exchange, no arrests would be made. Hedgewood then entered the stadium with his head down, looking defeated.

The sporty Baron, Zack, did a back-flip off his carriage. Then he puffed his chest pecks up and down. The girls nearly fainted.

I slapped my hands in my face. But the crowds went wild as Zack ran back and forth, giving high-fives to his admirers before cart wheeling away, causing me to retreat inside the carriage and slump into my seat.

Second to last was Kipp. My carriage was right up front, so close that I could hear Yenna and Sir Takaya talking from the steps, but I had to wait for Kipp to go inside before my special moment.

When Kipp's name was announced, the entire empire—stretching to all Seven Cities—yelled at the top of their lungs. Illegal fireworks went off. Flowers were thrown at him. He picked up as many flowers as possible and clasped the hand of every citizen he could reach.

Every. Single. One.

After ten minutes of this, Sir Takaya, the head of security, became antsy. "It's a security threat," he grumbled to Yenna behind barred teeth.

Two guards tried to usher Kipp on, but Kipp was insistent on seeing. Every. Person.

One guard grabbed his arm, but Kipp shrugged it off. The crowds started to yell in protest, so the guards pulled back. Finally, the constable growled into Kipp's ear that, "The longer you take, the longer the princess must wait!"

Kipp stepped away with a handful of flowers and gifts. But instead of coming to the entrance, he put the gifts in his carriage, then went out to retrieve more.

"I swear, the things I'd do if he wasn't a contestant." Takaya sneered.

Meanwhile, reporters wrote down everything that happened.

Finally, the trumpets sounded, and my carriage pulled up. "I love you, Princess Qloey," some yelled.

"Marry me instead!"

I twirled around, showing off my glittery green gown.

"Well done, Your Majesty." Yenna greeted me at the bottom step.

Suddenly, the crowds became rowdy.

"Down with Empress Qloey!" angry citizens hollered.

A handful of opportunists threw tomatoes at me. The guards quickly pursued them as Yenna scarified herself and took the brunt of the tomato punches.

In the chaos, Qinrel made a daring leap down the stairs, and scooped me into his arms. The heroic gesture drew applause from romantics who loved his cute elf-ness.

"Your Majesty, are you harmed?" He was trying very hard to get my attention after the recent events with Glynnda.

"No. But why are they angry with me?" My reign hadn't even begun. I wasn't even the empress yet. What did I do to anger them?

"Your Majesty," Takaya said, "we'll take you to the safe room until the riots are over."

It didn't take long for the soldiers to tame the crowds. Yenna, on the other hand, was riddled with red goo from the tomatoes. She stomped her feet and murmured profanities under her breath. "My good outfit. Ruined!"

The twelve contestants now sat in two rows across from each other. They each had a workstation setup with a desk, parchment, quills, ink, along with servants at their disposal.

As much as I wanted more private time with contestants, the competition was arduous and seemingly unending. After this game show, I had a private date in the evening. At seven in the morning, we had a council meeting on the centaurs movements, nonetheless, I would put my best foot forward and go on with my tiring day with a smile.

My family sat on a raised platform with our honored guest—King Edward and his family. To many, it showed biased favoritism toward Prince Edgar, and it was. People might start thinking the RMC was rigged, if they didn't already think that. I knew my mother and King Edward were working closely on a new deal to open more mines together, but they hadn't filled me in the details yet.

As I looked over, my mother and King Edward were leaning over as they chatted with each other. She then laughed at something he said.

Their faces were so close they almost touched as they amused each other. Then she reached over and lightly tapped his arm and just as quickly pulled away with a smirk on her face.

My father, on the other hand, leaned the opposite way with a frown on his face. As emperor, he had to put up with the empress's demands and flirtations without complaint. Even more, he had to show unconditional support and appreciation toward her in public, no matter her mistakes or flaws.

Nobility and paparazzi filled up the remaining spaces in the auditorium as the game show was about to get started. To Yenna's right was a wooden scoreboard with each contestant's name. She explained the rules:

"There will be three parts to this competition. The first section will be true or false. If you answer 'false,' you can write the 'true answer' to receive an extra point. Only the top eight contestants will move on to the second round." She cleared her throat. "First question: True or false, Her Majesty, Princess Qloey, is fluent in six languages."

All contestants scribbled away, then gave the board to the servant to reveal the answer. Well . . . everyone except Kipp. When it was time to reveal the answers, Kipp stood next to his servant and said, "False, Her Majesty knows five languages fluently."

The aristocracy sniggered. He did the job of his servant.

"Dear Kipp." Yenna walked forth. "You are to write on the board, not speak aloud."

Kipp tapped his foot nervously, but he held his head high to avoid more humiliation. Finally, he strode up to Yenna and whispered into her ear.

Yenna nodded slowly, then came to the royal box seating. "Your Royal Majesties, dear Kipp cannot read or write."

"Insolence." My father spat in annoyance, but I didn't think it was the game show that he was upset about.

"Your Royal Majesty, if I may?" I took control to display decisive leadership ability to my parents. Never waste an opportunity. "Have a scribe ready to write his answer for him."

My mother waved a hand approving this, and Yenna ran back to give the orders.

Now I had the opportunity to see the other boy's answers. Only one got it wrong, Alejandro. How disappointing! Did they not study my profile? I memorized ALL of theirs. Even an illiterate peasant knew the correct answer.

"My darling . . ." Alejandro got on his knees in a dramatic profession of his love. "Don't see this as a lack of love for you. I only expected you to have the highest of all knowledge. Six, seven, eight languages. It doesn't matter. You are the woman of my heart."

This sparked amusement from the audience.

He's so silly. I love it. "I forgive you."

There were twelve questions for the twelve contestants, with each getting more challenging as they went. On the last, it became clear who would pass to the second round and who wouldn't.

"Last chance to win points for this round," Yenna announced. "True or false, the 'Law of One' is a religion based on one of the most ancient elven religions of the world?"

Only Edgar and Kipp got this correct with: "False, it's an ancient Atlantian Religion." Again, Alejandro was terrible at this game; he guessed wrong, and was now in last place. Kipp and Edgar were tied for first.

"I will win your heart," Alejandro shouted as he walked to the sideline. "If not by truth and lies, then by my passion for you."

Everyone laughed, except the other boys.

Round two was the most exciting section. It involved personal questions. Alejandro whistled from the sidelines as I walked down to the contestant's area to participate.

"That's my future wife, right there." Alejandro pointed at me, indulging in the audience's attention with his fanatics. Yet I loved it! His attention made me feel loved and appreciated in ways my family never did.

Yenna explained to the boys: "In this section there is no right or wrong answer. You'll be asked a question, and Her Majesty will choose her favorite."

"Question one: If you married Her Majesty Princess Qloey, where would you take her on your honeymoon?"

Some answers were practical but not romantic and didn't win points, like: "On a carriage ride up the coast of the Pearl Sea," from McKinley, but I didn't want to spend a vacation inside of a carriage. Meanwhile, others knew no bounds and expanded their imagination with: "Transform into mermaids and visit their queendom inside the Pearl Sea;" or, "Spend the night inside the Emerald Caves of Nololay;" but my favorite was, "On a magic carpet ride over the Phoenix Pyramids," which was Edgar's answer.

Is Edgar a romantic? I grew lighthearted and giddy inside.

"Question twelve," Yenna continued. "What is your favorite characteristic about Her Majesty, Princess Qloey?"

"How you made my heart stop." Alejandro interrupted the game from the sideline. "You will never be out of *my* running."

The audience laughed again.

Kipp won my favorite: "The mighty strength and power Her Majesty displayed standing by the throne, despite the challenging situations that ensued."

Unfortunately, one of my favorites, McKinley, didn't make enough points in order to move onto the next round.

After the four eliminated contestants moved off the stage, Yenna stepped forth with a blank expression and announced in a dull, drawn-out voice: "This last round is the most challenging. You must answer correctly on various subjects to receive a point." She pulled out a card. "First question: In ancient folklore, where do all hybrid creatures originate from?"

Everyone answered correctly: Ancient Atlantis.

Five more questions in and there were two clear leaders with Kipp and Edgar neck and neck.

"How does a boy who cannot read or write know so much?" I turned back to ask Victorya, who shook her head not knowing.

"For the win." Yenna looked between the two leading the scoreboard. "What is the official name of a winged unicorn?"

The crowd found amusement when Hedgewood—who didn't know the answer—made up the name: "Unipeg?" with a question mark.

"Oh, Hedgewood!" I chuckled. It was a cute answer; at least he tried to come up with a name.

Kipp answered correctly with: "Alaricous Unicorn." Edgar wrote: "Alicorn."

"The winner of the game show is Kipp," Yenna announced.

Edgar's servant leaned over to whisper to him.

"Nonsense!" Edgar pushed his chair back and stood up. "His answer isn't even spelt correctly. It's A.L.A.R.I.C.U.S. It is not fair for him to win. In the first round of questions at the beginning of the game, Kipp delayed in responding. After we showed our answers to the audience, Kipp *read* off *our* answers. Kipp cheated."

"He can't read," I whispered to Victorya. Kipp could not have read off the other contestant's answers if he couldn't read, but I didn't want Kipp to be humiliated by announcing to the entire aristocracy that he as illiterate.

"I didn't spell the answer for Alaricus, Your Majesty." Kipp looked up to me, pleading with his eyes for me to defend his win. "It was my scribe who wrote my answer. All I know is the name, not the spelling of Alaricus."

"Then it's not a real answer! This is cheating." Edgar pointed at Kipp while walking toward the royal seats. "He didn't follow the rules. Between this misspelling and his cheating on the first answer, he must be deducted two points. It means I win!"

"I do believe he's correct." My mother stood, then glanced back at King Edward. King Edward stood up behind her right side, supporting her response. My father saw Edward's support of his wife, and as if jealous, stood up on her left side. All three of these powerful people, in support of Edgar, proclaimed him the winner and started to walk out of the royal seating area.

"This isn't fair!" Kipp was furious, but couldn't argue with the empress, emperor, *and* a king.

"Your Royal Majesty." I swiftly stood up, making them all turn back to look at me. Then I quietly spoke to my mother with my eyes downcast. "From what Yenna said, Kipp has the most admirers outside. The people will revolt if we don't give Kipp this win. How about I extend the date to both of them?"

"If you'd lower yourself to sit at the same table as a commoner . . ." she sneered, then waved me off. "That I'd have to associate with a daughter with no self-respect . . ." Her words trailed off as they walked away.

It is only fair, I thought and walked to the edge of the seating area and announced the two winners with open arms. "I shall extend my date to both of you."

Chapter 18

Fairy Goddessmother

As we stepped outside, Edgar's nose was stuck high in the air—which I noticed he did often—and he looked at nobody but the carriage. He didn't even bother taking my arm, as if he forgot I existed and that he was only here to accept his win.

Suddenly, from behind, Kipp offered his arm for me to take with the biggest smile I ever saw. He continuously thanked me for accepting his win and was especially thrilled that the crowds screamed his name.

The game show winner's prize was a ride inside the late Queen Cinderella's magic pumpkin carriage. Kipp's jaw dropped, and his eyes grew wide when he saw the sparkly white pumpkin carriage waiting for us.

Edgar was about to enter the carriage, but turned back to see Kipp escorting me. His face grew flush, with either embarrassment for not being the gentleman or anger that Kipp was by my side. With one foot ready to enter the carriage, he stopped and waited for me. Once I reached the door, Edgar helped me inside, slid in behind me, and slammed the carriage door on Kipp.

Kipp's smile fell away. His eyes questioned if I'd actually leave him, but I opened the door myself and held my hand out.

"Down with Princess Qloey!" The crowd became rowdy again and started pushing and shoving each other in order to get past the guards and overrun us.

Takaya gave the orders, and the carriage quickly sped off to escape the mob.

Queen Cinderella's old pure white pumpkin flashed blue like a moonstone crystal when the light hit it right. A miniature chandelier hung from the roof, barely swinging about, even though the carriage bounced on the cobblestone streets. It was a smooth ride on a scenic route through wealthy neighborhoods and over bridges throughout the city. The date was supposed to be a magical ride into the forest, along the same road that Cinderella once took on her way to the ball when she was but a farmer's daughter, but centaurs were roaming about, antsy for us to deliver the criminal, so we returned to the palace instead.

I was most eager to speak with Edgar now that he won, especially so that I could learn more about his views on the ruby mines. *But his treatment of Kipp entering the carriage was unbecoming of a gentleman, and there was also breakfast where he interrupted me and over-talked my ear off…* I lost my optimism. *But he still has great qualities as a husband, and his piano performance was divine!* I saw the glass half-full and kept my spirits up … *But then he discussed boring topics at an inappropriate time, and… he was a sore loser at the physical competition…* I flip-flopped trying to figure this out. *But my mother is so close with King Edward that I cannot afford to harm my relation with Edgar and must seriously consider his hand … but what if he agreed with the conduct in the ruby mines? I know!* I optimistically imagined. *Together, Edgar and I can convince our parents to fix the ruby mine problems. Between his influence and mine, the empire will become a shining beacon of hope for the world.* I smiled at him, then at Kipp; such thoughts gladdened my heart.

As our carriage whisked along to the palace, Edgar wouldn't dare look at Kipp and seemed content in his own thoughts. Kipp, on the other hand, glided his hand along the frame of the door in admiration of the architecture, jingled the chandelier on the ceiling of the carriage, and bobbed up and down on the seat cushions as if testing their buoyancy.

Once at the palace, Edgar jumped out of the carriage and took my arm before Kipp could. We headed to the rooftop when Edgar turned to me and said, "Both of us? I earned private time with you, not shared."

"Yes, but you both won—"

"This isn't part of the bargain! I demand alone time," Edgar interrupted me.

He. Interrupted. Me. Again. I growled inside, but remained calm when I spoke. "Yes, but—"

"But I will not tolerate it!"

I was growing irritable myself and gritted my teeth.

"Your Majesty." Kipp saw my annoyance and offered a solution. "Why not split up our time? One hour with Prince Edgar, and an hour with me?"

"A wonderful idea, Kipp! Thank you for your diplomacy and *mature way* of addressing the issue." I stressed, hoping Edgar would get the hint.

"Well, I'm going first." Edgar stomped his foot.

The setting on the roof was set up for the perfect fairy tale romance with a trellis of flowers hanging above us to walk through, and a red love seat looking out toward the city below. We could see houses and smokestacks stretching for miles until it cut off on the horizon where the sun would set later. Two goblets filled with champagne were bubbling to the rim. It could spark romance in even the worst of compatible matches. "Chess?" I reached out to a board set up at another table.

"I do not engage in trivial pursuits or childish games. There are simply too many important matters to discuss. I've wished to address so many issues with you. Together, we can improve this empire," he said.

"I couldn't agree more."

"I'm glad we see eye-to-eye. Why not start now?" He put both hands on his coat flaps and looked into the distance. "One issue is how to address the increased homeless population. Not just in Baylor, but the entire empire. Did you know our taxes are wasted on free housing for the homeless? Free? Since where did we get the money to freely hand out homes to people? I pay a pretty penny for my palace and think the people ought to as well. I think we should give the homeless jobs in the mines. Force them if we need to . . .”

“They are homeless shelters, not homes!” I barred my teeth, but he ignored me. The way he spoke about taking from the homeless and making more slaves in the mines was very disturbing.

“You know what happens when we give out free housing?” he continued. “People become lazy. They stop working, stop being productive to society. It was imperative I bring this situation to you as it needs immediate addressing.” Edgar continued talking about how our taxes were wasted on shelters, on food for the needy, and how the needy were being enabled instead of helped by us giving services to them. Somehow that led to the need to tear down the ghetto and rebuild attractive mansions to increase the greatness of the empire. That led to tearing down historic buildings and erecting a new council hall with a shimmering golden rooftop in its place.

I tried to interject a few times, but he only spoke louder making sure he was heard. I held back a volcano of anger that was bubbling inside. Edgar constantly shifted from one subject to another, a constant chatter of annoyance and ill-conceived intentions.

How can someone make a mess of a romantic setting like this?

After listening to his rant, I checked my jeweled pocket watch, knowing that at least half of our date must be over, but alas, only eight minutes went by!

Dear heavens.

“Working together, we can extend the ruby mines to all cities. Although, not all cities have rubies. Whatever gems we can find. Why should Baylor limit themselves to rubies? We must extract more.” Nine minutes. “We can remake the rules. Extend our lands into Ogarz and Tildon territory, they don’t use the land anyway. Especially with your power. Technically, you own all the land. I'll open a diamond mine next—"

The ruby mines. Yes, we needed to discuss this.

"How *are* the ruby mines going?" I finally got a sentence in!

"Ah, yes. They could be more productive. The ungrateful miners simply don't work hard enough. All they do is complain. My father and the empress are working on a Dwarf Relocation Plan right as we speak." His cheeks puckered into a smile. "To remove the vermin from Baylor city and into the mines—"

I turned away from him, acting like I was admiring the city.

A relocation plan? Enslaving all dwarves? They'd go after gnomes after that. I felt queasy listening to him. This whole time, he knew about the dwarves, and he was okay with it! And I would've married him blind if the RMC didn't exist. But all I could think of was how loathsome he turned out to be. Every word he spoke was more detestable than the last. What kind of heartless person would allow this to happen?

"Perhaps we can do away with that Hedgewood too." Edgar chuckled. "I can't bear being in the same room as a dwarf."

"EDGAR!" I spun around and yelled. I never yelled. But my face was burning hot from anger. *Okay, just calm down. Speak gently.* I breathed. "It's about time we sign the mutual rescission."

He finally shut up. "Insolence! I haven't had my first date yet!"

"This *is* your first date."

"It is not! This is the game show date! I have a right to a private date in addition to this. And you can't offer the rescission until *AFTER* all twelve dates are complete."

"You didn't technically win the group date today!" I bit my tongue, trying not to overreact. "You forced yourself to be the winner. And we're clearly not compatible. Best to save us the—"

"Outrageous!" He interrupted me again! "This is absolutely unacceptable, intimately objectionable, unfairly incursive to my rank and status, my reputation, my . . . *oh*"—he moaned and pulled out a hand-kerchief to cope with this traumatic news—"I will not sign on unfair terms."

I calmed down before speaking. *Restraint. A princess doesn't shout.* "I've decided we're not—"

"I signed an agreement for the RMC to have—"

"How DARE YOU continually interrupt me!" Every ounce of anger I had been holding back now exploded in a violent burst. "You don't take a moment to listen to me! And I cannot take a moment more of your incessant babble!"

"How dare you insult me!" Edgar's mouth hung open.

"I am your EMPRESS! I can insult whomever I wish!" My finger pointed into the air as if it made the point more clear. "You on the other hand . . ." I used the same finger to poke his chest multiple times in warning. "Better watch your tongue. Learn to OBEY *me*."

I turned to leave when he grabbed my arm. The guards pounced on him faster than a jackrabbit.

"OFF! Or I'll have you thrown in the dungeon."

He pulled back in fright.

"Never. Touch. Me. Again." I wagged a finger in his face. "Or else . . . Guards, take him to his room. He's to remain in custody for the remainder of the day."

I was angry, tired, stressed, needed time alone, and wasn't in the mood to see Kipp. It would've been an insult to send a servant to cancel my date after Edgar's forced win. Therefore, I went to address Kipp personally. But after he opened the door, everything fell apart.

"Dear Kipp, I do not mean to be rude or set you apart, but may we move our date to tomorrow?" I held myself together, but was fuming inside.

I expected an affirmative answer, but Kipp was different from all others, and so was his reaction. "What happened? You two just began your date ten minutes ago."

"Everything is fine it's—"

"It's not fine, you're upset."

"I'm not upset." My voice began to crack.

"Qloey." He forgot all formalities and wrapped his arms around me. The act made me come undone. I released everything in a pouring stream of tears; it wouldn't stop, no matter how hard I tried. I dug my face into his tunic to hide it from servants whose eyes were downcast.

He rocked me side to side comfortingly. After the weight of the stress fully released, he pulled me to the window seat and urged me to open up.

"I'm so sorry. This is so embarrassing."

"There's nothing embarrassing about crying. You're human." He wiped my tears up with his handkerchief.

"Edgar has a different vision than me. He has the worst ideas for the empire. I fear for the people." I choked on more tears. "And he's so . . . BORING. And he keeps INTERRUPTING me. The nerve! His ideas are REPULSIVE."

Kipp suppressed a smile as if he were glad I didn't approve of him. "Just eliminate him."

"I requested he leave, but he was offended. My mother will be so angry and disappointed in me. Maybe I'm just being stupid. All I want is her approval, but I keep messing up." I threw my face in my hands.

"Now, now." He rubbed my back. The very touch of his hands relaxed my every nerve. "You've been a wonderful surprise this entire competition. I can't imagine anyone showing disapproval toward you. Your mother must be proud."

But she wasn't. I knew. In fact, I couldn't recall her ever praising something I did. And now Edgar's imprisonment would set her on edge.

"You just went through two attempts on your life. And now whatever that oaf Edgar said to you . . . you just need to de-stress and enjoy yourself more."

"Perhaps I need to spend time in the crystal chamber," I said.

"Can I come along to support you? Besides, I'm curious about these 'chakras,' and it'll give us time to chat."

"Really?" He was so casual, it was refreshing. "It's not much of a date. You deserve better. I thought maybe we could go pet the kitten-fairies."

"Forget the date, I'm here as your arm to lean on. Your support," he said.

Support? I like that. A relationship must also be about supporting each other emotionally. I now added that to my must-haves in a husband.

Two human-sized clear quartz crystals lined the entrance-way of the crystal chambers. We came to a hallway with nine different doors of different colors ranging from red to purple. Each door led into a private healing chamber. The first room was filled with red jasper, ruby, and other red crystals sticking out of the walls and making designs on the floor. The next room was filled with orange crystals, then yellow, all the way to purple, making up the rainbow. After that, there was a white room of clear quartz crystals, a black room of tourmaline and obsidian, and a gold room made of real gold.

I explained their meanings. "Each colored room helps heal different aspects of yourself. Like, for instance, green heals your heart, which affects your sense of self-identity. Blue heals your throat, and your ability to express and speak. The white and gold are . . . well, like master rooms for the quickest healing. But it's tiring if you're in there long. Too much energy. You might not want to do it before bed or you won't fall asleep. Black is to release negativity."

"How come this isn't accessible to the common people?"

"I didn't realize the people didn't have crystal chambers available to them," I said.

"You don't know a lot about your people, do you?"

"I—" my answer hung in the air as my thoughts caved inward and I drew silent.

"I didn't mean to be mean. Never mind. Which room shall we try?" He quickly changed topics, but the question continued to weigh on my mind.

"Orange for emotions or green for my self-esteem." We chose orange.

Orange citrine, calcite, and topaz crystals were situated everywhere; they sat on tables, hung from the ceiling, and were woven into the floor. There were three beds made of crushed orange crystals that made me want to drink a glass of orange juice just looking at it. Two healers placed certain crystals on our bodies, then performed a healing ceremony. Other female maids waited at the door. Few knew, but the maids-in-disguise were highly trained fighters here to protect me.

"If you want to heal, you shouldn't keep your emotions bottled in all the time," Kipp advised. "It's important to cry and talk with someone. Hug someone."

"It's not proper." I had very little human contact growing up.

"Oh, forget propriety! Your health matters more than etiquette. Everyone needs a good shoulder to cry on. Did your parents raise you to suppress it?"

"No. Yes," I corrected. "It's expected to not show emotions in public. But my parents didn't really raise me."

"No? Who did?"

"My governess, a fairy goddessmother, over five tutors—"

"A personal fairy goddessmother? Five tutors?"

"Yes, to become fluent in different languages," I explained. "I had an elf tutor help me become fluent in the elven language and learn about their culture and politics. Then a tutor for archery, sword fighting, and equestrian. Plus, I had to learn law, mathematics, poetry, singing, dance, and everything really."

Kipp gave a low whistle. "You are impressive. I just had my mum and dad," Kipp admitted. "Fairy goddessmothers are hard to come by, even for a royal. They treat everyone with love. When love is given expression, no discrimination is possible and all problems correct itself."

"Yes, she offered a gift to me as a babe, the gift of *compassion*. But she didn't stick around. Well . . . really, my parents scared her away. They said my fairy goddessmother was teaching me nonsense. Inappropriate things, but I was too young to remember what."

"Fairy goddessmothers only teach beautiful things," Kipp added. "Compassion originates from love."

"I really . . . don't know. It was a long time ago. Anyway, growing up, I always wondered what the purpose was for giving me 'compassion.' Is it useful? I didn't receive much compassion growing up. I mean, my governess was compassionate and loving, and my elven teacher was also very loving. More than my parents."

"Or . . ." he said, "she granted you the ability to GIVE compassion to others. To have compassion. I've seen it in you. It's a very powerful gift."

"Hmm. Perhaps I was selfish in my thinking," I admitted. "I always wanted compassion given to me and never thought of how much compassion I should give to others."

"The more good you give, the more you receive."

"You are now my teacher too." I turned my head to see him, trying not to let the crystals fall off me. "You show me things I've never conceptualized before."

He showed off his teeth in a smile, making me chuckle.

"Can you tell me, Kipp, since you understand the people better than I do, why did they throw tomatoes at me today? Why do they not like me?" I asked.

He was silent.

"Kipp. Please tell me. I want to be a good leader."

He inhaled deeply. "The crystal chamber is a good example."

"I don't understand. Explain."

"You have this amazing healing center to heal all your wounds. The arrow wound at the opening ceremony was gone the next day. But why don't the people have it? It could possibly heal almost any ailment. You dress in opulent clothing. Gorgeous, yes. Yet, the people starve. To which is more important, clothes or food? Excess consumption or a roof over every citizen's head?"

This came as a complete surprise. I planned to impress him with my gorgeous dress and perfect mannerisms, but now I saw an imperfection in . . . perfectionism. I had everything backward.

I didn't respond for some time, so he looked over. "Did I upset you?"

"No. My emotions are comforted in this orange energy." Another pause.

"Yes," he agreed. "My anger from before is dissolving."

"Anger from what?" I asked.

"The way others treat me."

"Like how Edgar tried to take your win?"

He nodded.

There were so many problems in my city, internal problems in the palace, and turmoil within myself. I now wondered if it were possible to truly fix any of it! But I had to start with healing the inner turmoil before the outside problems would go away.

"Can I help with any of that?" I offered.

"Can you . . . get rid of all the bachelors I don't like?" He chuckled. "Actually . . . just being here with me now is helping."

"How so?"

"Because you defended me at the game show today. And helped me prepare for the competitions. Without your support, I would be the laughingstock of the competition."

I never realized what an impact little deeds of good would do for someone. "How is it you know all those questions at the game show without being able to read or write?"

"I grew up as a servant in a theater," he said. "I've memorized most of Pippa's plays and other fairy tales from listening. You'd be surprised how much wisdom you can get from a fairy tale. Every question in the game show was based on some moral lesson. It's how I won a spot in your Matchmaking contest too. I clearly have a knack for it."

"What was the commoner's competition for the RMC like?"

"There were three days of it. The first day was an interview to see if we were competent, attractive, and still virgins." He snorted. "The second day was a series of questions like the game show. It helped sniff out any incompetent boys. The last day was public speaking. Being in theater, I was a natural."

"I'm glad you were chosen." I reached over and grabbed his hand without leaving the healing bed. "I'm feeling better. What do you say we go see the litter of kitten-fairies?"

We explored the Secret Garden and played with the kittens until our hands were all scratched up. Kipp rubbed the kitten's belly, but it kicked its feet up and bit him in the process.

"The belly is a trap," I explained. "It's so cute and fluffy, but when you go in for a pet, the kitten will capture your hand."

Kipp lifted his hand up and the kitten opened its paws, then he went in and scratched the belly again and the kitten closed its paws and bit him. They repeated this gesture several times, playing a game.

Then we searched for cherry tomatoes and fresh green beans to munch on. "Fresh green beans are the best." I bit off the end of one and savored the crunchiness.

We then took a boat ride in the pond until the sun drew low on the horizon. It proved to be more enjoyable than just running to my room and brooding over how my parents would react to my imprisoning Edgar in his room. Our extended date was abruptly ended when Yenna came to inform me it was time to prepare for my private date that evening.

"I had such a wonderful time. Thank you for lifting my spirits." We held hands, but found it difficult to say goodbye. Kipp looked to the ground and wouldn't let go for a moment. Yenna was standing not too far away. I surmised he wanted to say something, but Yenna was ruining the moment.

"Meet me at my quarters." I commanded, and Yenna walked off.

Finally, Kipp looked up. "I . . . wanted to say . . . that I didn't initially come into the competition expecting to marry you, or even to like you. We all know, or knew, that my admittance was just to appease the working class. And that no royal member would actually choose someone like me. It was more of an opportunity to . . . increase my social standing."

The truth came out. But I originally had my own biases and intentions, thus I couldn't hold his initial feelings against him.

"But . . ." he stroked my hands. "You've been fair to me. And I . . ." he breathed heavily. "I've grown to have feelings for you."

My heart beat so loud, I couldn't hear my own thoughts. "Perhaps my view at the beginning of this was also distorted. I don't blame you at all," I confessed. "Since meeting you, I also feel . . . something . . . for you."

He stroked my hand more, thinking of how to proceed.

Then he reached in and gave me another hug. A long hug. A warm and delicious hug.

As he pulled away, our cheeks rubbed against each other. Our noses came inches from each other. His lips slipped by, teasing my mouth. How I craved him to go a little further.

But I was nervous about making the first move.

"I look forward to our one-on-one date." He left me wanting.

Baron Zaccaria of Tildon

Chapter 19

Kipp the Beggar

Zaccaria, Baron of Tildon. Human. Age 15. Goes by "Zack." Completed a free solo-climb up the highest peak of Mount Tildon. Interests: Boxing, jousting, tennis, violin, & calisthenics.

Things were awkward with Zack after the Pegasus investigation and his infamous talent show performance. And . . . well, everything else too. He was too young and childish to be a serious competitor. Perhaps in a few years he'd mature.

On this particular night, he was a bundle of energy and hopped all over the place like a bunny rabbit on steroids.

"I'm so excited to see you again!!!" He did a front flip. "Really, I'm so grateful you're still giving me a private date after the Pegasus incident."

He probably shouldn't have even mentioned it.

"Truly, I only meant the best. I mean, a Pegasus! Have you ever heard of such a gift?" He sat down next to me.

"No. I truly have not." I sipped on some *Mermaidlout* wine in discontent.

"I mean, can you imagine flying in the sky on the back of a horse?" He just couldn't sit in one place for longer than ten seconds and jumped up again to look over the balcony.

"It was a *grand* idea." My tone was monotonous as I watched him spin around on a single foot. "Except when our entire party almost got killed," I whispered under my breath, but he didn't hear.

Zack continued the discussion of the Pegasus and centaurs, the same touchy subject that I'd personally feel ashamed to keep throwing in someone's face. "You'd no longer be a swan, but an angel. But I suppose there's a reason nobody has tamed a Pegasus before. The centaurs keep a close relation to them. It's an insult to ride one."

"Indeed, as we found out." I felt more like his mother monitoring a child than his actual date. He took a seat again for the tenth time. "So . . . you're a talented violinist?" I changed the subject. "Shame you didn't do that for your talent show performance. I would've preferred to hear it."

"Ah yes." He hopped up again. "And I hoped someday you could dance to my music."

"Well, it is possible." I chuckled uneasily.

"How about now? Can you dance?"

I squirmed in my seat and tried to make an excuse why I didn't want to dance right now. "We don't have music."

He clapped his hands and ordered his violin to be brought to him immediately. I exhaled and closed my eyes for a moment, while the servant grabbed his violin.

Then he played a slow song. "Come dance."

"Uh? It's not a song I'd dance to. The beat isn't right."

"How about a fast song?" He changed tune and played allegro, but the mood still wasn't right. I didn't feel chemistry with him, and my long pink gown had a train that was designed to impress others with its elaborate embroidery and rich paisley brocade. It was not for dancing. Plus, the sparkles would fall off.

"Let me show you." He put the violin down and started solo dancing by jumping from side to side as though he were hopping on lava stones.

I pulled a hair behind my ear and uneasily chuckled to one of the maids who gave me a look that read, *"Please tell me this isn't going to be the next emperor?"* Then she politely drew her eyes to the ground and retreated to the wall.

Then Zack tried to jump into the splits but wasn't quite flexible enough and stopped himself before he tore something. "Argh."

"Are you alright?" I reached out to him.

"Oh, yeah. I'm fine." He slowly pulled himself up, but winced in pain. "No worries. Come." He shrugged the pain off and flipped back on his feet with a huge smile. "I know you can dance! Why are you being shy?"

I searched for the exit with my eyes.

"How about partner dancing?" I tried to smooth out the date with a compromise. So we danced without music together.

He twirled me around, and around . . . and around, until I was sick to my stomach. Then, he stepped on my gown and it ripped.

"Oh, I'm so sorry, Your Majesty."

"No worries. It's perfect."

"Perfect?"

"Yes. Perhaps we shall call it a night," I said and used this "perfect" opportunity to escape.

(The Bachelors)

Forgetting the game show results, the headlines of the next morning's newspaper focused primarily on Kipp hoarding flowers, Qinrel's valiant rescue, and the tomatoes.

"Listen to this." Alejandro read off an article called *"Kipp the Beggar"* from *The Royal Times Newspaper* to the entire room.

Alejandro and Zack laughed together.

Several boys looked up from their breakfast conversation, but were uninterested in the lack of maturity from the other boys and returned to the poached eggs and spinach soufflé.

When Kipp entered the *bachelor pad*, as the boys called it, the room went silent . . . except for an occasional snicker from the two mischief makers.

Kipp immediately knew something was up. Since arriving, he was met with bullying from some contestants. And now, all eyes were on him, making him uncomfortable. Although he couldn't read, there was a moving drawing in the newspaper of him picking up, not flowers the contestants threw at him, but piles of trash. The drawing showed him eating the trash on the way to his carriage. This was followed by a picture of Velazian Waste Management shaking hands with him.

Kipp turned beet red and slapped the newspaper on the table and stormed out of the room.

Hedgewood, as usual, sat in a rocking chair in the corner. His round spectacles were hanging low on his nose as his eyes darted between the newspaper and the bachelors. Always analyzing, studying, and recording information.

"He's not just a peasant, but a vagabond. I think it suits him." Zack and Alejandro cackled together.

Edgar walked up to the two troublemakers. His nose stuck so high in the air they could see up his nostrils. As the next emperor—as he saw it—it was his attempt at "looking down" at those inferior to his excellence. "It's about time we bring this issue to the empress. Something must be done; Kipp is out of control. To allow such scum in the same room as our esteemed selves, or let alone the same building . . . It was an outrage from the beginning. The empress will understand if he's removed."

"Or do you think it's best to bring the situation to the Princess herself?" Alejandro suggested, for he'd rather be around her than the aging empress. "There's no way she'll want to associate with a vagabond. She has high standards."

But Edgar thought differently. After her reaction following the game show, his faith in her waned. To him, she desperately needed him to rule by her side, to ensure she didn't make any more bad decisions like yesterday. "No. We must address this with the current empress. Princess Qloey might not understand."

"Nonsense!" Zack wanted to make amends with Qloey, as he wasn't certain why she ran off so quickly during their date. He wanted to show his support directly. "She must offer Kipp the mutual rescission herself, as it's her RMC."

Alejandro agreed.

Edgar turned to the remaining royalty in the room, since these boys couldn't be reasoned with. He desperately needed to bring this up to the empress, along with Qloey's lack of mental well-being. It was a serious concern that she didn't accept his political stance. Only someone insane would reject him.

"Each of you are to address this unfortunate situation with her Royal Majesty today. It's imperative we eradicate the beggar before this gets out of hand," Edgar commanded the other bachelors.

And that was that. Edgar expected everyone to comply with his order.

The elves, who chatted in the elven language, ignored him and continued their discussion about elven religions. "Others have a right to their own thoughts without invasion," Qinrel said.

"So says *you* who feel our every emotion." Zazan defended his position. "Hypocrite!"

"I'm not digging into others, only receiving what they give me."

"Well, aren't you holier-than-thou?" Zazan said in an angry tone. "When in reality, it's the same thing. They express thoughts. I pick up on it."

"No, you dig into them!" Qinrel barked. "You violate their precious thoughts."

The two continued to argue.

"Can you believe Edgar would actually try to eliminate Kipp for the lies in the newspaper?" McKinley asked the others sitting at his table, but received no response.

Hedgewood finished the last two articles in the newspaper. The first article was on how Qinrel heroically saved Qloey from an avalanche of tomatoes. It was complete with a moving fairy-drawing of him sweeping her into his arms. Lastly, the *Royal Times* went on to list the ratings of each twelve bachelors: *"Breaking News Update: Who will be the top candidates and who would be eliminated first?"* Edgar was at the top as the most likely to win, with Hedgewood and Kipp at the bottom.

Hedgewood tossed the newspaper down and picked up the *Fairy Tale Times*. This second newspaper was more of a citizen's opinion than an aristocrat's. They ordered the contestants based on who received the greatest applause at the game show, down to the least: Prince Edgar.

Now, this is more accurate. He smiled and turned the page, noting his position at number seven. An improvement.

Every morning they received one newspaper from each news agency. But on that particular morning, there were five from the *Royal Times* showing Kipp stashing trash in the carriage. Someone had intentional motives to hurt Kipp by ordering more from these harsh critics, and Hedgewood suspected it was Alejandro.

The very last page of the newspaper was a small blurb on the dwarf, gnome, and human protesters who were arrested, despite the soldier's promise to let the dwarves leave the game show unharmed if they stopped their protesting. Frustrated, Hedgewood folded the paper and went outside onto the balcony.

Kipp looked back as the door to the balcony opened and he heard the elves yelling at each other. He saw Hedgewood approaching.

"Reporters are brutal," Hedgewood began.

Kipp clenched his fists. "I wasn't hoarding trash; I was carrying flowers. I was expressing gratitude to the people. Do you know what happens to all the gifts they throw to us? Most aristocrats probably throw it away! Ungrateful trolls. The people's gratitude and love and money are swept under the carriages. It makes me wonder why any person would care about the aristocracy at all. I wanted to show I care for the people." He stared at his hands.

Hedgewood leaned against the balcony with him. "You have good intentions. Not all nobility are gracious or deserving of what they possess. The aristocracy needs fresh perspectives like your own. But they'll resist at every turn."

Kipp finally looked up. He bonded with McKinley for his assistance, and now found an ally in Hedgewood and sometimes Octavio and Lancelot. "But how could reporters make up such an idea about me?"

"Reporters are biased and greedy. They sell lies to achieve their agenda. They sell lies to get people to *think* certain ways. They sell lies to maintain control over the population. Being used for their whims is the price we all pay for being in the spotlight. And the price we pay for buying their newspaper. We get both positive and negative attention depending on if *you* agree with *their* opinions or not. You haven't seen the article on Qloey, criticizing her ability to lead the empire because she allowed you to join Edgar on their date."

"She only did what's fair!" Kipp slammed his fist on the edge.

"That's precisely why they criticized her. She was fair and honest. I have both hope for her and fear for her," Hedgewood admitted. "Keep your head up, kid. Watch, learn, and display confidence even where you feel none."

"Kid?" Kipp raised an eyebrow as the nineteen-year-old prince walked away.

CHAPTER 20

The Maze

(Qloey)

"Oh, it was dreadful!" I said to Hedgewood. "Pardon me, I shouldn't . . ."

Hedgewood laughed. "Don't mind, Prince Edgar is a stiff board."

"That doesn't begin to describe! It was purely a conversation between him and himself. One topic rolled into the next. Always about reallocating wealth away from the people and into his own pocket. I hadn't gotten a single word in."

We sat under the gazebo in the garden. There was no competition on this day, simply a garden party so I could get acquainted with each contestant and relax. But I was required to talk with all of them at least once.

"*You* dealt with him only ten minutes, *we* deal with him every day." He pointed out.

"These are unlivable conditions you're all in." I joked with my nose in the air like Edgar. "*Unacceptable.* A change must be made."

He laughed.

"I offered him a mutual rescission."

"Before his one-on-one?" He leaned forward in disbelief.

"It was painful! I cannot imagine another date with him."

Hedgewood glanced at Edgar. "Yet he remains. Did he . . . turn down—?"

"YES!"

Everyone stopped talking to look at us. I shouted a little too loud. My mother was drinking tea with King Edward and my brother when they paused to glare at me from across the grass. Farooq then stood up and went over to Clayton, who he often found good conversation with, while my mother turned back and put a hand on Edward's arm. My father grumbled to himself in the corner, occasionally giving both of them a darkened glance.

I hadn't yet told Hedgewood about Edgar's relocation plan of dwarves. Such a conversation wasn't right for the moment. It was a sensitive topic. But eventually, I'd have to warn him.

I grabbed his hand. "Oh, please do save me if he approaches. He insisted on his right to a date."

Hedgewood shrugged in agreement. "Our agreement as contestants says . . ." he left the words hanging.

"Whatever shall I do?"

"Go on the date with him. End it early again. Then, after all the contestants have their private date with you, reintroduce the mutual rescission."

"Hmm. By 'end it early,' how early can I end it?"

His smile reached both ears, and I was struck by how adorable his dimples were. "Five minutes tops."

I laughed. "Oh! I have an idea. I'll go on the date and . . ." I whispered a plan into his ear.

"How brilliant, he'll *love* it!" He joyously affirmed.

"I'm actually looking forward to my date with him now." And I *was* looking forward to this new plan. I smirked mischievously. *I'll show Edgar.*

Everyone at the garden party whispered as they glanced our way. No doubt they gossiped about how I became close with the dwarf.

"Ah, we're drawing too much attention. Perhaps you should spend time with your real contestants," Hedgewood suggested.

"But I'm enjoying our conversation, and I don't see anything wrong with having your attention." I toyed with my necklace.

"I am enjoying our time as well." He inhaled deeply.

We held eye contact for a moment, then both drew away.

"I thought of all people, you'd win the game show yesterday, Prince Hedgewood. You're too smart to lose such a game."

He nodded. "I already won mine. So unless I'm actually a contestant …"

"I don't know, are you?" I chuckled.

The question lingered in the air.

We both got up, and he dropped me off near a gaggle of noble girls. But my thoughts remained on that last comment, *"unless I'm actually a contestant." I* pulled a hair back from my face, but couldn't let the smile go.

"Your Majesty."

I turned to see Edgar, who smiled with his buck teeth and a putrid expression like he just bit into a sour lemon.

"Perhaps a walk around the pond is most suitable at this time." He put an arm out for me to take.

"Oh, I have an appointment with another first."

"I know you're evading me. It is my humblest duty to rectify my mistakes and display my greater qualities. I know our partnership will benefit the empire. I have a plan to save tax money and redistribute it."

"Oh really?" My insides squeezed inside out. *No wonder he looks a juiced lemon.* I had to spend time with each bachelor thus, with a sigh, I allowed him to continue.

"I analyzed the situation last night and realized …"

I held my breath thinking he was about to reveal some profound epiphany about his poor behavior, but instead he said:

"I don't know your view on property taxes."

All the blood drained out of my face.

"Your Majesty, the drink you ordered us arrived." Hedgewood came to the rescue. "Allow me to escort you to the drinks."

Edgar immediately protested. "We were in the middle of an important discussion—hey! Wha—"

We hurried away to gather drinks from a servant and chuckled as Edgar complained from afar.

Clayton and my little brother gave us dirty looks for our foolishness. We each took one sip of the lemonade but Edgar was on our tail again.

"It appears . . ." Hedgewood put the drinks down. "We'll drink later!" He rushed me toward the maze.

"Hey! Hey! I'm not done." Edgar chased.

Once inside the maze, Hedgewood took my hand, and we ran between the hedges without direction. "Where are we?" he asked.

"I don't know."

We ran into a dead end and laughed. Quickly, we retreated when Edgar spotted us. "Hey. Stop this nonsense."

We laughed more and ran down another route.

"Go left." I shouted directions. "Right. Now left."

We reached another dead end. "I thought you knew the way." Hedgewood exclaimed.

"No." I giggled.

We were about to turn back but saw Edgar facing the other direction. "Back, back, back." We retreated behind the bush before Edgar turned around to see us.

It was a small space. We heard Edgar's footsteps approaching. Hedgewood pulled me close to his body so we could hide.

"Wait. How do I get out? Your Majesty. Your Majesty! Oh." Edgar stopped on the other side of the hedge. Then he cried about the inappropriateness of this behavior. A moment later, he realized, not only could he not find us, but he was lost. "Help! Help! Oh, dear," Edgar cried. "I'm lost." He whimpered like a lost puppy.

I put my hand over Hedgewood's mouth to prevent him from laughing. I felt his warm hands around the curve of my waist, as his drumming heartbeat pounded against mine.

Finally, we heard Edgar's footsteps trail off into the distance.

"I think he's gone." I moved my hand onto his chest. We were nearly the same height and stared directly into each other's eye. Our faces only inches apart.

CHAPTER 21

Controversy

I felt his chest rise and fall. His big warm hands held me close. His beautiful green eyes glistened in the sunshine.

The moment seemed to last forever. I wondered if I should make a move and in what direction; away from or toward his lips?

My eyes found his mouth.

A moment later, Hedgewood pulled away and looked at the ground. "Uh, perhaps we shall return before . . ."

"Uh? Yes." I felt a little embarrassed for my lustful thoughts. *He pulled back, not me.* My passion at the moment must be a one-way road. *It would never work between us, anyway. What do I care? I don't have feelings for him.* I straightened my dress out. "Thank you for saving me." I pulled a hair behind my ear that had come loose; a nervous habit. It immediately fell again.

He reached up and arranged it for me. "It's my duty." His hand lingered on my face for a second too long.

After finding our way out, he quickly left me and headed toward Lancelot.

Duty? Just a duty. Okay. It was nothing . . . just escaping Edgar. His duty.

"Help me." I heard Edgar yelling from within the maze. "I feel faint. I—I can't breathe," he cried. Guards quickly ran into the maze to save him. "I think I'm dying. Hurry. *Oh.*"

With Edgar now lost in the maze, Prince Qinrel invited me for a stroll around the pond, but my thoughts were lost, unable to help thinking what Hedgewood's comment, *"It's my duty,"* meant.

Does that mean he has no feelings for me? Why would he? He's not attracted to humans. I was the Crown Princess to an empire, a desirable woman, yet, I still felt rejected. Vulnerable.

Qinrel talked on, but I heard nothing.

"What do you think?" Qinrel asked with a smile. But I had no idea what he was talking about. "You're quiet."

"Oh, I . . . uh, do, tell me more about Nololay." *He was talking about Nololay, right?*

"I do not think you were listening," he said with a smile. "Your mind is off in Wonderland."

"Oh, I'm so sorry, Prince Qinrel. That is rude of me."

"I don't take it offensively." His face shined down on me without an ounce of anger. "I can sense that someone else is on your mind right now. If you want to stroll the rest of the way in silence, I'll allow you to have your thoughts."

"Oh?" How do I respond to such understanding and patience? I felt that he felt an attraction to me but all chances were over already.

But Hedgewood didn't respond equally to me today. I brushed all feelings of him away. It was time to take my mind off of Hedgewood and the maze and focus on real contestants, so I took another look at Qinrel and said, "That's alright, let us chat and enjoy a good walk." We continued to walk at a slow pace, but I didn't know where to start. "Tell me something . . ." I searched for a topic to discuss. "What is your honest opinion about our compatibility?" Perhaps that was a little forward, but I was curious as to his response.

He looked up into the clouds, thinking of what to say. "I want you to know that I have great admiration for you. Especially after the way you handled the Glynnda issue. We have chemistry, and I'm attracted to you.

You need a husband who is supportive and knowledgeable in many areas, which I am. We have similar hobbies and thus will have plenty of things to discuss. I don't just want a wife, but a friend as well. There's much potential here if we allow it to blossom."

"I suppose you're right." I glanced back and observed the elder aristocrats rocking in chairs on the porch, while the bachelors found entertainment playing quoits; a game of horseshoes but with circular metal rings to throw instead. McKinley took his turn and successfully threw the ring over the stake. He showed no excitement over his successful throw and retrieved his rings with a blank expression on his face.

"But I see that you're still soul searching," Qinrel responded to the silence between us.

"I am attracted to you. Can a human not help but have admiration for an elf?"

"Physical attraction can only maintain a relationship for so long." He scanned the clouds for thoughts. "But like how the moon and earth are in an eternal dance with each other, there must be another force holding them together, something not visible to our eyes. Likewise, two individuals must be mentally and emotionally attracted and in an equal understanding of each other in order for their gravity to hold them together."

"You hold me speechless." All the other boys left my mind as I soaked in the depths of his soul. He proved to be so interesting that I intentionally guided us along a path I knew to be longer. "Tell me more."

Within forty-five minutes, our conversation shifted from one subject to another, until we found ourselves back in the grassy area near the quoits game.

"Ah yes, you must come to Nololay someday," he said. "We have the most marvelous emerald crystal trees. They're translucent emeralds that protrude from the earth and stretch fifteen feet out of the ground. They look like trees, hence the name. We don't mine them because they're such a spectacular sight. We hope to make it a tourist attraction and bring in wealth.”

“Yes, I’ve seen pictures. But I’m so busy, I’m not sure when I’ll make it there.”

“When you’re empress”—he smiled down at me—“you will have the power to do whatever you wish.”

“A day I’m looking forward to.”

“Oh, dear. It was tragic.” We overheard Edgar as he laid across a lounge chair looking faint as others fanned him. “I never experienced anything like it in my life. *Oh*.” He groaned.

“Thank you for your time, Your Majesty,” Qinrel said his adieu as he watched Alejandro approach.

“No, thank you for your patience.” I quickly said before Alejandro reached us. Qinrel may not be the first boy I thought about when I woke up in the morning—or the second—but he was slowly making his way up there.

When Alejandro reached me, he twirled me around and around, then pulled me into his arms. “My princess. My love. My soulmate. It tears at my heart to see you with other boys. When will I get a turn for a private date again? It’s been too long.”

“Well then, you better win the next competition.”

He put a hand to his chest. “My heart burns. You were supposed to choose me in the talent show.”

I giggled. How could I forget. “Your Paso Doble Pegaso was fabulous, and you almost won.”

“Well, you *already* won *my heart*, baby.” He flirtatiously raised an eyebrow at me with his cheesy one-liners. He pulled me closer. Too close. People were watching . . . We were in public!

“Alejandro!” I playfully put a hand on his chest and pushed him away. But he just took my hand and placed it on his heart. “You are so bad.”

"Ah, I see we're on personal terms now. Does that mean I can call you 'Qloey,' instead of 'Your Majesty?'"

I blushed. "Only in private."

"As you wish, My Qloey." He kissed my hand five times. Then his hand stroked my face.

People were still watching.

"Not out here!" I whispered.

"You're right . . . I'll have to find somewhere *private* for us." He gave me a crooked smile.

"Behave yourself." My body was boiling hot with passion.

"This is an outrage!" My mother glared down at me with my father standing quietly to the side—as if trying to earn back his position as emperor, which King Edward unofficially stole, by being more obedient to his wife. "That's exactly what Prince Edgar said. What made you think it was a good idea to run off unchaperoned into the maze? Especially with a dwarf? What is this sudden interest in him anyhow? He's a dwarf, Qloey. A DWARF!"

"He's a contestant, Your Royal Majesty." My hands remained clasped, and my eyes downcast as I spoke in a soft and submissive tone to her.

"Yes, but not a serious one. Nobody expects you to marry a dwarf, of all contestants. Let alone touch one. I saw you put a hand on his."

Anger boiled up inside like pot of water set over a flame, but my facial expression remained as neutral as my tone of voice. "He's an intelligent and proper gentleman—"

"Proper? Making a scene in public, running, and laughing hysterically, you call that proper? Edgar almost fainted because of your recklessness, the poor boy."

"Prince Edgar—"

"Prince Edgar claims you requested a mutual rescission. Before his one-on-one date. Before your twelve dates are complete. He claims you imprisoned him in his room. Is all this true?" Her hands rested on her hips as she looked down on me.

"I will never marry him!" Finally, I looked her in the eyes. "I detest him."

My mother growled. "You will reconsider! Look at what the tabloids are saying." She reached for a special edition breaking news pamphlet that showed a drawing of Hedgewood and myself running around laughing together by the maze with the title: "How low has the Crown Princess stooped?"

"No one told me the press was at the garden party?" I tried to find an escape, but it only backfired.

"Because they weren't supposed to be there! As a royal, you must act proper at ALL times, even when you think nobody's looking. That means keeping your distance from that dwarf. The paparazzi snuck in. We're pressing charges, but the *Gremlin Times* claims it was an anonymous tipster we can't pursue. This we'll deal with later, right now, Prince Edgar has a right to a private date. And you NEVER should've offered the rescission this early!"

"I'm sorry. I will go on the private date with him tonight." And I was looking forward to it too. I had a plan. My mother studied my response. "And then I'll offer it again."

My mother slammed the newspaper down. "If you ruin our relationship with Baylor city, it'll only make your reign more difficult. Do you see the repercussion your actions will cause? He's your best prospect. None of the other boys compare to him. Or are you too stupid to see this?"

Or are you too stupid to see this?

Was I being stupid? It would be stupid not to consider my parent's advice. They were far more knowledgeable than me in their mature age. I looked around the room at other council members and Yenna glaring down at me and stepped backwards. Alone. Singled out. *She's right, I was being stupid again,* I admitted. For a moment, I actually thought I might like Hedgewood and him me. But after he rejected my closeness in the maze, I felt embarrassed. Therefore, I concluded that my mother was right, he wasn't proper at all in running around a maze with me. *Why can't I ever make good decisions? I always mess up. If I was only smarter.*

"I recognize my faults and apologize for my behavior in the maze. I'll act more proper from here on out, Your Royal Majesty. May I be excused?" For some reason, my own words hurt myself, as if they defied everything my heart wanted.

"No. There's another issue." She snapped.

This time my father opened the newspaper showing a magical image of Kipp at the game show picking up trash, placing it in the carriage, then getting more, but he let my mother do the talking.

"He made a fool of himself. People are calling him 'Kipp the Beggar'." My mother said.

"I'm aware."

"Get rid of him immediately," she declared.

"You said yourself I must wait until all contestants get a date." I wasn't ready to let him go, even if it was another stupid idea of mine.

"He's a peasant and doesn't have an army to rebel with if relations go sour."

My mother didn't realize, but Kipp was officially a real contestant now—possibly even the future emperor. He was proving to be a kind, loving, and an interesting individual. Breaking down one boy was one thing, but two? What if she disapproves of Alejandro and McKinley as well? Her double standards etched me from the inside out. Now the pot of anger and pain within was nearing its boiling point. "He has the people behind him! Did you not see this at the game show? Everyone cheered for him." My tone grew higher than it should have against her, but I tried to find patience and calm down. "I will not harm his image or my future reputation with the people. All relationships must be held sacred."

She had a sour expression on her face, but considered my view. "Very well. After the twelfth date, give him a speedy exit. I don't want to see him ever again."

I wanted to cry of frustration now but didn't dare speak up against her any further. I stopped in the hallway on my way out to pound my fist against the wall. The guards who always followed me stopped to wait.

They're being so unfair! I raged inside. Why was it all the contestants I didn't want pre-competition, I wanted now? And all whom I did want were not to my expectation?

"Handkerchief?" Clayton held a gold-embroidered cloth out.

"I'm sorry." I wiped the tears away.

"Come, let's go somewhere private where nobody will see." He opened a door to a room overlooking the garden and the maze. My thoughts immediately returned to the moment Hedgewood and I were in each other's arms. Why couldn't I get him out of my head?

Clayton ordered the guards outside for privacy. "Whatever is bothering you?"

I never thought Clayton would turn out so sympathetic. As a child, he was obnoxious. We never really saw eye-to-eye. But now he showed serious concern for me. How my perceptions kept changing.

I shook my head, as my thoughts were too private.

"I understand. We were never close growing up. But I hope someday that will change, and you can confide everything in me."

"Do you truly wish to marry me?" I bluntly asked. For if he did, it came as a surprise. In actuality, I didn't expect him to accept the position as a competitor. I rather hoped he wouldn't.

"You are my cousin. I care about you. Despite how snobbish you were growing up."

"I was not snobbish."

He smiled in response. "You rarely talked to me. And when you did, it was often in disagreement."

"I was . . . reserved as a child." I was shy, but didn't want to admit that to him. My mother was outgoing, with a booming voice. Everyone in the council saw this quiet, reserved nature of mine as a weakness. Everything about me was constantly condemned as inferior to her. "Why did you come to the competition?"

"To see you," he said. "We only met at banquets and royal engagements, but after growing up and seeing potential matches for myself, you popped on the radar. I, too, only have limited choices in marriage. I was . . . curious how you grew up to be."

"Oh?"

The entire time, he kept glancing around the room at different doors, vases, weapons on the walls, chairs, then back at me. "After seeing you at the opening competition, well, you looked . . . pretty."

Pretty? *At least the opening ceremony was partially successful.* I prided, but I rather hoped he said "beautiful" or "gorgeous." Except, I didn't impress Kipp.

"Why did you give me the invitation?" he asked.

"My parents and advisors chose."

He looked down, defeated.

"Don't get me wrong, it is wonderful to rekindle our relationship," I said.

"If you will"—Clayton finally looked me in the eye—"please give me a real chance. I wish to be of service to our empire."

"I will."

And I planned, like everyone else. No more prejudice or judgments.

Except toward Edgar.

But what if . . . I had an epiphany that would satisfy my parents and myself, *what if Edgar doesn't want to marry* me *and pulls out of the competition himself?* My date with him tonight would be my opportunity to get him running back to his city. I smirked inside. *After tonight, he'll be begging for a mutual rescission.*

Prince Edgar of Baylor

The Ruby Mines

Edgar, Prince of Baylor. Human. Age 18. Second son of King Edward. Family owns several ruby mines, two castles, a palace & three estates bordering the Centaurus Forest. Interests: Playing piano & listening to opera.

"Truly, you will enjoy this date. I especially prepared it based on the topics you're most passionate about." I could barely see Edgar with only a single small lantern bobbing back and forth to the rhythm of the carriage as we rode down the cobblestone streets, meaning . . . he could barely see the mischievous smirk on my face. "And it's my way of showing gratitude for you being here." For once, Edgar allowed me to get a sentence in.

"I don't fancy surprises. Please tell me where we're going. Not knowing is unquestionably alarming, emphatically perplexing, indubitably horrifying. To speculate what'll happen next, *oh* . . ." he said as if in pain from the unwelcoming feeling of not being in control of the situation.

"You'll see in no time." I sniggered under my breath.

This. Will. Be. Fun.

He cringed as we stepped out of the carriage and into the dirty streets, which had fecal matter splattered about from lack of proper sewage systems and wood barred across the windows of every building to keep criminals out. The homeless slept in every crevice and cranny they could find, while the sick dragged themselves down the street as if it took every ounce of strength they had left in their feeble bodies.

"What *is* this filthy place?" Edgar exclaimed.

A beggar with large warts all over his face walked toward him asking for money. Edgar was informed to 'dress down' yet he still wore a silk doublet and gold rings studded with blood rubies from his mines, letting everyone in the neighborhood know that he had money to spare.

"Guards! Guards!" He shouted, but I pulled the guards back with the wave of a hand.

"No need. This is our building, here." I stepped inside.

Edgar leapt in the air as if ants chomped into his derriere and hurried after me.

The large room housed two dozen wooden tables and a low wood ceiling. It had an overwhelming smell about it from the homeless who were several years overdue for a bath or some perfume to hide their body-odor. The homeless now lined up to receive their dinner and secure their bed for the night.

The shelter staff were explicitly told not to follow royal etiquette and treat us as volunteers. Soldiers wore regular gear and disguised themselves as homeless for my protection. Nonetheless, the staff still curtsied. I joined the assembly line to provide porridge and bread to the clients.

"What are we DOING HERE?" His voice trembled with trepidation.

"You wished to know more about the homeless shelter, did you not?" I batted my eyelashes at him.

"You MIS-interpreted my—" He went quiet as a homeless woman walked by. He was so disgusted by the dirty rag she wore, he rushed to my other side.

"Our dear Edgar needs a job to do," I informed the staff. "Why not clean the dishes?"

"This is an outrage! I . . ." He grabbed a spatula and started slapping porridge onto people's plates instead; causing the food to splatter everywhere. "I will NOT clean dishes." He went silent and barely looked at the plates which he flopped food onto, then began scanning his surroundings as if keeping a quick eye out for enemies.

This was the first time he didn't annoy everyone around with incessant babble.

Peace.

So wonderful.

After everyone was served bowls of porridge, bread, and lettuce over the next ten minutes—in silence—I walked to the other side and grabbed my own bowl. Edgar chased after me, afraid to be alone.

"Let us go now. There's a fantastic restaurant I'll take you too . . . what . . . what . . . what is this?"

I handed him a bowl of porridge and took one for myself. "This is our dinner. Come."

"What? What? This isn't food!" He followed me to a table so we could sit with the homeless.

"Are you really the crown princess?" a dwarf woman sitting with her five children asked. She was plump and so short that her chin was only a few inches above the table.

"I am Princess Qloey. And this is Prince Edgar. Just the other day Prince Edgar, here, mentioned how the homeless were lazy; if you all just got a job, we wouldn't need this shelter and he could tear it down." I innocently tilted my head.

Everyone within earshot went silent. They turned to glare at him with darkened eyes and furrowed brows. They were ready to eat him alive.

Possibly me too.

"Ah—ih—nuh. Noooo! That is not what I said! Ha ha ha." Edgar chuckled it off, but he sounded more like a wounded puppy crying. "I simply said, 'I hope we can create *more* jobs so you all have a place to live and sleep and eat and live and . . .'" He whimpered.

A woman started to cry. "You think we're just lazy? You think we want to be here? In this dirty shelter every night? This sloppy food? Not knowing if I'll feed my five children or we'll starve? Not knowing if child protection services will kidnap my children because of our unfortunate situation?"

"Yeah!" Another man joined our conversation. "We never be knowing if the shelter will be full that night or if we'll have to sleep on the streets. They give beds to women every night, guaranteed, but not us men."

"Ah, yes. These are great questions, Edgar." I faced him again. "Didn't you think this shelter gives too much to those in need? I do believe Edgar, here, mentioned tearing the building down and replacing it with a luxury home complex."

Someone behind him sharpened a knife.

The guards uneasily drew closer to us for our protection.

"No. No. I did not." Edgar whimpered. "You misunderstood me. I wish to bring *more* jobs. More! Great jobs to you all!"

"I has a job!" The man next to me slammed his fist on the table while glaring at Edgar with bestial eyes. His hands were dark brown from dirt and he wore a jacket with a huge hole in the chest. "I has a job. But they moved the location across town to make way for that ruby mine! I can't afford a horse to travel. I can't afford a home near work because there are already too many mansions. Cost of living is too high. I be working seventy hours a week just to send remittances to my wife and five children. It means I has to sleep at the shelter or the street every night because I ain't got spare money!"

"I had a job designing beautiful gowns for wealthy women," the dwarf woman said. "But once the ruby mines opened, many dwarves were forced out of their jobs. Our jobs were given to elves. I was forced to work in the dirty underground every day at one-fifth the pay. My husband

and my daughter died in there last year. My kids had to pick up their father's work and quit schooling to pay for food. The youngest is only six, working a full-time job! They kept us like prisoners in there. My kids and I managed to escape last week, but now I can't get another job. Nobody else will hire me." The woman placed her face in her hands and sobbed.

I was close to crying too. There were so many issues I never knew about . . . because I never took the time to listen to my own people. I hid myself away behind glamour, wealth, and armed guards.

"I'm so sorry. Edgar, isn't that your ruby mine? You mentioned a plan to increase productivity and decrease costs, by that, did you mean more forced labor and decreased salary for dwarves?"

"Aye . . . uh . . . mm . . . uh."

Everyone inched closer to him as they popped their knuckles.

"I tell you," a different man with black soot all over his face said. "I used to cut gems. Real talented too. But dwarves are cheaper to pay. They haven't the skills I have. Yet I lost my job and they put me in a coal mine. I'm unlikely to make it to age thirty. No point in getting married. I always wanted a wife." He hung his head and poked at his slushy porridge in defeat.

"Well Edgar, what do you plan on doing about that?" I flowered him with my attention.

"I will . . . I will . . . I will build free housing for all mining employees. Yes, so you can save your money. And increase pay. Definitely." Edgar laughed erratically. "Right away. I'll go do that now!" He jumped from the seat. "Help you ALL get higher pay! Ah, ha, ha, ha." Edgar cried as he ran out of the building.

"How can I be of help to you all?" I didn't say "we" because I was certain Edgar wouldn't do anything about it. And anything *I* achieved, I would make sure *he* wouldn't get credit.

"Are you marrying that man?" One man pounded his fist on the table. "Is he the next emperor?"

"Absolutely not! He's a thieving scoundrel, and I wished to address his wrong thinking by bringing him here and showing him the harm he's causing."

"Want me to take care of him for you?" Another man flossed his teeth with a knife.

"That is alright, I'll take care of him. But I do have a plan to help you all." I smiled. "Every single one of you."

CHAPTER 23

New Policies

"What are your plans to prevent the centaur attack?" a reporter asked during the press conference the next morning.

I wore another impressive mullet dress with breeches and a yellow vest that accentuated my girlish features and made me feel more confident when I answered their question. "We're going to hand over the mastermind and his accomplices to the centaurs, as we agreed upon."

"So you know who the man behind the assassination is?" the same reporter asked.

"We are very close to having the evidence we need to convict the culprit." Really, we didn't, but I wanted to make the perpetrator *more* nervous and the people *less* nervous. I called on another reporter.

"Who is your favorite candidate?"

"I cannot answer that; it'd ruin the surprise." I smiled. But really, I didn't know.

"Who do you want to send home?" another asked.

Oh, how I wanted to say Edgar's name, but I already humiliated him enough. "That I cannot answer either. But before we adjourn, I have an important announcement to make."

All reporters got their quills ready and leaned forward.

"I have a new mantuamaker extraordinaire who'll be designing my gown for the Royal Matchmaking Competition Ball, and I've hired a new gem cutter who will be overseeing the rubies that come out of the mines."

"Who is it?" The reporters excitedly jumped out of their seats and tried to guess which famous designer it was.

"Let me introduce Gappy and Fred." The dwarf I met at the shelter and the male gem cutter who lost his job to the dwarves, walked onto the stage all clean, wearing new royal garbs.

The room went silent.

Nobody applauded.

I clapped vigorously and looked at my staff members to follow suit. None of the reporters wrote the information down as I explained the dwarf's expertise and qualifications.

"Who's Fred?" A woman asked as she squinted her eyes at the meek looking man to my side, whose shoulders caved inwards as he stared at his toes. "Only nobles oversee this position."

"Do you really think a dwarf is capable of sewing?" another reporter asked.

"Capable? Absolutely. Dwarves create and design all clothing and art in Adonis Peak, do they not? They have a beautiful and thriving society. Gappy has already designed many fabulous dresses for noble women in Velazia and I look forward to her great expertise and originality for my new gown at the upcoming ball. Our empire needs to recognize the great talents ALL dwarves and commoners bring to our society, including literature, wood carving, metallurgy, and more." I smiled and took Gappy's hand and walked off. Fred trailed behind before the press ate him alive.

"Thank you, Your Majesty, but why are you doing this for us?" Gappy asked once we were behind closed doors.

"Because you deserve it. And by making you a royal mantuamaker and Fred a manager, it'll inspire others to hire dwarves and commoners for similar professions and bring love as a whole to our society. Before, I was ignorant, but I recently met a wonderful dwarf prince and commoner named Kipp, who opened my eyes to areas needing attention in the empire. So thank them."

"I want to thank you, Your Majesty. This means everything to me and my people. You have no idea," she cried.

"And now you and your children can live and grow up in this beautiful palace. A safe place to call home, where they can be properly educated. And you." I looked at Fred. "You can live in a more prosperous condition and find yourself a wife." He smiled.

It was time to head to the croquet game outside. Each bachelor underwent their own interviews while others were already finished and watched my speech.

"The beggar, Kipp, publicly disgraced, yet he's STILL here." That was the first thing I heard stepping outside. I looked over to see as Edgar wore another aristocrat's ear off with incessant complaints on the porch. "Meanwhile, I've been humiliated. The experience was absolutely horrifying, totally terrifying, monstrously mortifying. *Oh*." He wiped his forehead with a handkerchief. "I will not play croquet so long as a debased commoner is among us."

Ignoring him, I stepped in the opposite direction. Then my attention was drawn to Lancelot who finally made a move. "Y-Your Majesty, I—"

"Your Majesty!" Clayton, Zack, and Alejandro jumped in and pushed Lancelot aside. One boy took each arm so I couldn't escape. "We all wished to address an important issue with you."

"Sorry, let's talk later," I told Lancelot who nodded. "What is the issue?"

They led me to a private corner of the porch.

"We wish to help your image in the empire . . ." Alejandro began as he placed a hand on my back. "And we feel that . . ." He stroked my hand.

Clayton jumped up. "After what happened in the news with Kipp . . . 'Kipp the Beggar,' we're afraid if he remains here, it'll harm all of our images."

It was difficult to hear this. "I do see it differently; his presence here improves my image with my people."

"Not of the nobility," Clayton said. "We are the ruling class, and we're afraid that by supporting him you're . . . stepping on the wrong toes. You need *OUR* support to rule, not the peoples."

"Kipp's presence here is part of a century long agreement. He has a right to remain until the end of the RMC and get his private date." I wouldn't budge in this view.

Alejandro leaned in. "Then why did you ask Prince Edgar to leave?"

I stepped away to look at all three together. "There was an altercation. He acted inappropriately. It's also in the agreement if my life is in danger, I may dismiss a contestant. That is exactly how I felt when he inappropriately manhandled me. Now, please."

They looked at each other, wondering what Edgar did. Perhaps I exaggerated a little.

"May I whisk Her Majesty away?" McKinley came in for the save and quickly escorted me away. "I saw you were uncomfortable," he said after we stepped into the grass, away from the royals.

"Thank you Sir M—"

"Please, call me McKinley."

He led me to a table sitting underneath an umbrella where we could drink green tea and eat crumpets. "McKinley, we haven't spoken enough these last few days. But your presence now is comforting."

He had a masculine protective feeling about him. Perhaps because he was so big and strong or because his eyes said, "I want to keep you safe in my arms," and I, too, wanted to curl up in them.

"I have a confession to make." He put a hand on mine. "I've been holding this for some time, but mustn't conceal it any long. I apologize, for I failed to protect you during the centaur attack—"

"No." I stopped him. "It's just the opposite. If you didn't have that whistle, we . . . may all be dead. You also risked your life for Kipp. You saved us all. And now you're doing your duty to protect the empire from centaurs by working with our constable, training our soldiers, and offering secrets in warfare we never knew. All, in addition to participating in the competition. That's a lot you're putting into all this."

"As much as I don't want this to happen . . ." he said. "Wouldn't it be best for your safety to end the competition until the centaur issue is over? Otherwise, you *could* end up choosing an assassin."

True, what if I married the one trying to kill me? What if he secretly poisoned me in the night? I shivered.

"Your Majesty." He held my hand. "I didn't mean to upset you."

"You're only telling the truth, I appreciate it. But if everyone leaves, we'll never know. And it'll give him greater time to create a plan when the competition commences later. It's part of the treaty after all; the competition must continue. Let's put this all in the past. Now, how about a game of checkers?" I changed topics to see if he could enjoy casual time with me, unlike Edgar. "Best out of three?"

"If I win, then I get an extra date with you." He played.

"I'm not sure the competition works that way. But I'll agree anyway." I wrinkled my nose.

McKinley ended up winning two of three, to my delight.

"Until our date." He kissed my hand.

Upon leaving, Hedgewood was the first to jump in.

"You're supposed to give me time with those seeking my hand, unless you ARE seeking it?" I batted my eyelashes . . . but was actually curious what his response would be. Either there was something between us or I truly was stupid and ought to put all feelings away.

"Maybe I am?"

My heart raced.

"What can I say?" he continued. "You're irresistible and I couldn't wait to speak with you."

I struggled to believe my ears. *Did he actually say that?*

We sat at a table visible for all the gossiping aristocrats to watch us.

"I'm glad you're here." I reached across to take his hand.

He took it.

Then he stroked my the back of my hand.

Every nerve in my body worked in overdrive to calm me down.

"What you did for Gappy was . . ." he lost the words.

"It is the first of many steps down a long road."

He squeezed my hand tighter. "And what you did for Edgar . . ."

We both laughed; the paparazzi caught the image from afar.

"There's no way he's still here because he likes me. I'm not certain why he didn't go running back to Baylor after that life-altering experience last night."

He sighed. "He's expressed interest in becoming emperor. He also finds your perspectives to be misaligned with the empire's needs, as he openly voiced during breakfast."

The gall! I suppressed my anger. With paparazzi watching, they'd assume Hedgewood angered me. We couldn't afford that.

He studied my hand as if wanting to know every detail about it. "I considered him as the assassin, but . . . he's too frank about his views. I think he's a regular politician interested in power, wealth, and control; but I don't think he's capable of rounding up centaurs."

"I'm afraid the dinner party three years ago, when my mother publicly insulted me, has eschewed Edgar's opinion of me." I recalled. At the dinner table, there were many deep discussions—discussions that shouldn't have been reserved for a dinner party—one being the rising crime rates of the Gremlin Gangs. We also talked about how Velazia should hire trolls to collect tolls on bridges. I suggested listening to the grievances of the people to find out why they join gangs in order to solve the issue from its origin. Also, I pointed out how trolls are bullies, and shouldn't be given power. The thought so enraged my mother that she condemned every word I spoke for the remainder of the night. She then ranted on about how we don't negotiate with criminals, and that bridges shouldn't be used by commoners without being profitable. *"Only an idiot can't see these facts,"* she said. This was supported by my father insulting my intelligence in front of the guests. Thereafter, many disliked me.

"Ah yes, I heard about that," Hedgewood said.

I gasped. "You heard? I hadn't realized such a tragedy reached so far as the dwarf kingdom."

"The incident brought up many questions about the future of the empire. One was whether you'd be capable of maintaining control of society, as your mother so openly questioned in front of the dozens present."

This was hard for me to listen to.

"The other, was hope," he said.

"Hope?"

"Yes, hope," he explained further. "Hope that your reign would be different. As you see, problems in Velazia are growing. Places like Payonna Queendom are simply waiting for Velazia to crumble from the inside out to claim their power in the realm. Velazia's internal problems originated during your, what was it, your great-great-grandfather's time? The RMC was a last-ditch effort to keep the empire together. And now, the empress and King Edward's policies are pushing things to the brim. What they see as 'strength' others see as 'destructive' and 'harmful'. There will be another revolt if this doesn't change. A revolt will bring opportunists from foreign regions."

Opportunist from the dwarf kingdom? It almost sounded like he was the suspect in the assassination case, as there was a clear motive. *But no, Hedgewood would never do something like that.* I threw the thought away.

"But you, my dear . . ." he traced the lines on my hand. "You're our shining beam of hope. You have the power to alter things for all of us."

There it was, the confirmation I had been seeking all my life that maybe . . . just maybe, I wasn't so dumb or incapable as others always said. His words filled me up with confidence and optimism.

In the distance, my father looked disgusted that I held a dwarf's hand. His eyes turned away and back onto my mother, who was walking arm-in-arm with King Edward and Farooq. Surprisingly, the two had the exact same curved nose. They looked oddly similar.

Our time together was too long, and the croquet game was about to begin.

"Well, we should start the croquet game. But . . . before I go. I wanted to ask you something." I trusted him more than others. "Did you see anyone by the horses before the race during our picnic?"

"Yes."

"Who?"

"Everyone." He patted my hand. "But I didn't see who rubbed poison on its rear."

"How do you know about the poison?" This alarmed me. The High Council didn't inform many people about the poison. Again, I emptied my mind of any other suspicions of him as the assassin, confident he would never commit such crimes.

"When we returned the Pegasus to the centaurs, I saw the rash. It's not difficult to piece together someone intentionally tried to leave you as bait, especially after it started bucking all over the place, irritated by something."

We stood to leave and saw Zack punting pine cones using croquet mallets. "Speaking of good prospects in marriage . . ." Hedgewood said.

"Now, now. I always imagined my husband doing cartwheels up to the alter on our wedding day." I retained all seriousness.

He raised a single eyebrow. "You know, he can bench press your throne while you're sitting on it?"

"I expect nothing less from a husband."

"Well, if anything, Edgar is a GREAT choice!" Our attention now turned to Edgar, who was receiving a foot massage from the servants, while being fanned. "You'd never run out of things to talk about . . . I mean, to listen to him talk about . . ."

"You're right," I said. "But you must know of his great reputation, Hedgewood."

"Oh, I do hear it is astonishingly stupendous, staggeringly prodigious . . ."

"And highly empyreal." I finished his sentence.

"*Oh*." We both groaned at the same time to imitate Edgar, then burst into laughter.

"Oh, Hedgewood. You're too much."

Prince Zazan now approached. "Shall we choose our colors for the croquet competition, Your Majesty?"

"Oh, it seems everyone's eager to start the game. I suppose we shall." I took Zazan's arm, and he escorted me to the game where the other bachelors were already gathering.

Croquet Game

"**M**y darling…" Zazan's silky multi-layered elven garbs fluttered as we walked up to the croquet setup where the other boys were. "How can I prepare to serve you on our date, if I don't know when or where it'll take place." His voice held an air of irritation, as though he was on edge about the situation.

"Take heed. I'm aware your customs believe in giving, just as Prince Abdulla's, but everything will work out fine."

"A meeting between two lovers is a sacred act. I wish to have time to prepare." He pressed on as we reached the croquet mallets, clearly not liking the new procedures after the centaur attack. "We had a pre-arranged schedule. Now I'm left in the dark. Such was not the agreement when I decided to come."

"Let me know how you wish to proceed, and I'll honor it."

A moment later and I was caught in his hypnotic charm. The world seemed to dissolve away. I was aware of being in a trance but didn't know how to escape from it.

"Your Majesty!" Prince Qinrel grabbed my arm, which shook me out of the enchantment. "Will you start the game for us?" he asked me while glaring at Zazan, like a lion protecting his den from a predator.

Zazan puffed his chest up.

"Absolutely." I stepped in between them. "Let's begin the croquet game."

"Very well." Zazan walked away in defeat.

"I'm sorry." Qinrel looked down in shame.

"Sorry about what? It's not your fault he's charming me. Perhaps I should be the one to discuss the inappropriateness with him in private. Come."

"If you do, keep your guards close with explicit instructions on how to free you from his charms if he does it again. Or better yet, allow myself or another elf to come."

"I'm afraid that inviting a Nololay elf to the discussion would only offend him. Already, his life was in jeopardy during the centaur attack, and he's unhappy with his situation here." I grabbed the purple croquet mallet and ball.

"I'm concerned for your safety, Your Majesty. What if he's the assassin?" Qinrel brought up a good point, as we knew nothing of the Eldoren Elf Queendom or their motives. But we also couldn't act rashly when dealing with foreign relations, especially from a powerful neighbor who wielded elven metals.

"I would love your input, Prince Qinrel. Perhaps when we don't have listening ears," I whispered and placed my ball on the starting line. The other boys followed suit.

Qinrel stayed by my side. Every time Zazan went near me, he became protective and stood guard like he was my knight and savior. I said nothing to discourage this behavior and looked kindly upon Qinrel for his gallant affection. Then Alejandro came from behind and wrapped his arms around me. I laughed as the reporters in the distance quickly recorded the scene.

"This section is tricky; allow me to help you." He showed me how to hit the ball . . . even though I played croquet every year since childhood—I knew how to hit the ball. Nonetheless, I allowed him the chance to feel like a heroic prince.

"Prince Alejandro, you embarrass me."

"Embarrassed? Don't be embarrassed by my love." He lightly tapped my chin and pulled me in closer for a kiss. Quickly, I pushed him away. No public affection allowed for a princess. "Get used to me smothering you with affection."

Each bachelor tried to capture my attention somehow or start a conversation. Kipp gave me pleasant smiles, Zack did cartwheels all the way to his ball, and Qinrel rolled his ball alongside mine so he could protect me from the other elf.

"You should be trying to win, silly." I became amused with Qinrel's behavior. Qinrel looked around at the other boys and suddenly realized that he was falling behind.

Kipp was doing very well until his ball came up against Alejandro's. Alejandro wasted his turn, knocking Kipp's ball into the pond.

"Poor Kipp." I felt sorry for him, so I picked a pink chrysanthemum flower and went over to put it in his coat pocket.

"You just made my day." He kissed my hand.

"Where's my flower?" Alejandro tried to pull my attention back to him.

"It fell into the pond."

He fell onto his knees and touched his heart. "My heart is broken." Then he flopped onto the ground as if he died.

I laughed it off, then spoke to the group. "If I end up winning, I get to choose my date!"

Everyone expected the most physically fit to win, but McKinley missed two wickets and had to redo the shots. Qinrel fell behind, since he was more concerned about my protection. In a lucky shot worth a pot of gold, Abdulla came in from behind, shot his ball through the last wickets, and hit the stake, securing the win.

"It is a happy day!" Abdulla picked me up and spun me around in the air. I screamed with glee, but hushed up, hoping my parents didn't hear from across the pond.

Abdulla always smelt delicious and wore the most colorful garbs. We waved to the aristocrats, who sipped on their teas, then stood by the paparazzi to get a good drawing.

Our date was at the stables where two gryphons awaited with their trainers.

"We get to ride them." I nearly skipped in excitement because my parents were too far to witness this unruly behavior.

"Ride them?" He stopped in his tracks with his mouth wide open in surprise. "Uh, is that safe?"

"Of course it is. The trainers will be right with us." I grabbed a sardine and fed one of the gryphons so that the press could draw our pictures.

Finally, it was time to mount them. But Abdulla was frozen like a statue, too afraid to get too close to the beast.

"Don't be anxious. They're sensitive like horses." I was a confident rider of any animal.

"I do prefer the camel myself," he admitted but wasn't as much of a thrill seeker as myself. The trainers helped him mount. He closed his eyes and prayed.

"Do we get to fly?" I asked the trainer as I sat behind him on the double-seated saddle.

"Fly? What?" Abdulla panicked. "That's a little risky, don't you think?"

"If you wish not to, we won't . . . but how often do we get the chance?" I shouted in joy.

The gryphons now walked into the open field. But we weren't allowed to travel too far because of the centaurs. The only adventure we could have was upward.

"We can fly, Your Majesty, if you wish," the trainer said.

"How about it?" I encouraged.

"Are you sure it's safe?" Abdulla's voice squeaked.

"Absolutely! Let's go!"

The trainers led the gryphons into a gallop. The gryphons spread their wings and leapt into the air. We flew high above the palace and over the capital. I never realized how far-reaching the capital was, or how extensive the palace grounds were in comparison to the city.

The gryphons flew north toward the mountains, and we overlooked a large lake I had never seen before. Further west was a castle lying in ruins, and even further beyond that, we could see the Pearl Sea in the distance. We flew over the Centaurus Forest and even made it to the northern part of Baylor before we circled back around.

Below us, I saw a herd of galloping horses, but on further inspection, I realized they were centaurs clad in armor ready for battle. And they were headed to the eastern side of Velazia. From the eastern side, they could bypass the city and intercept the palace directly.

This wasn't good, but I could discuss these dangers later with the council. Right now, was time to have fun!

This was a miraculous experience. A nice breath of fresh air. A whole new view compared to the confines of the palace. I could see everything from up here.

I took a chance and let go of the saddle. My arms reached up, and I relished in the freedom as the wind went rushing past my hair. "Freedom!" I hollered in satisfaction, then a bug flew into my mouth. "Gross." I spit it out.

I turned to look at Abdulla. "Isn't this fun?"

Abdulla was screaming with his eyes closed as he hugged the trainer for fear of his life. *Poor thing,* I thought.

"Let's return," I said to the trainer even though I was having a blast.

Abdulla's trainer made a soft landing, while mine did a running landing and then galloped back to the palace. The press captured the image even though my hair was a frizzy mess from the wind, yet all I could do was laugh the whole way.

Abdulla was frozen stuck, holding onto the trainer even after the gryphon came to a halt, and had to be pried off like ice.

"Come, let's retreat." I escorted him away from prying eyes. His hand was still shaking.

Then he heaved.

"Are you alright?"

A moment later, he ran behind a bush and puked.

McKinley, Knight of Centaurus City. Human. Age 19. Voted the most eligible bachelor by citizens in Centaurus City for the RMC. Interests: Spending time outside, jousting, horseback riding, chess, & archery.

McKinley dressed his best. He had a square-shape to his face, yet was humble about his attractive features and wore a white and black doublet, matching feather hat, and buckle boots.

He stopped breathing when he saw me.

I wore a fluffy deep-red gown that revealed my chest. My sleeves slightly hung off my shoulder as the heavy bliauts stretched to the floor.

"You're making it impossible for me to let you go if you don't choose me, Your Majesty. I'd never recover."

"Do call me Qloey . . . in private." I gave him a seductive smile.

He inhaled deeply, as if trying to hold himself together; the fear of revealing too much emotion weighing on his conscience.

We entered the entertainment room for a private opera concert with his favorite opera singer, Sophya. Our hands joined as we sat on a vintage love-seat in the center of the room with red rose decorations set about the room. A servant dimmed the candles for a more romantic setting and served us chocolate coated cherries.

My mind was more on McKinley's warm body against mine on this small couch than on that actual opera. Occasionally, my attention returned to Sophya when she reached a high note, but then I'd glance up at McKinley and his attention immediately went to me.

Halfway through the concert, he reached an arm around me. It sent a river of emotions though my body. *He likes me. He really likes me, even after my mother's open criticisms.* I felt that I could trust in him, and responded by resting my head on his shoulder. He lightly stroked my arm, giving me a thrill.

Sophya sang a famous love song in her last piece. Then she curtsied and left the room so we could have privacy.

With his arm still wrapped around me, we moved to the window for wine.

"White Zendolf or Red Mermaidlot wine?" he asked.

"Red."

He poured a glass for me. "It's my hope that once it's safe, we can go on a longer horseback ride together and I can show you around Centaurus City."

"With you, absolutely." I took the chance and snuggled right into his big, burly arms. Unable to resist him any longer.

He took the opportunity to stoke my hair.

"Tell me, what do you hope to find in a husband?"

"It's shifted." I looked up at him. "At first, I looked for someone capable of taking on the work of a politician, like my father . . ."

After my parents married, they had me within the next year, but it took another seven years before they had Farooq. It seemed they were rarely intimate with each other. It was likely that my mother chose my father for a political alliance. He agreed and supported everything my mother did, so it seemed like they were compatible in one sense of the matter.

"After you all arrived, I realized my parent's plans don't fit my own. Perhaps . . . I'm enjoying how you all surprise me. Now I want a friend, an ally, support, and a lover. What about you? What do you want in a wife?" I turned the tides on him.

"The Centaurian royalty only had daughters; the next choice as the bachelor to the RMC in my city was a man in love with another, then a boy not of age. So our city had a poll. I was proclaimed the most eligible bachelor. But it was quite a surprise as I wasn't thinking of marriage yet and thus never considered that question. I had no idea people thought of me in such a way."

"But you spent a lot of time with your people. You're always out on the streets, are you not? The people must know you. They know you are kind." My eyes sparkled. "And handsome."

His lips went flat. "It appears so. I had many doubts coming here, but I realize now . . . that I want my wife to be you."

My cheeks went flush. Although he didn't show much emotion on the outside, he seemed to have a flowing river of passion within that he was forever trying to hold back.

"I don't think I could love anyone else but you. Do you . . ." He paused. "Have feelings for me?" He weighed the risk of revealing so much.

"I do."

He put his wine down and gently coddled me into his muscular arms; treating me like a precious flower. In response, I wrapped my arms around his large torso and further embraced him on the lips.

It was gentle, soft, yet meaningful.

In the silence, I enjoyed the remainder of our date with my lips on his.

Knight McKinley of Centaurus

CHAPTER 25

Moonlit Swans

The soft moonlight fell across Qinrel's face as he gazed out the window.

My date with McKinley just ended; a date filled with many passionate kisses and warm hugs. My heart was still singing, and I floated on cloud nine.

On my way back to the opposite side of the palace, where I planned to return to my room, I found Qinrel alone in one of the hallways; I took a moment to really soak him in. He shifted his weight to one side and rested an elbow on the windowsill. A sword hung off his hip as his other hand clutched the handle. Not only was his skin as smooth as silk, and his face perfectly symmetrical, but the tall frame of his body screamed of ecstasy. I tried very hard at that moment to push my attraction to him away for I just left the date with McKinley—who might possibly become my husband—and to me, my attraction to the elf meant I was cheating on the knight.

I tried to slip away unseen, but my skirt rustled as I turned and alerted him of my presence.

"Your Majesty?"

Once he saw me, his empathetic abilities amplified my giddiness from my wonderful evening. "You look radiant." His eyes scanned my deep red dress, and the way my sleeves barely hung off my shoulders.

Now I noticed his shirt was slightly open, revealing his bare chest underneath, as though he were preparing to head to bed. "You look strapping yourself."

"Something wonderful is out there, you must see." He pointed toward the pond. "Something is glowing in the water."

"Oh, yes, the glowing swans."

"Glowing swans? I must know more." He smiled oh-so-cutely.

"It's truly a special occasion." It was late, but I was in a good mood, so I decided to introduce him to this rare event. "Come, I'll show you." I lightly took his hand, and we ran down the stairs like little children.

The guards at the door gestured to Qinrel's sword and took it from him. No contestants were allowed to have weapons around me anymore. They then flung open the doors, and we made our way onto the dirt path around the pond.

Fireflies lit the path, but most of the light came from the full moon. "Did you know, even the fireflies in Nololay have elf ears?"

"They do?" My eyes grew as large as an orange.

He laughed.

"You're joking?"

He laughed again.

He had a sense of humor, who knew?

I pointed at the moon. "Every full moon, the pregnant swans glow iridescent blue."

"Now you're joking."

I leapt forward to the water's edge, then spun around like a swan dancer, with my silky skirt flailing about beneath me. "Nope."

"Perhaps *your* true nature is a swan, Your Majesty. And every full moon you wait by the pond for a prince to offer you true love's kiss."

I chortled. "True love's kiss to save me from my parent's rigidity." I playfully danced in the moonlight, letting loose and forgetting everything my mother had taught about etiquette. But my mood was so amorous I didn't care. Somehow Qinrel brought that inner child out.

Qinrel marveled at my every movement as I danced along the dirt path. "Do you dance, Prince Qinrel?"

He answered by putting his arm around my waist. Being so close to him made me become aflutter. It made no sense; I danced with many men before. Why be nervous in his arms? But it was fun. Together, we twirled down the moonlit dirt path to the music of the crickets and croaking frogs.

"Is this *your* happiness I'm feeling or mine?" I wondered how his charm worked.

"It's yours. It's your pent up happiness coming out. All the joys you've always wanted to express growing up but couldn't. I can tell that your parents always suppressed your excitement."

"Amazing. What about negative emotions?" I asked. "If you felt it, would they be amplified in me?"

"Only if you wanted to accept those negative emotions," he said. "But I try not to be negative, because it'll harm others around me. I must be responsible, so I may be a blessing to others instead."

"You have a beautiful heart, Qinrel." How quickly things could change with these bachelors. "Tell me something about you not on your profile!" We fell out of the dance and skipped over to some wild red roses. I shoved my nose inside a rose to get a good whiff of the scent. He clipped one off the stem and put it into my hair.

"I'm not full elf; one distant ancestor was from the Moonstone Queendom before it was conquered." I already knew everyone's lineage as part of my research. But I listened anyway. "And . . . I'm connected with forest nymphs. But that's a secret, please tell nobody."

"What do you mean?" I asked.

"I met a forest nymph as a child. We became friends, and she eventually invited me to their secret underground queendom."

"Do you still talk with them?"

"The underground is connected like roots. It doesn't matter where I am on the planet, they visit me," he clarified.

"And have you seen them at the palace?"

Nymphs were rare to view, and they usually avoided the cities.

"Yes, I saw them at the picnic. One was ushering me over prior to the attack, probably to warn me about the centaurs. But it happened too quickly. We never spoke."

"What? Wait! Can you ask them something?" I stopped twirling about. "Did they see anyone . . ." It meant I had to reveal the secret and trust him to give me the truth . . . *unless he is the culprit*, I thought. But he was so sweet; there was no way he could be the mastermind behind all the assassinations. I discounted him as well as the others whom I held in my heart. "Did anyone rub toadstool poison on the Pegasus' rump before the horse race?"

"Toadstool poison? Huh. When I see them next, I'll ask." He said. "But they don't always emerge. It's usually up to them to find me."

"That would be most helpful."

The clock struck midnight, and we heard bells in the distance. "Hurry, it'll end soon." I took his hand and ran toward the swans. We found a nice spot to watch as five swans gently swam past us. Two of them glowed iridescent cobalt blue colors.

"You weren't joking." He rested a hand on his belt.

"No. Only pregnant female swans glow on the full moon. So you can't see them all year round."

I felt him appreciate me for showing him such a miraculous event.

"You're cold." He took his cloak off and wrapped it around me. Our hands brushed against each other and sparks of chemistry flew between us. His cloak smelled like a fresh pine forest. I gazed up into his eyes, so blue that they almost glowed in the moonlight. I wanted to reach up and touch his adorable pointy ears. The way he protected me against Zazan was endearing and won him points. And now his body was warm against mine, and I couldn't help but want to get closer.

Then I quickly pulled back. McKinley and I just had a wonderful date. How could I immediately move to another boy like that? It wasn't right. Were these even my true feelings or some elf charm again?

He saw my change of tone and stepped back to give me space.

Then I realized that his power could have many dangers to it. What if he controlled me emotionally like Glynnda did, while playing innocent? I realized the soldiers who followed us were further away than usual.

"You're scared. Shall we go inside?" Qinrel attended to my emotional needs.

"No! I . . ." One look into his face, and the fear went away. He didn't have maleficent feelings toward me. It was all appreciation and gratitude. I didn't want to be suspicious of every contestant. I wanted to enjoy every moment with them. So I chose another emotion: joy.

"I recognize you've developed feelings with many others . . ." he started to say.

"Are none of my feelings private when I'm around you?"

"I'm sorry. I . . ."

"No, it's okay." I stopped him. "Perhaps part of me is still frightened of these elf charms. But, in another way, your empathic powers create transparency. It is refreshing as well, for I feel that we understand each other on a deeper level that we haven't fully discovered yet. Then again, you probably feel that way around everyone." I chuckled.

"No. I don't. Some people are closed and emotionless. Heartless too. But with you, it's different. I can sense you even when you're not in the same room. This has never happened before."

"What does that mean?"

"I don't know," he admitted.

One swan fluffed its wings up as if getting more comfortable as it floated by.

"But I do think you're a special person. You're gorgeous, intelligent, and courageous. And above all, you're yearning to let your inner child out and enjoy life. I would love to help you achieve that. If not for my own interest in you, then for the empire that needs a good leader," he confessed. Again, these boys helped validate that I sometimes did things correctly. If only I had parents that nurtured that instead of bringing me down all the time. "You are the best choice in marriage for me, but I screwed up in the beginning and it seems there's little gaining ground against my rivals in this competition now."

It wasn't really his fault. "If we were to start all over, and pretend Glynnda didn't happen, what would you do now?"

"I'd invite you to dance under the moonlight again."

I put my hand out with a smile, and he escorted me to a flat spot on the grass. "Then let's savor this beautiful moment together and act like Glynnda never existed." We twirled and danced around until we were giddy with joy.

CHAPTER 26

Updating the List

Was I drunk? I was awake in bed as I recapped everything from the previous night, both with McKinley and Qinrel. *Since when do I dance around the pond or get so excited over swans? I see swans every day.*

"I only had two glasses of wine with McKinley," I recalled. Not enough to get drunk. But enough to feel *passionate.* Yet, my heart beat loudly thinking of both of them. I was starting to like Qinrel. But how could I choose a husband if I kept falling in love with a new boy every day?

I unraveled my pre-competition list of bachelors in my journal. It was originally written in black ink and now scribbled over in purple.

Qinrel's name was first hearted, then crossed out, and now re-added. I definitely felt something for him. My "duty-inspired" list involved the black hearts. Now those like Abdulla had an extra heart now in purple.

Alejandro didn't offer much in return for how much Ogarz would gain by marrying into the royal family . . . except steamy romance. The only reason I didn't cross him out pre-competition was due to his handsome portrait. And now, my heart sang every time he drew near.

Maybe Lancelot wasn't completely out of the running. He might be shy, but what if our date was as spectacular as McKinley's? Increasing relations with Moonstone City would greatly benefit the capital in that they were rich in education, knowledge, and spirituality. But at this point in the competition, adding another boy I loved to my heart would confuse me to oblivion. I wanted to start eliminating the boys I wasn't interested in.

A.K.A. Edgar.

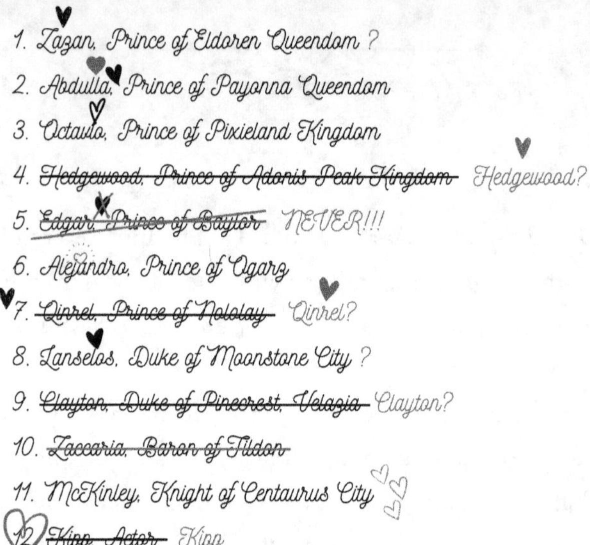

"Who is it that took your heart this time?" Victorya came in unannounced to wake me up and found me lying on my stomach with a girlish smile and my feet dangling in the air.

"Nobody." I laughed and threw a pillow over my face to hide my large grin.

"Nobody?" Victorya didn't believe me and lifted the pillow to see me beaming brighter than the sun. "Hmm, would it be your date with . . . Sir McKinley?"

I giggled and hit Victorya with the pillow, not ready to reveal my feelings.

"Your Majesty?" Victorya's mouth stood agape for a moment before curling into a grin. This was unusual behavior for me. Nonetheless,

Victorya had a fun personality. She grabbed a pillow and hit me back. "Somebody's in *love*," she sang.

"With eleven boys." I kicked my feet up in the air and hugged the pillow.

We both burst into laughter.

"I kissed McKinley."

"YOU DID WHAT?" she shouted, but all I could do in response was plant my face in the pillow while giggling, and kick my feet behind me.

THE CROWN PRINCESS QLOEY IS UNSUITABLE TO RULE. THE PRINCESS IS DISTURBING THE PEACE IN VELAZIA BY REDISTRIBUTING SOCIAL CLASSES. UNICORN-FORBID IF PRINCESS QLOEY CHOOSES A DWARF TO RULE BY HER SIDE, THEN ALL STRUCTURE IN SOCIETY WILL FALL APART. DO WE WANT DWARVES TO RULE OVER HUMANS? DO WE WANT DWARVES CONTROLLING THE VELAZIAN EMPIRE? DO WE WANT DWARVES IN OUR ROYAL BLOODLINE? IF WE CONTINUE TO ALLOW THIS, DWARVES WILL REVOLT, EXPECT SPECIAL TREATMENT, SUPPRESS HUMANS, AND ASK FOR AN EQUAL SAY IN GOVERNMENT. WE NEED A RULER WITH SELF-RESPECT.

My mother read off the front page of the *Royal Times* to the council. Next, she read off a quote from Edgar, *"She put our lives in danger and lowered my value by meshing with city scum. Not an example any ruler should set."* She slammed the paper down. Several council members jumped in fright. "What is this nonsense about a dwarf living and working in the palace? An a filthy miner taking a nobleman's job? Has Hedgewood gotten into your brain?"

"As next ruler, it's my duty to improve the living conditions of my people," I said, defending my position.

"As ruler, it's your *duty* to hold the Empire together. Not offer our home as a shelter to vagrants and destroy your rapport." She towered above me by several inches.

We were not only different in philosophy but also in temperament. People questioned if I was her real daughter or a changeling swapped at birth. Some even suggested I was dropped on my head. But in reality, many were frightened that my reign would be different, and therefore insulted me as an excuse to lessen my influence in court. I was starting to see this in another light now.

"It goes on to say . . . 'Is the princess falling for the dwarf, or is he manipulating her with dwarf propaganda to destroy the fabric of our highly functioning society? Some wonder if he's the real assassin, attempting to create discord so the dwarves can break the empire apart'." She looked up at me. "So, tell me do you have feelings for this dwarf? Is there anything we should be concerned about?"

"It's best to ask individually about each contestant than to single out a dwarf." I lightly stated, yet my eyes remained downcast.

"What's with your behavior?" My mother's voice grew irritable, she then ordered Yenna to hand me a list of bachelors. "Since you're too daft to figure this out, after the twelfth private date, we're reducing the contestants to this list."

Her list included Edgar, Abdulla, Lancelot, and Zazan. Zazan was . . . well, he was Zazan, and somewhat manipulative, Lancelot was unresponsive, and Abdulla was the only one I connected with, but not my favorite. And Edgar was an absolute NO.

Finally, I hit a fuse.

I ripped up the list and raised my voice for the first time in my life. "This is MY competition! I get to choose. And Edgar harmed *your* image as well as mine! I would expect you to discipline Prince Edgar for his defamation of the crown instead of supporting his inappropriate comments to the press!"

Everyone in the room stared at me in stunned silence, including the guards. Nobody ever saw me speak up against my mother before. Everyone waited for her to retaliate. To my surprise, her words came out calm and collected, yet with a threatening undertone of caution that said I went too far."

"Finally, you've grown a backbone. You've grown too soft over the years. You've always been a push-over, a wimp. I started to question if you were capable of ruling the people." She was going easy on me, probably startled by my change of behavior. "No more of this social justice image you're putting on for the people's entertainment.

Nobody spoke.

She continued, "Quite frankly, I'm being kind to you. I only had *three* options in my competition. My parents wanted to strengthen our hold over the empire. That meant I couldn't choose any of the bachelors from the four-foreign-nations. Ogarz and Nololay are weak impoverished cities and have no chance at rebelling, so those bachelors were out. I fell in love with King Edward of Baylor." That explained a lot. The two were inseparable since he arrived. "But Baylor already won the competition two out of three times before me in the past. And your grandmother chose a Velazian royal. People started questioning the legitimacy of the competition. Thus, I wasn't allowed to choose someone from Baylor or Velazia either. So I had *three* choices. Three! And I chose your father from Tildon, despite having no love for him. So by giving you *four* options, I'm being kind. Very kind. *You* have one more option than *I* had!"

For the first time, I realized she was in pain. All these years, she suppressed all her torment and suffered in silence. Then she'd lash out at others because of this unhealed pain. She didn't know how to be happy or enjoy life. Her life was all about "duty," thus mine had to be too. I was just like her in this respect. Yet I felt compassion for her, as it explained why she was so bitter inside.

Her three choices in marriage also explained her deep connections and business dealings with Baylor. She wanted to keep King Edward close. Edgar reminded Ezmorelda of what she loved most.

"Why not Sir McKinley from Centaurus?" I asked. None of my favorite boys were on the list, and I wouldn't tolerate this. Just because she was limited didn't mean I had to be.

"He undermined his own authority by having the centaur whistles. We can now threaten them to comply with anything we demand. If they don't cooperate, we'll hand McKinley over to the centaurs as the assassin. Thus, we no longer need their alliance."

Such thoughts sickened me! Everything was about gaining power over others. Gaining wealth. Gaining advantage. Not about helping the people! This was exactly why the empire was falling apart. Because my family always sided with greed and power over the well-being of others. The people were suffering and needed help.

It felt like an earthquake ripped a hole between my mother and myself.

But I was ready to stand up for myself for once. "I've developed feelings for many of the boys and can—"

"THIS. IS. YOUR. LIST. And I will hear no complaints about it."

"I won't—"

"ENOUGH!" The woman that I once knew as my mother bellowed. But I no longer desired her affections anymore. Not when she was trying everything possible to take love away from me.

The empress turned to Yenna. "Yenna, inform Prince Edgar, that if he doesn't change the reporter's view on the crown in the next three days, he'll be named the 'number one suspect' in the assassination case."

"Yyyyeees, Your Royal Majesty." But it was just a threat; Ezmorelda wouldn't *really* harm him. Just nudge him in the right direction.

"And I want *you* to get that filthy Gappy out of this palace! She's to work in the ruby mines per our new Dwarf Relocation Mandate." She pressed a finger against a paper on the table. Their business agreement with Baylor.

I wanted to cry.

She saw my hesitancy and continued. "You WILL openly support this policy and are required to announce our new mandate to your bachelors. Yenna will give you the details. Once the last private date is over, you are to immediately send that dwarf prince and peasant scum home, or I'll ensure your coronation never happens." She turned to leave but stopped to say one more thing. "And don't think"—her eyes sent bullets into mine—"that you can ever raise your voice to me again."

CHAPTER 27

Turning the Tide

Pressure was mounting inside of me. I was ready to explode. There was no time for the crystal chamber or to process my emotions. Yenna would oversee as I properly addressed the candidates with the "new mandates" during breakfast today.

How can I stand up to her? I questioned. *How can I let go of the boys whom I love? How can I not obey the empress and still come out on top?*

All I wanted my whole life was Empress Ezmorelda's approval. I did everything she asked; I listened, obeyed her, and even behaved in ways unbecoming of my true nature. I studied hard, put on a smile even when I was dying inside. I tried to be "perfect." Yet despite this "perfection," she still disapproved of everything I did. It was never enough, and neither was I.

Perhaps I had faulty ideas. I examined my behavior at the shelter. My mistake of allowing Gappy in the palace. My stupid childishness with the swans. I wanted to align myself with those whom I loved the most, whom had values like myself, but a peasant, a knight, a dwarf, and two lowly princes couldn't offset the influence or power of the council, other aristocrats, and the empress and emperor. *Can I really remain true to myself and stand up to the most powerful influences within the empire?* Perhaps it was true, I needed the support of the ruling class, not the peasants, otherwise, I would be ousted.

I struggled to find the truth amidst the chaos in my thoughts and emotions that said I was *incapable, insecure, and weak,* and that if I just *follow the empress's orders now, she'd finally approve of me. This must be my opportunity now,* I concluded, as if all the other times that I obeyed her weren't prime examples of my worthiness.

Oh, I'm so confused. My face fell into my hands as I leaned over my vanity.

Yenna brought me the list of the four bachelors.

I wanted to scream, but instead, I crumpled the list in my fist, put it to a candle flame, and then threw it in a bucket.

"Your Majesty, I wouldn't . . ." Yenna knew this wouldn't go well for me if I disobeyed. "Please. Breakfast is almost over. Our Royal Majesty said you must fix your mistakes at breakfast or *she'll* fix them for you."

My face went pale. *What do I do? I'm too scared to disobey her.*

Yenna led me into the breakfast room, where the boys stood to greet me. There, I took a seat at the head of the table and instructed them to sit.

"Some things were brought to my attention . . ." I couldn't look anyone in the eye. "Concerning what you all read in the newspaper. Much of it was a fabrication."

"We know they lie about you," Kipp said, but his words failed to comfort me. "We believe in you, Your Majesty."

It hurt hearing that. It hurt because of what I was about to say. "It's best that the homeless shelter closes as it takes too much of our funds. The money will go towards hiring trolls to patrol the streets. And the homeless clients will be given housing and jobs in the coal or ruby mines."

"Have you been to the mines? They have worse conditions than the shelter. That's no way for anyone to live. And what of the elderly and children; they'll die!" Hedgewood stood in frustration.

I put a hand up to hush Hedgewood. "Gappy and Fred will also be relocated there."

"What?" Kipp stood. "How can you say this?"

"It is the *proper way* to do things. As future empress, I must show myself as a true ruler and make difficult decisions—"

"Your mother's forcing you to do this? Isn't she?" Kipp was enraged. "This isn't you talking. You can't—"

"If you cannot accept this, leave!" Edgar stood to face Kipp. "This table is for *real* leaders. And you simply cannot understand what it's like for us to manage people like you."

"People like me? I will not stand for this!" Kipp looked ready to fight, but McKinley grabbed his arm and held him back.

"Don't Kipp." McKinley warned. "They'll throw you in prison for hitting a prince."

Kipp turned to me. "Stop this nonsense, Qloey. How can you—"

"Address 'Her Majesty' with respect!" Alejandro joined the fight.

My eyes remained downcast.

"None of you deserve to rule if you support this. You sicken me!" Kipp angrily stormed out of the room.

Now Kipp was angry with me. I just couldn't get anything right. Every time I pleased one person, another was upset. I couldn't bear the dramas around this any longer and left the room before I cried in front of them. I felt overwhelmed and weighed down by the world with an endless sea of problems.

"Qloey! Qloey. Qloey. What was that about?" McKinley chased after me in the hallway.

"This is the way of things. How things are intended to be." The interaction with Empress Ezmorelda weighed on my mind.

"There is no 'intended way'." He remained gentle with me in speech. "You decide the way as Empress."

"I'm not empress yet, and if I'm ever to be, I must make good decisions and be headstrong. That means doing what must—"

"That's your mother talking. Not you!" He spoke a little louder.

"Well, the empress is right. She knows the best way, and I must take after her." I kept my tone calm. Trying to hold everything together. But a volcano erupted inside. "What matters is the ruling party, not the people."

"How can you say that? How can you flip upside down in a single day? You hurt a lot of people just now. And you'll hurt a lot more if you continue this behavior."

"My actions the past few days hurt people."

"No! You hurt some aristocrat's *ego*. To the people you gave hope. Don't follow your ancestor's example. The empress is losing support. She's abhorred by the people in all Seven Cities. If something doesn't change, you won't be the ruling family anymore."

"How dare you say such a thing?" I defended my family.

"It's not me, it's what I hear." He spoke with calm determination. "I'm more connected to the outside world than you are. And I can tell you that by promoting Gappy and Fred, by giving Kipp and Hedgewood a chance, by hearing the voices at the shelter, you bring light to the people. Or at least you did until just now. Now you're being a tyrant. And the current tyrant on the throne is destroying the empire and the people just as she's destroying you."

These were dangerous words. Very dangerous. If the empress or the wrong person heard our conversation . . . it would not bode well for him.

A burning sensation welled up behind my eyes. Before the RMC, it was easy to hold everything in. Other than Kipp, the last time I cried in front of another was after my brother was born. My father threatened to claim I wasn't his real daughter if I ever cried in public again. So I held it all in. And now I was ready to burst like a broken dam.

"Why are you being so harsh? Why can't you accept I'm trying to prove myself as a capable leader? And If I don't correct myself now, the empire will fall apart. My mother will—"

"Then DO IT correctly. Do it Qloey's way. The way you've been doing it all along." McKinley said.

"You read the newspapers? You hear what they say. If I don't . . ." I started hyperventilating. "You heard . . ." The tears started cracking through the dam. "She threatened . . . if I didn't say all that . . ." I couldn't finish the sentence. "When I please one person, it only angers the rest. Why can't people just be satisfied for once?" I leaned against the windowsill for support.

He pulled me into a hug. Just like with Kipp, it caused all the tears to pour out. He stroked my hair and rocked me in comfort.

"You don't know this, but I read about you my entire life. I researched articles about you before I arrived. They critiqued you from the moment you were born. They said you were 'too small,' only a five-pound baby. Then you were 'too artistic,' perhaps they should put you in the freak show. You're 'too quiet,' how can you ever be a public speaker? Every step of the way, they tore you down. Your mother tears you down. Your father tears you down. I'm of a royal line and see it in the princesses and princes of Centaurus. I see it in every royal family. The pressure you're under is immense. But if you seek validation from any of those critics, you'll *always* struggle. You have to find validation from being YOU. The YOU every one of us loves."

"I need to go." I tried to escape, but he held tightly onto me.

"Don't run away."

"I'm not running away, I . . . I need to be alone."

"No, you need help with your burdens."

"I . . . I'm . . . unfit to rule." My knees collapsed, but he was right there to pick me up. He found a seat but kept me wrapped in his burly arms.

"The news lies. Edgar lies. Don't believe a word they say. You're on your way to becoming the best ruler the Velazian Empire has ever known. Do you know how I know that?

I shook my head.

"Because you care. You listen. You're smart. You make bold moves that help the needy." He rubbed my arms. "The aristocracy has everything they need, yet they complain the most. They will fight back when you take their toys away but . . .

I chuckled through the tears.

"But in the end, you'll be known as the bravest, most daring, and benevolent ruler our empire has ever seen. I'd advocate for leaving the empire if you ruled like your mother. But if you rule like Qloey, I'll support you every step of the way."

"You really think I'm capable? That what I did for Gappy was right?" It felt better listening to him than the empress, as if his words breathed truth, and that the truth manifested as harmony itself.

"I know you're capable! I loved every decision you've made up until breakfast," he affirmed.

"But why has this competition taken such a toll on me?"

"Because you need to stop reading the lies in the newspapers. And start listening to your conscience." He wiped my tears up with his sleeve. In the distance, I saw a moving figure eavesdropping on our conversation. *Hedgewood?* "Come, let's talk in private." He lifted me up in his arms and carried me somewhere that we could talk.

Kipp

CHAPTER 28

Pippa's Play

Oh Hedgewood! How he must be hurt. And Kipp. Everyone I adored. If Edgar agreed with me, I must've been delusional.

McKinley stayed by my side for several hours and helped me find myself again. I canceled the group date for the day and ordered a time of rest for the participants. After Qinrel heard about this, he came to comfort me. We now sat on the window seat together. Immediately, my emotions were lifted, almost healed by his presence. It was much different from McKinley. McKinley was rational, protective and supportive. But Qinrel was like an elixir which offered emotional and mental support.

"You were . . . off this morning. Confused. Hurt."

"Yes, and . . . in my own pain, I hurt others," I said.

"As pain usually does. It's when we're in higher emotions, like happiness, love, and compassion, that we make better decisions."

"Compassion?" I looked up at him.

"Compassion, yes." He smiled. "That's what you're often in. Like when you saw Kipp being ridiculed because he couldn't hold a bow and arrow during the archery competition. When you brought Gappy to the palace. When you pardoned my mother and me."

I hesitated before revealing personal details about my life. Perhaps because I felt powerless to his charms and wasn't sure if my attraction to him was his doing or natural. But one look into his kind eyes and I decided to open up. "When I was a baby, my fairy goddessmother gave me the gift of compassion. But my parents didn't like the things she was teaching me. So they made her leave."

"You must be special." Qinrel pointed out. "Fairy goddessmothers only come to those who have big destinies. Often they'll give magical gifts to babies for their innocence and purity, or grant one wish to a kind-hearted adult who withholds moral values even through difficult life-challenges. She became a ruler who bestowed kindness unto her people, and her reign was one of the greatest that any kingdom ever saw."

"So . . . you also think I was doing the right thing, allowing Gappy here and taking Edgar to the shelter?" I needed assurance that more opinions sided with me, because at that moment, I felt entirely weak inside; unable to see right from wrong. So far, it seemed like I was gathering a large support system.

Qinrel laughed. "It's quite amusing, actually. I would've loved to have seen Edgar get a taste of his own medicine. And yes, you were amazing with Gappy and Fred. It's what I love most about you."

"It helps to hear it." It wasn't just McKinley, Qinrel also thought I was doing the right thing before the empress's criticisms got into my head. Then I told him why I said all those things, including the Dwarf Relocation Mandate in Baylor, and the list of four bachelors she was forcing on me. "I think she's trying to lead me into Edgar's hands to ensure this business agreement goes through."

"This breaks the treaty. Does she realize the repercussion of this?"

"Not if she keeps it under wraps."

"Then don't keep it hidden. Listen, during this competition, you've made alliances with Nololay, Adonis Peak, Centaurus, and Moonstone; you've impressed many commoners of Velazia with your display at the homeless shelter. Even Abdulla and Octavio adore you. All of us will back your right to the throne if it means there will be positive change. Now's your chance to solidify support from the other cities. Getting support from the politicians in Velazia isn't enough for your mother to hold on to power."

These were very encouraging words.

"Why does your mother treat you this way anyhow?" He asked.

"She's like this to everyone, including my brother. She's just bitter, unhappy. My grandparents were the same way, so she learned from them, but I also think it's because they stripped her of her happiness by forcing my father's hand on hers. She went through an entire RMC and couldn't even choose the love of her life! She despises anyone who challenges her, and now . . . I'm standing up for my happiness, something that she was to weak to do herself."

He made a humming sound. "I do sense a lot of pain in her."

"While I wish to continue our conversation, I have to prepare for a date. Unfortunately, Kipp hasn't responded to my invitation yet."

"Several boys were hurt today, Kipp the most." He clasped his hand on his knee. "From what I heard, he's packing his bags and leaving the competition."

"What? No!"

"As much as I want to be selfish and remain with you, I think it's best to rectify the damages with him before it's too late."

I went to Kipp's door and told the staff I'd knock myself. Never in my life had I knocked on a door before. My staff always did it for me.

But Kipp was worth it.

"I'm not to be disturbed," Kipp shouted through the door. I knocked again. "I told you, I'm stepping out of the competition." I knocked again; this time he answered. "Tell Her Maj—Qloey?" Once he saw me, his heart changed tune by letting me inside. His bag was already on the bed and fully packed with the few leather jerkins, doublets, trousers, and tunics that he owned.

"Please stay," I pleaded.

"I'm done." He sat on the bed and looked at his fingernails as if not willing to admit that he wanted me to convince him to remain.

"Leave," I told the staff. "What I'm about to say could ruin my chance at becoming empress someday."

He stopped fiddling with his fingers. "You're the crown princess; nobody else can inherit the throne."

"Not if the empress and emperor do something about it. You see, I've always swum against the grain. The ruling class who influences the crown always controlled what I did, how I did it, and when. But as of late, I've made my own choices that they don't like. They're pressuring me, forcing me, really, to agree to certain protocols and even to choose certain bachelors. But I don't want those bachelors. Or their mandates. I want you. I need you. I need you to help me understand my people. I need your help to fix wrongs. I need your support and advice, because I can't do it alone."

"What you said earlier—"

"I was wrong. I did it because of the pressure. And I was confused." I sat next to him and took both of his hands in mine. "I was forced to say that at breakfast, or the empress would've done it herself. And I . . . well, I wouldn't have been in a good position after that. But I was wrong. It wasn't the real me. And that's not how I'm going to rule. Even if . . . things end up badly for me. Please stay. If not for me, then for our people."

"Before this morning, you inspired me. I liked you . . . well, I still do. But I couldn't stand hearing you say that and I wanted to rise up and rally the people against all you idiots."

My lips slightly lifted into a smile. "Perhaps you can help bring in more positive change."

He looked away. "Only if my presence means you idiots will stop making dumb policies, perhaps I'll stay."

I took no offence to his insults, knowing he was hurting inside. "This idiot sitting next to you will try."

He chuckled, but still wouldn't look at me. "Fine. I will stay a little while." He crossed his arms as if he wasn't ready to fully forgive me yet.

"Thank you. Perhaps this idiot over here should also spend more time in the crystal chamber. Not sure which color to choose to heal idiocy."

"You don't need more time in the crystal chamber." Kipp finally looked at me. "And you're not really the idiot, the people trying to control you are."

"Does this mean you'll still go on the date with me?" I gave him a pouty look. "I planned this one well in advance."

"I will."

"Good, because I have some things for you." I jumped up, clapped my hands, and ordered the servants to bring the presents inside. I gave Kipp the most expensive date. He was a commoner, after all, and I wanted him to experience the royal treatment for once.

"This outfit was tailored for you." I gave him an entirely new outfit, fit for a prince. It consisted of large puffy canions, with a matching navy-blue and silver doublet and cloak, plus a feathered hat, and blue leather gloves. It also included new boots and a special gift. . . .

"I wanted to give you the gift of a nobleman." A servant handed me a sword. The casing was studded with sapphires and engraved with the story of Kipp's life. It showed him growing up at Orb Theater, adventures to the palace, and the magic pumpkin ride after the game show.

"Wow!" Kipp admired all the intricate detail. "This is fabulous!"

"You're famous now. As a gentleman, you need your own sword. But I'm afraid because one of the bachelors is trying to kill me that we can't take it on our date."

"Fair enough."

"And . . . there's one more thing." The last servant brought out a warm apple pie.

"Bribing me with sugar, I see." He licked his lips.

Kipp, Actor. Human. Age 17. Won the Velazian commoner competition. Actor at the Orb Theater. Interests: Theater, fairy tales, & apple pies.

Kipp smoothed out the rich brocade doublet with silver leaf designs while standing at the top of the stairs. He looked confident in these garbs as he descended the palace steps—a new man. The servants bowed and curtsied to him as he came, as if he were the next emperor. This moment was for him to feel special; therefore, I waited to receive him at the bottom of the stairs.

My large gown had a low v-cut with ruffles on the sleeves and was made of the same fabric as his so that we looked like a couple.

"Your Majesty." He kissed my hand. "Do you really see me as a potential husband?"

"If you'll accept *me,* then you're one of my top choices."

His eyes glistened in the light. "I'm forever grateful simply to be in your presence." He held my hand to his heart.

We entered the royal carriage together and then I opened up a conversation of interest to me. "Tell me about your acting life."

"Really, I'm not an actor. My parents are servants to actors in the theater; I follow in their footsteps. They put 'acting' on my profile to make me look better. I was born in the theater, you know. The first sentence I ever spoke was a line from Pippa's play."

"Have you ever thought about writing your own plays?"

"Writing my own play? Well . . . if I ever get the opportunity, yes. But I'm illiterate," he said.

I grabbed his hand. "You made it to the palace already; you can make it further."

The four horse carriage stopped at our destination. "Your Majesty." Takaya knocked on the carriage door and encouraged us not to linger too long.

We made our way to the royal box seats in the Orb Theater. "I figured you never watched a play from the box seats before and wished to give you the royal treatment."

"The best part is that I'm sitting next to you." He offered me a smile.

We watched Pippa's play about two lovers from different classes who find a way to marry and live happily ever after. It was my third time watching this play, yet I'd watch it three more times if Kipp were by my side. After the play was over, Pippa, the great writer, came onto stage and curtsied to the audience. Then she motioned to us. "To the future empress of the Velazian Empire!"

We waved down to the cheering audience.

"Your Majesty Princess Qloey, His Greatness Kipp, my friends . . ." Pippa opened her arms to the audience. "If you would, please join us on stage to read the lines from my new unpublished play."

Everyone roared in excitement.

I didn't have time to read her play yet, but was enthralled by this chance. It was my greatest hope to be on Pippa's good side, so she would write a play about me someday.

"Your Majesty, it's too dangerous." Takaya warned.

"It's safe in here—" Kipp began.

"You have NO idea of the dangers!" Takaya snapped.

I put my hand up. "Sir Takaya! Address His Greatness Kipp with respect. I will not have you talking to the candidates in this manner." I defended. "Now, did you not secure the building?"

"We did, but, Your Majesty, please," Takaya pleaded.

"I trust you. It will be alright." I smiled tenderly at him.

Kipp and I stepped onto the stage while holding hands.

"Before we begin"—Pippa turned to Kipp and announced to the audience—"Kipp, I wish to offer you a position as my personal assistant after the competition."

Kipp's mouth fell open. Winning the spot on the RMC surely had its advantages. "That's so gracious of you Pippa, but I was planning on becoming the next emperor." Everyone burst into laughter, with the silent knowing that it would never actually happen.

Or would it?

Then I imagined him ruling by my side and smiled to myself knowing such a scenario would make me happy.

Pippa offered us both one page from the play, but Kipp gave it to me. "Can you read it to me?"

"As we go along?" I asked. This piqued my curiosity.

"No. All at once. I'll remember."

I didn't believe him, but read the whole page, anyway. He soaked in every word, then stepped into the spotlight and spoke with perfect fluency.

I read my first line like my other speeches, as though this was a serious matter that must be addressed immediately, but it was a play and didn't come out right. "It's not a speech to the press, it's acting." Kipp came and whispered in my ear. "Speak with emotion. Feel the character's passion as you go."

Kipp recited his next line with spirit, using the whole stage as his playground.

Next, Pippa narrated that a sorcerer put a spell on Kipp. The woman was supposed to cry over her lover, who had lost his memory.

Kipp whispered into my ear. "Say it as if I died, and you were heartbroken."

I closed my eyes and looked at him with this new perspective. If Kipp died, my heart would tear into pieces. This time, I spoke fervently. "For thou art my lover, my confidant, my courage. Without thee by my side, I shall never love again."

"Awe," the audience murmured.

Then Kipp faked being ill from the spell. I was to break the spell, or he'd forget me forever. Real tears formed in my eyes. The crowds became thrilled.

"You!" Kipp said. "A faint recognition. Who art thou?"

"Thy fiancé!"

Kipp lifted a hair off my face. "A faint remembrance. But how shall thy ever know the truth?"

We reached the end of the page. Pippa then handed me the last line on a new sheet of parchment. I looked at Pippa in shock. Then back at Kipp. Then to the constable.

We were in public.

The crowd leaned in closer, waiting.

"What is the line?" Kipp asked.

It's okay. It's okay. I gathered the courage.

"Thou shall know from a kiss of true love." I stared deep into his eyes. "A kiss to break thy spell."

Kipp gulped. There was silence on the stage for a moment, and then Kipp made up his own line.

"Dost thou speak truth? A simple kiss is all ye ask? If true, thy love shall return. If not, thy shall bid thee farewell. But how can thy ask this great maiden for such a favor?" Then he whispered to me. "You don't have to. We can make up a . . ."

"No." I put a finger on his lip.

He looked at me with bright eyes. "Are you sure?" he asked.

I put an arm around him. "Without a doubt."

Our lips touched. The audience jumped up in applause. But the kiss didn't end there. We stood transfixed in each other's embrace, enjoying the moment, as the world around us erupted into applause.

How I wanted to do that again.

"Her Majesty and His Greatness Kipp." Pippa curtsied to the audience.

Pippa did this on purpose. But I was glad.

Meanwhile, Takaya's arms were crossed with steam coming out of his ears.

CHAPTER 29

The Most Compatible

(The Bachelors)

"Truly, I thought everything in the empire was spiraling into despair." Edgar wore off the ears of everyone at the breakfast table.

Alejandro sometimes tolerated Edgar's incessant babble, but having too much wine the previous night as he partied with Zack, Clayton, Octavio, and Abdulla on the rooftop, meant he was in no mood to absorb Edgar's early morning dissertations.

"But my position has changed." Edgar almost formed a smile while talking with food in his mouth. He was pleasantly surprised with Qloey's last stance the previous morning; but became fearful when the empress threatened to release him to the centaurs if he didn't fix his mistake when he criticized the crown. However, Qloey made it easy for him to speak kindly about her; all day yesterday he had nothing else to speak about except this one wonderful change of tune to the RMC.

With his neck tall and his eyes glancing off into the distance, he continued to express the wonderful feeling of gratitude his heart felt. "Yes, changed indeed. The princess will make an indelibly excellent, fantastically fantabulous, eminently estimable empress, especially if she increases the wealth of our people." By "our people" he meant his own pockets. And with that, he cut up another pea sized bite of his sausage.

McKinley and Kipp glanced at each other from across the table in annoyance, both withholding a roll of their eyes. McKinley inhaled deeply and returned his focus to his poached egg smothered in hollandaise sauce.

A maid with the cutest dimples on her cheeks returned to the room to place more sausages on the table. Alejandro reached over to grab a sausage, but instead rubbed his hand against the maiden's. She blushed and batted her eyelashes. Alejandro winked and then watched as she walked out of the room, his eyes fixed on her backside.

Qinrel witnessed Alejandro's salacious eyes wander, but said nothing to avoid undue drama.

Only one seat was empty at the breakfast table. Zack just finished his morning wall squats and was flexing his muscles in the mirror when he suddenly decided to run and leap over the backrest of his chair. He collapsed into his chair with a thud, jiggling the entire table. His hand landed on the edge of his spoon, causing it to fling into the air, and whiz right past Zazan's head.

Zazan froze mid-bite.

"Dear heavens, Zack!" Clayton burst out of his hawk-like focus on his food. "If you spilt my breakfast all over my new purple velvet—"

"You'll survive." Zack patted Clayton's arm so hard, Clayton had to rub it.

Clayton was almost annoyed, except Zack always had a bright smile and positive outlook on life that it was hard to hold a grudge against him for too long.

Finally, Lancelot stood to leave the room. Hedgewood decided to follow suit when the crown princess entered the room.

(Qloey)

"Qloey," Hedgewood whispered as I stepped inside. I hoped he was the one listening to me and McKinley yesterday; so he may know my true stance. This was confirmed when he escorted me to the head of the table without any animosity toward me.

"Excellent position you took yesterday. Simply—"

"Shut it, Edgar!" I hushed him up.

"I—ih . . ." He hushed up and obeyed.

I addressed everyone. "Yesterday my words were very harmful to a lot of people. I want to make it clear that Gappy will continue to be employed as my personal mantuamaker, and Fred will have a position somewhere cutting gems; where he's most qualified. Our civilization needs all the talent we can find. This empire has digressed in the last hundred years, and I will do everything in my power to repair damages and improve the lives of our people. It's expected to rain today and the group date will be held inside the drawing room. It will commence in an hour." I left the room to prepare.

This time, Alejandro followed me out the door.

"My beautiful flower." He kissed my hand five times, which made me glow inside. "My heart aches when I'm not with you. May we spend this time together before the group date?"

"For a few minutes. I have something to attend to before the date."

"I sleep with your painting on my wall. Always wondering when we'll be with each other in private again."

This moved me. "You're such a sweetheart. Tell me about yourself, Prince Alejandro, something I don't know," I said.

"I am a simple man who enjoys the fruits of life." He had a slight accent that added to his attractiveness. I decided to speak in his native language of Ogarzian to enjoy a more private conversation. Yet, I did so *without* a Velazian accent.

"What are your aspirations in life?"

"To make you happy." His flattery never ended, but as endearing as it was in the beginning, I was ready to find a serious partner with realistic views, and parading around with one-liners would only last so long. He continued, "Ah, but I do work on many charities, one for an orphanage in my city and for a school. You like charities, yes? Always wanting to help the people." Again, he put a hand on my back and walked as close to me as possible. I felt the heat of his chest. "But really, I want to focus all energy on helping my wife. For you have a big role to fill."

"That is wonderful to hear." But was he mentioning it because I liked charities or because he liked them?

"You inspire me. From the moment I saw you, my heart was stolen," he said. "It is my greatest hope you'll choose me in the end."

Choose him? I tried to imagine him as the emperor, but it brought up some issues. His profile didn't disclose that he was a politically active person, and I didn't like how he attacked Hedgewood during their sword fight. Luckily, the competition today would help me determine everyone's true stance and the extent of his political knowledge. I had hopes for him.

Rain lightly tapped against the window as we walked by. Abruptly, he stopped me by placing an arm on the glass behind me. Servants kept their eyes downcast as they strolled down the marble floored hallway. Despite the servants being respectful of my privacy, public affection still made me self-conscious. My shoulders caved in, hoping he would wait until we were somewhere private, but I quickly corrected my posture and stood tall to face him. As the empress, I had to be strong and never cower away from situations, or the court and my parents would continue to try and control me.

He came on so strong in the beginning, and even tried to kiss me on the first date, but was it a long-lasting love or a fling?

He gave me the most charming crooked smile. "You don't know how badly I want you." Our faces inched closer together as he stroked my chin. "I'll give you all my time. All my attention. All my love." His lips lightly caressed mine. They felt fuller and softer than the other boys.

Our kiss didn't last long. He pulled away, just as quickly as he came on. "I will win today's group . . . for you."

"Prove that with your actions." I smirked, then turned to walk away.

"Councilwoman Sonya." I pulled Sonya aside before the competition began. All the contestants were already gathered inside the drawing room, on-time. Punctuality was important. "I had no idea Prince Alejandro was into charities. He didn't seem like a . . ."

"Charitable type?" Sonya wore a light green-colored vest with trousers since she had to run around the palace all day.

"I just want validation." If Alejandro cared about them, why didn't he tell me earlier or make a more impressive profile? I wanted to believe he would make a great emperor, but needed proof. "Also . . . see if any servants know if my picture is on his bedroom wall."

"I'll look into it, Your Majesty."

To my delight, Hedgewood now approached me. I desperately wanted to discuss the events of the previous morning. But before we could say anything, Yenna made an announcement: "The quiz is about to start."

"Afterwards," I said.

He squeezed my hand. That one simple touch made my heart flutter like a butterfly.

I stepped in front of the contestants. "It's vital that whoever stands by my side is compatible with me in our views and shares similar world-views. Becoming the next emperor is not a simple task. The emperor must also have the ability to problem-solve, think on their feet, and be of service to our people. Thus, you'll all be given political scenarios, and you must write down your solution."

I handed the floor to Yenna, who wore a gray and white dress today of its usual dull nature. "The answers are anonymous, but your boards will be numbered on the back, so we may identify the winner. You'll have one to three paragraphs to write your answer. The first and second place in each round will receive ten points, third place will receive nine, fourth place will receive eight, et cetera, et cetera. The most points after seven rounds wins private time with Her Majesty for the remainder of the morning. Several scribes are here to assist you."

I invited the scribes mostly for Kipp, but offered them to everyone, so he wasn't singled out.

"First question." Yenna stood before the boys. "There's a natural disaster that has completely destroyed a small village to the west side of the capital. There are hundreds of survivors now seeking aid. Most lost their homes, their livestock and they have no food or water. How would you address the situation?"

The bachelors scribbled away. Kipp was placed in the corner of the large room so nobody would hear his answers as he spoke to the scribe. Afterwards, a servant picked each paper up, rearranged them, and handed them to me. I instantly began reading them and then sorted each answer on the table in order of favorite to least favorite. Then a servant recorded their points. While I read, Yenna was already giving the next scenario to the competitors.

"Second question," Yenna sounded bored by her job as she read the questions. "The Gremlin Gang is harassing people in the ghetto, forcing people to pay tolls. Crime rates are increasing in this area. How do you effectively handle the issue?"

The answers on each question were diverse. Some wrote a detailed plan like: "building a new Crystal Healing Chamber to heal the victimized people," (likely to be Kipp), to one plan—which won "zero" points—it involved declaring martial law, not allowing anyone to leave their home unless the sun was up.

So disappointing, I couldn't wait to see who that might be, later. While the actual competition was anonymous, I could see who said what afterwards.

Other questions in the quiz were focused on corruption in the palace, how to address decreasing wages and increased poverty, corruption in the military ranks, various issues with the ruby mines that had been brought to me, and the last question was on dealing with the centaurs.

I was a quick reader and could almost finish reading the previous round before the bachelors completed writing their next answer down.

With some answers, I could tell who wrote them. Lancelot's answers were majestically poetic and always received high points. Kipp's were passionate and always advocated for the people and eliminating funds from the palace. Sometimes his plan worked, other times it didn't. I already knew what Hedgewood's handwriting looked like, plus some of his policies were things we already discussed together. Edgar always over emphasized his points with *exorbitantly excessive* adverbs and adjectives. Three bachelors had no political future at all as they clearly put no thought into the answers, but I wasn't sure who they were yet.

After the last round, the servants tallied up the points and quietly informed me of the winners.

Impressive, but not surprising. I happily stood in front of the bachelors. "This was no doubt, the least joyful of all our dates, but it was necessary. I thank you for your time. To congratulate you, I'll reveal the top three choices. In third place, His Highness Prince Octavio of Pixieland." Everyone applauded. "In second, His Grace Lancelot, Duke of Moonstone." More applause. "And for the winner"—I smiled too much, revealing my deep affection—"with the most thought-provoking and realistic answers that will benefit the empire the most, is His Highness Prince Hedgewood of Adonis Peak Kingdom."

Edgar's jaw dropped, but he quickly closed his mouth and looked around, probably hoping nobody saw his fly trap wide open. Clayton leaned against the back windowsill with his eyebrows furrowed and his arms crossed like a sore loser.

I couldn't wait to find out who the last few places were! But right now, it was my alone time with my beloved Hedgewood.

A cool breeze sprinkled mist on my face as the rain turned to a drizzle. The sun peaked out of the clouds, creating a double rainbow arching over the palace. We held hands while we walked across the roof of the palace.

The palace was built on a hill overlooking the city. We could barely make out the far end of the city where a wall protected the inhabitants. Behind us were rigid mountains with sharp points and a little bit of snow resting at their peaks. There was an assortment of wine, grapes, figs, and dates spread across an extended coffee table with green cushions for us to sit around, and because Hedgewood won, I ordered that fresh berries be picked for him.

I remembered what the empress said about choosing one of four contestants, but I couldn't. Just couldn't. My heart went out to five *other* boys not on the list, and their support showed me that I had allies. Plus, this was *my* Matchmaking Competition. Not hers! There was no point in having the RMC at all if I couldn't choose. She has to give in to at least *one* of these boys. If not . . . well, then I'd reveal the truth to the people that the RMC treaty wasn't being honored. It would put the empress in a very bad position. But would she truly give the crown to my younger brother? Could she legally do that?

My stomach curled thinking of it.

Clearly, Hedgewood was one of the best choices for me in terms of a political partnership. Except our match would be the most controversial and would come with many challenges from critics. Yet the more we interacted, the stronger my feelings for Hedgewood became. Recently, I couldn't help feeling the desire to impress him more than the empress. He was amusing, smart, eloquent, princely, handsome, strong . . . and from this quiz, I knew he was "perfect."

Just perfect.

Thus, I went on this date, knowing full well there was a possibility for marriage here. But a question weighed on my mind: does he have feelings for me or was this a one-sided affair?

We stopped at the railing and absorbed the beauty of the rainbows that arched above us. Two doves flew by.

"I'm not surprised you won." I stood close to him, just as Alejandro always inched closer to me.

"I'm surprised you chose me," he admitted.

"Why? Do you doubt me? Although, after my poor actions yesterday, I can see why. I'm so sorry for what I said . . ." I glanced downward.

He gently touched my back. Almost in a half-hug. He spoke in a gentle manner, "Your words were hurtful. But I know your burden. And you rectified your ways. That's what matters. Learn. Grow. Correct yourself. That's life. I forgive you."

"I . . ."

"No need to say anything more. You're here with me now. That's what matters."

He was so close. Close like in the maze.

I inched even closer. "Your opinion means more to me than anyone else's here."

His eyes lit up.

Realizing.

What might be there.

My chest slowly rose and fell. Our closeness was suffocating.

"Hedgewood..." I had to tell him. Had to know which direction to go in, to either let him go and focus on other bachelors, or pursue him "I'm ... I'm sorry if this is wrong. Please tell me if my feelings are misplaced. And if I should let you go . . ." My heart raced, not knowing if I was making a mistake by revealing this. I felt too vulnerable and wrung my hands together trying to come up with what to do. *Okay, just say it.* "I'm ... I'm falling in love with you."

He stood there for a moment; saying nothing. Then he turned away from me, took his hat off, and stared at the ground in silence.

Oh dear. He doesn't love me. Tears welled up inside, but I pushed them back down.

"I'm ... I'm sorry," I apologized. *Oh, I feel so stupid. And embarrassed.* "It's a matchmaking competition after all, how could I not think of you in this manner?" I pressed my fist against my forehead. "But after what you said on our first date, I understand why you don't find me appealing. It's just ..." I kept explaining, hoping it'd take away the stain of him not returning the feeling. "Not only do you fit the position of the emperor perfectly, you're smart, knowledgeable, and have great ideas, but you fit everything else I want in a husband; you're handsome, humorous . . ."

I never got the rest of the sentence out. He threw his hat on the cushions and spun around. "Do you mean it? Is this real?"

I nodded.

He took two large steps toward me and devoured me. I melted into his warm body as we passionately kissed.

Unlike the other kisses, I fully put myself into it, wrapping my arms around his neck and pulling him in, molding my body into his. Our lips worked in unison, perfectly aligned to each other as if we were two stars who made up a constellation.

This time, no audience watched us, and thus there was no holding back. Just his lips against mine.

We shared a passionate embrace for quite some time.

And I never wanted to stop.

Prince Octavio of Pixieland

CHAPTER 30

Making Choices

Octavio, Prince of Pixieland Kingdom. Human. Age 16. Survived a winter while living in an igloo amongst polar bears and penguins. Interests: Playwriting, dancing, snowball fights, & listening to nature wisdom.

"Prince Octavio, we finally have time together." I was overly excited . . . not about Octavio, but about the recent development with Hedgewood!

Hedgewood loves me too! Oh, the joy! I sang inside with a smile superior to Octavio's, even on the brightest day.

The sun was setting with the most beautiful orange, purple, and pink hues that I ever saw before. Octavio and I were to have dinner in the Secret Garden. The fireflies added a wonderful decorative touch to the hundreds of candles which lit the area for us.

"Your knowledge in politics is impressive," I complimented.

"It is delightful to know we share similar views, not simply for the competition, but overall, for the relations between our people." He smiled brightly.

I didn't want to leave Hedgewood after our date. We spent the entire morning together, then we ate lunch. After lunch—where we kissed so much my lips hurt—Hedgewood and I went over the books he gave me at the opening ceremony. Most were on dwarven literature and fairy tales unheard of in the human realms. But I enjoyed them and wished to learn everything about dwarven culture now! But one afternoon with him just wasn't enough. Only a lifetime could satisfy my passion for him. I barely had time to change for Octavio's date. Victorya kept my hair the same and just changed my dress to a striped gold and white one.

Octavio was a well-rounded individual, but my thoughts kept straying to Hedgewood. After looking over the dwarven literature, we cuddled on the couch and shared stories about when our feelings for each other first began, also what doubts we had, and overall thoughts about the competition . . . and, well, everything.

We literally shared everything!

"Something wonderful came over you." Octavio ended my daydreams.

"Ah yes, well I had a wonderful day today. But enough about that . . . this is your special day," I said.

"You're in love aren't you?"

Octavio caught me red-handed. My smile reached to the moon. "I . . ."

"It's okay to admit it. You've developed deep feelings for the other bachelors already as you've had more time with them than myself." Octavio was so mature about it.

"I'm sorry. Are you upset?"

"Pixies teach happiness." He beamed in delight. "It's their hope everyone can experience it. I can only be happy for you. This is wonderful news!"

"I'm afraid I'm falling in love with a few of the bachelors. Oh, how I never realized I could love several boys at once, let alone one," I admitted.

"The heart has unlimited space for love. Always expanding. But I imagine it's too late for me to enter that space."

"Oh, Octavio, I will give you an equal chance." I now believed in giving all the boys opportunity.

"It's okay." He smiled kindly. "You're a beautiful, powerful, smart, and a promising leader to your people. Any of us will be lucky to end up with you. I didn't act quickly enough when we arrived. But perhaps the stars simply weren't in the cards for us."

"It's okay, we have time to get acquainted now."

He chuckled. "That's so sweet of you. Oh, Princess Qloey, I'm happy for you. Do not waste time on *me*. You need to use what time you have left to choose which of these lovers you want the most."

"You're such a sweet and wonderful man, Prince Octavio." We both knew what this was coming to. "But I don't want to break this off too early."

"It's okay. I'll accept the mutual rescission, knowing . . . someone is out there for me, waiting for our love to blossom." He smiled as his mind drifted into the clouds. "Perhaps you and I can remain friends and help each other where needed."

"I would love that. You are welcome to visit Velazia anytime."

At this point, I was ready to start letting bachelors go and focus on my favorites.

The evening was still early, and I thought about knocking on Hedgewood's door, but then I saw a glimpse of Prince Qinrel standing outside on the balcony. He was deep in meditation, as if his mind soared into the ethers where none other could visit.

Qinrel was wonderful to be around, but he wasn't at the top of my list and I might have to let him go too. But at that moment, the moonlight created a halo around his masculine energy field, and he vibrated with spiritual wisdom. Just being in his presence and I filled up with everlasting joy. He was irresistible to my feminine instincts. *I can't let him go yet. Not until I have a ring on my finger, and I know for sure.*

I stepped onto the porch, and he swiftly jolted out of trance. "Your Majesty." He bowed. His light skin was perfectly smooth and bright, and his long black hair was lightly taken by the breeze. "Your date with Prince Octavio ended early."

His charm made me forget all troubles in life. It was addicting. "I'm coming into more understanding of whom I'm compatible with and whom I'm not. Whom my heart belongs to and whom it doesn't. Prince Octavio is a wonderful human, but we've decided to sign the papers."

He was surprised. Then, as if I could feel his thoughts, I sensed he was afraid I'd let him go prematurely too.

"Worry not . . ." I took his arm. "It was a mutual decision."

He eased up.

"What are you doing out here?" Whenever we were alone, I only spoke elven so staff couldn't overhear.

"Looking for the nymphs. I haven't seen them yet to ask your questions, Your Majesty." His eyes glanced into the forest again.

"Do you think they'd let me see them?" My eyes twinkled.

"Would you like to take another walk and find out?"

We stepped onto the path together. The guards never liked when I went out here at night. "You had some very interesting answers in the quiz." I brought up. "Some perplexed me, and I wasn't sure if they would get past the council. Yet you had limited space and time to write your answers, perhaps if you elaborated more I'd get a clearer picture. Nonetheless, they were all concepts that could bring light to the people. I know now that you're reliable and will offer the empire a lot. Not to mention, you help lift me up emotionally in hard times."

"I try to hold the space for you. Love is the greatest remedy. I held love for you while McKinley spoke to you after your breakfast speech, but I knew you'd eventually come out on top," he said.

During the regretful speech, I pushed compassion and love aside; that's why my words hurt so many.

"I will need assistance like that in the future." I said as our boots crunched on rocks underneath us, while we traversed the pathway. "Facing the aristocracy. Challenging the court. Gaining the courage to pick my own husband. Changing the way we do things. The common people need a real leader who stands up for them, and I can't do it alone. More than once you've demonstrated that you have the ability to help with this change. How is your elf kingdom faring?"

"Reduced wealth from the empty mines made some go into survival mode and commit acts of corruption," he admitted. "This ultimately lowered the consciousness of our elven people. But we're trying to stamp out corruption and reintroduce spiritual values. If I may be frank, the treaty between our cities contributed to it. But we're resilient."

"Perhaps together, no matter what happens in this competition, we can work together to create a solution."

His eyes became brighter. "I've no doubt from what you told me about your fairy goddessmother that you have an important destiny." He pointed down a dirt path. "Can I show you something down there?" The path forked in many directions. We could essentially take the path all the way around the palace; some servants claimed one went to the city gates. "I want to show you a beautiful area."

We playfully skipped down the dirt path leading away from the pond. The soldiers tried to keep up with our pace while smacking bushes out of their way. Qinrel stopped before an overhead trellis and pulled grapes off of an overhanging vine. Then he fed one to me. His warm body was so close; I could smell his cologne that smelled like fresh raindrops after a storm.

He put a hand on my back. "You're fun to be with, Your Majesty." We stared each other in the eye for a moment. "Other princesses don't

. . . enjoy trivial things like this. I once courted an elven princess from Zazan's city, but . . . she was as stiff as a board."

"Like Edgar?"

We laughed.

"Perhaps you have it worse." He joked, then picked some fresh raspberries and threw them into the air. I tried to catch them with my mouth but kept missing.

"Are you out here a lot? You seem to know every bush and path," I asked.

"I've been trying to find the nymphs to ask them your question, but none appeared. Then I discovered a beautiful seat by the pond. Let me take you to it." His face became softer as he smiled. It looked so innocent and cute when he got excited.

He led me to his special location, where willow trees hung over the pond and dipped their leaves into the water. A natural seat formed on the grass between the willow tree roots. Lily-pads rested on the water's surface with a frog croaking nearby.

He sat down on the grass and placed our lantern nearby.

"My dress will get dirty," I protested.

He took his cloak off and made a seat for me.

The grass smelt fresh, like a rainstorm had just passed through. It was cold to the touch and of a deep green color, as if filled with nutrients.

"Ah, look!" He pointed to an indigo-colored glowing goldfish that was three feet long. "I thought only swans glowed."

"As far as I know, only swans can. This is truly magical!" We drew closer to the water's edge.

A second multi-colored goldfish of gigantic proportions swam up. The two glowing fishes swam in circles. Then the lily-pads started to glow. And the leaves on the willow trees glowed.

"What is happening?" I marveled.

"I don't know. But it's beautiful."

We laid down side-by-side to look at the glowing vines and leaves. Our fingers brushed against each other, causing my nerves to jump on end. I was desperately attracted to him but was too afraid to make the first move. Already, I kissed four boys and worried about adding another to the list. But he could feel my desires for him. Just as I could feel his unending attraction to me.

Did I like him because of my lifelong elf fantasy, because of his charm, or because he was smart, fun, beautiful, and marked off many must-haves on my list?

In the next moment, I felt our chemistry pulling us together like magnets and determined it must be my real feelings.

He responded by moving his fingers on top of mine. He then reached his other hand to my cheek. Our foreheads rested against each other. My heart pulsed rapidly, desperately wanting his body against mine.

Several fairies flew around us; giggling. One released pink dust out of her wand like Cupid. The feeling of love filled the air.

Is the love real or just magic?

Fireflies flew around us in a magical dance. After that, the frogs and crickets sang an entire concert for us.

My hand rested on his chest. Our noses rubbed against each other. I momentarily recalled the other boy's kisses, comparing them, but lost all sense of the outside world once Qinrel wrapped his arms completely around me, drawing my entire body against his. All I could think about was how much I wanted him at that moment.

Our lips smacked against each other in a violent dance. Our passion was unstoppable, overpowering, intoxicating.

I gripped the back of his vest and felt the fine contours of his sculpted body. He responded by kissing my neck, then we both pulled away, knowing the guards were nearby and we were going a little too far.

Yet my body loudly screamed; wanting more.

After a while, we laid together under the trees as he stroked my hair. Both of us absorbed the beauty of the night, occasionally joining in another round of kisses.

CHAPTER 31

Eliminations

"Your Majesty." Councilwoman Sonya came into my bedchambers before breakfast. Victorya and the other ladies-in-waiting were busy attending to my hair, coloring my toenails, and preparing my makeup for my day, while I sat back and relaxed. "I have information regarding Alejandro's painting and charities. I've confirmed that the painting *is* in his room. Also, it appears *his family* does charity balls every year."

"So it's a good cause?"

"Mmm." Sonya pursed her lips.

This didn't sound good. He had the worst score out of anyone during the political quiz. He might be good support as a husband, but had no political motivations, no practical talents, no ambitions except being my husband. I wondered if he was acting with me some of the time. After all, the position as "next emperor" was tempting.

"Some interesting information came in," the councilwoman continued. "He gets a huge tax cut from his donations, however . . . the money from his charities is donated back into his own company."

"So . . ." I looked at Sonya through the mirror. "He's basically getting good publicity for his charities, while donating money to himself, and getting a tax cut in return."

"Correct. And . . . it's not really a charity, it's a lavish ball."

"I don't like this." But . . . my heart was attached. How do I let go of someone I've grown fond of? It was easy to let Octavio go, but not Alejandro. He made me feel loved and cherished at times. I just wasn't ready yet. If anything, he was fun to have around for the remainder of the competition.

"I do have other news. Unfortunately, your mother ordered me to give this list to you." Sonya held out the list of four bachelors I must choose from. "Yenna snitched on you and told your mother how you burnt the previous list she gave you. To this, the empress warned: 'Immediately after the twelfth date, you must reduce the list to these four contestants. You have three more dates left'."

I said nothing.

"Now that I've officially brought the list to you . . . would you like me to burn it?"

A slow smile formed on my lips. This was why I liked Sonya.

"I have a better plan," I said. "There's going to be a few alterations to this morning's schedule, and I need you to enlighten me on the RMC Treaty rules."

"Spoken like a true empress." Sonya smirked. "What are your questions?"

Zazan, Prince of Eldoren Queendom. Water Elf. Age 19. Second child of Queen Biva and King Tolyn. Interests: Water activities such as swimming, cliff diving, & partaking in elven water ceremonies.

On this hot summer day, I wore a lavish light pink and white gown with peplums falling off my stays and decadent lace falling from my elbows.

I never wasted a moment for a fashion statement. Then I addressed my beloved contestants after breakfast with Yenna and Sonya by my side. "Under normal Royal Matchmaking Competition procedures, the first twelve dates are completed within the first two weeks. The contestants who are compatible with the crown are invited to the second part of the competition. We normally offer a ball to celebrate all of you, but . . . we are a few days behind schedule due to the centaur attack. Under article eight of the treaty which states that 'in the event the crown or contestants are in danger or threatened by danger, alterations may be made to accommodate our safety'." I smiled.

Sonya stood right behind me in support of our new arrangement.

"Seeing that hosting a large ball—while the mastermind behind the assassination attempts is running loose—will threaten all of our safety," I said, "we decided to continue on-schedule with the ball tonight."

"We did?" Yenna rummaged through her memory. The council didn't decide on this, in fact, no date was selected regarding when to host the ball.

I continued. "And, to eliminate the potential threat to a large gathering, we'll begin the first round of eliminations today."

"We will?" Yenna's eyes grew to the size of a grapefruit. This was my way of maintaining control of who remains and who doesn't. The decision was made *without* the empress's approval.

"We'll skip the competition today as I wish to spend more time getting to know those who will remain. Now, I will invite you in, one-by-one, for a private discussion on the elimination process."

"Right now?" Worry filled Yenna's face. I knew she was calculating whether or not she had time to run to the empress and warn her of these recent developments.

Knowing Yenna might escape to tattle on me, I continued. "Yenna will be handling all the paperwork for our mutual rescission."

"I will?" She shifted through her papers looking for the right ones.

"All the papers are in the next room, already prepared."

"They are?" Yenna's jaw dropped.

"Come now." I stood tall and walked inside.

Yenna reluctantly followed me inside the room. Sonya remained with the bachelors and invited them in one-by-one in the order of rank from the opening competition.

"Prince Zazan." I smiled as he walked toward me.

Zazan and I weren't compatible at all and I didn't like his charms, especially after experiencing Glynnda's charm. His answers on the quiz were unimpressive, but since we didn't have our date yet and I wished to have good relations with this people, I requested for him to stay; then I'd eliminate him after our private date.

"Your Majesty, it's been a pleasure getting to know you and receiving your hospitality, but I must decline." Zazan had a frown on his face. "You did not receive my elf charms. We are not compatible. Additionally, until this centaur-human issue is absolved, I wish to retreat into elf territory."

Well, he definitely wouldn't be a husband I could depend on!

We only had a few days left to solve the issue before an all-out war with the centaurs, and we had no more leads on the issue.

"I respect your decision, and am pleased to have become acquainted with you," I said.

Zazan politely bowed, causing his ocean blue robes to brush across the floor. After he left, Prince Abdulla was called in.

The handsome prince wore sand and gold colored loose-fitting garbs with part of his chest showing. He stroked his goatee once and bowed to me.

"Dear Prince Abdulla, we had such a great start to our relationship and I've enjoyed playing music with you, but . . . I'm afraid we don't have much else in common." I spoke in the kindest voice I could, for I wasn't familiar enough with his personality to know how he would handle rejection.

He looked forlorn, with his eyes falling to the ground before looking up again to respond. "Music is everything. It makes the world turn. What else is there?"

That answer said enough. He scored second lowest on the quiz because he didn't take political affairs seriously. As the fifth child of a queen, he had fewer responsibilities than his five elder brothers.

"The role for the emperor would take you away from music. Music would become an irregular pastime, and you'd be forced into many responsibilities," I explained. "Do you really want that?"

"I suppose you're right. Although I like you, I desire music more than the role of the emperor."

That went easier than I expected.

"Hedgewood!" My arms went up, and I stepped toward him with a huge grin to welcome one of my favorite contestants.

Yenna noticed my informal greeting with the dwarf and opened her mouth in shock. After I hugged Hedgewood, Yenna fell off balance.

Hedgewood was an absolute yes! And he accepted my invitation to continue the RMC with near tears forming in his eyes.

Then came Edgar. I was surprised to find he did better than Kipp in the political challenge, perhaps because he was a politician and knew the limits of what is permissible to accomplish within the court. He probably "trod lightly" to make himself agreeable to win my favor. It still didn't convince me, so I re-offered the mutual rescission.

"You have not given me a proper chance, Your Majesty. I am here to support and protect you from the dangers lurking about the palace; I have extensive political connections and knowledge, I will make an excellent emperor! And I demand a REAL date. Not some social justice trick," he said.

"Being a politician means addressing ALL social justice issues you're presented with, not complaining about them," I said. "And you've had *two* dates. One forced upon me. But since you're staying, all is well. Now

we'll have someone to hand over to the centaurs when the time arrives."
I playfully tilted my head with a grin.

He whimpered. "Absurd! The Empress will never agree to it. I know
your tricks. You cannot get rid of me that easily! With *me* by *your* side,
the empire will be restored to greatness!" He stomped his way into the
adjacent room.

I gritted my teeth at Yenna. "If I didn't know any better, I'd say Edgar
is up to no good. Maybe he *is* the assassin?"

Despite the controversy surrounding Alejandro, I wanted to keep him
around longer. If anything, we could be friends. Qinrel and McKinley
were both a definite "yes" and Octavio had already left the palace after
our date.

Lancelot, the poor boy never had his opportunity for a date. But he
was such a beautiful writer with a great plan for the empire. Nonetheless,
I needed Lancelot as a safety measure. He and Edgar were the only two
boys remaining on the empress's list. I wouldn't give her such leverage
by eliminating Lancelot.

I was prepared to send my cousin home. We had no chemistry. He
never sought me out and spent the majority of the time with my little brother. Not to mention, his answers on the quiz were disturbing;
even worse than Edgar. He was the one to suggest martial law to suppress peaceful protesters (which wouldn't solve anything), hiring more
troll-bullies to monitor bridges (which would create more violence), and
increasing taxes for the already starved people. He worded things in such
as way as to exclude dwarves, gnomes, and commoners from prosperity,
and enact strict punishments for wrong doers.

When Clayton came in, he was shaking. "Dear cousin, are you well?"
I began.

He stood tall and stern yet was rattled with nerves. "This elimination
came as a surprise. I'm afraid we haven't spent much time together and

now you'll send me home. But I truly wish to stay and try one date with you. Just to get to know you better."

I rather hoped he would've made this elimination easy for me. But compassion won over me again.

"Dear Clayton of Pinecrest, I will honor your request."

And then I'll eliminate him after our date.

He exited the room and Zack bounced in.

"Baron Zaccaria. I do thank you for your gift of the Pegasus," I said. The room suddenly went cold and my face turned white. That wasn't the best way to begin . . . "Despite everything that happened . . . you're thoughtful and entertaining. But I've developed deeper relationships with the others."

"Oh, don't send me home." His arms slumped at his side like a little child who was being punished. "I don't know what happened on our date but—"

"We're . . . simply not compatible." I tried to explain. "I'm looking for something different in a husband."

He dropped his head low. "If it's the Pegasus thing?"

"It is all forgiven. I wish you all the best."

"But . . . but . . ." He didn't know what else to say and walked away with his head down.

"Kipp!" My toes lifted me into the air with a bounce in a way my parents would scold me for. "You look strapping in your new clothes."

Kipp proudly strutted in with the outfit I gave him.

"I would be so honored to have you stay," I said.

"That would make me the first commoner in history that has made it to the second round. You're constantly surprising me," he confessed.

"Oh Kipp, how is this a surprise? After everything we've been through? I wish to keep you close to my heart and thoughts forever," I said.

Kipp happily returned to the bachelor pad.

Yenna cleared her throat after the last contestant left the room. "I'll . . ."

"Report me to Her Royal Majesty now?"

Yenna gave a single nod.

"Just remember, Yenna." I gave her a cold hard stare, "Ezmorelda may be empress now, but *I* will be the empress in the future. Let that settle on your conscience."

I watched from the third-floor window as the eliminated participants departed, hoping Edgar was one of them. Still, I didn't count him as one of my seven boys remaining.

This'll prove to the empress that I'm decisive. I affirmed with my head tall and my back erect, as I doused myself in confidence that I never knew before. *This is my competition! Not hers. She always wanted me to be strong and my actions here prove I have that strength.* I wouldn't allow myself to feel belittled anymore.

Zazan floated down the stairs. He was a full-blooded elf and the difference between him and Qinrel was notable. Qinrel was graceful, but Zazan had more magic about him that was difficult to take one's eye away from. He glided effortlessly with his elven robes fluttering in the wind.

The news reporters rushed to the scene when they heard about the quick and random elimination process. Hopefully, it would send a message to the people that both the dwarf and commoner were accepted by the future empress. A first in the RMC history.

"The elf from Eldoren Queendom also withdrew from my competition before our private-date."

The room seemed to fill with ice as the empress approached from behind. Every muscle in my body froze in fright.

"I, too, watched from this window as the elf stepped into the carriage and returned home without giving me a chance. Not a single Eldoren elf was seen again for nineteen years," the empress said as she paused to watch him. "They enjoy our hospitality; observe our behavior, study the next empress or emperor, and leave."

My legs began to shake with trepidation and my nascent confidence quickly flew out the door. In her presence, I suddenly felt small and worthless again.

"I suppose I should be furious at you for not getting my approval first." She held malice in her tone, yet spoke with soft determination, knowing she was the ultimate potentate.

"You wanted me to be bold and decisive." I defended myself. "You wanted me to be strong and rule with an iron fist. I am."

"The bachelors whom you asked to leave show me that you have *some* intelligence." That was an improvement in her perspective toward me. "Zack will never be allowed to step foot here again. And that Octavio is too cheery; it annoys me."

That wasn't my reason for letting Octavio go. I loved Octavio's cheerfulness. But I wouldn't tell the empress about that.

After Zazan's carriage rode out of sight, Ezmorelda finally turned to face me. "Nonetheless, there remains two contestants who I expect you to eliminate in due time. Toy with their hearts all you want . . . but you will not like the manner in which *I'll* eliminate the dwarf and peasant if you don't do away with them soon." Her threat pierced the air like needles. "And only two remain whom you can choose from in marriage."

A shiver went down my spine; because I wasn't planning on following her orders this time.

Prince Zazan of Eldoren

CHAPTER 32

Gossip

(The Bachelors)

"I shared the first kiss with Her Majesty." Alejandro cockily leaned back in his chair and rested his feet on the table.

The boys, who were participating in the second round of the competition, were slowly trickling inside a room adjacent to the drawing room, where Qloey was talking with each of the contestants.

"Yes, the feel of Qloey's soft pink lips on mine. The gentle touch of her hand as she caresses my arm. Did anyone else experience this?" Alejandro looked around. "No? Nobody kissed the princess? Just me? Well, that doesn't surprise me at all. Our love has no bounds."

Nobody answered, not because they hadn't kissed Qloey, but because they had more respect for her than to gossip about it.

"Well, I guess she wanted to give you all a chance. But . . . I don't mean to get your hopes up." He smirked and rested his hands behind his head. "Seems like this competition is coming to a close."

Clayton now entered the room.

"My man! I knew she had good taste." Alejandro leapt up to pat Clayton on the back, while the other boys gritted their teeth.

McKinley entered the bachelor pad next, followed by Kipp a few minutes later.

"You're supposed to use the servant's door," Alejandro told Kipp as he entered and sat back down. "That's what you are, right? An actor's servant."

Kipp clenched his fist, but he'd be imprisoned the remainder of his life if he hit a royal. Unless he became the emperor . . .

"Enough of this; we're all gentlemen here." McKinley leapt up in Kipp's defense.

"Oh, McKinley, a piece of advice, you're only as good as those you associate with. And mind you, I'm a prince, so show *me* some respect." Alejandro said.

Finally, Prince Hedgewood stood up in support of his two friends. "Don't bring more problems into this palace than there already are. We're here to—."

"I WILL NOT BE SPOKEN TO BY A DWARF!" Alejandro yelled. Meanwhile, Clayton lingered in the background, not getting involved.

(Qloey)

I entered the room where my remaining contestants waited and was surprised to find it filled with tension.

McKinley's hand was on Kipp's shoulder, as if holding him back from a fight. Kipp was red in the face and both of his fists were clenched. Next to him was Hedgewood with his eyebrows furrowed.

To the opposing side of this group was Alejandro, who casually leaned back in a chair, so much that the backrest was pressing against the wall. Edgar was completely red like a tomato, and he faced his opposition with his nose up in the air.

Qinrel, Lancelot, and Clayton stood on edge in the background, staying out of the fray.

"Lords, gentlemen?" I asked the room.

"Oh, my darling." Alejandro leapt out of the chair walked up to kiss both of my cheeks. Every boy in the room watched Alejandro greet me with jealousy in their eyes.

"May we go for a walk?" Alejandro asked.

"In a moment, but I wish to speak about today's schedule first." I smiled to everyone to help ease the tension, turned to Edgar, lost my smile . . . and then smiled again as I addressed the remaining boys. "I'm so grateful you're all . . ." I paused, glared at Edgar, turned away, then corrected my sentence, "that *most* of you are here. Because of the good weather, let us relax together in the garden. There are two more private dates left—"

"Three." Edgar corrected me, adding himself to an extra date. "Just saying, there are *three* dates left."

I ignored him. "*Two* more private dates after tonight. Those *two* being with the Duke Lancelot and Duke Clayton. Let us proceed to the garden."

Now that I was finished, Alejandro held an arm out for me to take.

(The Bachelors)

The bachelor crew—except Clayton and Edgar who chatted alone about Zack's elimination—sat under the gazebo and chat. From afar, they uncomfortably watched as Alejandro slid his hand lower on Qloey's back.

They all cringed.

Alejandro's nose inched closer to Qloey's face while they laughed together. Alejandro kept pulling Qloey's body closer to his in a way that caused the boys to grind their teeth together in irritation. Qloey kept pushing him away, but to no avail.

"We need to do something about this!" Kipp shouted out loud.

"How shall we proceed?" McKinley asked.

"We can all individually bring up Alejandro's bad behavior and illicit intentions to Her Majesty," Qinrel said, finally joining the fight. "Just as Edgar planned to do against Kipp that one day."

Kipp looked about. "What day?"

"After the game show, when the papers said you were a beggar," Hedgewood explained, while Lancelot sat back, not speaking as usual. "They rallied against you and approached Her Majesty to get you eliminated. But she clearly sided with you. I have faith she'll listen to us."

"Her Majesty is intelligent and upright," McKinley affirmed. "But I cannot sit around and let him"—Alejandro put his hands on Qloey's lower back, again. Again, she pushed him away—"to let him fool with her heart."

"I'm not certain who is worse, Edgar or Alejandro." Kipp huffed. "Why *is* Edgar still here?"

Hedgewood sighed. "He won't leave. She offered him the mutual rescission after the game show and again today, but he's insistent on winning the crown. I cannot believe Her Majesty would ask him to remain after her many complaints about him."

None of the boys realized how close Hedgewood became with Qloey, or that she revealed so much to him.

"Do you think he's the assassin?" Qinrel searched Edgar's emotions, but he was too far away.

"It'd be too obvious," McKinley said.

"Unless we're overlooking the fact, because he is so . . . so . . . what's the word?" Kipp noted.

"Vexing," Hedgewood answered.

They all stared at Edgar and Clayton chatting away.

"Clayton can be the culprit as well."

They all turned at the same time to stare Clayton down.

"He's a nervous creature. But what's his motive?" Qinrel asked. "All I sense is anxiety and fear."

None of them answered.

Qinrel scratched his chin. "Separating the empire or causing centaurs to attack wouldn't benefit Clayton. But I also don't feel that Alejandro's truly in love with her. He's faking it. What if *he's* the culprit?"

They glared at Alejandro again.

"It can just as easily be one of us," Hedgewood said.

They all shifted glances between each other, now suspicious of each other's motives. They were so busy judging the boys whom they didn't like that they never considered if one of their friends was the assassin?

McKinley stood. "It's time to end this."

(Qloey)

McKinley and I headed toward the archery range together and I ordered the bow McKinley gave me during the opening ceremony to be brought out. This rare jewel was made of petrified trees from the lost city of Atlantis. As I shot the first arrow, a light streaked through the air, tracing along the path my arrow flew. "What was that?"

He made bullseye, then turned to me. "The Atlantians had far superior technology than us. Some say they even had flying chariots. The light that comes out of the arrows is part of their mystery."

My new bow was powerful. I reveled in the feeling as each arrow was released from the quiver. "I wanted to thank you for knowing who I truly am inside, even when I didn't know," I said.

"I will *always* be there for you." He put down his arrow to address me directly with his lips flat across his face. "And in my concern for you, I wish to bring up a touchy subject."

"You have the freedom to speak candidly."

"My concern is with . . ." He took a breath. "Prince Alejandro."

"Alejandro? What did he do?"

"Well, they are higher ranked humans than all of us."

"They?" I asked and glanced at Edgar, Clayton, and Alejandro chatting to see who McKinley was referring to. Then I looked at the strange group of friends underneath the gazebo: a dwarf, a peasant, an elf, and a human who never talked. A strange crew, indeed. He clearly meant the former group.

"All three of them?" I asked.

"Well . . . I understand that you have feelings for Alejandro, but I'm not certain that his values align with yours. Presuming he *has* values in the first place. He doesn't treat those beneath him with dignity or respect. Perhaps I'm defensive, and I wish to . . . protect you from him and his ways."

But Alejandro always made me laugh and showed great interest in me. *I'd get rid of Lancelot and Clayton before him.*

"I will consider your concern," I said.

We continued shooting more arrows with no more talk of Alejandro.

"You parent's put you to bed every night as a child?" I asked, as this was a new concept for me.

"It is *normal* for parents to do this," Kipp said. "Have your parents never read you a bedtime story?"

"No. I'm . . . not entirely sure my parents love me at all." I thought this was the norm. Kipp's eyes drooped as if he was sad for me. "I mean . . . they are concerned over my well-being. When I was almost assassinated, they were very upset. All those years of training and educating me would go to waste."

"It's not about money or training . . ." He stopped walking to address me directly. "It's about love!"

"Well, my governess loved me." I tried to cheer *him* up since he seemed so upset by this. "My governess told me several times she loved me and offered lots of hugs. But we never told my parents. But now that you think of it . . . my governess did tuck me into bed occasionally, like when I had a nightmare or after a challenging day."

Kipp still had a sad puppy dog expression on his face.

"But now that I know it's normal, I'll tell my children bedtime stories and tuck them in too." My voice became chipper.

"*Our* children," he corrected.

His statement struck me to the core. *Our children*? I'd have children with one of these men. This competition suddenly became real. Then the question became: *which one do I want children with the most?*

We leaned up against a tree away from the other boys. "About the kiss on the stage . . . did you do it because of the pressure or . . ."

I didn't say anything. Instead, I made sure nobody was watching and gave him a peck on the lips. "I did it because I wanted to."

We locked arms on the way back to the group.

"Before we return"—Kipp slowed our pace—"can I bring up an issue that happened today? An incident with Alejandro."

"Oh, no. What happened?"

Qinrel walked me all-the-way around the pond, laughing and sharing in playfulness together. Somehow we ended up behind a tree where the other bachelors couldn't see us. His arm reached around, pinning me between the tree and himself, then he gave me another taste of his lips.

"Your Majesty?" The soldiers cleared their throats. They didn't like the precarious situations I kept putting myself into, like hiding behind trees, going on stage at the Orb Theater, or going on midnight strolls around the pond.

We giggled as we returned to the path.

As we neared the garden where everyone conversed, he kept looking at my hand while stroking it, as if lost in thought. Then he stopped walking, and cleared his throat before bringing up an issue.

"Before I hand you off to one of my competitors, I wish to bring up a touchy subject with you," he said.

Oh, no! The boys were getting vicious with each other.

"You may speak openly," I said.

"There's a certain individual here who may be acting. I just don't sense that his feelings for you are genuine."

"Please explain?"

"I *feel* that Alejandro is attracted to you." He slowed his speech as if treading carefully. "But he doesn't love you."

"That doesn't make sense. He's always so . . . so affectionate. And welcoming. And romantic. He says the most adorable things to me and he's charming."

"Yes, but charming doesn't mean he cares. But love?" He squinted. "I'm sorry, but he's faking it with you as much as he does with the maids."

The maids?

"Dear Hedgewood, have you ever heard of elven charms?" We stopped at the edge of the pond to feed the goldfish. A large one with black, white, and gold splotches puckered its lips.

"Heard, yes. But I cannot say I know much about it. Why?" Hedgewood asked. "Has the elf charmed you?"

I chuckled. "Indeed. I just wonder if it's my true emotions, or his emotions, or if charms act like spells, or if we were being manipulated by fairies."

He nodded. "Fairies can be mischievous. I can research it for you."

"Oh, that would be wonderful. I am so busy with the dates and council meetings that I haven't had much time to myself."

He rubbed his arm against mine. It wasn't like Alejandro, it was . . . warranted. I could kiss him right there. Wanted to kiss him, but couldn't in front of the others.

Perhaps I can find another tree?

"But while we're on the topic of charms . . ." Hedgewood hummed. "That Prince Alejandro, he's quite charming, isn't he?"

"There again with Alejandro! You all planned this, didn't you?" My hands moved to my hips.

"My love . . ." His arm slid behind my back and pulled me closer.

Oh, I love it when he calls me that!

"You asked me before to analyze the boys. Even though I'm a candidate now, I must point out that an empress needs a man who won't . . . gloat about his experiences with you to the public. Romance should remain private. He hasn't a filter."

I remembered how Alejandro told everyone about our paintings and rose petals on the first date. Did he gloat about everything we did?

"But . . . he's so charming and . . ." I defended.

"You should always be wary of the *charming* ones. Although I'm uncertain if 'human charming' and an 'elf charm' are under the same category yet . . ."

"But...I thought charming was a good thing," I said matter-of-factly. This was the norm in romances. "That all prince charmings are to be desired. What of all the fairy tales where princes are heroes?"

"Charming is often promoted in human fairy tales, but in real life, the charmers know how to woo women, sometimes without caring about them. He's a wolf."

I soaked this in and analyzed my relationship with Alejandro to connect the dots better. Alejandro tried to kiss me on our first date. It was as if he developed feelings before getting to know me, but I did the same for Edgar in the beginning. Perhaps it's the idea of a perfect match or the thought of becoming emperor that appealed to him. Wealth, power, and influence could be tempting, tempting enough to marry someone without caring for them. Something did seem off about him, but I was so taken by his affection for me that I failed to see who he truly was on the inside. My family never showed me that type of warmth.

"He's toying with me."

"Maybe, maybe not. He knows how to flirt and has no boundaries with *whom* he flirts with; princesses, maids, doesn't matter, as long as his lust is satisfied in the end. After that, he'll have nothing to do with the woman. He doesn't have values. No ethics. No restraint. Are his politics even aligned with your own?" he asked.

"He flirts with the maids?" That's what Qinrel implied. "What exactly did he do today?"

"Well, aside from gloating about having the first kiss with you, he—"

"WHAT?" I felt the flame of embarrassment. He told them about our kiss?

Every boy brought up a different negative aspect about Alejandro. There were too many charges on him now that I wouldn't tolerate another moment of his presence.

I turned on my heel and headed straight to the Ogarzian prince with my fists together, like I was ready for battle and had one target. The boys in the gazebo grew alarmed and sat at the edge of their seats. Alejandro was smiling with his buddies, but took one glance at me and dropped his goblet.

"Prince Alejandro! Did you gloat about kissing me in public?"

"P . . . public? I said nothing to news reporters," Alejandro said.

"But you were gloating to all of us." Kipp abruptly stood up.

"You openly talked about all your experiences with Her Majesty to anyone with an ear," McKinley said and stepped out of the gazebo.

"Prince Alejandro, it is imperative to support and protect your wife, no matter the occasion." I said. "You should seek to improve our image, not your ego's image. This means keeping romance private, unless it's agreed upon beforehand. Normally, I wouldn't bring this matter up in *public*, but seeing you already did, I'm inclined to address it likewise. Do you understand?"

"Ye—yes, Your Majesty. Please forgive me, my love," Alejandro pleaded.

"I would. However, it's also been brought to my attention your illicit behavior and mistreatment of the other bachelors, and illegal siphoning of funds from your 'charities,' among other things, which I won't tolerate. You don't have what it takes to make a benevolent leader, emperor, or husband."

"What did that dwarf just say to you?" Edgar tried to turn the focus on Hedgewood.

Suddenly, every boy joined in the argument. There were two sides to this fight, my group of favorite boys vs Edgar, Alejandro, and Clayton. Each side brought up something they didn't like about the other group. Many harsh words were spoken.

"QUIET!" I raised my voice above their bickering. Then I turned to the silent one. "Your Grace, Lancelot, Duke of Moonstone, there are at least five different accusations against Alejandro, including bullying and mistreatment of the other bachelors, and flirting with my maids, are any of these true?"

He stood up and nervously squeezed his hat in his hand. "Y-yes, Your Majesty. All."

"So that's five witnesses. You and Edgar are invited to leave before the ball. I'll have nothing to do with either of you." I started to leave, but stopped myself. "And for the record"—I smiled at my boys with a seductive look in my eyes—"Alejandro didn't have my first kiss."

Alejandro got on his knees. "Please, my darling. I meant nothing wrong. Only to share my love with you."

"You meant to share our love with the rest of the world and my maids." I ascended the stairs.

"No, I . . . they . . . they're lying to you!" he shouted from behind. "You dare listen to a dwarf and knight over me?"

I spun around with a menacing glare, as if ready to eat him alive.

"I—I—didn't mean that." He pulled his arm back, retreating his statement.

At that moment, I was the core decision maker with five wonderful boys backing me. I felt like a real, powerful, decisive empress for the first time, and it felt good.

"May I safely escort you back?" McKinley, Qinrel, and Kipp eagerly ran to my side, satisfied by Alejandro's elimination. I looked back and saw Lancelot and Hedgewood going back to get their hats on the table.

"Of course." I gently put my hands out for them.

"Suits Alejandro for wearing trousers two sizes too small." Kipp laughed.

With my heart lifted and a huge grin on my face, I took McKinley on one side, Qinrel on the other, and Kipp nearly skipping near the windows; we strode down the hall in jubilant laughter.

CHAPTER 33

The Royal Ball

McKinley, Qinrel, and Kipp may have been the ones to escort me from the event, but it was Hedgewood who pursued me afterwards. I leaned back, cuddling with Hedgewood on the couch as we read Pippa's new play. We weren't allowed to be unchaperoned together, therefore, Victorya silently hand-stitched a skirt on the other side of the room while we snuggled by the dead fireplace. In due time, Victorya attempted to pull me away to prepare for the ball.

"I don't want to go to the ball. Or my date with Lancelot. Or Clayton. I'm ready for this to end." My head rested on his chest.

"For this, I may advise one of two things." Hedgewood measured. "Ditch both of them after five minutes and return to me. Or . . . scare them away by mentioning their aristocratic crimes to the homeless."

We both cracked up in laughter. He squeezed me tighter.

"Oh, I suppose I must get up." I tilted my head up, and he leaned down to kiss me. "Five more minutes," I pleaded.

"Royal duties first." He urged me on.

At the door, I gave Hedgewood one last kiss before preparing for the ball. "I'll see you in one hour, my love." I was head over heels.

My ladies-in-waiting dressed me in an extravagant sapphire blue dress with translucent wings that resembled a fairy queen—designed by Gappy, who was still employed.

"Forget the new ruby and moonstone jewels; I'll wear the old sapphires," I told Victorya.

It was a political statement, as the former gems represented Edgar and Lancelot. But sapphires were mined in the dwarf kingdom. And it was a discreet way to test the empress's reaction.

Despite the reduced list because of the attacks, there were plenty of nobility present to make an enjoyable party. Nonetheless, each attendee, servant, and soldier would remain accounted. There were also sword-fighting maids stationed around at all times. No masks were allowed to this magical creature themed ball.

Each bachelor was announced on entry. Edgar was first, as decreed by Empress Ezmorelda. He was dressed like a green extra-terrestrial, in bright green trousers and a tunic, with two antennas sticking up off his head. He looked ridiculous. The empress greeted him and his family with warmth. "Dear Edgar's been working with us on a new private date plan. It'll be much enjoyable for you both."

"We've already—"

The emperor pinched my arm and bared his teeth, then spoke in a tone of great severity. "You will give him his time, or we'll resort to other methods to ensure it."

Surely, the emperor had to know that once I was empress, I would be higher ranked than him, but he also had to remain on the empress's good side.

King Edward stood at my right and happily joined in conversation with our families. They were all planning something, I could feel it. *But it's my competition.* I clenched my fist.

After all contestants greeted Edgar and my family, the emperor led me in the first dance. After this, I was required to dance with each of the contestants.

"I'm disappointed with your choices lately," the emperor said as we danced. "You disgrace your family with your associations."

"The empress always condemned me for not being strong and decisive enough. Now that I am, you condemn me further? Why can't you ever be happy with me?"

He paused for a moment, as if wondering this himself, then gave a half-hearted response. "She gave you an order, to ensure the dwarf and commoner wouldn't make it past the elimination ceremony, which you disobeyed. We hope you're . . . mentally sound enough to make a good decision in this competition. If not . . ." He left the words hanging as he escorted me to Edgar for the first dance.

Mentally sound? Would they make the case I'm not mentally healthy enough to inherit the throne?

A shiver of anxiety ran through my body.

Edgar was a perfect dancer. Perfect on paper, that is, just as I was. But I learned that there was so much more to a relationship.

"One more dance," Edgar said.

"You. Will. Comply with the rules or I'll send you to your room again." He let go. "All contestants get one dance." I put on a fake smile and walked off to the next contestant, who should've been the first to dance with me since he was a foreign participant.

"I see you chose sapphire." Hedgewood was dressed like a golden sphinx. His entire outfit was gold, with faux cat paws resting on top of his hands. Two cat ears also stood on top of his head.

"Yes," I murmured. "This sapphire necklace was a gift to my grandmother during her Royal Matchmaking Competition."

"Ah . . . and of course you wore them to honor her?" He smirked.

"Of course. Why else?" My smiling eyes found his. He looked so handsome in his gold outfit. His strong, thick arms held me in a protective embrace, yet I wondered if they could hold up to what was coming for us. Nevertheless, my body drew closer as we danced; never wanting to leave his embrace.

"You certainly make the gems look more beautiful than they are, my love."

"I love it when you call me that." It was hard to hold back from rubbing my lips or nuzzling my nose against his. If anything, our foreheads could rest against each other, but, no! Such was too dangerous while so many watched us.

But then I wondered how the two of us could ever make it in a world so vicious as my own.

I didn't want to stop dancing with him but had to leave for the next contestant.

"The princess has the most hideous dress." Ednnys gossiped loud enough that I overheard. "I wouldn't touch anything made by a dwarf."

I spun around and walked right up to her and her group of princesses. We were so close that she had to step back to honor my space. "Oh, look Ednnys, you're wearing rubies mined and cut by dwarves. I bet they put their cooties all over it and now you have warts."

Ednnys quietly rubbed her ruby necklace, while looking around embarrassed. As the crown princess, she couldn't argue with me.

The princess of Moonstone smirked from my jab at Ednnys. The Moonstone people had never held animosity toward dwarves and traded often with their kingdom.

My dress was gorgeous. If a human made it instead of Gappy, everyone would want it.

Next up was Qinrel. As he approached, all anxiety from my parents' threats suddenly dissolved. "You always turn my life right side up." I exhaled.

"As I hope to do for the remainder of our lives."

I almost missed a step in the dance, hearing that. *The rest of our lives?* Yet one bachelor stood out in my mind more than the rest.

Qinrel was the most ravishing man in the room, and I felt important dancing with him, as if he wore the crown to the empire, not me. He was dressed as a unicorn in white elven robes but danced like an angel, swift, smooth, and gentle in every movement.

I looked up at the single unicorn horn strapped to the top of his head and chuckled.

"You can wear it later if you want," he joked.

"And look as silly as you do?" I said, making him chuckle.

The room applauded when our dance was over. They would approve of an elf on the throne. But not a dwarf.

"What a beautiful couple they'd make," I overheard Princess Isabella say.

The next song began with Lancelot at my side.

"What is your costume, I cannot seem to figure it out?" I asked.

Lancelot was dressed in blue canions and tights and had a blue Mohawk wig that fell to his waist. "A . . . a hipp—hippocamp," he stuttered.

"Ah, yes, a horse-mermaid hybrid. Wonderful, I see it now." The remainder of our dance continued in silence. My joy returned when he handed me off to McKinley.

"A phoenix, how brilliant! Quite literally," I exclaimed. Bird wings extended from his arms whenever he opened them. But it sometimes made it difficult for him to spin me. I kept running into the feathers and occasionally had to spit one out of my mouth. McKinley was definitely rougher around the edges in terms of dancing and was stiff and humorless in his expression. Nonetheless, I felt comfortable with him.

Clayton was as excellent a dancer as Edgar. He donned a red dragon costume that had several pieces of fabric that looked like scales hanging off of his doublet.

"I knew at least one individual would show up as a dragon." I chuckled in amusement.

"And I knew at least one would be a fairy." His sharp tone sounded more like an insult, especially when coupled with his grave facial expression.

"Are you enjoying yourself?" I asked.

"Yes." He kept his attention on something else—or someone else—in the room. When I turned to look, he quickly spun me in the opposite direction, and I lost sight of where in the room his attention went.

He didn't seem to enjoy the dance and hastily escorted me to Kipp, dropped me off, then just as swiftly walked away without even bowing. For wanting to be in the competition longer, he sure didn't have an agreeable attitude.

Kipp was fast-tracked in his dance lessons and knew all the basic steps and some twists and turns. But his feet movements were choppy. "You make me look better than I am," he admitted.

"That's the goal."

His aura grew brighter. "I'm sorry, I'm just repeating the same moves. Suddenly, I forgot everything I learned. No doubt you want a more exciting dance."

"Nonsense." I rubbed his arm reassuringly. "The joy isn't just in the dance, but in spending time with you."

He blushed.

After our dance, my parents pulled me over to make small-talk with Edgar and his family. "Only two contestants on the list left." The empress whispered a threat into my ear. "I wonder who you'll choose."

Fear coursed through my body, making me shiver despite being hot after dancing. It sounded like she had a plan to eradicate Lancelot.

I didn't say anything and glanced about the ballroom, wishing to be out there with my favorite guests. *With one whom I would marry.*

"Qloey, don't you agree?" the empress asked.

King Edward said something disagreeable, but I couldn't express my true opinions without being controversial myself.

"Pardon, I just saw the Centaurian princess and haven't spoken with her in years. If you will excuse me." I left. My discussion with the princess was short, then I found myself on the dance floor with Hedgewood, once again.

We had a splendid time and didn't fail to display it openly. After the dance, I found the empress sneering at me from afar. Her burning glare tore into my skin; I was taking this too far. My hand started to shake. "Perhaps . . . I shall ask another to dance. Not to cause controversy."

"Controversy?" He was left bemused by my sudden departure.

Edgar had his eyes set on me and weaved himself through the crowds to reach me, so I rushed over to the closest bachelor I saw.

"Prince Qinrel." My voice was shaky.

Qinrel interpreted my distress and saw Edgar approaching. "How about we go to the balcony for refreshments," he said and shuffled me through the crowds until Edgar lost sight of us, then we snuck onto the balcony.

"My parents are . . . planning things behind my back. I—" I gripped the railing for solidarity.

"As I sensed. Around choosing the right bachelor?"

I nodded.

He stroked my arms. "Many guests notice how the empress keeps Edgar's family as company, and that she arranged for you to dance with him first, out of turn, might I add."

"This competition didn't go as they planned." My legs stopped shaking as his energy soothed me. "They're planning something. My stomach is queasy. Let's talk about something else. Anything."

"Anything?" He thought about what to say. "Okay. I contacted the nymphs."

"Really? What did they say? This could change everything!"

"They were alarmed about centaurs roaming about the forest, ready for battle. They claim they hid themselves and waited for the signal of the whistle. Although they were too distracted by the centaurs to see who blew the whistle, some were at the picnic watching us and claimed nobody used *toadstool poison* on the Pegasus."

"What? Nobody? Then how?" My voice quavered.

"Pardon, allow me to clarify. They said it wasn't *toadstool poison* but another. They can tell a plant just by smelling it. The poison on the Pegasus was slow acting and is very rare. It's called *gowler*."

"*Gowler*? I've never heard of it. This means . . . it might not be a competitor. It could be *any* staff member! Or a guest. It makes finding the culprit more difficult." This only added to my stress.

"But still." He stroked my arms and pulled me into a warm hug as the gentle breeze brushed past my hair, taming the sweat from dancing. "If they could pay off the family of a suicide archer during the opening ceremony, they must be rich, indeed."

"You're right. Thank you for the information, but we're still nowhere close to finding the culprit, and the centaurs will attack in a matter of days."

"Not necessarily," Qinrel continued. "They also told me the *gowler* can only be found in one location, so this should narrow our search."

"Where?" I spoke rapidly, as if it'd help find answers to all of this faster.

"Unfortunately, I don't know this region at all, as I'm not from Velazia. Nymphs don't use human names of cities or places. They say things like: 'go through this stream, around this rock, over this hill.' I'm sorry, but it's all unfamiliar terrain to me. But don't let that discourage you; an herbalist might know." He kept trying to soothe me and it was working just by being with him. A moment later and my nerves started to drain out of my feet and onto the balcony.

"Qloey!" We turned to see my little brother and Clayton walking outside together. "Guess what, Clayton's invited me to his estate next summer to learn sword fighting, boxing, and javelin."

"Those are dangerous sports."

"So is archery, and you do that!" he snapped.

This wasn't an appropriate way to speak to his superior. He started being more prickly around me lately. "Right. This is very exciting news." But this meant . . . Clayton had no intention of being *here* next summer and did nothing to get to know me like he said he wanted to. Yet I appreciated Clayton taking the time to get to know Farooq, when I never could. "Dear cousin, if I didn't know any better, I'd say you came to the competition to become acquainted with Farooq." I chuckled.

"We've discovered many things in common, haven't we?" Clayton looked down at Farooq.

"Indeed," Farooq said flatly. "There are secret passages in his estate. And we both climb trees."

"Tree climbing, now, now, that's not a princely activity."

"You sound like a whining mother." Farooq's tone turned callous toward me. I didn't like how either of them were treating me tonight.

"Well, dear brother, the empress and emperor would also say that we must dance together tonight. Formality. Shall we?" I put my arm out, and we took the floor for the next song, while Clayton remained outside on the balcony.

Farooq was still shorter than me and managed fine during the dance, but he could barely twirl me around without getting on his tippy toes. Just as the song picked up, I heard the sound of two metal chains clanking against each other. Suddenly, a piece of glass fell on my head. Then shards began to fall from the ceiling.

I looked up to see the chandelier directly above us. The chains were breaking apart, like someone was sawing away at the metal. Suddenly, the last chain ripped apart with a loud snap and the full weight of the chandelier fell down on top of us.

CHAPTER 34

New Clues

I grabbed Farooq and pulled him to the side. We fell on the ground as the chandelier glass shattered everywhere. The huge metal chains came crashing down, rupturing the granite floor and leaving a large crater where we stood a moment ago.

People screamed and ran in every direction as glass splattered about. The chandelier caught the train of my dress underneath it. Shards of glass sliced through my clothes, making a bloody mess on my back.

Neither of my parents gave me any forethought as they ran toward Farooq and pulled him away.

"He scraped his elbow. Take him to the healing chambers immediately," the empress ordered.

Emperor Ricardo looked down at me, saddened by my state, but then the empress ordered him away and he obeyed. Like he always obeyed. Because not obeying was what led me to the position I currently was in, ostracized, criticized, and abandoned. That was the price to pay for standing up against the empress. He turned away, and the three walked out of the ballroom together while I bled on the floor.

They just left... without me.

My eyes burned as tears poured out.

The guards finally lifted the chandelier off my train to free me. But my family was already gone and I didn't know how to get through this chaos alone or to find my happily ever after.

The empress ordered all of the palace healers to assess my little brother's scraped elbow, leaving me bleeding on my bed as my maids and ladies plucked the glass out and applied alcohol to the wounds. I gnawed at my pillow as the alcohol stung my back. Luckily, my stays prevented the glass from cutting too deep. Nonetheless, my family's abandonment hurt me more than the shards of glass wedged into my skin. My heart caved inward and caused me to choke up with tears.

A knock sounded at the door and Victorya answered it. It wasn't the healer but the five of the bachelors, Hedgewood, Kipp, McKinley, Qinrel, and Lancelot.

They gathered around my bed.

"How are you doing?" Kipp asked.

I tried to wipe my tears on my bed sheets, but it was too late; they already saw them and heard my sniffling.

"You feel betrayed by your parents," Qinrel interpreted in my silence. "But never forget how we adore and love you."

A tear dribbled down my cheek.

Kipp spoke next. "It's a terrible thing for any parent to do. I'll never forgive them for that. We're here for you."

"Your family is just frightened of the positive new direction you'll move the empire in when you have the crown. Don't ever let that invalidate your worth," Hedgewood said. "You have support on all sides."

McKinley stood nearby. "We'll support and stand by your side the rest of our lives. You have many who love you, both friends and admirers."

I sniffled. "Thank you. Thank you all." They stayed with me until I fell asleep on my stomach. The healers didn't come until the next morning.

"Universal fairy dust," Takaya explained how the assassin manipulated the chandelier to fall at precisely the right time. "Anyone in the room could've plucked it out of their pocket and used it to cut the chandelier."

"But how could the fairy dust get from someone's pocket to the ceiling of the room without flying up there themselves?" The empress didn't accept his response.

Councilwoman Sonya answered for Takaya. "The Fairy Protocol Investigators say that *universal dust* can be used for multiple purposes in one jar. Once universal fairy dust is given a purpose, it transforms into the right solution. The investigators found that it was used for three purposes: flying dust, invisibility dust, and cutting dust."

"This is absurd! Where would they get the money, knowledge, and ability to use universal dust on my son?" The empress fumed. "Even if they left the palace to acquire those supplies, how could they do it so quickly?"

"Leaving wasn't necessary. Many guests entered the palace for the event and could have brought it in." Takaya looked between the empress and myself. "Plus . . . Prince Octavio gave Her Majesty Princess Qloey universal fairy dust as a present during the opening ceremony."

"So it's Octavio!" She jumped to a conclusion.

"Unlikely, Your Royal Majesty," Sonya explained. "Octavio left two days ago. It had to be used by someone present within the room."

Takaya turned to me. "Your Majesty, do you still have your fairy dust?"

I motioned to a soldier who knew what to do and went to look for the fairy dust in its hiding place.

Ezmorelda paced about. "So it's quite clear someone wants both of my children killed. Does anyone have any clues who it is?"

"There is . . ." Takaya appeared hesitant to mention it. "One royal in the competition who we've observed leaving the palace frequently. He keeps going to the pond and scoping out the forested areas. Although he never left the property entirely."

"Who?" Her voice became a low hum as her neck creepily creaked to the side to glare at him.

Takaya glanced between the empress and me. "Prince Qinrel."

"He did so on my account," I said, swiftly stepping forward.

"Explain." The empress's nose twitched, not at all amused by the development.

I had to keep my wits about me with the pressures of being disinherited looming over the horizon. "He discovered information about the poison. It didn't come from toadstool poison as we once thought."

"How does he know this? Why is a prince frolicking about the shrubs, it's inappropriate behavior." Ezmorelda was not in the mood for any funny business.

"He just knows. I trust him." I said, hoping to end it at that.

"Not. Good. Enough." The empress leaned over the table toward me, testing me.

"What he told me is confidential, I can't—"

"You will tell us, or he'll be arrested for suspicious activities around the third assassination attempt," she said.

Oh, Qinrel, I'm sorry. Please forgive me. He explicitly said he didn't want others knowing. "He has connections with forest nymphs. Part of an earth elf connection. They were at the picnic and provided new information about the poison on the Pegasus." I repeated everything he said and grew resentful that the empress made me break Qinrel's trust in me. I wanted to be as supportive of him as he was of me.

"And where did the nymphs say this *gowler* poison is located?" She interrogated me with an air of suspicion.

I inhaled deeply, then recalled my memories: "Over a river, through the woods, around a rock, past some flowers . . ."

"Dear heavens, is anyone in here sane?" The empress pressed her temples.

"It's rare and only located in one area. When we find it, we'll narrow down the culprit." I said, then turned to Sonya, ignoring anything the empress would say on the matter. "Begin an investigation immediately and question every herbal and fairy shop in the city. And learn where it's naturally located in the wild."

The soldier returned. "Your universal fairy dust is missing, Your Majesty."

"This narrows it down to someone in the palace." The empress now moved the meeting forward. "Now onto the topic of the centaurs . . ."

Takaya took over again. "Unfortunately, Centaurus City turned down your request to send more soldiers than they've already supplied."

"They have no right to turn me down." Her face became red at the audacity someone had of turning her down. "The royal family is in danger! Along with dozens of royal guests. Send a royal edict to supply us with every soldier they have to defend against the centaurs."

The centaurs were seen to the east, west, and south of Velazia, along with the southern border of Centaurus City and north of Baylor. They were active and prepared to attack any moment.

"If I may," Takaya tried to explain. "The Centaurian leaders claim that if we supply them with any more soldiers, they'll be too weak and the centaurs might attack *them* instead. If this happens, the centaurs might breach their walls and attack the inhabitants. We can utilize King Edw—"

"What matters is that the royal family and our guests are protected!" She slammed her fist down. "Send the royal edict, NOW. If they don't comply, we'll completely disband their military. Then they won't have *anyone* to defend them ever again."

"Your Roy—" I tried to step in.

"I'm done with your opinions!" She bellowed at the top of her lungs, then turned back to Takaya. "What of our battle plan?"

"We can't leave them to die!" I yelled.

"Shut your trap!" the empress screamed at me. "Or you'll be dismissed from all future council meetings."

Everyone in the room was now looking at the ground.

Takaya pursed his lips but obeyed his empress anyway. "Tomorrow we're closing the city gates. All farmers and outlying residents have been notified to be inside the walls by midnight otherwise there's no guarantee they'll be safe. As soon as the centaurs attack, the gates will be locked until this is over. We can expect all farm houses within a twenty-mile radius to be completely destroyed . . . along with all of Centaurus City; women and children included."

I gritted my teeth. As empress, I wouldn't let such a tragedy happen! *How will the other cities react once they find out we allowed Centaurus to be defenseless during an attack?*

"What about offering a prisoner in our dungeon as an offering to the centaurs? We can claim he kidnapped the Pegasus and be done with them." The empress suggested.

"If the centaurs discover he's not really the assassin, then war is imminent. They could attack Baylor too and will never trust our word again. Reports also claim nearly a hundred different herds of centaurs have joined in the fight," Takaya warned. "A small herd managed to get close to the palace this morning, but we scared them off. They aren't counting the days left and will attack any moment now."

"Well then, prepare for a fight." With that, the meeting adjourned.

Takaya rushed out of the room. I could tell he was furious about the decision to leave Centaurs City defenseless, so I followed.

"Takaya," I called to him in the hallway. We stepped inside the frame of a doorway to hide from onlookers. "We need to do something for Centaurus City."

He exhaled deeply as if waiting for someone, anyone, to speak up against this atrocity. "What do you suggest, Your Majesty?"

"The Centaurian whistles, do you have them?"

"All of them." He showed me three whistles that resembled fragile seashells.

"Go yourself to Centaurus City and secretly return one whistle to them. After the battle, have them return it to us. In the meantime, if the empress asks, tell her that one of our soldiers at the wall has it."

"Thank you, Your Majesty." He gave an exasperated sigh of relief.

"Also, inform the Centaurian leaders what Empress Ezmorelda's edict is, and then . . . tell them that their *future empress* orders them *not* to follow it."

His eyes swiftly found mine.

"If the empress asks, tell her that all Centaurian soldiers came to our aid. There's so much going on, she won't notice how many are fighting at the wall. If she doesn't ask, say nothing. If she finds out, blame it on me," I explained.

He said nothing.

"Now go."

"Yes, Your *Imperial* Majesty." He gave me the title of the empress and dipped into a low bow. I just gained the alliance of an important council member.

"This is a most unfortunate predicament we're in, and I'm sorry for the discomfort this is causing you." I addressed the contestants. Whoever this assassin was, he was ruining my competition! All I wanted was to spend time with these astounding young men and sort out my heart's true desire; not deal with centaurs, my parents abandoning me, the threat of my crown being given to my brother, or a contestant trying to kill me! "Rest assured, we will catch whoever is the mastermind behind this and put an end to this centaur attack. All we can do now is live in the present and continue with the RMC. With a small group as this, we can get to know each other better." *And narrow down who the culprit is.* "Thus, the yellow drawing room is set up for a card game."

We were in a small room away from the busyness of the palace. A card table was set up with only a few chairs.

Kipp hurried over to take my left side at the table, while Hedgewood took my right. Edgar immediately saw there wasn't a seat available for him.

"Your Majesty?" Edgar stood embarrassed.

"Oh, sorry Edgar, this group date is for contestants only."

Kipp chuckled under his breath. I was making a bold statement.

"Ih—" Edgar's nostrils flared. "This is—"

"But . . . since you're Empress Ezmorelda's guest . . ." I motioned to a servant to bring in a rickety worn-down chair in—a part of the plan, before he inevitably ran off to our parents and tattled. "I'll allow you to join for fun this time."

He looked at the ripped up chair with disgust. "Utterly preposterous, positively unseemly, altogether indecent; the treatment of such esteemed members of my house. *Oh*." His words were barely audible under his breath.

"What was that, Edgar?"

"Uh, nothing, Your Majesty. Nothing." He hushed up and gently placed a handkerchief down and settled his bum on it.

I shuffled the cards for the first round, and each person at the table was given coins. "We're playing Velazian Hold'em. The winning contestant gets to keep the money and have a tour of the restricted areas of the palace." The use of the word "contestant" was purposeful, since Edgar was not one and thus couldn't win.

"I wish to buy more coins." Edgar snuffed.

"Everyone starts out equal. Once you're out, you're out. So play smart." I passed the cards out when Hedgewood rubbed his knee against mine, causing a thrill of sensations to run through my body. Qinrel glanced over, sensing my exalted emotions. "Kipp, you're left of the dealer, you bid first."

"You know, I think it's about time *we* get to challenge *you* in a competition." Kipp peeked at his cards.

My smile reached ear to ear. "No, no, I think things are fine the way they are."

"I do think this is a rather good idea," McKinley playfully agreed.

"So far," Kipp continued, "you put us through a grueling political quiz, a game show, a talent show . . ."

"An archery competition, a horse race . . ." Qinrel joined in the fun.

"And during the physical strength competition"—Hedgewood eyed me precariously and rubbed my knee more—"you forced us to take off our shirts."

"I did not *force* you." I laughed.

"You enjoyed it," he winked.

"I have no comment."

Clayton raised a single eyebrow with a putrid expression from across the table, as if disgusted by the table's conversation.

The first card was placed face-up on the table. Everyone went about another round of betting. Edgar threw in a large stack of chips, raising the bet. Qinrel and Hedgewood folded their hands.

"How about a questionnaire?" Kipp accepted Edgar's raise. "We each get to ask you one question that you must answer honestly."

"Yes, yes, indeed." McKinley threw chips on the table, accepting the raise. "The first question I want to know is who *did* you kiss first?"

Everyone at the table stared at me.

I folded my hand of cards with a smile difficult to tame. Without answering, I flipped the second card over. "Second card is three of diamonds," I announced.

Edgar raised the bet again.

"Also," Qinrel continued questioning, "How *many* of us have you kissed?"

My face went flush. "My, my, that's quite a lot of money on the table." I ignored them.

"Don't change the subject." Kipp accepted Edgar's raise again.

"You didn't kiss more than one of us on the same day, did you?" Hedgewood wondered aloud.

"I'm especially not answering that one," I whispered under my breath and pulled a hair behind my ear.

Only Kipp and Edgar remained in the hand with a bucket-load of coins on the table.

"We're waiting on an answer." McKinley raised a single eyebrow while he fiddled with his stack of coins.

"I don't know what you're talking about sir." I uncomfortably shifted in my seat.

"All in." Edgar pushed every chip he had to the center.

"Boys, boys, it's just the first round!" The last thing I wanted was Edgar winning twice as many chips as everyone else during the first hand and me having to explain him why he's not eligible to go on the date.

"I accept." Kipp pushed all his chips in.

Duke Clayton of Pinecrest, Velazia

CHAPTER 35

Comparison

"Are you sure?" I reached a hand out to Kipp. *You better win, Kipp!*

"Do you doubt me?" Kipp showed off his marble teeth.

"No, I—"

"Reveal your cards." Edgar demanded.

"No. Rules are, you raised the bet last, therefore you must reveal first." Kipp demanded of Edgar. After the recent eliminations of contestants, the room was full of friends and supporters, and I noticed that he got a boost of confidence.

Edgar pursed his lips.

"Come on Edgar," I urged. "You must show first."

Edgar slammed his cards on the table without revealing them. "This is an outrage! He's cheating. He cannot afford to play at our table! It's a gentleman's game."

"Quite frankly, *I'm* funding this game for *all* of our enjoyment." I remained firm with him.

Edgar stomped his way out of the room, probably to tattle on my mommy.

"Did you actually have the win?" I asked as Kipp happily pulled in all the money and arranged them in stacks.

Kipp revealed his full house of sevens and threes to me.

I gleamed. "You all better watch out for this one."

"What will you buy with your winnings?" Kipp and I walked through the palace with our hands intertwined; after he decimated the poker game.

"I'll save the money for something of great need in the future. Or possibly buy my mum a new dress or my pop some boots."

"It would've killed me if Edgar won."

"I knew he was bluffing," he confidently said.

"How?"

"I've played with guys like him before. They come in with big pockets and bet large. Sometimes they go all-in every hand, scaring everyone else away. If they lose, they'll just buy more chips. But the real issue was that Edgar didn't want to lose to a commoner. It caused him to act recklessly. In any case . . . you dealt me good cards, just like you've done this entire competition." He squeezed my hand.

"For you, always." I tapped his nose. "Come, let's go down this hall." I brought him to a large gallery. The walls were filled with paintings of queens, kings, empresses, and emperors of the past.

"Where will our portraits be placed?" Kipp half-joked.

I giggled. "Right there." I chose a spot on the wall. "But I was thinking of putting a statue of you out front too. Perhaps reciting a line from a play."

He stroked my hand.

"Over here . . ." I led him deeper into the palace. "This is the north wing; it's not used as much. I used to hide back here whenever I was trying to avoid my parents or escaping from my tutors."

The north wing was dank and dusty. White sheets covered the furniture and artworks to protect them. I led him to a library which overlooked the northern mountains.

"Beautiful." He gasped.

I motioned for the soldiers to stand further away so that we might have some privacy.

"When I started this competition, I never realized . . ." he breathed deeply, "how deep my feelings for you would become. Actually, I wasn't expecting to like you at all."

"Me neither. I'm so happy we have this chance to be together."

Our foreheads touched.

"I think I'm falling in love with you," he admitted.

Our noses nuzzled against each other.

"And I . . . I'm falling for you."

Our lips lightly caressed each other.

But the competition was serious now, and I couldn't rely solely on my feelings anymore in choosing a partner, since I had feelings for four of them. It was a matter of which of these four had the capabilities of becoming an emperor and serving the people and myself the best. It was time to narrow my list down to the one.

"Qloey, to what do I have the honor?" I stopped by Hedgewood's room after I dropped Kipp off at the bachelor pad. We had spent quite a bit of time exploring dusty statues, looking at paintings, and sifting through old books in the library, yet I was eager to come see Hedgewood before my private date tonight.

"Leave," I told the guards.

"Your Majesty, we're not allowed to," the guard protested.

"His servants are in the room with us."

They nodded and obeyed.

"I wanted to see something before my private date with Lancelot," I confessed.

"See something?" he asked. Instead of answering, I brought my lips to his and we found a delicate rhythm with each other.

"That's what I thought." I beamed. "I need to go to my date now."

"A five-minute date, right?"

I chuckled and skipped off like a love-struck child.

Clayton, Duke of Pinecrest, Velazia. Human. Age 17. Heir of the Pinecrest Estates inside the eastern Centaurus Forest. Interests: Hunting, new technology, calivers, politics, & investment.

I really didn't care about what I wore; maybe jewelry was too much effort.

It was supposed to be a fancy dinner, but since Lancelot didn't talk much, I decided on dancing to pass the time. It came as a surprise when I entered the ballroom to find my cousin in place of Lancelot.

"Clayton?"

"My dear cousin." He nervously wrung his hands. "Duke Lancelot was so gracious and allowed me to switch dates with him. I . . . wanted to see how you were faring, but your staff members wouldn't let me visit."

"That is kind of you." My staff never said he came by. Besides, the other boys were able to come see me. Clayton seemed to flip-flop. He wanted to go on a private date with me, except during the ball he kept snapping at me to the point of being rude. Whenever Farooq and him were together, Farooq behaved similarly. I was completely confused by his intentions.

"You're all better? How is Farooq?" His voice sounded desperate.

"You two have grown very close, haven't you?" I said and stepped closer to him. "He had a small bruise on his elbow. That's all."

"Thank goodness." He put a hand on his heart and shook his head.

Something also wasn't natural about the way he talked to me, as if his cares were forced. I never knew him to be a nervous person either, but then again, what did I really know of him?

We stepped onto the ballroom balcony to watch the setting sun and discuss life growing up. "I met Edgar and his siblings a few times, both at my castle and once when I traveled to Baylor," he explained.

"You two get along very well." Which concerned me.

"He talks too much, but really has great ideas, you know. He'd make a great emperor." Clayton kept looking out at the pond while we spoke. His eyes always wandered whenever we were together like he was thinking, processing, and analyzing our surroundings.

Even aside from his political views, I wasn't interested in talking with him and hoped to sneak out of this date early to pay my favorite four a visit.

"Dear cousin." I became formal. "I've enjoyed reconnecting with you"—I hesitated, that wasn't the truth—"but . . . I have risen in love with others who are more suitable for me."

"I know . . ." he looked away from the pond and onto me for once. "My feelings . . . aren't there either. But"—he reached a hand out for me—"it doesn't mean we can't spend one last night together, as family. How about a stroll outside, we can walk to the old fairy mine we used to play at?"

The old fairy mine was a stream with large cottonwood trees, surrounded by crystals, which we dug up together *once* as kids.

"I haven't visited that area in years." I delighted in the adventure. "Why not?"

We grabbed a lamp and headed downstairs.

(Ezmorelda)

Takaya pounded on the door. Within two seconds, he pounded again. Then again. *Hurry up.* He was ready to barge into the room, but no matter the urgency, he knew that wasn't a good idea.

"This better be good. I already took my hair down for the night," Empress Ezmorelda answered.

"Your Royal Majesty, we know who the mastermind behind the assassinations is."

"Who?" she barked.

"The *gowler* poison was identified by a local herbalist to be of a rare variant of poison. When rubbed on the skin, a rash will appear within thirty to sixty minutes, as it did on the Pegasus' rump. When ingested, it causes imminent death. It was the same poison the archer used to commit suicide. It's found in only *one* location in the world . . ." He took a breath. "Pinecrest."

"Clayton?"

CHAPTER 36

Dark Path

"Pinecrest! If you want to make a bold statement against my nephew, Clayton, then you better have more." The empress became defensive.

"There is more, Your Royal Majesty." Takaya was nervous giving this information. "Please bear with me, but what would happen if Princess Qloey was killed?"

"We already went through this! Prince Farooq would take his place." At that point, she wanted that to happen.

"And as we know from the ball, the assassin wants both of them dead. What would happen in that case?"

She was ready to sack him for such suggestions. "My brother, Pennington, the Grand Duke of Velazia, would be emperor."

"Yes, Your Royal Majesty, and Pennington's health is declining. You'll likely live well beyond his years. That means the crown will get passed onto—"

"Clayton!" she murmured under her breath.

"If you consider, he invited Prince Farooq to his estate next summer to learn javelin and sword fighting. If an accident happened, who would be there to testify? Clayton has access to our soldier's uniforms. He lives along the border of the centaur forest where he goes hunting, and can easily access Rainbow Mount . . ."

"Bring him in for questioning!"

(The Bachelors)

Takaya and his soldiers slammed open the door to the bachelor pad and looked around. "Where's Clayton?"

Lancelot stood. "O-on the p-private date."

"You were supposed to be on the date!" Takaya yelled.

"He insisted on changing dates w-w-with me."

"What is the meaning of this rude intrusion?" Edgar grew annoyed. "I'm a prince and must be tr—"

"Clayton's the assassin!" Takaya interrupted. "He's under arrest."

Every bachelor ran to the door at the same time and bumped into Takaya in the process, trying to save Qloey before Clayton hurt her. But they ended up crashing into each other instead. Nobody could get out the door.

"You fools!" Takaya bellowed. "Out of my way."

They eased up and slipped out the door. The blush of boys ran to the ballroom but it was empty except for a few maids cleaning up.

"Where's the princess?" Takaya yelled.

"They went on a walk outside, m'lord." She curtsied.

Again, all boys piled out of the room.

"Would-you-get-out-of-my-way!" Takaya hissed. Once outside, they looked around but didn't see the two. "Where'd they go?" Takaya asked the guards at the door.

"Fifteen minutes ago, they walked in that direction."

"Fifteen minutes! She could be dead! Guards, find the princess and arrest Clayton." Three dozen soldiers jumped to attention and went running in Qloey's direction.

Kipp, Edgar, and Hedgewood ran down the dark path with them. "Get back. Leave this for the guards. We can't protect you too." Takaya spat after them, but they all ignored him.

"Wait!" McKinley shouted, but only Lancelot and Qinrel waited to hear him out. "It's faster on horseback."

All three of them ran to the barn together.

(Qloey)

"The path is so dark. I've never been here at night." I was hesitant to go off the path to the fairy mine. It was in a secret location only Clayton and I knew of, but it required us to venture into the forested area where centaurs were spotted this morning. "Let's come back in the morning."

"It's right there, Qloey! I can see it from here." Clayton pointed.

I didn't like this idea one bit.

"Your Majesty, centaurs were spotted around the palace today," one of the guards warned. "It's harder to keep you safe here."

"Agreed. We'll return in the daytime," I told Clayton.

"As empress, you can't play it safe all the time!" Clayton snapped. "You must take a bold stance or people will question your ability to rule!"

He hit a sore spot.

"Excuse me?"

"It's just . . ." He nervously wrung his hands. "I wanted to show you—"

"We can visit later." My tone became stern.

"It glows in the dark!" He blurted out in a final attempt to persuade me. "You can only see it at night."

"On a day centaurs aren't running around. We'll try tomorrow at dusk if—"

"You're being a coward!" Clayton yelled.

"That is enough, Clayton! We're going inside. That's an order." I turned back with the guards, when suddenly we heard a bird screeching. I flipped around to see Clayton shove something in his pocket.

"What is that?" I reached for his hand, but he became defensive and pulled back. "Guards, search him."

He tried to run but the guards wrestled him to the ground. They pulled a bird-shaped whistle from his pocket.

He was the one who alerted the centaurs during the attack.

"Clayton? It's you? How could you? *Why* would you?" It made no sense. "We're family!"

But it was too late; we heard the sound of centaur hooves galloping in our direction. The three guards forgot Clayton and took up arms against the approaching herd. I turned and ran back to the palace.

Clayton chased after me. He stepped on the train of my dress, and I flung backward and onto the ground.

I quickly got up and punched him in the face.

He was dazed, but the intensity was not enough to put him out. He punched me in return. I plummeted to the ground. The world spun around as my head felt the impact from his fist. Clayton came over and pinned me to the ground. The four centaurs had already knocked the guards unconscious and now came for me. They had ropes with them in preparation of my capture.

This entire time, we assumed the culprit wanted to destroy the empire or create an uprising. But what could Clayton's motives be?

"Clayton, why?" I struggled against him as he tied me up. I elbowed him in the stomach. He responded by slamming me onto the ground.

"I realized at the dinner three years ago just how much of a threat you are to the empire. You'll bring it to ruin. Your parents see it. Everyone sees it! You've only confirmed my assumption with your stupid behavior. Taking Edgar to the shelter. Your *disgusting* affection for the dwarf. Allowing 'Kipp the Beggar' to remain with us. Well, not under my watch! I will assure you, no dwarf or peasant will ever rule our empire. They will not become part of *our* royal line. Your mother will understand. Already she wishes you were dead. We already had a discussion that it's best if we find another to take your place."

"We? You and my parents discussed this?" I gasped.

He didn't answer and focused on finishing tying my hands behind my back, then prepared to gag me. I let out a scream to alert any guard who might be within range.

"This girl is the one who kidnapped your Pegasus," Clayton explained to the centaurs. "She's the one who rode your Pegasus. She's planning on taking over your land, and to use your people as horses to ride on. As the next reigning emperor, I promise to protect your land from *her*. Take her and be gone from Velazia, as we agreed upon." Clayton handed me over to the centaurs.

CHAPTER 37

Taking Charge

(The Bachelors)

The boys heard a scream. There was enough moonlight to see several soldiers lying unconscious on the ground ahead, while four centaurs galloped away into the forest.

McKinley, Qinrel, and Lancelot tested their horse's speed and raced past Clayton and after the centaurs.

"Whistle!" Qinrel shouted to McKinley as they galloped along.

"They took it from me. Suspicious of my motives."

A sharp feeling spiked up Qinrel's spine and spread to the others. "How will we fight them with no weapons?"

McKinley didn't know.

Hedgewood outran all the humans. He was the first to reach Clayton but cared more about Qloey's life than imprisoning the duke. He grabbed a guard's sword on his way and continued after the three riders.

Soon, the other humans made it to Clayton on foot.

"They took Qloey . . ." Clayton played innocent. "Quickly, run after her." The soldiers continued running past Clayton.

Kipp came in with a running punch, knocking Clayton off his feet. He flew through the air landing on his back.

Edgar caught up, completely out of breath. He stopped to look at Clayton lying unconscious.

"Finally, I got to hit a nobleman!" Kipp gleamed as he held his hand, which hurt from the impact.

"Hit a nobleman?" Edgar took two steps back. He looked around. It was completely dark, and the two were alone. "Uh?" Edgar gulped.

(Qloey)

Mist floated across the dark forest floor. The trees reached up to the stars, which gave off a soft white light, guiding the centaurs along their route back to their herd. The centaurs trotted slowly, knowing that human soldiers were constantly patrolling the forests around the palace and because I kept squirming and making it difficult for him to hold me. He carried me in his arms because it was an insult to have a human ride on their back, and while centaurs had powerful legs, they didn't have much strength in the arm department.

"Stop moving," he demanded.

Knowing he was struggling, I intentionally wiggled back and forth like a fish out of water. He stopped galloping to try and get a better hold on me.

"Stop, human."

I flip-flopped every which way, trying to free myself from his arms.

"What is she doing to him?" One centaur looked back at his comrade, wondering if he should help. "Dear Pegasus, she's a lunatic."

"I hear humans do magic, what if this is spell?"

I kicked and thrashed until he dropped me on the ground.

"Hurry, pick her up. We must get out of here," he said whilst standing there doing nothing.

The centaur who was carrying me crossed his arms. "No! You pick her up."

"No, you pick her up."

"Why did I get this job? You carry."

"I don't want to carry her, you carry her."

I rolled my eyes as they argued.

We heard the sound of more horses approaching, but they came from the direction of the palace this time. The centaurs pulled out their swords. In the distance, three men on horseback galloped toward us.

"Hurry." The same centaur picked me back up, and they took off. But his arms were tired, and I was intentionally going to make this hard for him.

Showing off his great horsemanship, Qinrel stood on his horse's back. When he was close enough, he jumped onto the centaur's back who held me captive.

Completely enraged, the centaur dropped me again and attempted to fight off his rider.

"Ugh!" That was the second time he dropped me and it really hurt.

"Get off me, elf!" The centaur struggled to reach behind him.

Lancelot jumped down to untie my bindings.

The other centaurs forgot about me as they sought to defend their insulted comrade with the elf on his back.

"Blasted elf! Get off!"

Qinrel put his hands over the centaur's eyes so he couldn't see. The centaur kicked its hind legs up trying to buck Qinrel off. Qinrel looked like he was riding an angry bull.

McKinley swept the sword off the ground and stood his ground to defend Lancelot and me.

Lancelot finished untying my hands, then put his arms in a wrestling stance, like he was prepared to fight with his bare hands.

The centaurs were trying to jab at Qinrel, but because Qinrel was covering the centaur's eyes and the centaur was jumping around; they couldn't get a good shot at the elf without also hurting their companion.

"You dare insult us you pointy-eared bipedal!" The centaurs heckled at Qinrel.

Hedgewood soon caught up, completely out of breath. Unfortunately, in the opposite direction, a dozen more centaurs emerged from the forest and galloped toward us.

"We need to get Qloey back to the palace!" McKinley hollered.

As the centaurs charged at us with their weapons, all three boys braced for impact and then . . . all the centaurs put their hands over their ears, dropped their swords and ropes, and screamed.

"Stop! Stop that noise!"

We looked up and saw Takaya running toward us with more guards as he blew the seashell whistle until the situation was under control.

All the bachelors sat in the Gold Healing Chambers with me . . . except Edgar. Edgar determined the event was over and I'd be just fine, thus retired for the night.

My body stretched across a bed made of pure gold. Hedgewood sat in a chair next to me, holding my right hand, and Kipp intertwined my left hand in his. The others sat around the room, not willing to let me get too far from their protection.

"He's not working alone." I touched my black eye. "Ah." It still stung. "He said '*we* became more motivated and realized *we* need to try again.' He also said that my parents want me dead." Hedgewood gripped my hand tighter. "But who was he scheming with? If it were up to me, I'd run an investigation into all his acquaintances, including Edgar but the empress won't allow that to happen."

"Edgar, Zack, *and* Alejandro," Kipp scowled.

"Zack may be overzealous, but he has an innocent heart," Hedgewood pointed out. "And Alejandro may have his bad sides, but killing Qloey was unlikely one of them."

"It doesn't have to be another bachelor." Qinrel leaned forward. "His staff was very loyal to him. I always felt Clayton was anxious, but assumed it was a part of his personality, not because he was nervous about getting caught. He had connections with many Baylor politicians."

"I think we ought to charge Edgar for conspiring with him," Kipp said. "The two agreed on too many things."

"It's likely everyone from Baylor that Empress Ezmorelda's acquainted with could be conspiring against me. Thus, convicting Edgar isn't even possible." I lifted the ice pack—frozen by fairies—off my eye, and a servant came to retrieve it. I hoped I wouldn't have a black eye for the remainder of the competition. The Gold Healing Chamber would hopefully heal it quickly.

"I've angered a lot of aristocrats in this competition." My mind raced over the different politicians who criticized and disagreed with me, no matter what. "The RMC has been confirmation to many people that we're on different sides. This might . . . might be a long-term issue. But to run a full investigation means we'd have to interrogate many royals, including the empress's brother. She won't do that. At this point, she wants my brother to inherit the crown. It wouldn't bother her if another assassin had a second chance at me."

Everyone went silent and absorbed the deep meaning of this.

"Your eye's looking better." Kipp brushed my hair aside. "It's not black anymore. More like a navy blue."

"Thanks, Kipp. But don't worry about me. You can all go back—"

"NO!" Everyone spoke in unison.

"We're staying here with you." Qinrel remained firm.

"And if you choose to go to your bedchambers, we'll sleep outside your door and protect you all night." McKinley played champion.

"Well then, you all better get comfortable."

All council members and commanding officers were gathered inside the council room the next morning.

Sir McKinley was dressed in his military uniform with different medals dangling off his chest and made his report. "Your Royal Majesty, we found that Clayton made an unannounced visit to the training camp in Centaurus City earlier this summer. He arrived claiming he was injured while hunting and was so embarrassed, he asked the guard if this could remain off record. During his visit, they received a false alarm. The guard temporarily left Clayton alone in his office where the whistles were being held."

"Plenty of time to snatch a whistle." Takaya stroked the hair on his chin as he contemplated these matters.

"Additionally, there is . . . another important matter I'd like to bring up, Your Royal Majesty." McKinley took a deep breath. What he said next was risking his reputation, but I knew he felt obligated to help me. "Clayton mentioned several times his connections with the Baylor royal family including, Prince Ed—"

"Enough!" The empress fumed. "It's a mere speculation. Remember your place. You're dismissed."

He bowed and left.

Takaya now stepped forward to make his report. "After searching Clayton and his servant's rooms, we discovered two different whistles: the bird whistle used to alert the centaurs, and the seashell whistle that annoys them so much. We also found a bottle of universal fairy dust, mostly empty, but enough to use one more time. All his staff have been arrested. But we're still investigating if there was anyone else who assisted him outside of the palace. We know for certain he paid someone to sell the Pegasus to Zack."

"Thank you, Sir Takaya." The empress acknowledged his efforts with a nod.

The door opened, and a soldier rushed in with his sky-blue cloak billowing behind him. "Your Royal Majesty, the centaurs are arriving."

We all poured outside just as seven centaur leaders galloped up. Clayton was brought out in chains. A huge black eye was smothered across his face—courtesy of Kipp.

The empress waved, and the guards dragged Clayton before the centaurs' hooves. "This is the thief who stole your pony." She assumed her traditional stance of threatening, insulting, and demanding. "Now take him and leave our land or we'll wipe your entire herd out!"

The centaurs neighed and jumped on their hind legs in response. "This is not the thief. She's the thief. Hand her over!" They pointed to me.

"As much as I'm inclined to do so, you can only have one criminal today. Take your thief, you filthy half-breeds or—"

"Your Royal Majesty, allow me." I interrupted the empress before the centaurs pulled their arrows out since I knew she didn't have the diplomatic skills necessary to solve this peacefully, but I did.

I'm not stupid. In fact, I'm smarter than you when it comes to diplomacy, I affirmed in my mind as my insecurities dissolved.

"If you don't succeed . . . whatever blood is spilled will be on your hands," she warned. If I messed up, she'd have a stronger case against me to not inherit the crown, so I better solve this.

I held my wits, straightened my back, held my head high, smiled, and stepped forward to greet them.

"I'm not the thief!" Clayton shouted. If the centaurs doubted that he was the real thief, they might still attack. "She's lying."

The guards threw a gag over Clayton's mouth.

I put my hand up. "I haven't said anything yet. Therefore, how am I lying? Let him talk." I wasn't afraid. "Oh, Great Centaur, wise and mighty ones that you are . . ."

Empress Ezmorelda's eyes rolled into the back of her head. She pressed her fingers to her temple in defeat.

"This man here is Clayton, the Duke of Pinecrest, a nobleman, a member of my family, fourth in line to the throne, and my own cousin. A very important man." I had to make Clayton seem desirable enough that they would accept him as their prisoner. "We found enough evidence to convict him of many crimes, including stealing the whistles that irritate your ears." The centaurs cringed. "We've confirmed he was in Centaurus just before *he* attacked your precious people, as he lives right along your borders. We have evidence that *he* kidnapped the Pegasus and sold him before it was given to me as a gift, where he then tricked me into riding it."

That last part we didn't have evidence for, but the centaurs would never ask for it.

"And again last night, *he* tried to fool *you* into taking *me* as your prisoner instead of *him*. He's the liar."

The centaurs forcefully dug their hooves into the soil as if agitated. A few of them trotted in a circle and regrouped in a huddle and discussed something amongst themselves in the Centaurian language.

"She's lying." Clayton pleaded. "She's responsible for all that and will attack your lands if you don't kill her."

"If you want some proof"—I smiled at the centaurs—"we also know that Clayton traveled to Rainbow Mount during the Spring Equinox when the Pegasus was captured." I reached over, having already prepared this in advance. A soldier brought out Clayton's painting of the mount during the talent show. Although, it wasn't really proof, it did spark curiosity how he knew what the mountain looked like in the springtime with the blooming flowers if he hadn't been there. "Clayton painted this. See how the light touches the tip of the mount at the perfect moment causing a rainbow?" Except Clayton's rainbow was black, white, and gray.

"It happens only on the equinox," one centaur exclaimed.

"The poison found on the Pegasus' rump is called *gowler*, and it is only found in Pinecrest. If you don't believe me, ask the nymphs who witnessed it. You trust nymphs more than humans, right?" I couldn't help but show off my teeth is a huge grin.

The centaurs discussed again, piecing all this together. I overheard a few words from the occasional Velazian that they spoke. Some of them didn't believe me and thought it was a trick, but another pointed out that this was real evidence, more than Clayton ever provided. After a few minutes of this, I tried another tactic.

"Clayton is the thief, we know for a fact, however"—I crossed my arms and turned to the side—"if Clayton is not *your* thief, then you cannot have him!"

"Qloey! Unless you plan on handing yourself over . . ." The empress stepped forward with her fist clenched.

"You would take the thief from us?" The centaurs growled.

I continued with my plan. "You see, the Duke Clayton is a *very impor-tant* family member. He's a *major criminal* to us. And to you. He was trying to start a war between us. So if you don't want him then fine! Let's go to war."

"GIVE HIM TO US!" The centaur demanded. "You promise, now you lie!"

"No. He's too important." I shook my head in defiance.

The centaurs drew their weapons and the palace soldiers followed suit. "HE'S OURS! Hand him over NOW!"

I put a hand up, telling the soldiers to hold back. "If you want Clayton, you must agree that all of this is solved and agree not to attack; you'll withdraw from all of our territories immediately."

"We leave only if you give him to us."

Good.

"Do you keep your promises? Or are you a liar?" I now questioned them.

The centaur spit on the ground. "You dare question us! We keep promise! We'll leave. Never return."

"Then we have an agreement. Takaya, hand over this *great man* to them. Oh, and remember," I warned the centaurs. "He lies a lot. Don't listen to him."

"How do we carry him?" The centaurs tried to organize between themselves.

"Take him by the hoof. Here, you carry him."

"No, you carry him!"

"No, you carry him!"

"He'll cast a spell like the crazy lady." They looked like a bunch of bumbling idiots trying to arrange how to carry him without putting him on their backs. Finally, one picked him up by his legs while another grabbed his bound arms. He hung like a hammock between them as they galloped off.

"You'll pay for this!" We heard Clayton screaming as they carried him away.

It appears the rumors are true: it was bad luck to commit a crime on Rainbow Mount. Keep the holy places holy.

A smile lit up my face. I succeeded where Empress Ezmorelda never would have.

"Reverse psychology," Hedgewood said to Qinrel, and loud enough for myself and the other aristocrats on the porch to overhear. "Handing Clayton over to the centaurs wasn't satisfying enough. The centaurs only wanted someone *important enough*. Someone worthy of taking as a prisoner. An excellent way to manage the centaurs. Excellent indeed. Her Majesty Princess Qloey completely evaded a war."

The empress clenched her fist and took one long menacing glare at Hedgewood before turning inside. It caused a pang of anxiety ripple through my body. Suddenly, I feared for Hedgewood's safety.

"Do you know which bachelor you'll choose out of the six contestants left?" a reporter asked after all questions on the centaurs were exhausted. Now the attention was turned onto the romance in the palace.

"*Five* contestants," I corrected. "Prince Edgar is here visiting the empress. I've already requested his mutual rescission twice. The remaining *five* are the only options I'm considering." I publicly discounted Edgar from the competition so that if my parents tried to force me to choose him, the people would know that the entire competition was fake.

The empress gave me the most menacing glare I ever witnessed. A dark cloud formed over her head. Even her eyes seemed to turn black with venom.

Sweat dribbled down my back. I knew something wicked was brewing in her thoughts. But I continued to smile at the reporters and called on another.

"Is it possible you'll choose a peasant to become the next emperor?"

"Do you doubt it? From now on he shall be called, 'His Greatness Kipp'." I used Pippa's title for him to increase his importance in the eyes of the people. "And he's proven to be an intelligent, good-hearted, and talented candidate in marriage. His advice is valuable. There is a possibility that he'll reign by my side."

The empress now clenched her fist so hard it turned white.

"Some say you love the dwarf above all others?"

"Please address him as 'His Highness, Prince Hedgewood,' as his honorary title indicates. And yes, my heart belongs to all *five* contestants left." I had to push the *"five"*.

"Who do you love most?" Another reporter jumped to the forefront.

"You will know by tomorrow morning." I chuckled.

Everyone jumped up with more questions concerning this last comment.

I simply waved and turned to leave the press room. It was time to make my final stand. I knew who I couldn't live without. I knew who would be the best ruler and was ready to end the competition and ask the *one* to marry me.

The empress's lip curled into a snarl as I headed out of the room.

Duke Lanselos of Moonstone

CHAPTER 38

Dreams Falling Apart

I wore my favorite violet day dress with white ruffles; it had small dark-purple polka-dots all over it that were only noticeable if you were paying close enough attention. Victorya made me look extra beautiful today—as beautiful as I felt—with matching eye shadow and a purple flower in my hair.

My heart was made.

My choice finalized.

All I had to do was ask him to marry me. Of course, he'd say yes!

After the events with the centaurs and Clayton, I realized that I simply couldn't live without *him* by my side. In the Gold Crystal Chamber, I wanted him to hold me. I wanted him to offer his wisdom on how to proceed with the centaur negotiations. Today was the last private date. Therefore, I was allowed by treaty rules to ask him to marry me *today*. By tomorrow morning, my engagement would be announced.

My heart glowed, and my mood was extra chipper as I hummed an opera song under my breath.

After reaching his door, I patted down my dress one more time, making sure I looked perfect, then centered my sapphire necklace on my chest and impatiently waited for him to answer the door.

Hedgewood's head hung low as he answered. "Your Majesty!" He bowed formally.

"Hedgewood! Since when did you start referring to me by title? I thought we were on less formal terms?" I nearly pounced on his lips, but he didn't kiss me back.

Everything was planned out: I'd take him to where we first kissed, feed him some berries, then reveal my heart's desire for him.

"Are you not prepared for our date? The servants informed you, didn't they?" His demeanor was solemn, and his heart hung low. "What is wrong, my love?"

He turned away from me. "I must cancel the date."

"Oh, do you prefer the evening? I have the date with Lancelot, but can end it in five minutes."

He didn't laugh at the joke. Instead, a weight pressed him down. "You were supposed to have a competition today, not a private date with me. If you cancel it, others will think something is between us."

"What do you mean, Hedgewood?" I pulled him closer. "There are *many things* between us."

He pulled away again.

"Hedgewood?"

"My title is 'Prince Hedgewood;' it's imperative we return to formal terms and end this nonsense!"

"What . . . do you mean?"

"I'm leaving this evening. You must go on the date with Lancelot today or people will question the authenticity of this competition and turmoil will break out."

"That doesn't make sense." I pursued him, not willing to give up on the one I loved. "Why are you acting this way?"

"You have duties!" His eyes teared up, but he turned away to hide it. "You must take Lancelot seriously; otherwise your mother will strip your title!"

"Stop this! I love you Hedgewood."

"No, you don't."

"Hedgewood, I do love you."

"You're being naive. I'm a dwarf."

"Do you doubt me?" His back was to me, so I lightly put a hand on his shoulder "Hedgewood, I love you more than the others. I choose you! I wanted to tell you on our date. Ask you . . . to marry me. My heart belongs only to you."

"We can't. We're of different species. We can't ever get married." His voice croaked.

"So now you're openly discriminating against me?"

"Even if you choose me, I'll turn you down." He took three large steps to cross the room and escape from my embrace. "I don't want to be here anymore. I'm done. I'm leaving."

"What happened?" I pleaded. "There are plenty of elf-human marriages and other inter-species marriages. You've never been this way? Did the empress put you up to this?"

He shook his head. "I. Don't. Want. To be here anymore. I don't want to live among humans. I want my own kind. I don't want you. I never loved you. It was all a lie."

"Don't say things like that!" I maneuvered around the bed to get closer to him.

"I was toying with you the entire time."

"No. You're lying."

"I'm not."

"Hedgewood, stop this!" Tears formed in my eyes. "This isn't you. Something happened. The empress put you up to this, didn't she?"

"What happened was . . . I was faking it the entire time." He solemnly stared at the floor. "Leave me. Please."

"No! You're lying." My eyes burned as they flooded with tears.

"I'm tired of your recklessness. You need to behave properly. Like a real empress. Find someone else who will love you. Because I never will."

"Stop it." I didn't believe him. "Why are you hurting me?"

"Go! Get away from me, will you? Leave me!" he yelled. "You disgusting human."

"Hedgewood?"

"You filthy human scum. Guards, get her out."

"You can't order me out. I'm staying right here until you tell me what happened. What did Ezmorelda say?"

"The empress is higher ranked. If you don't leave, I'll request her assistance." He finally looked at me.

"You would never do that." I challenged.

But then he turned to a soldier and gave the order. A soldier quickly ran out of the room.

This isn't real. This isn't happening. Tears streamed down my face. "Talk to me. Please. Hedgewood. We can solve this." I bawled. "Just tell me what she said."

Two minutes later, imperial guards arrived with Empress Ezmorelda's orders that I was to leave immediately.

"No. I won't comply."

The empress's word was senior to mine, so the guards grabbed my arms and dragged me out of the room, out of the Bachelor Pad, and down the hall. I struggled against their might in vain. I felt as fragile as a toothpick in their hands that could easily be broken in two.

"Hedgewood!" I cried out in pain. "Hedgewood! Please. Talk to me." But he wouldn't come out. "Please!"

The other bachelors came out of their rooms and tried to reach me, but the guards held them back as they dragged me further away.

I collapsed in another hallway, weeping in anguish.

"HEDGEWOOD!" *What happened? This? How?* I hyperventilated as tears poured down my cheeks. *This can't be happening.* My heart shattered.

Lancelot, Duke of Moonstone. Human. Age 16. The sword fighting champion of Moonstone City. Interests: Poetry, archery, horseback riding, & reading.

"You're required to complete this date." Yenna stood above me as I stared out the window. The sun was setting. Hedgewood was leaving soon. But I didn't have the energy to move. "If you don't . . . Her Royal Majesty will . . . ensure Hedgewood won't make it home in one piece."

My eyes were bloodshot from crying all day. The sapphire necklace remained on the ground where I had thrown it. I didn't change my gown or let Victorya touch my hair.

I knew Empress Ezmorelda was behind this. But no matter how hard I tried, I couldn't get to Hedgewood. Every hallway leading to him was blocked by soldiers. He returned every one of my letters unread. I was helpless. There was nothing I could do. And if he didn't want me . . .

A few tears onto my arm. I sniffled. *Why did you do this to me Hedgewood?* What hurt most was thinking that he didn't actually like me.

"Your Majesty, please," Yenna begged. "She's going to harm Prince Hedgewood if you don't. How will you feel then?"

Even if he didn't love me, I still loved him enough to not jeopardize his life on the road home.

Without saying a word, or changing into a proper evening gown, I got up from my perch and headed to the date.

Lancelot sat ten chairs away in the dining hall. I didn't care. I wasn't obliged to talk, so I plummeted into my chair without even looking at him. My head hung low over my bowl as I twirled my green soup in circles until it was mush. My stomach felt empty but I couldn't eat. Couldn't think. And didn't want to feel anymore.

Nothing mattered anymore. Nothing.

Without looking up, I heard Lancelot drop his spoon and push back his chair. Then his boots clanked against the floor as he walked toward me and pulled up a seat next to me.

"Y-you love P-prince Hedgewood, d-don't you?"

I stopped twirling the spoon in circles.

He continued. "I-I watched as bachelor-after-bachelor returned from their dates with you, overfilled with joy. H-Hedgewood, Qinrel, Kipp, all of them returned with . . . with bright eyes and newfound views of you. It made me jealous. All except Edgar, of course.

A spark of humor welled inside, but I didn't dare allow it to blossom.

"I watched as y-you and Prince Hedgewood grew close. How . . . how you two spoke and laughed often. Truly, it is remarkable you have such a big heart to allow a dwarf in despite the protest of the world. Your mother takes a harsh stance on dwarves. She and King Edward manipulate people to follow their agenda to open mine after mine at the expense of the pa-people. But she's not acting alone and is part of a large network of political abuse. Her and King Edward's policies cause hardship for many people. In my city, dwarves and humans work alongside each other with ease, which is why I can see this situation with more clarity, for the blinds of discrimination don't cloud my vision like it does others.

Why is he talking so much? I wondered.

"Everyone said you were different. Still, coming here I was skeptical of you. Honestly, I didn't think I'd like you. But I do. Now I see that *you* have the ability to make great changes in our empire. *You* have the vision necessary to know what those changes should be. *You* have the courage to step forward. We need you. All of us. But I can see that if your heart is weak from losing your true love, you'll never make it. So I'll say it: Hedgewood loves you.

Finally, I looked him in the face.

"I—I don't talk much, but . . . but I see. I see many things about this palace. Your mother summoned Hedgewood after the press conference today. He returned quite in a different mood. Following your mother's usual stance, she likely threatened him if he didn't convince you he didn't love you. He immediately went to pack his bags.

My hands shook with fright.

"Hedgewood was saying his goodbyes as I left for our date. The guards didn't follow him. You can still catch him.

I didn't dare move.

"Don't worry. I'll gloat about our date to your m—mother. Perhaps try to convince her of Edgar's incompetence. Go, now. Go talk to him before it's too late." Lancelot's soft eyes held so much love and compassion in them.

The last time I ran indoors, I was Farooq's age. The emperor smacked me so hard, I fell to the ground. *It is unladylike,* he had said. But I didn't care anymore.

Every servant and guard in the hall stopped their activities to watch me sprint as fast as my heart would allow.

My heart and my life depended on it.

CHAPTER 39

Goodbye

(The Bachelors)

"Did you ever imagine the possibility of being chosen as the emperor?"

The manner in which the reporter asked Hedgewood this question was insulting. For the other candidates aside from the commoner, they would expect this much. But for a dwarf, the word "imagine" was used. Could he "imagine" such a reality?

"Her Majesty, Princess Qloey, gave each of us the equal opportunity, displaying her openness, wisdom, and loving heart. With her as empress, we can expect a bright future for the entire empire and prosperous relations with foreign nations. Without her, such a future doesn't exist," he concluded.

The next reporter moved in. "Did you fall in love with the princess?"

He paused, not knowing how to respond. Should he risk hurting Qloey further . . . or tell them the truth and risk the lives of Velazian dwarves?

Luckily, he never had to choose. The answer came on its own.

"HEDGEWOOD!" He heard a young woman yell from behind.

"Princess Qloey . . ." The press tried to get her to answer questions, but she ignored their pleas and went straight to Hedgewood.

(Qloey)

"Hedgewood! Don't leave!" I descended the stairs and came face-to-face with him. "I know that the empress threatened to kill you. But . . . I can't live without you. Please." Then I made a daring move and wrapped my arms around his shoulders and kissed him.

There was no point in hiding his love now. He pulled me into his arms and pressed his lips against mine.

After a while, my forehead rested against his with my arms wrapped around his neck. "Don't break my heart. It's too much for me to handle right now."

"Princess, do you truly love Hedgewood?" Reporters tried to pry answers out of me.

Wasn't it obvious?

"Please tell me you love me, or I can't go on. Not another day." I held onto him as tight as possible.

"Come. Let's talk in private." Hedgewood submitted and we returned inside.

I curled into his lap on my bedroom couch and intertwined my legs through his, so he couldn't escape.

"Your mother threatened to enslave all dwarves in the empire and to throw Gappy's children in the mines, if I didn't convince you I wasn't in love," he admitted. "Knowing you'd be empress someday and possibly reverse the slavery, she also threatened your life. 'Accidents happen,' she said."

"She already has a Dwarf Relocation Plan and will do it anyway unless I stop it." I finally informed him. "Don't worry, we can make it work. We can still be together—"

"No, we can't." He spoke kindly as he stroked my arm. "While it is true, you can choose me, and I, you, and we can possibly even make it to the wedding alive, it is also true that I'll have to live the rest of my life looking over my back wondering if my food is poisoned or if an assassin is lurking in the night. We'll be killed. Any children we have will be killed. And before that, we'll experience great hardships within the palace and the press. I don't want to live that way. You can't live that way. It'll eat us alive. I want to help my people in Velazia, but if we got married, it'd cause them more harm."

How would my mother react if we got married? No. She'd never allow it. She'd be so enraged, she'd disown and disinherit me, then start attacking Velazian dwarves with brute force. I knew we couldn't be together. Yet I couldn't give him up either.

"What do I do without you?" I squeezed him tighter.

He rocked me until all tears finished pouring out. There was a puddle of water forming on his shoulder.

"We're both ahead of our time . . ." he said, stroking my hair. "Our era might be beyond medieval times, but the people still aren't ready for a royal marriage between humans and dwarves . . . not yet. Not even in Adonis Peak. But our love can bring hope to them, even while we live separate lives. So not all is lost."

I clenched his doublet sleeves. "I can abdicate the throne."

"No! You can't!" Those were rather drastic measures. "Think of all the good you can achieve if you were empress, and all the harm that'd continue if Prince Farooq became emperor. Already, he follows in your parent's footsteps. The dwarves in Velazia need you."

"But I love you and want to be with you." I felt like a child who couldn't get her way. So much had happened over these last two weeks that I was at my limit.

"Just as I love you. I never realized anything like this would happen. Or how wonderful you'd turn out to be. I love you with all my heart." He kissed the top of my head. "But it's impossible to be together."

"It's not just you. She won't let me be with anyone but Edgar or Lancelot. But I don't want them. Whatever shall I do?" Then I explained the list she gave me. "She could threaten the other bachelors to leave as well."

"Let's come up with a 'plan' so you can come out on top."

"Kipp!" Forgetting all etiquette, I pulled him into a tight hug. I preferred this method over traditional ways. Hugs felt so good. I was deprived of so many wonderful things growing up and wanted more emotional comfort, especially in these times.

"I heard what happened with Hedgewood today." He rocked me in his arms. "Are you alright?"

The night was growing old and Kipp looked exhausted, with bags under his eyes.

"It's . . . been the most difficult time of my life. I love Hedgewood with all my heart and want him as my husband. He also has a great political vision and would make a most benevolent emperor and supporter. But . . ." It hurt for me to finally admit this, but after a long, long discussion leading late into the night, I finally came to terms with letting him go. "We can't be together. I fear for his life and yours. Oh Kipp, my parents aren't open to new ways. This competition is a joke. I can't even choose the bachelor I want. Even without Hedgewood, I can't choose you because you're a commoner. We can't . . ." I let the words hang.

He held me tighter. "I'm in love with you, Qloey."

"And I love you," I confessed. "But at this time, my parents might have you assassinated. Also, if you became emperor, you'd struggle with protocols, learning strict etiquettes; you'd have constant criticism from the press and nobles gossiping in the palace. Everything you do will be condemned. You'd be miserable here and would have to quit the theater. Do you really want this?"

"I understand the gravity of this." He looked downward, processing everything I just said. "It's not fair to you. That you can't choose your own husband from your own competition. Although I don't want to let you go, I also never expected that you'd choose me. So, in a way, I was mentally prepared to leave."

"Oh, I gave you a fair chance."

"I know. I know." He examined my hands as we spoke.

"In order to ensure this RMC is fair to future generations, I need to make some sacrifices. But I wish to remain in contact with you. I'll extend your writing lessons and fund your first play. New boots for your father . . . whatever you need, don't hesitate to ask."

He chuckled.

"Someday, I hope to return to the Orb Theater; to see *your* plays, and watch *you* as the main actor," I said.

He clenched my hand even tighter. "You are"—he breathed deeply—"the most amazing woman I've ever known. I'm so grateful for the opportunity, for giving me a real fighting chance. You'll always be in my heart."

An eerie shadow flickered on the walls from the candles set about the throne room. It was cold and lifeless in here, with no sounds but that of the wind billowing against the windows. I formally requested an audience with the empress, and instead of meeting in the royal chambers where we saw each other everyday, she ordered me to the throne room to display her power and might over me. A cold shiver rippled down my spine as I gazed up at her.

The empress looked me up and down, mentally criticizing my improper evening attire. *Another reason to assume I was mentally unsound.*

"You. Disgust. Me." She clutched the armrest of the throne, my throne, as if my very presence threatened her ownership of it. Yet the rest of her body remained relaxed and confident in her position. "I never thought you'd fall so low. Of ALL the contestants, you had to fall for the filthy, revolting, riffraff."

I decided against making snarky comments, like, *"How come he was invited to the RMC in the first place?"* Instead, I bit my tongue and went with the plan that Hedgewood and I came up with to secure the crown and choose my own contestant. "Both Kipp and Prince Hedgewood will be out of the palace for good by tomorrow morning. Never to return." *Until I was empress.*

Empress Ezmorelda stroked a single finger in circles, questioning if I was telling the truth or not. She likely thought I had some secret plan to run away and elope.

"I knew something was wrong with you the moment you were born." Her voice echoed in the empty throne room.

Her opinion of me no longer held weight in my mind. Long gone were the days that I would try to impress her anymore. I was a woman now with my own ideologies and opinions, and she would have to learn to cope with our differences.

"I wished that archer killed you at the opening ceremony. It would've made things easier." She tested my reaction, but I remained silent. "If the two boys aren't beyond the palace walls by noon tomorrow . . . let's just say, it's a long road from here to Adonis Peak; accidents can happen."

CHAPTER 40

The Threefold Plan

"*It doesn't matter if she loves him more,*" Edgar's comment lined the front-page column of the *Royal Times Newspaper*. "*I'll never give up. Because Princess Qloey and I are destined for each other.*"

It became a race, not to find the right husband, but to ensure my parents didn't manipulate me into marrying Edgar, ultimately solidifying their business deal to relocate Baylor's dwarves.

Hedgewood put the paper down as he cuddled with me on the couch early in the morning. It was nine, and the cool air was breathing into the room through the open window as birds chirped outside. However, despite the peace at the moment, he had only three more hours to leave the city, otherwise chaos would break loose.

"My heart went out to you for some time. Between running around the maze together, to hearing your answers on the political quiz, I knew you were the one," I admitted.

"So politics turns you on?" He joked.

I chuckled. "No, silly. Your intelligence."

"Ah, it was the spectacles. I always knew wearing glasses would cause women to fall head over heels with me someday."

"Oh, you!" I wrinkled my nose at him. "But now that I can't have either you or Kipp, how do I choose a husband? Moreover, will McKinley or Qinrel be upset that I chose them second after you?" I rested my head on his shoulder as I contemplated this.

"I know both of them are in love with you. So much that they'll overlook the incident on the stairs with our kiss. And you screaming throughout the Bachelor Pad yesterday evening."

"Even Lancelot admires you. But don't be greedy, just choose one man. Tell me the pros and cons of each."

I went over the list in my mind. "McKinley knows the real me. He helped me find myself after . . . the incident."

Yes, how could Hedgewood forget that dreadful morning at the breakfast table when I threatened to throw Gappy in the mines? Both of us knew all too well how powerful the empress's threats were on people.

"He's an amazing support and understands politics. He impressed me with his answers in the quiz and even secured fourth place. He'd be the perfect emperor. The perfect image. And he'd be hurt the most if I didn't choose him."

"Weigh all options first," he advised. "What are the cons to McKinley?"

"He's . . . sometimes too serious. He doesn't show much emotion. While I wanted that at first, now I've come to desire to have fun once in a while and to feel emotionally free. This brings me to Qinrel. Oh, how I love him too. Whenever around him, my emotions heal. I feel lighter, brighter, as if no problem could ever touch me again. He brings me joy where McKinley cannot. Plus, he's . . ." I wasn't proud saying this after our first date. "A highly attractive fae prince." I fiddled with his neck collar as a nervous deflection from my elf-bias.

Hedgewood said nothing, so I continued.

"But there's some doubts weighing on my mind. Our love came on so quickly that I wonder if his elf charm is influencing me. Also, is he just trying to please his mother and help Nololay by marrying me? It's hard for me to fully trust him."

"Ah, with this I have an answer." He motioned for his dwarf servant to hand him a book on elf charms. Several tabs were saved, and he read off each marker as we cuddled.

"Did you read that *entire* book already?" It was a seven hundred page book.

"All in a day's reading, my darling." He adjusted the spectacles on his nose. "I knew it'd make you want to marry me."

"You must have some dwarf charm called the *impeccable reading skills.*"

He chuckled, then read off the page:

> *Elf races and religious ceremonies are classified based on the elements. This element is passed down to their offspring.*

"It goes on to say that Nololay elves belong to the *earth element.* That's why they mine minerals, while the Eldoren elves live near the ocean."

He flipped the page to a different marker.

> *Elf charms help elves find their soul-purpose. They may develop healing abilities, elemental-charming skills, or even the ability to communicate with crystals. Elf charms may also help two soul-mates become in-sync with each other and grow in understanding. For instance, if one is telepathic, their soul-mate will suddenly develop a telepathic link with them.*

"Well, I can feel Qinrel's charm. And he feels me. We seem in-sync. And he didn't force it on me like Zazan did," I explained. "With Zazan, he was drawing me in, seeing if I'd fall head over heels for him. But I didn't."

"Poor, poor Zazan, rejected by Her Majesty." Hedgewood joked. "But it gets more interesting on the topic of elf-romance:"

> *Once an elf finds their soul-mate and they become in-syn-chronicity with each other through their charm, the experience is spiritual in nature. If they are lucky to be around the element of their race during this synchronicity, often they'll witness the elementals glowing of a bright gold or blue color and experience a moment of deep love. An elf may or may not realize the true significance of this experience. It can happen anytime during the development of their relationship, even before they realize they love each other. Elves can also have more than one soul-mate ...*

I quickly stood up and walked to the fireplace to grasp this.

"I take it ... you've experienced this?" He closed the book.

"By the pond. The fish and trees began glowing. We didn't understand how or why it happened. Just a few days before, we witnessed the swans glowing. How different is that? The females glow every full-moon. And there were fairies around; they used some dust on us. So I wondered if our feelings were fake."

"It appears, his feelings are genuine. Additionally, the book claims 'their powers are known to have great healing effects on humans as it helps them lift in consciousness.' So I don't think he's forcing anything on you. However ... you must be informed that upon his arrival, there was this mysterious elf woman—"

"Glynnda. I know all about her. It's solved."

"Oh." He stood up. "In that case, it appears, he would be a great option, in love and in decision making. Rising in consciousness means that you'll experience even higher wisdom than a bookworm can ever hope to achieve. In a way, I envy them for their spiritual ways."

"Thank you for your help. Hedgewood." We held hands and gazed deep into each other's eyes, wanting more yet letting go. "But time is coming to a close and you must take your leave."

We gave each other our last hug here as we agreed on no more public displays of affection, and then walked arm-in-arm to the entrance where Kipp was already speaking to the paparazzi by the gates. The crowds went wild as soon we stepped outside. "Can you comment on yesterday's kiss on the stairs?" We heard a reporter ask.

"Princess Qloey, do you *really* love a dwarf?"

Kipp ran up the steps to meet us.

Ignoring the press, I bid Kipp goodbye with a hug. "I'll come visit you at the Orb Theater very soon."

"As soon as my writing and reading lessons are advanced"— Kipp clasped my hands in his—"I'm going to write a play about your life and the RMC."

"I'll be your biggest fan." I withheld the bubbling feeling to cry.

After that, Kipp entered his carriage and rode off.

Then I turned to Hedgewood. "I'll always love you."

"And I'll always love you. In our next lifetime perhaps."

"I'll continue with our 'plan.' The moment that the empress passes away, you are required to get on the first carriage back to Velazia and visit. Understood?" I ordered.

"Yes, Your Majesty."

"I have another plan as well." I held onto his hands so he couldn't leave. "A plan to open a school teaching young girls about the dangers of charming princes."

He released a belly of laughter. "Before I go, I must confess: before arriving, I was guilty of discriminating against humans in my thoughts and emotions, but you've helped me see that humans are actually very powerful and beautiful beings, capable of great love. Elves think they are so high and mighty but . . ."— he bit his lip— "I'm starting to think humans are the most intelligent of all creatures . . . second after dwarves that is."

Now was my time to laugh.

Despite our agreement, we still hugged in front of the crowds.

As he stepped into the carriage, I witnessed a tear fall down his cheek. Even well after his carriage was out of sight, I gazed into the horizon, wondering what life would be like if we were allowed to be but also knowing that I could still have my happily ever after, but I had to fight for it. The press asked question after question with no response from me.

If the plan went well, and I held onto the crown, I would ensure that all dwarves and peasants lived and worked in better conditions. That they'd have a chance at marrying the next reigning monarch. A chance at love. A chance at freedom.

Once I turned to go inside, I saw the emperor glaring down from the third-floor window. He quickly stepped away and out of sight.

This wasn't over yet. I had to act before my parents did.

The plan had three parts. The first part: I must choose my husband and make the commitment before dinner tonight or my parents might do something to manipulate the competition in Edgar's favor. The problem was I didn't know who to choose.

Takaya met me inside the palace door. "Her Royal Majesty requests your council immediately."

The empress was acting already, but I needed time!

"I'll meet her later." I tried to walk around, but he stepped in front of me.

"You must! Please, Your Majesty! She also gave me explicit instructions on what to do *if* you didn't comply. Please don't make me do this. Not in public." He looked toward the ground.

It was too late. I would never get the opportunity to ask one of the bachelors to marry me.

CHAPTER 41

Arranged Marriage

The throne room was cold, like ice, as if a winter frost were upon us. A disturbing silence washed over the onlookers. The only sound was the tapping of the soldier's footsteps marching in unison, with me at their mercy.

The empress slowly tapped her nails on the arm of our throne, causing a shiver to go down my spine. Prince Edgar, his parents, and all the High Council members stood next to the throne as they looked down on me. It meant something important was about to happen, and they wanted witnesses.

"Seeing your recent controversial behavior," the empress began, "such as risking your lives at the homeless shelter, your inappropriate behavior with the dwarf, disgracing yourself by running around a maze with a bachelor unchaperoned, your interest in a commoner, and the incompetent way you handled the centaurs—which nearly brought our empire to war—among other issues, we devised an emergency plan for the safety, prosperity, and well-being of the empire. His Highness King Edward and I came to an agreement. He's offering his son, Prince Edgar's hand, in return for the financial security we'll need in order to deal with the centaurs and keep your illicit behavior in check."

Sonya stepped forward to speak, but Ezmorelda waved her back.

"Pardon me, Your Royal Majesty, but the centaur issue has been resolved," I said, "There is no more—"

"They're a threat to our lives!" She bellowed like an angry God striking down a thunderbolt from heaven. "They can attack *any* day for *any* reason. Their continued existence is a threat that we must act on. They are to be exterminated."

"You can't do that!" I belted out with an ever-growing power building in my throat.

"I can. And I will. We will set the wedding date—"

"I will NOT marry Prince Edgar." I remained firm.

"You can. And you WILL marry him! You see, this competition has also brought to attention to how bad your . . . *mental illness* has become."

The council mumbled amongst themselves.

"I have no mental illness!" I kept my head tall.

Everyone glanced between us, bewildered by the accusations. One older council member named Haziz, who had been around since before I was born, used a cane to wobble his way down the steps toward me. He brought forth a piece of parchment and opened it for all the room to see.

"You've had one all your life," the empress said and glanced around the room, informing the onlookers. "As you see, it was signed on the day of your birth."

I quickly glanced it over the document claiming I was mentally handicapped and needed assistance making decisions. It was signed by this same old man and dated on my birth.

"You had a council member instead of a healer sign this?" I crumpled it up and threw it on the ground. "Nobody's ever seen this before today. You did a poor job concocting this unrealistic lie."

"We didn't publicize it, afraid it'd harm your image," she said. "But we can see your illness clearly now and must address this before it's too late. We'll make this information public, unless you agree to take a suitable husband who can support you in the manner you need."

Even Yenna sadly dropped her head as if in silent knowing that this was wrong. She knew this was all made up. I never had any illness.

"Interesting that I never knew about this fabricated illness my entire life. Tell me, how does it work?" My hands went to my hips, testing her.

"Those who are insane usually cannot comprehend the differences between reality and insanity." The empress was so casual about it, yet her tone was cold and heartless. "We don't expect you to understand."

"I have no illness. I never had one. And it is *my* Matchmaking Competition. You legally cannot choose my husband for me. You've been trying to manipulate the outcome this entire time. To fulfill your business agreement! But I assure you, I will *never* marry Edgar!" I spoke like the ruler I intended on being someday.

She sat on the edge of her seat. "You will, or you'll lose the crown!"

Not a peep sounded from the onlookers.

"The law states I'm the heir. You can't change that. The RMC treaty states a marriage cannot be arranged. You can't deny that. Besides . . ." I took a gamble and lied, throwing flames to the fire. "I'm already engaged. He agreed."

The empress swiftly stood from her seat. "You're making up stories." She rolled out the contract, a marriage and business agreement worth pounds of gold. Baylor would supply the manpower—or dwarf-power—to open a new diamond mine north of Tildon, while the empress would reap the profits without lifting a finger. The exchange was, Baylor got to maintain a high level position in the monarchy—the position of the next emperor—and a spot on the High Council. Through Edgar and his family's influence, they could control me. At the bottom was added that Baylor will help eliminate the centaur threat.

"Now sign." She slammed it on the table.

"It's too late." I stepped forward and clenched my fists, not allowing her to remain dominant over me anymore. Finally, I was displaying my true strength and power, yet still, she couldn't accept me. "My engagement to another contestant is official. You'd have to go through legal paperwork to undo it."

According to the treaty, after each of the twelve private dates, I could officially choose someone to marry; as Sonya explained before. Once I chose "the one" and they agreed to the engagement, it was official, as if on paper. Royal engagements cannot be undone easily.

"You never completed your twelve dates; you can't choose one." The empress's words contradicted her own attempts at an arranged marriage.

"I completed the last date last night. Ask the Duke of Moonstone if you don't believe me. After that I made my engagement official, just as I announced during the press conference when I said they will 'know by tomorrow morning'."

"YOU LIAR!" She barred her teeth like a rabid dog and towered over me. My legs shook with fright, but I gathered as much courage from within as possible and stood my ground.

"There is a way to see if she's lying." Yenna stepped forward to end this. "Bring in the boy she claims to be engaged with and test his response. If he can confirm the engagement without Her Majesty interfering, we'll know the engagement is official. Then nothing can be done."

My eyes sent daggers to Yenna. Yenna saw this and quickly looked to the ground. I wasn't sure if she was trying to help me or the empress, or act as intermediary to satisfy both of us. But once I was the empress, Yenna would be gone!

"So, which bachelor did you chose?" Emperor Ricardo asked.

The doors to the throne room opened and armed guards escorted a single bachelor in.

My stomach was ready to hurl up my breakfast. What if this doesn't work? If he didn't go along with the plan, there was little recovering.

"Prince Qinrel," Ezmorelda said, "what's your status with Princess Qloey?" She worded it in a way to see if he'd reveal a mistake.

Qinrel looked at me, a nervous wreck in the corner, then back to Empress Ezmorelda. These were unusual questions to ask, especially with the entire council and several royal members watching. His eyes slowly shifted around the room, as if absorbing the situation in its entirety and feeling everyone's thoughts before answering. I had a connection with him now and sensed him gathering information before speaking.

"We are in love." He tread carefully with his words.

"There's proof enough it's a lie!" Ezmorelda declared herself the winner, but it wasn't really proof that I lied, and I wouldn't give her the win that easily.

I stepped forth. "Be more specific in your question."

"Pardon, if I may." Haziz stepped forth and coughed. The empress trusted him for he always sided with her. *A suck up.* His thick spectacles sat at the edge of his nose as he spoke. "Have you had any discussions with Her Majesty Princess Qloey concerning her final decision in the RMC?"

Qinrel looked around the room again, assessing, analyzing, and interpreting with his charm. He knew Hedgewood and Kipp were gone. He knew my choice was between him and McKinley. He knew they were trying to force Edgar's hand on mine. Then his eyes found the treaty with Baylor hanging off the table. The emperor quickly rolled it up so he couldn't read it.

Yes, Qinrel. Say yes.

He spoke with delicate caution. "We have . . ." he felt my hope increasing " . . . discussed . . . the final . . ." He studied me further with his feelings and his eyes. "Decision . . . Your Royal Majesty."

In a way, it wasn't a lie; we discussed these matters more than once together.

"This is dumb. He clearly doesn't know." Ezmorelda prepared to end this.

Qinrel looked at Edgar and his family, then at the council.

"We agreed to keep the decision quiet." Qinrel stood tall, as if confident in his answer.

I felt so relieved. He interpreted this relief. But the council still wondered what he meant. He hadn't yet told them we were engaged.

"Elaborate," Yenna said.

"I wish not to discuss Princess Qloey's . . . decision"—he felt my excitement—"without her permission."

I stepped forward. "You have my permission to announce the winning contestant to the council. Just as we discussed last night, in your room, after my date with Duke Lancelot." I sent a million words to him with my eyes. We never even saw each other last night. From this lie, he must understand.

The unspoken words settled between us. I felt him asking, *Did you really choose me?*

I did, I thought to him with a nod.

A weight fell off his shoulders as he took a deep breath with the universe swirling in his eyes.

"We . . . are . . ."

I smiled and nodded again to give him motivation to say it.

"Engaged?" It sounded more like a question than an answer. But I'd take it.

I walked up to him. "See, he admitted we're engaged without me saying anything."

"She was stringing him along." The emperor stepped forth.

"We've already made an agreement with the *Fairy Tale Times* . . ." I lied again. "To publish the final decision . . ."

"It was announced to them before Prince Hedgewood left." Qinrel played along. "They're already printing it."

"Additionally, we've already made an elf bond of eternal love. It cannot be broken. And if we don't marry, he'll never find another soulmate. As the prince of Nololay, he must marry!"

Qinrel appeared shocked by this revelation. I might have stretched it a bit. The book said elves can have more than one soulmate.

The empress's face turned bright red.

Some within the room probably knew that we made the engagement up, but the empress had agreed to this dumb test. And now she lost. "We already have a marriage agreement!" She grabbed the contract from her husband's hand and waved it in the air like a scepter.

"Pardon, Your Royal Majesty . . ." Finally, Takaya stepped in to end this interrogation nonsense. "Baylor's not the only city we need relations with."

Now Sonya stepped forward. "And the RMC treaty states no arranged marriages or prior agreements are allowed. The crown princess or prince is the only one permitted to make the decision, Your Royal Majesty."

"She's mentally ill and cannot decide on her own," she said in quick desperation.

"I believe she's already proved that wrong." Another councilman joined the fire. "Her way of handing the centaurs saved us from war. And besides, Prince Qinrel is a fine choice and the people will be happy."

Sonya added more to my cause. "She already publicly stated her lack of feelings for Prince Edgar, how she offered two mutual rescission to him. If she marries him without consent, it'll cause dissension. All Seven Cities and the four foreign nations will rise up and proclaim the RMC treaty isn't being upheld by the crown. It will be the worst disaster for internal and foreign relations since the treaty was signed!"

"And the centaurs completely dispelled their attacks and returned to their provinces already." Takaya added the last weight to tip the scales in my favor. "Any further action against them will result in unnecessary deaths. Committing genocide against them will be a grave error. It would turn into a world war."

Now I clenched my fist together and took a bold stance against her. "I resolved issues with the centaurs *twice*!"

"YOU LITTLE—" Ezmorelda was steaming at the ears. "Fine, you can marry your elf, but I henceforth declare Prince Farooq the heir to the throne."

Another council member now stepped to the plate. "You cannot do that, Your Royal Majesty. According to the law—"

"Then I'll change the law!" She spit on the ground. "And if you don't agree, I will sack you. And you. And you. For your incompetence."

Now all council members looked at the empress as though she was mentally ill.

The second part in Hedgewood and my plan was to secure my crown. In order to secure it, I must win the trust and respect of the council members so no laws would be passed concerning rights of ascension. Already, many were turning to my side.

"I order all members to uphold this agreement between Velazia and Baylor, which makes the previous law illegitimate!" Her hand slapped onto the table.

Many in the room took a step back in disagreement.

She was losing support fast.

"Your Royal Majesty," Yenna whispered. "We cannot . . ."

Even Yenna stood up to her. This was big.

Ezmorelda crumpled up the agreement with Baylor and threw it at my feet, resigning her position. "Rest assured. So long as I'm alive . . ." She left the words hanging; she didn't dare threaten my life in front of so many witnesses. But what she really meant was my life would never be safe until she was dead.

CHAPTER 42

Wedding

Victorya was sent to arrange a secret deal worth a goldmine with the *Fairy Tale Times Newspaper,* for them to announce the winning bachelor. They came before dinner to paint our portraits and do an interview. We even snuck in a deal for them to be the first to announce our firstborn child, if they lied and said we arranged this "before Hedgewood left."

The interview, combined with a ceremony to sign the RMC marriage agreement, and a formal dinner with all royalty in the palace, meant that Qinrel and I had no time to ourselves to talk about the incident until late sundown.

I now snuggled into the arms of my fiancé and explained everything that lead up to the council meeting. "I'm sorry I couldn't have asked you to marry me in a more romantic setting. To ask you if you *actually wanted* to marry me."

"Of course I want to." He squeezed me tighter. "I love you. And I'm honored to spend the rest of my life with you. Besides, we'll have more time for romance in our future."

I blushed.

We watched the pink sunset through the library window where nobody would disturb us. "I thought you might be upset by what happened with Hedgewood on the stairs."

"No, no, no." His arms wrapped around me and pulled me in for a hug. "You've been so forgiving with me, as I said before, I could never hold anything against you. I knew something fishy was going on when a whole army escorted me into the council room. You mother had a strong feeling to prove you wrong. I listened to your 'hope'."

The way we connected was unlike anything I experienced. We were two peas in a pod. Maybe we were actually destined to be together, instead of Hedgewood and me? At least I'd still end up in a happy marriage. But I felt bad, because he wasn't my first choice, and he knew that. I openly shared this as well. Letting nothing hidden remain between us.

"You don't feel bad at all that I chose you second?"

We pressed our palms together, comparing my tiny hand to his rougher and calloused hand. "I sensed you loved Hedgewood more than us. Especially at the card game. But I hope you can grow to love me more someday."

"Oh, Qinrel." I burrowed my head on his shoulder in shame. "I have no doubt. But now that we're opening up about everything, I must confess something else . . . I harmed your trust. You asked me to keep the nymph thing quiet but . . ." I explained how Takaya found him searching for nymphs and planned to lock him away. "I didn't know what to do."

He laughed it off. "It's not the biggest secret in the world, and if they threw me in the dungeon, I would've had to tell them anyway. I prefer avoiding that experience."

He was so understanding! How lucky I was to be with a man . . . or elf . . . like him.

We shared a kiss together. "Now, I must talk with McKinley. He looked heartbroken at supper."

As I walked out of the room, I looked back to see Qinrel gazing out the window. He might not have been my first choice, but he was my best choice. I knew we'd be happy together. Hedgewood and I could never have had that happily ever after. He would've been miserable here and our lives would've be under constant strain.

Before this RMC, I never dreamed of having such support and love from someone like Qinrel. I smiled, knowing he would be at my side the rest of my life.

McKinley found out during supper that I chose Qinrel. Although his face was emotionless, he had stared at me for a moment absorbing the news. I sensed that a storm was brewing inside his heart and wanted to run up and embrace him, but couldn't with everyone else present. He hung his head and ate his entire dinner in silence, barely able to look me in the eye. A horrible way to learn about his rejection. It probably caused him further agony to realize he wasn't just second to my heart, but third or even fourth.

I now found him in the bachelor pad, deep in thought with only a single candle lit.

"How are you faring, Your Majesty? You've been through a rough couple of days. Or weeks." He retained all etiquette and formality with me and bowed with his usual poker face that hid his true feelings.

"I'm getting through it." I stepped forward while fidgeting with my fingers. "Lots of highs and lows, but I sympathize with the trials you're likely going through right now." I paused, not knowing how to say this. "Oh, McKinley, I have grown to love you. You are most remarkable and intelligent. I feel so safe around you. The decision was difficult, and I hadn't time to think. But when I was standing before the council this afternoon and my parents were forcing me into an arranged marriage with Edgar, I kept thinking of how Qinrel will be able to interpret what was happening. How he'd understand me on a deeper level. How he soothes me, lifts my emotions up. It's healing to be around him. And—"

"You don't have to tell me everything." He put a hand up to stop the comparisons as it pressed against his heart. "I don't know how I'll ever get over you. I thought . . ." He put a hand to his temple and closed his eyes, trying to reel in any sign of sorrow, yet I knew there was a river of feelings deep underneath the surface.

"We were so perfect together." He neither smiled nor frowned.

"We are," I said, trying to soothe him.

McKinley was twice as big as me in width from his muscle mass. I looked like a toothpick next to him. So when he wrapped his bulky arms around me, it felt like a bear hugging me.

"I don't know how to move on," he admitted.

"I'm so sorry. I never wanted to do this to you. For a long time I thought you would be the one."

"I respect you and your decision. And anytime you need me, I'll come. I'll come back to you..."

"Once the empress passes, I want to invite you by my side to help implement some challenging new laws. And give your whistles back," I said.

He lovingly took my hands in his. "I will serve you until the end."

The third and final part of the plan with Hedgewood was long term. It involved discreet political activism but nothing too controversial to help lift the dwarves out of the mines, and address the various issues brought up at the shelter. Also, I planned to open several trade and art schools as the literacy rate in Velazia was only ten percent. But none of this would come into full fruition until after I was empress. In fact, after the RMC, my mother kicked Gappy and Fred back onto the streets. I secretly helped both get settled into new jobs and homes, but having them in the palace was too big of a step too fast.

Lancelot was part of the plan. He took his rejection quite well—as we hadn't developed a romantic connection—and if I was able to secure my crown, I'd invite him and McKinley onto my High Council.

Our wedding took place three months after the RMC; I wanted to secure our nuptial as fast as possible. Our ceremony had just ended, and we waited on the third floor of the palace for our special moment.

"Look at this." I showed Qinrel a letter from the Eldoren elves and quickly ripped it open.

> *Congratulations to Her Majesty, the Crown Princess Qloey and her consort, His Highness Prince Qinrel, on your marriage. Please accept these gifts for you and your children.*

Qinrel was already opening the small box by the time I finished reading and pulled out two large necklaces. Both were made out of glass and filled with water, like a snow globe, with a pearl rolling around inside.

"That's . . . interesting." I rolled the pearl back and forth, not quite sure what the purpose was.

"As impractical as it is, Eldoren elves don't give gifts often, not even to Nololay elves." Qinrel put the present down on the table. "Perhaps it'll look good on the mantle in our room."

"I can break the glass and see if it's a real pearl." I shook the bottle and inspected it closely. There were at least four dozen wedding presents on the table with an overflow placed underneath.

"They also gave us this," Qinrel said and handed me a book.

"History of Laws Dating back to Antiquity, hmm." I opened it up. A note inside addressed it to: *Princess Qloey & Prince Qinrel's firstborn.* "Do they expect our children to be unruly?" I asked.

But before we could open another present, we heard a trumpet outside.

"It's time," Qinrel said and took my hand. Before we stepped outside, Qinrel reached over and arranged several curled hairs falling down my face. "Perfect." He kissed my forehead.

Together, we turned and walked toward the balcony. As soon as we stepped outside, a huge crowd cheered at the top of their lungs just outside the palace gate.

We walked to the edge and waved to our vassals.

According to the newspapers—except *the Royal Times,* of course—people were romantically inspired by my choice in the handsome elf and my approval ratings increased exponentially. *The Royal Times,* continued to condemn the way I handled the centaurs daily, as if unable to let go of this drama from two months ago, and went on constant rants about how I've developed dwarf warts after kissing Hedgewood. *"Are dwarf warts contagious or hereditary? Will Princess Qloey's children will be born with them?"* was the last article I read from them before canceling my subscription.

Meanwhile, the other two newspapers applauded my efforts in preventing a war and spoke about how Qinrel and my children would be so beautiful. *"The next RMC will be the most exciting competition in the history of the RMC. Watch as contestants fight for their chance to marry the next human-elf empress or emperor of Velazia!"* The Fairy Tale Times said.

All this meant that the aristocrats disliked us less, and the people liked us more. Yet I learned throughout this competition that I would need the support of both in order to secure the crown. There was an internal battle that I had to fight in order to get through this alive. This wasn't just about myself, but the people and my children's future as well.

"Should we give them a show?" Qinrel wrapped an arm through my waist and pulled me closer. I knew exactly what he was referring to because we talked about it beforehand.

Perspiration dribbled down my back just thinking about it. When I looked up at my tall handsome husband, my confidence returned. *I can do this.*

"Alright."

He stroked my cheek. Then he lightly lifted my chin and we kissed in front of our onlookers. A second later, his arms reached all the way around me and he dipped me, giving the people a show worth remembering.

This truly was my Happily Ever After.

Epilogue

Four years later

My shoes wore the rug down as I paced back and forth in the tent in the wee hours of the morning. I didn't get a wink of sleep. Too many thoughts roamed my mind. Too many uncertainties laid at my doorstep. History was about to be made, and I would either come out victorious as the next empress of the Velazian Empire or die trying.

My husband, Prince Qinrel, was asleep on the bed and my two children were sleeping in another tent. I was already three months pregnant with my third child, but our conditions weren't ripe for having another baby.

Not here. I touched my belly. *You'll be born in the palace, where royalty deserves to be born. Where I was born.*

When word had gotten out that Empress Ezmorelda had had a stroke and wasn't expected to survive, and that she had planned a last-resort assassination attempt on my life, my family and I had fled with our lives. In my absence, the empress had ordered the High Council members to sign a document claiming that in leaving, I had officially abdicated the throne, and that my brother, Prince Farooq, was the heir. But it wasn't legal. All twelve members of the council had to sign the document to make it legitimate. Two of the council members had escaped with me, and were therefore unavailable to add their signatures.

Nonetheless, I knew that the empress had other tricks up her sleeve. I needed more leverage to win this.

A week later, she was dead, and we were camped outside of the Centaurus Forest, waiting for a messenger to arrive before we stormed the capital.

I now had three armies at my disposal, from Moonstone City, Nololay, and Centaurus City. But word had gotten out that I was amassing troops, and Baylor followed suit. Baylor was prepared to defend my brother's claim to the throne. They would advance on us later today, slowly squeezing us between the two hostile forces, if I didn't make the first move.

Moreover, they had moved my brother's coronation to today, and I had to be there to stop it.

It was four in the morning, the moonlight only provided us partial light in the night, and we were waiting on a messenger to arrive with the evidence we needed to win this. Whatever pseudodocuments the empress had used to bypass the laws that recognized me as the rightful heir would be completely overturned if I had three witnesses to my mother's infidelity. It was obvious that my parents weren't in love. My mother had fallen in love with the king of Baylor, which she had publicly confessed during my RMC. What we didn't learn until recently was that she had been having an affair with the Baylorian king for quite some time. During an extended diplomatic mission to Baylor when I was six years old, the empress had realized she was pregnant and returned home. Six months later, she had given birth to my brother, Farooq. She had pretended it was my father's son. But rumors persisted that Farooq was conceived by another, which would completely disqualify him from inheriting *anything* from the royal family.

He would own nothing.

Three witnesses were needed by imperial law to prove a crime. If we could find them, we could storm the capital and reclaim the throne. But it had been two day, and we still had no word. Now the Baylorian army was on the move.

I paced back and forth, wearing down the grass beneath me.

Many were already calling me "Empress Qloey," but my brother was currently in control of all of Velazia, supported by my father, so I didn't feel like an empress. *Does he know Farooq isn't his son?* If he did, he didn't act like it.

Suddenly, I heard a horse galloping toward the tent and ran outside. *Is it him?* It was too dark to see without moonlight.

The knight, Sir McKinley, rode up. "I have it, Your Imperial Majesty." He dismounted with a thud, creating an imprint in the earthen floor from his great muscle weight. "Three witnesses arrived with me. Two maids and a steward."

"We have it?" My heart raced faster than a horse. I almost couldn't believe it. "We *really* have it?"

McKinley reiterated what he just said to soothe me.

This was our moment. "Tell the troops to prepare. We're heading out at once."

McKinley bowed and left to give the orders.

He's such a wonderful man, I thought as I watched him walk away. *Completely loyal to me.*

McKinley had been the ideal choice for me in marriage. I had always imagined a husband with his qualifications and countenance. He was serious, dutiful, but sometimes stiff, like my parents. But I later realized that that was exactly what I wished to get away from. Qinrel was my relief from my duties. He was my joy, my easement, my elixir—something McKinley could never be. The biggest and most important reason that I chose Qinrel was that we were like one soul in two bodies. Our love was like the relationship between the sun, moon, and earth. We revolved around each other. We were yin and yang, night and day, feminine and masculine counterparts. And we loved each other dearly. I never regretted my decision. It seemed, however, that McKinley had never gotten over me. He stuck by my side, always ready to serve me, and never married, even though I encouraged him to do so. My RMC was four years ago, and it would be good for him to find a woman . . . and take his mind off me.

Prince Qinrel—no, Emperor Qinrel!—heard the commotion as I flung the tent flaps about, and he slowly pried his eyes open. His fatigue was palpable as he rolled off the bed and forcefully got to his feet with every bit of energy he had available. His long, black hair fell loosely to his waist as the flames flickered on his muscular elven frame.

"We have it! We have it!" I ran into the room, far too energetic for this early in the morning. But I couldn't stop. I wouldn't stop until my illegitimate brother was off the throne and the crown was on my head. I was born for this. I had trained my entire life for this role and wouldn't back down now.

His voice was groggy. "When will you le—"

"Immediately!" I was on fire, as if I had drunk five cups of coffee and my brain was about to explode.

"Calm down." Qinrel put his arms around me. "It'll be fine."

"You need to stay here with the kids."

"No, I'm coming with you," he protested as I ran to the tent of our sleeping children.

Prince Zadkiel, the eldest child and heir to my throne, was curled up into a ball on a cotton mat. His adorable little hands rested under his chin as he slept soundly. His little sister, Princess Seqoiya, slept in the same bed. She took all the blankets and the majority of the mattress; Zadkiel was about to fall off. I fawned for a moment at the sight of the two of them. Especially with their tiny elf ears poking out, as they took after their father. The two siblings, born ten months apart, loved each other dearly. No matter how many times I put them into separate beds for the night, they always managed to crawl into each other's rooms and snuggle.

I kissed each child on the forehead, then redistributed the blankets so both were covered.

Qinrel held the curtain open so the soft fire in the other tent could light the room for me to see. I quietly slipped out and wrapped my arms back around his torso. He was my rock: tall, strong, and firm.

"It's too dangerous for you to come." I pointed out. "If something happens to me—" He started to say something, but I softly put my finger on his lips. "Please. If something happens to me, I need you to raise our children."

Such words scared Qinrel. I felt it. I felt his every need, desire, and emotion. With his elven empathic abilities, we had an even deeper connection; we hid nothing from each other.

"Even if I don't make it, our son *must* inherit the throne someday," I said. "It rightfully belongs to him. You must assure me he'll be raised with your spiritual ideals, that he'll go through his RMC and find someone he loves, just like I did. Promise me."

He held me tighter, not ready to let me go. "I promise."

PRINCE ZADKIEL

One prince charming searching for his true love.

Twelve beautiful damsels, elves, a dwarf & a commoner competing for the prince's hand in marriage.

One shadow lurking behind the scenes, trying to assassinate the royal family and take control of the empire.

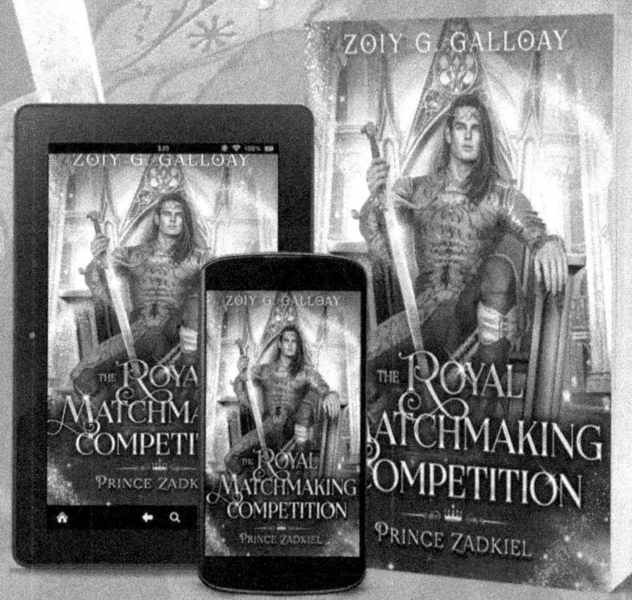

SNEAK PEEK:

THE ROYAL MATCHMAKING COMPETITION

PRINCE ZADKIEL

BOOK 2

COMING 2023...

Prince Zadkiel

"You look so fetching in blue," my mother said and set about fiddling with my collar, then straightening out my doublet, even though it had been pressed that very morning. "You and Nikko are, without a doubt, the most handsome princes in the entire realm. Absolutely adorable."

"'Adorable'?" I cleared my throat and now spoke to her in the deepest, throatiest voice possible. "'Fetching' is suitable. Perhaps even 'dapper,' but most certainly Nikko and I are not 'adorable.' After all, I'm almost nineteen. I've commanded ships and fought centaurs and I'm first in line to become the next Velazian Emperor. Girls can be 'adorable,' not grown men."

"I second that," my younger brother, Nikko, said from across the room.

"Oh, all right." She diverted her attention to inspecting my sleeves for lint . . . for the third time.

"Oh, we all know you're soft and sweet like candy on the inside." Saqoiya came in from behind and squeezed my waist in a tickle attack, making me jump and yelp.

"Hey! Stop that." My hands went up in fighting mode.

I can't believe I just yelped. I'm a warrior. A crown prince. And now my ego has been sufficiently deflated by the actions of a young maiden: my rascal of a sister.

Saqoiya chuckled and plopped on the sofa.

"Oh dear, get off." Our mother quickly motioned for Saqoiya to get up. "You'll wrinkle your dress." She now began flattening my sister's skirts and aligning her necklace.

The mother hen is at it again.

"This is an important day for your brother. I just want everything to be perfect."

"Everything is perfect, Mom," Saqoiya said. "Don't worry."

"The Royal Matchmaking Competition might be a month-long event, but the opening ceremony provides an opportunity to make good first impressions to our foreign guests," my mother explained. "This isn't just about Zadkiel choosing a bride among the eleven most eligible bachelorettes in the realm in order to serve a two hundred year old treaty, it's a chance to appease the cities in our empire, make alliances and negotiate trade with our foreign neighbors, all while—"

"Yes, yes. We know, Mom." Saqoiya huffed with her arms crossed. It wasn't the first time our mother expounded upon the importance of this RMC, not only for my love life, but for the greater good of the Velazian Empire as well.

I pushed the list of eleven contestants that sat atop the solid oak buffet table to the side and dared not pick up their profiles again—eleven, because the city of Baylor wasn't participating. Each city was allowed to nominate their own contestant. The first four girls were foreign noblewomen from the outlying queendom, kingdoms, and empire. Seven of the girls were noblewomen from the empire's seven cities. The last contestant was a commoner from the capital, Velazia City, who had won the opportunity to participate during a contest held by the crown. In total, there were five princesses, two duchesses, two countesses, a viscountess, and a baker.

Already I had read their profiles too many times. After all, they were designed to impress me, but there was so much more to a human that cannot be properly described in so few words. And once the contestants did arrive, they would be on their best behavior. Simply put, I wanted to know the finer aspects about each girl, including their quirks and imperfections *before* I chose the one. Therefore, I had done a little research and asked about each girl with other nobles who had met them before, hoping to gather some juicy insights.

"Princess Grace of Tildon is extraordinarily refined, regal, and intelligent," one woman from Tildon had told me. *"She has no imperfections. She's perfect for you!"*

"Have you heard about the Centaurian contestant commanding ships?" Sir McKinley of Centaurus (our constable) had said. *"She's the perfect leader. No need to look further for a wife."*

"The Nololay contestant is your perfect counterpart," my Nololay grandmother had said. *"If it wasn't for the RMC, I would have arranged this marriage myself."*

Alas, my questioning led me nowhere. Everyone was biased about the contestant from their own city. I would have to wait until the dates got underway to figure this out. My younger siblings had agreed to help and were pixieish enough in their ways to weed out the girls' deeper, darker secrets too.

At the moment, my entire immediate family was gathered inside the purple drawing room, overlooking the front of the palace from the third floor—checking that their shoes were tied and every last hair was in place—before we headed to the opening ceremony. Or in my three youngest sibling's case . . . pointing out the window at our noble guests as they arrived.

"What if we don't like the girl who Zadkiel chooses?" The three conspired together. "Can we frighten her into not marrying him?"

On second thought . . . perhaps I shouldn't involve them.

"Don't judge the girls based on their portrait or profile alone." My mother's silky voice hummed from the side, drawing my attention to her.

"I am trying not to," I said and shoved the contestants' profiles inside of the buffet drawer.

"Such was a mistake I had made in the beginning of my RMC, when I had predetermined that I'd marry Prince Edgar of Baylor. But, of course, my cruel mother had ingrained that absurd notion into my head." My mother pursed her lips.

"But luckily"—my father wrapped his arms around her, offering a kiss to her cheek—"Qloey wizened up and chose me."

She chuckled as their noses rubbed against one another. Theirs was a relationship that I wanted to emulate with whomever I chose to marry. Love. Friendship. Political partnership. Spiritual soul mates. Surely I could find all of that with one of these eleven maidens.

"Can you two get your own room?" Saqoiya raised a single eyebrow at our parents.

"Oh, *Saqoiya*," my mother sang with a chortle, waving her off as her cheeks flushed.

"I've been wondering, in the scenario that one of these girls refuses to sign the mutual rescission and leave . . . just as Edgar had done . . ." My words trailed off. This competition was a matter of international relations, therefore, I had to eliminate contestants *carefully*, with official documents stating that they agreed to it. Prince Edgar had refused to sign the papers three times, and hadn't given up until my parents were officially engaged. What if one of my contestants would become overzealous about winning the crown and caused trouble?

"He was the first in RMC history to do so," my father said. "It's unlikely to happen again. But if it does, we'll support you in whatever way we can, Zadkiel."

"I appreciate that."

The grandfather clock on the wall slowly ticked along. Every second made me more anxious to leave this suffocating room and begin the process.

Tick. Tick. Tick.

The closer it came to the top of the hour, the slower the hands moved.

I grabbed a string off the coffee table and began pulling my black, shoulder-length hair back.

"What are you doing?" Saqoiya rushed over and took the string from me. "Trust me . . . the girls will *love* to see your long hair down."

"Oh, yes. Do keep it down," my mother agreed. "Your hair is . . . *strapping*." She finally used my own terminology, even though it didn't quite work in this context.

I was outnumbered now, so I let my hair hang loose around my shoulders. Instead of fiddling with my hair, I decided to inspect my doublet and . . . really, *anything* to pass the time.

My attire today was made of royal blue velvet with slit sleeves that hung loosely down my arms. Occasionally, white fabric peeked out from underneath. Several military medals adorned my chest. Black leather boots reached up to my knees with matching trousers underneath, and a metal belt and scabbard hung loosely at my side. I wouldn't dare go anywhere without my sword. In times like these, with so many guests, I had to keep an eye out for the safety of myself and others. Being the crown prince of the Seven Cities meant that everyone had an interest in me, whether it be to attain influence, wealth, my heart, or my life. Nevertheless, I was not a suspicious man, simply a well prepared one. I would, overall, rather trust my companions.

My garb was perfect, so I experimented by putting on a serious facial expression, like I was headed into battle. *No, the angry look will turn the girls away.* Instead, I lifted my eyebrows and revealed a cheesy smile, with all of my teeth showing. *Now I look creepy.* So I put on a neutral face. This expression was the most suitable of the three. *Maybe a slight smile would suffice.*

To finish it off, I placed my crown upon my head—with a jewel that represented each of our empire's cities embedded on the gold rim:

amethyst, diamond, ruby, emerald, aquamarine, rainbow moonstone, and citrine.

"By the way, have any of you heard the rumors about *Baylor*?" Saqoiya asked while inspecting her red nail polish.

This was the perfect distraction from my man-vanity, so I pulled myself away from the mirror.

"A Baylorian contestant might show up today," Saqoiya said.

My mother's eyes darkened, telling me she hadn't heard.

"Which is worse," I asked, and made my way toward the window, "the city of Baylor boycotting the RMC, declaring their long-desired independence from the empire, or them sending a last-minute contestant, potentially taking the throne back through marriage?"

My mother growled, liking neither option, one considerably less than the other. "The latter will never happen. Rest assured."

I glanced outside. No carriage from Baylor was parked outside. Their carriages were easy to spot, with green and yellow flags that clashed with their red rubies. An ugly combination.

Because of our inimical relations, the Baylorian royalty originally planned to boycott the RMC. That action, however, only gladdened my mother's heart. She happily accepted their withdraw by announcing the satisfying outcome to the press. Perhaps it was because we were gloating about their intended slight that Baylor had suddenly realized the importance of this occasion, and thereafter admitted Prince Edgar's daughter into the RMC. In response, Empress Qloey sent a letter stating that, *"Because Edgar had tried to manipulate the previous RMC outcome, he won't be allowed to attend with his family."* His daughter sent her withdrawal letter stating that, *"If my father cannot attend, then Baylor will no longer recognize the RMC's legitimacy."* There was, however, no legal basis in this and we replied that we could still *"charge Edgar with treason for his actions years ago."* They swiftly dropped their accusations.

Since then, we'd been back to square one, with nobody from Baylor participating.

"They have a right to be here," Saqoiya said nonchalantly.

"It's all hearsay. No respectable lady will show up unannounced. It's time, everyone." My mother headed toward the door, yet her eyes remained downcast. I held compassion for the pain she carried from her past. But at some point, she would have to forgive, heal, and move on, instead of letting Baylor push her buttons so much.

The grandfather clock ticked on.

Tick. Tick.

It actually wasn't time yet. We still had one hundred and forty-four seconds and several milliseconds remaining.

Did she expect me to stand idle for that long?

My father came to stand next to me. He looked directly at me through the window's reflection and smiled comfortingly. "It's your big moment. Are you ready?"

Side by side, it was easy to see how my half-human body differed from his; I had broader human shoulders and more muscular arms than his slender, elven frame. But it was also because I practiced sword fighting, archery, and other sports several hours every day that I had built a bulky physique. I had similarities to my father as well; my siblings and I inherited his glowing blue eyes, his height, and his pointy ears.

"I've been impatient all day." I took a few deep breaths. "But I also grow weary wondering what they are like in person."

"Don't worry, every single woman is feeling nervous about the ceremony," he said. "Perhaps to an even greater extent than yourself, since they're vying for your attention."

"Did you feel nervous during your RMC's opening ceremony?"

He scratched his temple, going over the memories with a contorted expression on his face. "My time was a little different. Another elf had put me under her charm and . . . really, I don't remember much about the opening ceremony."

"Oh, yes. I forgot." An elven woman had wanted to marry him to become queen of the elven city, Nololay, so she had put him under hypnosis. "All right. I'm ready."

Truly, I was excited. I was ready to get married and build a family, to know a woman in full.

A trumpet sounded.

All of my family rushed to the door to line up.

Then a commotion could be heard at the entranceway outside. Instead of lining up, I glanced out the window to see dozens of guests heading inside the palace's front entrance, but one particular attendee stood out among them all.

Several aristocrats surrounded a young woman in a brilliant red dress, all trying to get her attention at once. She then began to spin around, causing the hem of her gown to ripple like water.

A contestant.

Acknowledgments

Special acknowledgments to my mother, for all of your help, and everything you selflessly do in life. To my father, for all the sacrifices you've made. To everyone who was excited about me debuting my first novel. Thanks to Clarissa Janeen for your suggestions.

To David Kondratiuk for your amazing illustrations, and to everyone who helped put this novel together.

To all my readers, fans, and reviewers. Reviewing this book is one of the single best things you can do to help me as an author. Until next time . . .

About the Author

Zoiy G. Galloay writes original fantasy and fairy tales with unpredictable endings and occasional humor. She is a die-hard Star Trek Voyager fan and has a BA in IAFS and Asian Studies, and lives in Colorado. You can occasionally find her sporting dorky costumes or sipping on tea in her homemade Victorian drawers.

Zoiy earned a place as a #1 Amazon Bestseller on her debut novel, The Royal Matchmaking Competition: Princess Qloey.

If you'd like to help the author, write book review on Goodreads, and wherever you purchased the book.

Receive a bonus scene *Princess Qloey meeting her Fairy Goddessmother*, when you join Zoiy's mailing list.

https://subscribepage.io/ZoiyNewsletter

THE WIZARD CODE

SEARCH FOR THE TRUTH WITHIN

A forbidden love, expanded across timelines.
An ancient wizdom, erased from history.
A profound Truth, illegal to receive.

One wizard's destiny
is entangled in a prophecy.
One maiden's fate
is bound to a red dragon and a rose.

The two are intertwined in a dance of the
cosmos, trapped in a chess game of power
and control. Only one can survive while the
other is destroyed. Beware, the Truth has
never been so dangerous to know . . .

FROM THE AUTHOR OF
THE ROYAL MATCHMAKING COMPETITION

ZOIY G. GALLOAY

www.ingramcontent.com/pod-product-compliance
Lightning Source LLC
Chambersburg PA
CBHW070239200726
48293CB00005B/1695